A BOND WITH THE DARK

BOOK ONE

THE BEAUTIFULLY BROKEN SAGA

INARA GAGE

TRIGGER WARNINGS

Trigger Warnings:

This book contains violence, gore, sexual assault (off page), mention of crimes against children (off page), cancer, suicidal ideations, and strong sexual scenes. This list is not exhaustive and other triggering circumstances or topics may be present within the work without any further warning beyond this point. You are important and your mental health matters. This story is recommended for mature audiences only.

PLAYLIST

A Bond with the Dark Playlist:

https://music.apple.com/us/playlist/a-bond-with-the-dark-playlist/pl.u-GgA5eNmhoZ05p4

Madness 3:31 Ruelle Madness Alternative
Walk With You 3:56 Janelle Kroll
Even Though I'm Leaving 3:45 Luke Combs
Let Me Hurt (Acoustic) 3:42 Emily Rowed Crying in Cars
Bone 4:13 So Below
Just a Dream 3:58 Nelly
Hide and Seek 3:04 Klergy & Mindy Jones
Cup Runneth Over 4:19 Kiki Rockwell
Hurricane 3:43 Luke Combs This One's for You
Kryptonite (Reloaded) 2:38 Jeris Johnson Kryptonite
Slip 3:09 JPOLND Slip - Single Alternative
Wild Ones 2:21 Jessie Murph & Jelly Roll Wild Ones -
Katana 2:07 KVPV Katana - Single Dance
All Over You 3:23 The Spill Canvas No Really, I'm Fine
Wicked as They Come 3:32 CRMNL Trouble - EP
Take My Breath Away 2:38 EZI In Between Everything

Shivers (feat. Jessi & SUNMI) 3:28 Ed Sheeran
Leave Before You Love Me 2:35Marshmello & Jonas Brothers
WDGAF 2:24 Dave East & G-Eazy Fortune Favors the Bold
vampire 3:40 Olivia Rodrigo GUTS Pop
The High 2:24 Bryce Savage The High - Single
Dies Irae 5:10 Apashe & Black Prez Requiem -
You Right 3:06 Doja Cat & The Weeknd Planet Her
Gasoline 3:20 Halsey BADLANDS (Deluxe Edition)
Hurricane 3:43 Halsey BADLANDS (Deluxe Edition)
She's Fire 3:33 G-Eazy, Diane Warren & Santana
Game Of Survival 2:59 Ruelle Game Of Survival - Single
Sinner & Saint (feat. Beacon Light & Moiba Mustapha)
Glass House (feat. Naomi Wild) 3:22 Machine Gun Kelly
Like A Villain 3:31 Bad Omens The death of peace of mind
Breaking Me 2:47 Topic & A7S Breaking Me - Single
Ashley 3:06 Halsey Manic Alternative 0 1 3:06
Bad Decisions 2:42 Bobi Andonov In Bad Company
Black Sea 4:14 Natasha Blume Black Sea - Single
Going to Hell 3:50 Bryce Savage Going to Hell - Single
Revolution (feat. Ruelle) 4:38 Unsecret
Monster 3:05 Walking On Cars Colours Alternative
Inside 2:36 Chris Avantgarde & Red Rosamond
I'll Make You Love Me 3:29 Kat Leon
Play with Fire (feat. Yacht Money) 3:01 Sam Tinnesz
lovely 3:20 Billie Eilish & Khalid

COPYRIGHT

Cover art by: Amber Thoma with 2Girls1BookCoverDsgn

Editing: Lisa Ingeme, Early Editing, and Black Quill Editing

Alpha readers: Naomi Pickett, Gauge Traw, Mara Angier

Beta Readers: Lynda Volkel, Donna Moos, Marie Muller, Jasmine Knell, Faith King

Proofread by Curious Minds Editing

Audio book by Jacci Prior and Gabriel Michael

DEDICATION

To the stars I've wished on, and now Mama who's become one, this one is for Mama.

And for all my Delena babes. Those who love to fix the broken. For those who've been the villain in someone else's story....

Here's to the villains.

MADNESS

SADIE

The ground beneath Sadie's feet was soft and moist. The trees above bent together like a canopy of blackness, obscuring the view of the moon that stood in mournful watch directly above her. The stars were abounding in the twilight, twinkling between the branches yet swirling together in the madness that had taken over her mind. There was a glow about the night that whispered to her delusions, peeling away at her soul and revealing her grave mistake. The giant trees in the woods bent slowly in the breeze, but the voices mixed within the wind belonged to Freya. She called Sadie's name, beckoning her to the darkest part of the forest.

The glittering bugs crawling across her skin were tickling and itching. Blood boiling, she fought the desire to scratch her skin open while searching the trees for Freya. Her white nightgown was ripped and torn from catching on low branches, the hem caked with mud and grass stains from falling a dozen times. Her heart felt ready to launch out of her throat every time she regained her footing before the creatures beneath the surface clawed out of the depths to get her.

Sadie had to thrash her way through overgrown vines and thorns, feeling the briars catch in her hair, dragging like talons across her face. One of the thorns caught the hem of her dress and caused her to fall. Panicking, she picked herself up and stumbled on loose ground as an ethereal luminescence dappled the scenery ahead, forcing her to stop.

There Freya was, hovering on a mound of moss and rocks. The fog danced around her, causing the moon's glow to almost illuminate her, painting her as the stoic goddess she was. Her white dress billowed in the breeze, and the moon's light clung to her skin, cascading down the long tendrils of her hair, her face like an ancient sculptor's creation. The moment Sadie stumbled to her, she fell to her knees, crawling up to the mound Freya hovered on.

"You have failed me," Freya whispered.

Though her lips remained still and unmoving, her voice emanated in adulations unlike anything Sadie had ever heard.

"Just give me another chance, Freya, please," Sadie pleads, futilely trying to crawl up the rocks.

"The balance of nature is off, and you were supposed to restore it." Freya's mouth was a firm, straight line.

The intensity in her gaze gave Sadie pause, and she listened intently.

"You were the chosen one," Freya continued, "and yet you ruined it by mixing your blood with the vampires. I cannot use you now. Now you belong to her." Her arm extended and her bony finger pointed somewhere over Sadie's shoulder.

Sadie slid her gaze to a dark forest corner, the breeze stirring her blonde hair delicately into her face. In the shadows, she could see the grimspawn, the dark hooded figure with a melted face watching her from the obscurities.

Paralyzing fear gripped her stomach, causing her to nearly wretch from the horror the creature emanated.

"No! Freya! Please . . ." her voice echoed in her madness. The trees swirled, and a hectic flush rushed to her cheeks.

"There will be another phoenix," Freya resumed, the clicking and growling coming from the shadows like a death knell—the reaper was on its way. "There must be. But you—you belong to her now. I cannot save you."

Freya's voice intensified the ringing in Sadie's ears. She covered them with her dirt-ridden hands, the soil thickly coating the inside of her fingernails.

The putrid being slid out from the shadows, followed by dozens more faceless wraiths with rows of jaggedly sharp teeth. Their movements were slow, monstrous, like serrated versions of what they used to be. They glitched when they moved, a stuttered migration where they'd lurch and bend, then creep and lurch again.

The air turned frigid, as though the demons had sucked the warmth from the atmosphere and filled it with ice water. Sadie's blood froze in her veins, and her limbs felt like they weighed a million pounds. She couldn't run if she tried to, so she fell to her knees.

More monsters lumbered out of the trees, darkening the clearing with a vile smog, their stench contaminating the air.

Looking to Freya for salvation, Sadie locked eyes with the goddess and waited for death to claim her.

The swarm of grimspawn closed in on Sadie. They hissed and snarled as they drew upon her, swirling around her like a repugnant plague.

The largest grim, with disintegrated facial features, secured Sadie's hands behind her back, grabbed her neck, and pulled her toward his rancid mouth. "You're mine now."

The blackness of his soul cinched around her, tightening and strangling every molecule of her being. The evil was drilling into her bones and stealing her marrow, agonizingly ripping her soul from her body. She watched as the grimspawn extracted her soul piece by piece, each and every particle, until there was nothing left.

1

THE DARKEST DARK

SAYAH

Waves of nauseating grief threaten to drown me.

This doesn't make any sense.

My mom isn't supposed to die.

The police say it was an accident; the fire started in the kitchen.

I can see Dan downing a bottle of rum while cooking and forgetting to turn the stove off. My parents are alcoholics—one of the reasons I am sober. But something about it doesn't sit right in my soul. It's crooked and wedged into a place that doesn't fit.

Five minutes have passed, and the phone is still lying in my trembling hand. The meaning behind the worst call I've ever received is slowly sinking in, and I'm waiting for it to annihilate me.

My mom and stepdad have perished in a fire.

Perished.

What an awful fucking word.

My mom is gone.

Everything slows, becoming boiling hot while a searing, soul-deep pain swells up inside me.

My bones are mush; they've melted. My face, arms, and feet feel like they've turned to liquid as I topple out of bed. In a compulsory gait, I amble toward the stairs where my knees give out, forcing me to tumble to the top step as I try to wrap my mind around this. Feverous tears spill from my eyes, and my breath hitches; overwhelming agony rips me apart from my marrow outward.

Another witch in our family has died by fire.

It *is* our way.

A witch's way.

I have to call Mama's sisters.

Fuck!

I have to tell my son, Gauge.

This is quite possibly the worst thing imaginable. This is Gauge's first experience with death. And it's hers.

Death.

That is the only word I can cling to.

My thoughts lapse into the aching silence.

My mom is gone, and the world is turning dull and dreary right before my eyes, leaving an irreversible hole in her wake.

It's three o'clock in the morning, two in Washington, which is too early to call my aunts.

What else is there for me to do right now? Go back to sleep?

There's not a chance in hell that's happening. My heart is fracturing; the shards are suffocating me, constricting my airways.

My mom died, and I'm just supposed to go back to bed, shut my eyes, and pretend like the world isn't ending. Like it isn't tilted on its axis or spinning around the wrong way. That gravity isn't thrown off, or the air isn't broken.

I begin to sob, taking a sharp breath, but it does not quell the hitch I have in my heart. This suffocating feeling. The strangulating grief weighing down on me and crushing me alive. She was my best friend.

When I beat leukemia five years ago, my mom was by my side for every bone marrow biopsy, blood transfusion, lumbar puncture, and chemo treatment for two and a half years. My mom had been there for me through all my trauma. My first baby dying, my sexual assault, the abusive relationships, my son almost dying, my cancer—all of it.

There are no words that will suffice as a raft in this rogue wave that is monstrous and threatening, engulfing me within its treacherous waters. The crushes of heaven and Earth are weighing me down beneath that water, and the splintered moonlight is piercing, like a beacon I can't reach because the waves are too strong.

I watch the snow billowing outside through the giant picture window in a stupor, rocking back and forth. My left hand is clutching my heart, trying to prevent it from leaping out of my chest. There's a pain in my jaw from crying so hard and gasping for air, screaming the next breath out.

Somehow, I find myself stumbling back to my bedroom. I collapse at the foot of the bed, my phone still in hand, as though it's the life force keeping me anchored in this realm. If I drop it, I will become untethered and end up somewhere time, space, and walls don't exist.

The winds outside my window whistle.

It's unclear how long I lay on the floor, the darkness of the room closing in on me, the weight of my sadness crushing my bones and snuffing out my light. It takes all I have to peel myself off the carpet and retreat downstairs to get another weed gummy—my only vice. It helps me on the nights my mind wakes up and doesn't let me go back to sleep.

My drinking adventures began in my teens, but it never became a problem until I realized I was miserable in my marriage. Paired with the chemo that caused insomnia, the alcohol had me in a chokehold. When I finally managed to break free, I never wanted to return to its clutches.

I fill a glass of water and pad back to the living room, flicking the TV on. Mindlessly, I scroll through my different streaming services, trying to find something funny. Something comforting.

Friends.

The sitcom had been there for me in my darkest hours while I walked with leukemia, slaying the beast I fear will return for me one day.

Neither here nor there right now.

Right now, I have to focus on holding myself together while everything I know comes crashing down around me.

I let my mind relax while I watch my favorite show, losing myself in the quips and banter of the actors on the screen.

After three episodes, my eyes get heavy and I feel as though I could possibly sleep again.

As I drift off, I wonder if Mama will come to me tonight and tell me she made it safely to the other side.

But it isn't my mom who comes to me.

I'm standing in a field at the foot of the mountains, fog resting on the ground. The moon is high in the sky, illuminating the fog eerily in a pearlescent glow, like it is glinting off newly fallen snow. It looks like a field of fallen stars. A black shadow is silhouetted against the moon. Whomever he is, the savage aura about him runs me through to my bones.

His face slowly comes into focus. The merciless beauty of his face unhinges me with a sharp jawline, jet-black hair, and lashes that frame the most crystal-blue eyes I have ever seen. Behind the sinister smoothness in his smile, something beckons me to him. I try to marshal the thoughts to run but as much as I fear this, I'm afraid I will never want anything more.

My white dress billows out in front of me in a beguiled breeze as I await his approach.

Perhaps he is the angel of death, coming for me, too.

He's tall and muscular; his black shirt makes his eyes pop, striking against the dark midnight blue of the sky. The moon bathes his face in light, contrasting the midnight black of his hair. He looks formidable as he draws closer to me, something fatal in his eyes foretelling a disastrous end.

I *should* run.

"Hello, I'm Sebastian," his cruel voice reverberates through our misty midnight encounter. There is beauty in the deadly, smooth cadence.

I freeze in place as all-consuming, all-encompassing passion weighs me down like gel in a heating pack, warm and heavy, soothing yet passionate. Wanting nothing more but for him to reach me, to pull me up and kiss me urgently as though his life depends on it, I beckon him closer with a glint in my eye.

"I'm Lasayah," I hear myself respond. "But I go by Sayah."

"A beautiful name for such a beautiful woman," he speaks through luscious lips, but the words don't register.

The danger in his eyes, the destructive darkness, is like looking at something terrible for you, yet wanting it all the more because of that. He is darkness, and I want to be in darkness with him.

He inches closer, his cool voice coaxing and enticing, sexy and deep, "Sayah, what are you doing in my dreams?"

In *his* dreams? Isn't this my dream? Is this a dream at all? How is this possible?

He reaches me.

My breath hitches.

He is more beautiful up close than he was far away. The smell of roses and violets swirls around me, reminding me of a wild menace. This has to be part of my protection spell, but what does this gorgeous man have to do with it?

"Am I in your dream, or are you in mine?" Even in the dim light, I feel myself pale two shades.

"Oh, love, you have been in many dreams of mine," he laments. "Yet you have never spoken. Until now."

The knowledge of what he means escapes me. English is the language he's speaking, but the meanings are foreign to me.

He leans in and my heart races, wanting those lips to press into mine more than I want to draw another breath into my lungs. His eyes sparkle with malevolence. He grabs my chin, and I brace myself for the kiss, letting the rushing warmth of love and lust consume every pore.

Who is this man, and why do I want to go to the ends of the Earth for him?

Suddenly, he turns my head, and out of the corner of my eye, I see fangs protrude from his cuspids.

He's a Vampire.

His breath lingers around the yielding hollow of my neck for a few seconds. His fangs puncture me, and warmth expands inside me. It begins at my toes and then enters my knees; the heat intensifies by the time it reaches my waist. When the feverish incalescence scorches my middle, the heat burns me. Crawling up my torso, it reaches my neck as flames burst from my skin, bubbling up from the inside, torturing me with the agonizing torridity.

I am burning alive, and the agony ripping through me is causing a pain I have never imagined I could ever feel.

Sebastian backs away; the hurt in the depth of his eyes is like watching someone falling off a cliff. Sorrowful, scared; his face contorted with a resonant grief.

It's the last thing I see before the flames consume me.

2

SHADOWS I CARRY

DOM

The blanket of night devours the light down the dark alley we've ventured into, chasing our next meal. Sounds of the city pass by in an echo as we hunt our prey, careful to use our powers of stealth and speed to muffle our approaching footsteps.

As predators, being lithe and fast is almost as important as our alluring looks. Most of us get our meals by drawing people in with our haunting appeal, veilweaving them with magick to trust us, and then pulling them to the brink of death, only to let them go with mists of a memory. It's only those of us who are addicted to the high that comes with killing that do it. When someone's life perishes on our tongue, it delivers a chemical reaction that is like an opioid high.

The latter is not my style.

I avoid taking innocent human lives at all costs.

Killing is one of the things I detest about being a vampire, but it comes with the territory. I know I have to feed on humans to eat, as that is the only way to get sustenance, but ending a person's life is optional.

My sisters love to kill.

If Scarlet wasn't my twin, I'd be scared of her shoving a silver dagger into my heart without breaking a fingernail and using my lifeless eyes as a mirror to touch up her lipstick.

My sisters have resolves of steel; they can take human life and embrace their high. I have no such compunction. That first taste of their death on my lips makes me fly off the deep end, leaving trails of bodies in my wake without any mercy. It's only after the high has subsided that I fall into the blackness of self-loathing, wanting to end my infernal life to redeem my soul for the horrors I've caused, the shadows I carry in my soul.

It's not pretty for anyone, so I avoid it.

Ollie, our brother, doesn't mind the high and can do with or without it, but he doesn't like killing innocent people. He'd settle for a rapist or pedo. But killing innocents isn't easily blended into his DNA.

Tonight's prey is a lonely, drunken hipster with khaki pants, a flannel shirt, and a man bun who stumbled down this back alley behind the city's bars.

Scarlet spotted him as we emerged from the Neverdusk Dominion—the dark fae realm—and followed him into the dimly lit and narrow street, us sailing behind her as a unit.

Always better to hunt in packs.

Especially these days.

Even though Scarlet has that otherworldly beauty and can use it to her advantage to lure poor souls like him into her clutches, she loves the hunt and the thrill of the chase. She is crouched down and about to pounce on him when Hattie bounds into the air above her, landing on the victim's back.

Before he can scream, she snaps his neck. The breaking of bones and popping of tendons tangles with the city noise of crowds and traffic.

"Hattie!" Scarlet shouts as Hattie commences draining the man. "Fucking bitch, he was mine!" Her eyes flash white, and her fangs emerge.

Ollie, always the peacekeeper, steps between them before they can fight. "Scar, chill. We'll find more."

"One that isn't tainted with grim blood?" Scarlet scoffs sardonically.

The grimspawn population has been rapidly growing in the last few months. We're in New York City to figure out what to do and how to stop them.

That's the thing, though. The only way to stop them is to stop the warlock producing them, and *they* are impossible to kill. Warlocks are created by the fae, which is why we were in Neverdusk.

"What are we going to do about that?" I ask as Scarlet visibly calms, the color of her eyes seeping back to green.

"So far, we've come up with nothing," Ollie answers, his lips pursing in concentration. "Checking the Neverdusk haunts is proving to be pointless. The fae don't even know where these fuckers are coming from."

"We gotta do something," Hattie responds, wiping her chin of the excess blood and dropping her meal to the ground with a thud. "Those twats got Amanda."

"Not to mention," Ollie expands, "if we don't get a handle on this, they'll overrun not only the mortal realm but the supernatural world as well. It will be the end of the world as we know it."

"What happened to Amanda?" I ask, heaving the lifeless body of the poor mortal who crossed my sister's path into the dumpster.

"She was marked," Hattie answers.

Being marked means the mortal has been marked for necromancy, to be a grimspawn. While the warlocks are producing the grimspawn, they pick out humans to mark by applying their brand on that person which compels them to do murderous things. The more heinous the crime, the better, as it desiccates their soul to the point the warlock can attach themselves to the mortal. The grimspawn ends up being a mindless zombie doomed to roam the Earth to kill for the warlock, feeding it youth and eternal life. When they're in the state of being desiccated to be a grim, they're called trackers; the stage someone is in before the mark kicks in.

They are also cloaked by magick, so normal humans don't see the awful creatures they are.

The grimspawns look and smell differently from each other; no one grimspawn is alike. Some have melted faces and no eyes, but rows and rows of sharp teeth. Others take on the appearance of whomever they've been feasting on. Some have rotted so far beyond belief it's impossible not to know when they are near; their rancid smell permeates their presence. All of them have gray skin that's thin as a drum, revealing black veins that spiderweb underneath.

The dangerous part of this is that the newly marked humans are impossible to ascertain. If you bite them and drain them, killing them in the process, the mark then transfers to you, and then *you* are doomed for necromancy.

"Is there any way Amanda can help us find one of the warlocks?" I ask Hattie.

"Even if we find them, Dom, what would we do?" Jasantha questions, her midnight-kissed skin glimmering in the moonlight. "Mom doesn't know of anything that will kill these things."

Ollie's head snaps up like he scents something—or someone—and flashes away.

"There's got to be a way to kill them," I respond, watching Ollie's trail of colors as he zips off. "We have to find a way."

"We've tried everything," Scarlet says, her blonde hair backlighted by the lonely amber light above us. "There's no way to get close enough to kill them. And even if we did, they're playing with a kind of magick we know nothing about. I'm afraid there's no way to kill them."

Ollie returns with two women, young twenty-somethings with tight skin and bright eyes. It's obvious by the vacant expressions on their faces that Ollie used his veilweaving magick on them—putting them in a trance with his voice.

"Dinner, Dom?" he offers.

I look at the blonde one hesitantly.

"You don't have to kill them, Dominic," Ollie murmurs, drawing the brown-haired girl close into his arms. "Just a snack." His fangs elongate, and the eerie crunch echoes off the walls of the alley as he sinks them into the soft flesh of the brunette's neck, the sound of his feeding piercing the night.

"Oh, all right," I concede. I am hungry.

Grabbing the blonde by her neck, I yank her toward me, feeling my fangs elongate and sink into her, savoring the sweet nectar of her blood on my tongue.

3

RESOUNDING SADNESS

SAYAH

Opening my eyes the following day, the first thing that floods my mind is those bright blue eyes.

That fire.

A vampire?

While I know there aren't vampires in the world, the dream was so fucking real. So real. The ones you wake up from and wonder if part of you crawled out of your skin and entered a new dimension, fell from great heights, or flew around the sky.

Gods, the flying dreams are great!

That's what this feels like.

I've had dreams that I've woken up from and they staggered me, my muscles still tense from that crippling fall or my heart still racing from the near drowning in a tsunami.

But this. . .

This is something else entirely.

My skin feels different. It feels like I've grown inside of it, stretched it out to be too big and now my existence is smaller somehow. It's as though I've found a new part of me in this other dimension, part of me that clicks right into place like it was always supposed to be here.

Then there's the pain.

What exquisite torture that fire had been!

One of those agonizing kinds of pain you hate and love—you love it because it makes you feel alive, a tangible force of nature that can bend and break and bleed and come back stronger from every rip, every slice, every burn.

The sting of the fire still scalds my every inch, the invisible blisters lap at the bends of my arms. I hold one out in front of me to check for singes of hair or marks, any indication I've been burned.

But there is nothing.

Is there some coincidence between dreaming of being burned alive and the way Mama died?

My mom's face comes to mind and my chest constricts, breath caught in my throat as the wave of sadness drowns me once more, dousing the fire with a hiss.

The tears take hold and asphyxiate all other thoughts, and I struggle to keep moving, burying my face in the pillow to scream once more. Laying here with only the sound of the fan humming in the background, I picture Mama dying in an agonizing blaze of fire.

Please let there have been no pain.

Please, Freya, tell me you came to take her before she could feel anything at all.

I don't know what to do now. How to move on. To rise and carry on as though nothing has changed even though my entire existence got upended.

I have to tell my aunts.

And Gauge.

For once, I am thankful for the split custody schedule. Gauge is currently with my ex, Derek. As much as I would love to snuggle my little guy up and hold him, the anguish I'm feeling is too much. It would seep off me and into him, and I don't want that.

Grabbing my phone from the nightstand by my bed, I find my aunt Hilda's name in my phone and press the green call button, steeling myself for this conversation.

"Hello?"

"Hi, Aunt Hilda," I say, though my voice doesn't sound right. It's higher than usual and strained.

"Sayah? What is it, what's wrong?" That's my aunt Maggie. They're always together.

I try to hold on to my composure, but as the words form on my tongue they freeze. Splinters from the jaggedness of them slice me, knowing that after I utter these words, we'll never be the same.

The world is different now.

Taking a deep breath, I say, "Mama and Dan passed away last night." The words are no less frigid and venomous as they'd been unspoken.

"What?" they both say on a breath.

"What happened?" asks Maggie.

Tears prick my eyes as I borrow strength from the air to keep talking. "There was a fire. The police said someone left the stove on."

"Oh my god," Hilda sighs.

"That wrecked curse," says Maggie in the background.

"Oh, Sayah," Hilda replies. "Do you need us to come out there?" She sounds strange. As though her voice is caught in a vice, strained with a tension that could burst at any moment.

My brows pinch together as I stifle my sobs. "Yes, please," I whisper, tears tumbling down my cheek.

It would be nice to have family around me. I have a small family. My dad is in Kansas with my stepmom, and my sister and I are estranged. Besides my aunts in Washington, the only other family I have is Claire, my best friend.

"We'll leave right away," Maggie says, her voice audibly contoured with sadness. This is their second sister and the third person in our family to have died by fire. "Just hang in there 'til we get there, okay?"

I nod like they can see me.

"Sweetie?" Maggie says, her sweet voice perforating the silence.

"Yeah?" I answer, my voice breaking.

"I know you're barely hanging on right now." She swallows as though she's speaking of herself as well. "But do everything you can to not fall apart, okay? Do your magick, it will help."

Making a noncommittal noise, I sniffle and wipe the tears away with my sheet.

"We'll see you soon."

"Okay. I love you."

"Love you," they both say and end the call.

Wrapping my arms around my shoulders, I let myself fall apart.

As I topple out of bed a few hours later and descend the stairs, I glance through the windows. The winter storm has unleashed chaos on the outside world. A thick blanket of twelve inches of snow veils the ground, transforming roads into slushy, icy paths. Given the early hours, the snowplows have yet to reach the neighborhoods. I find my driveway untouched, a stark reminder of mundane tasks deferred, relics of average days when the world wasn't on the brink of upheaval.

After making some coffee and snuggling with my cat, I go to my spell cabinet. When my aunt mentioned magick on our call, it sounded like a good idea. Maybe it will help me feel better. Magick is like coffee for your soul.

I've always known my aunts are witches, but because I didn't fully embrace the craft, memories seem hidden away, like I've been under a spell. Every time I practiced, more of that fog lifted and memories would resurface of my childhood and my mom.

One time, I was doing a healing spell and a memory of Hilda and Maggie cut through my vision and took over my mind. They talked to my mom in my old childhood house while I listened through a crack in my bedroom door…

"You're either fully in or fully out; there is no in-between," Maggie told Mama.

"But she's just a child; she doesn't know what she wants yet," my mom answered.

"She's too powerful, Fran. She can't be halfway in. It will eventually consume her even if she is out right now. She is the balance. She has to fully want it, or it will never work. Time will bring her into it when she's ready. We have to trust that."

While I have no idea what that memory means, it still haunts me.

Grabbing the sage, a few herbs, some incense, and the oil I need for my altar spell, I begin to arrange them on a small wooden table by the floor-length window. The plants in my dining room give me the most comfort when I do spells.

Magick certainly isn't a new concept to me. I've known I'm a witch for a long time, but the idea of spell casting, herbs, and magick circles hadn't called to me until I almost died. Even when my aunts would come out twice a year to work magick with Mama on solstices, there was something about it I couldn't wrap my mind around—almost as if an invisible force wouldn't let my mind embrace it until the right time. Now that I'm finally embracing it, my instructors aren't around to guide me.

Even though I don't know if I'm doing it right, practicing magick makes me feel better. It's as though I am getting reacquainted with an old friend; like I'm getting in tune with the world around me, and the moon herself is locking into my veins and seeping comfort into my blood.

Mama didn't practice the craft after she met Dan, and my aunts stopped visiting around that time as well. It wasn't that she was hiding it from Dan; he didn't believe in it and made us feel sillier for it.

Magick had been one of the best parts of my mom. The sheer power of Mama's soul could knock people over when she entered the room. When I was a kid, I loved watching her conduct spells.

Even though I loved watching Mama practice, the few times I did it with her or my aunts, I didn't feel I was doing anything. I felt silly. For that reason, I never participated, and because Mama always left it up to me to choose my path, she never forced it on me.

Once Mama met Dan and stopped practicing her magick, it saddened me. When I got sick and began to embrace that side of me, I felt something was blocking me, like a fog surrounding some aspects of my witchy side.

I read everything I could about the craft and kept it under wraps as to what I was reading and discovering. But my mom must have picked up on things because she began to give me candles and incense on my birthdays instead of clothes and jewelry.

When I found my ex-husband, and we had Gauge, I began showing more and more of my true colors; knowing he was cool with me, my craft, and my spirituality. Though, after the cancer diagnosis, everything changed. I wasn't afraid to let people know that I was a witch and practiced magick; that was what I believed in and how I live my life now.

Anointing the candles with violet oil, I light the same scented incense and place it in the holder.

As the incense burns, I close my eyes and picture Mama.

She's in the park she grew up near as a kid—Bartram's Garden. The park is brightly lit and littered with daffodils. The trees bend in the breeze like they are whispering secrets to each other. Her sister, mom, and dad are waiting for her.

The sweet, pungent aroma of violets swirls around my nostrils, and I tilt my head back, trying to hitch the crescendo of grief at the thought Mama is heading to a place where she will be with her sister, Janet, again.

As I clear my mind and think of only that, a vision of fire flashes, and a sharp whisper—almost a beckon—cuts into my reverie.

There is light in the darkness.

When I open my eyes again, I'm not in my living room anymore.

Green grass is all around me and the sun is cascading her warmth down, oozing into me and filling me with overwhelming ease.

I feel comforted.

Gazing up at the robin's-egg-blue sky, birds flit across my vision and call out a sound.

A sound I recognize.

Mama's favorite bird, the Red-Winged Black Bird, soars in the air and frees her beautiful song; the melody mingling with the sun's rays, adding to the depth of ease I'm feeling.

Tilting my gaze back level with the rolling hills of the park, Mama is sitting with me on a blanket.

We're having a picnic.

"Mama?" I say questioningly as she digs in the basket for something.

Looking up, her eyes are young again, her wrinkles gone, hair bright and curly. "Yes, darling?"

Taking a deep breath in to stanch the unraveling, I say, "I don't know what I'm going to do without you."

The sobs threaten to rip me apart and I'm afraid if I let it out, I may never stop.

"You'll never lose me, punkin," she says through a smile, and I feel the seams straining against the weight of my sorrow, threatening to burst.

She reaches out and strokes my face; her hands feel soft and tender. I lean into the embrace and close my eyes again. A tear determinedly leaves my eyes and she wipes it away, pulling at my chin.

"Why are you so sad?"

"I don't know what to do," I repeat, clinging to the calm in her voice. That soothing agent in only my mother's words that can quell whatever's ailing me. That balm to my burns.

"Oh, sweetheart," she whispers, clasping my hands in hers. "You will always prevail. I know you. You have the strength within you to overcome whatever is in front of you. Remember leukemia?" She lets out a slight laugh. "You kicked its ass and made it your bitch, remember?"

My chest lightens with the memory. "I did make it my bitch."

It was one of the things I said to her when I first found out I had cancer.

I called her and told her, and while she fell apart I told her not to worry. I said, "Fuck you, Leukemia, I'm coming for you. You can come in for now and teach me things, but you cannot stay. I will kick your ass and make you my bitch."

"See," she says, nudging me with her shoulder. "I've watched you rise up after being knocked down and come back stronger since the day you were born. It's been the greatest honor of my life, being the witness to your soul's authority. No matter what comes for you, it stands no chance. Especially now that you're a mother too. That fire in your being only got brighter with Gauge. And for him, you would dismantle the world. Just like I would dismantle the stars for you."

I heave a sorrowful sigh. "I don't know how to do this without you, Mama."

The pause in her smile stuns me, the look in her eyes telling me she believes in me and is forever proud of everything I do.

"Of course you do, darling. You're you. That's always been your answer. When things get dark, you find the light and keep on keeping on. Your own well of strength comes from the essence of who you are. I knew I'd made something special when I made you. You are destined for greatness."

"Yes, but I've always had you to cheer me on, to hype me up. I can't fathom a life that doesn't contain my biggest fan." My shoulders slump and my head falls to my chest, the sadness enveloping me.

Her arms embrace me, pulling me into her and it mimics the feelings the sun gave me. "Shhh," she says, rocking me. "I'll always be there, even if you can't see me. I exist in you." She pulls my chin up again, her green eyes searching. "No one can ever take me from you; we're bonded, you and I. Remember? I'm the Cooder to your Wade."

The laugh that spills is soaked with that memory of her and me, telling a joke, reenacting southern accents to each other, and laughing so hard our cheeks hurt.

"Okay, Cooder," I say with the accent, though this time it's dejected and sad.

"I love you, punkin pie." She then recites the poem we'd adopted from a children's book we read when I was young. It's how we ended every letter, every text.

I recited the poem with her and let her rock me some more.

"Everything will be all right," she says, and the weight of her arms lessens like she's fading away.

"No, Mama, don't go, please," I plea, grasping at straws as she dissipates.

"Keep on your path," she whispers, her face fading into the clouds. "We did not have you crawl through shards of your own brokenness to prepare you for mediocre magick."

A chill through the air gnaws me out of my vision and places me back at my house, before my altar.

I shiver and collapse back on my knees, physically feeling the effects of seeing Mama.

The candles are dancing in the ghosts of the air, and even though I know it was a vision, it feels like she was here.

That was Mama.

4

WE ARE MONSTERS

DOM

"So, what did you find out?" Mom asks. She's in her spell room, muddling something together in her mortar and pestle.

"Absolutely nothing," Hattie responds despondently, plopping herself down on one of the chairs by the fire.

"Hattie, I told you it was a bad idea," Dad answers gruffly. He has a penchant for making Hattie feel childish about everything.

Ollie shifts in his chair uncomfortably.

"Everett darling," Mom scolds him, "try to be nice. She is only thinking of ways to help us with the grimspawn problem."

"She's only after trying to save her girlfriend—whom she met a week ago."

"It was a month!" Hattie replies childishly. "And it's also to help us figure out this problem. You guys don't have that much of a problem since you have endless supplies of blood, but we"—she circles her fingers around at Ollie, Scarlet, Jasantha, and I—"still have to worry about dining on a human who's been marked. You don't want us to get marked, do you?"

"I'm not even entertaining that with an answer, Hattie," my mom responds, adding some herbs to her spell that she's babying on her old wooden butcher block.

"Guys, c'mon," Ollie pacifies, picking up the poker and stoking the fire. "We're all on the same side now. Hattie, you need to stop—"

Hattie scoffs, "But he—"

"No!" Ollie scolds her. Being the middle sibling but the eldest vampire, he often plays the role of putting Hattie in her place when she is acting like a bratty teen, even though she is eternally twenty-six.

"Adaline," Dad says to my mom, "would you like a drink, darling?"

"Yes please, my love, thank you." She moves from the spell to the grimoire lying open on the table, taking up half of one end of it.

"Anything interesting in there, Mom?" I ask, making myself a bourbon on the rocks. The bar is in a corner of the expansive space that takes up almost the entirety of the west wing of their home.

"No, nothing we didn't already know." A smile reaches her eyes, which is rare for my mom.

She is a hardened warrior woman who wears her tragedies on her skin like armor against the rest of the world. Each and every scratch and scar and catastrophic event meant to kill her molded her into the fierce protector she is today. It's the softened edges that hardships haven't whittled down where she keeps her tenderness for her family.

We all hide our love for each other underneath our sharp actions and jagged words.

"Is there no one you can talk to back in England?" I inquire, "Maybe your old coven that you haven't seen in ages?"

Before moving to the States, we lived in England for a long time. It's why everyone in my family has a British accent except me. It wasn't something I held onto. Once we came to America, I shed the accent like an old skin.

"Esmerelda is consulting a shaman there, and Isobelle is working on tracking down another vampire who's lost his whole family to the grims. But so far, nothing."

"It may come down to us leaving the area," my dad says.

My mom's face falls. She loves living here.

"I won't be driven out of my home by monsters," she replies tersely and takes the wineglass filled with blood that Dad hands her.

"We *are* monsters," Jasantha adds, a sinister glimmer in her purple eyes.

Jasantha is our adopted sister. She is part siren, so her jagged words hold more weight than ours. When her temper flares, we don't just have to worry about how her words can cut us. We have to worry about where her anger will send us, often waking up outdoors with little to no clothing. Her siren's sunder is not just something that can lure soldiers to their doom, but entrance someone so they have to do whatever she says, and not remember it until later.

"Yes, but," my mom replies stolidly, "we aren't the kind of monsters that suck the souls out of other monsters and walk around like zombies feasting on the flesh of the mortals."

"And if we don't do something about it soon," Dad adds, sweeping Mom's hair to one shoulder and rubbing her shoulders, "we will all become extinct one day, and those fuckers will run the Earth."

"We can't let that happen," Ollie says.

"This is dire," Mom adds, her gaze flitting around the room to all of us. "Two of my friends were marked and now are mindless grimspawn. And if you lot aren't careful out there, you could be next."

"I've never seen it this bad," Dad adds, still rubbing Mom's neck, the muscles in his own shoulders tense and locked through the black T-shirt he wears.

"They've been around for centuries, but never like this." The tone of Mom's voice fades into a desperately somber one.

Scarlet's eyes lock with mine and our psychic twin connection buzzes.

I'm worried about this Dom. It's getting scary.

Retaining our eye contact, I move over to her on the brown leather sofa.

I know. Me too.

It's easier for us to talk like this rather than whisper. With everyone's excellent hearing, this is the only way we can have private conversations when we're around other vampires.

It scares me to see him like this. Even her voice in my head is uneasy and stiff.

She's referring to our father. Like my mom, he wears an armor made of thicker steel than hers. The only time we see the softness in him is toward my mom. She seeps through the cracks in his armor like sunlight. As we noticed more and more grims popping up and truly threatening our existence, we saw more cracks appear in his shield. It's like seeing a sunken battleship underwater. Something once fierce and threatening that's now vulnerable and innocuous. It's unsettling.

We're going to get through this. Even if we have to leave. We'll always have each other. Her green eyes soften and lift with an inner glow.

Scarlet carries herself with the grace and wit of an assassin princess. Her bold but flawless looks paint her as the immortal creature that she is, and she embraces it with every ounce of her villainous being. Scarlet has no soft side for anyone except for me.

"Oh, this is interesting," Mom quips. "This says only a phoenix can stop a warlock."

The room falls into questioning silence, feeling tight as though it is filled with something heavier than air.

"What the fuck is a phoenix?" Jasantha finally breaks it.

"A supernatural being with powers beyond the mundane. They are stronger than vampires, formweavers, sirens"—Jasantha scoffs—"and warlocks alike. But one only comes around every few hundred years —when . . . " she trails off.

"When?" I press.

Her eyes collide with mine, and I see nothing but worry in that gaze. "When it's bad enough it could cause a pandemic."

5

THE CARTWRIGHT WITCHES

SAYAH

Guilt is creeping up my bones again, settling into my marrow and severing all everyday thoughts, making processing this absolutely fucking tragic event nearly impossible. All the things I should have said, should have done, should have . . . Should have . . .

Should have . . .

The days have passed by like seconds and like years all the same. They've simultaneously been the slowest days of my life, and yet I look back to that dreadful phone call, and it's been a blur.

The aunts arrived last night, and while we've been processing and grieving and going over funeral plans for my parents, we've tried to look for light in the dark.

Hilda and Maggie are both in their seventies, shrinking violets and fading looks; their faces don deep-set wrinkles and missing teeth punctuate their smiles. The two women are short and stout, Hilda with strawberry-red hair streaked with silver that she wears with bangs and always in a pony and Maggie with boy-short white hair forever in disarray, as though she sticks her head out the window of a car after a shower.

We're going through an old box of pictures my mom gave me

when I had Gauge. Pictures and her grimoires and other magickal objects she'd passed down to me once she stopped practicing the craft as much.

"And there she was," Hilda goes on through tears and laughter, "in that little red car, moving to Colorado, and she takes off with all her stuff in the back and stalls the car 'cause she didn't know how to drive a stick!"

Peals of wheezing laughter erupt from Maggie, Hilda, and me as we continue our reveries and funny stories about Mama.

"I'll never forget it! I ran to her window and asked, 'Are you sure you want to move across the country without anyone?' And she said she was sure. She started that car back up and drove off into the sunset."

It feels good to keep Mama's memory alive. It's keeping that monstrous cloud of destruction from ripping my walls down and flooding me with grief.

I have to keep going like this. For Gauge.

"How long do you guys plan on staying?" I ask, sifting through the pictures.

Maggie lifts her glasses to wipe the tears from under her eyes with a tissue. "We're probably going to leave Monday morning," she says, cleaning her glasses off. "We have to get back soon to help with the kids."

After Aunt Janet died, Maggie and Hilda looked after my cousin Francine, Janet's daughter. Since Francine had children, they have helped her look after them as well. They are doing what they think Janet would have wanted.

The fact that they're leaving so soon catches me off guard. "Well, I can't plan a celebration of life in two days," I mention.

"You don't have to, honey," Hilda replies, tipping the cup to her lips and chewing on some crushed ice. "You can plan it for a few months out, and we'll make sure to return for it."

"You guys would come back for it?" I ask as I inspect an old photo more closely, deciding if it's good to show at my parents' celebration.

"If we can, we will," Hilda answers.

"Well," I add, putting the picture into the pile I want to show, "we can do something in the meantime. Like a balloon release or something."

"Oh, that would be lovely," Maggie responds. Her voice sounds strained, as though she's trying to sound excited, but it's taking every ounce of her to do it.

Hilda stands, putting the pictures she's looked through into the box and grabbing a new one. "I've never done one of those," she replies, sitting with her new pile. "I've always thought it'd be cool."

We lapse into a comfortable silence, pictures sifting and a dog barking outside the only sound.

An emptiness in the shape of Mama that weighs heavier than anything I've ever lifted pulls at me, and I fight with every ounce of who I am to not be pulled down to wherever that force wants me to go.

I know once I fall apart, it will take me a million times as long to put myself back together.

Seeing a beautiful picture of my mom in her twenties, before my sister and I came along and left lightning in her skin and wrinkles by her eyes, sets my heart to the metronome of life without her. Ticking by and empty, drifting aimlessly and heedlessly into the unknown.

Tears accumulate and fall onto the table.

The chair squeaks on the floor as Hilda rises, grabbing a tissue before she hands it to me, enveloping me in a hug.

"I don't know what I'm going to do without her," I cry, holding the picture before me and letting my aunt rock me.

"So, let's do some magick," Hilda says, releasing me from the hug and playing with my hair.

Dabbing my eyes, I look up at her skeptically. "Really?"

"Yes, later tonight," she says, combing my long locks with her fingers. "We'll do a safe passage spell for your Mama and Dan and one for us for healing."

"That sounds wonderful, Aunt Hilda," I reply as she takes her seat, resuming her walk down memory lane with the pictures. "I found her runes and rowan wand in a box I had downstairs."

Maggie's eyes grow inquisitive. "The rowan wand she inherited from Grandma?"

"I believe so, yes. It was with all the other magickal things she gave me when I got cancer. Since she didn't practice much after she met Dan. I can grab the box if you want to see it."

"Would you please, sweetie?" Hilda requests, pouring more tea from the glass pitcher into her cup.

"Of course," I say, scooting my chair back to get out.

I bound down to the basement to retrieve the box and return, setting it down on the dark stone dining table. "She's got a bunch of stuff in here," I say, shuffling through the contents until I find the wand and velvet pouch of runes.

When my skin touches the wand's wood, a zap of electricity moves through my body like a live wire, a flash of those crystal blue eyes and thick dark lashes take over my vision. It stuns me for a few seconds, and when I look back at the aunts, they stare at me as though I've grown another head.

"What?" I ask.

"You've just been staring at nothing for a few minutes," Maggie says, her magnified eyes behind her glasses all the larger to stare at me strangely. "Wondering if you're all right."

"Oh. Yeah. I'm fine," I stutter, trying to hide my confusion about what happened.

Sitting down to join them, I hand Maggie the red velvet pouch, and Hilda takes the wand.

As Maggie unties the pouch and pours the stone runes into her hand, I pick up the pictures I was looking through and pull out one of my mom and Janet.

Teenagers. Babies. At the beach in New Jersey. Mama's curly golden locks are alight by the sun, and Janet's fiery red hair burns just as brightly.

"They were so beautiful," I say, turning the picture to show my aunts.

Maggie moves her glasses to her head and squints at the picture.

"They were," she says, her mouth turned upside down in concentration. "Otherworldly."

"I wish I had a sister I was close to," I reply, adding the picture to the Yes pile.

"Well," Hilda says, switching with Maggie to look at the runes, opening the pouch with her knobby, arthritic hands, "you have a sister. Just not one you're close to."

"Understatement of the year," I add, shuffling to the following picture.

It's hard not to acknowledge Laureya when the box is filled with pictures of the two of us as kids. Although there are more pictures of me smiling and laughing with my longest friend, Ayris, than there are pictures of Laureya among them. Always scowling, never smiling. It's as if she was born with a dark soul and succumbed to the darkness.

"Have you heard from her at all?" Hilda asks, pouring the runes onto the table and flipping over the ones that are face-down.

"I tried calling her earlier today," I reply, coming across another picture of a younger Mama. "It took five calls for her to finally pick up. I was so frustrated that when she answered I blurted out, 'Our parents died.' She said, 'Cool, gotta go, bye,' and hung up."

"Do you think it's because she doesn't care?" Maggie asks inquiringly, setting the wand carefully back down on the table. "Or is it something else?"

"Honestly, it doesn't matter to me if she cares. She's had so many chances to be a part of our lives. And somehow, she always seems to fuck it up." I wrinkle my nose at the way she blisters me. "You know she's never met Gauge, right?"

"Yeah. We knew that," Hilda replies.

"I'm at the point where it wouldn't bother me if I never saw her again."

"It's too bad," Hilda says soberly. "There were five of us, so we always had a friend. Maggie and I have always been together since we were the eldest. And your mom was best friends with Janet and Pricilla, though not always at the same time, since Janet and Pricilla never were close."

"I knew Mom and Janet were close during their teenage years," I say, setting down my pile of pictures. Shifting in my chair, I say, "So, when did you all get into magick?"

I think it's a good segway into the topic I'm intrigued to learn from them. I have known some from my mom but never got to talk about it with my two eldest aunts. My cousin, Francine, isn't too keen on the whole witch thing, so the aunts keep it under wraps around her.

"We all came into it at different times," Hilda states, picking up a rune and looking more closely at it. "Our mom was Wiccan, but our father was Christian, so we never got to see her practice much. She did her spells in private. But it's funny how the path picks you because no one ever told us about it; we all happened upon it."

"I started in high school," Maggie says, leaning back and crossing her arms. "Just with tarot and herb magick. Hilda got more into the crystals, and your mom was into all of it. Janet was into altars and seasons and celebrated the solstices. But Pricilla never got into it much. Your mom and Janet were the two of us most into the magick."

"So, you don't come from a long line of witches or anything?"

"Not that we know of," Hilda says, gathering the runes and funneling them back into the pouch. "We knew Mother had a gift. She was able to talk to spirits and see the dead. It was enough to scare her, but she never talked about that or if her mother was a witch."

"And what is it with the fire?" I ask timidly. I've been hesitant to bring it up.

Maggie and Hilda exchange looks then glance elsewhere, avoiding my eyes.

"What? What is it?"

"We believe a curse was put on us," Maggie replies tersely, shifting in her seat. "Every witch with a child in the Cartwright line seems to die by fire."

"But that would mean . . ."

Is that what the dreams are trying to tell me? Are they foretelling my end?

"This is why we didn't want to bring it up," Hilda says, reaching for my hand across the table. "Please don't think that way."

I take her hand, but it doesn't quell my fear that the fire will come for me too. "That means I have the same fate?"

"It's not set in stone," Hilda says soothingly, grabbing my other hand. "Don't scare yourself thinking like that, okay?"

"But if it's a curse, who placed it? And how do I break it?"

Maggie looks at me with consternation. "We don't know. We think it was placed on us before Grandma's time."

I let go of their hands and hug my chest. "She died by fire, too, right?"

"She did," Hilda answers solemnly, her voice a low whisper. "Her sister and their mom also."

Nox, my black cat, bounds into my lap, purring as though trying to comfort me.

"And beyond that?" I ask as I pet his soft fur.

Hilda swirls the ice around in her glass. "We're not sure. It's in her journals at home. We'll bring them when we come back for the celebration."

Nox stands and stretches, jumping on the table.

"That would make me feel better," I reply, picking him up and setting him on the floor before he can knock anything down.

"The Cartwright sisters," Maggie says maudlinly, holding up a photo of the five of them.

They're young and carefree in the photo, posing by a sign that says *No Loitering*, laughing at something one of them had said. A moment frozen in time.

"The Cartwright Witches," I correct, leaning on Maggie's shoulder and gazing at the picture.

The wind blew their hair around in a soft breeze, the Pacific Ocean at their backs. The three shorter sisters were Hilda, who had strawberry blonde hair in a pony, Pricilla with dark long hair and bangs, and Maggie, who had short, spikey dark hair. The two taller, skinny women had wild curls of fiery red and the other with golden blonde.

While admiring the picture, I absentmindedly pick up my mother's wand from the table. An invisible shockwave blows through the house, causing my hair to rush off my shoulders. It feels so real I swear my mom's hair moves in the picture as well, her eyes glittering like a cat's in headlights. I hear a phantom voice in the wind: *There is light in the dark.*

Shaking my head, I look at my aunts; Maggie's holding the photo still, unfazed by the sudden blast of wind, and Hilda is staring off into space, oblivious as well.

I must be exhausted.

That picture didn't move.

Did it?

6

BRINK OF A PANDEMIC

DOM

"So, what is a phoenix, and how do we find one?" Ollie asks as we sit on the back porch, sipping bourbon and smoking cigars. Well the men are; the women are drinking blood from wine glasses and chatting in the kitchen.

"Your guess is as good as mine," I respond, swirling the bourbon around in my glass, watching it leave behind the most beautiful cathedral arches on the side of the glass.

The lake my parents live on, Lake George, is peaceful right now. The water is still and quiet, and the only sounds are a distant hoot of an owl and the wind rustling the trees.

"Well, if the grimoires say something about them, then there has to be other knowledge somewhere," my dad says, his blonde bushy eyebrows furrowing.

"Like, is it an actual bird?" Ollie asks, taking a puff of the cigar, the blue smoke whirling around his head in the amber light of the porch. "Or is it a person who has phoenix powers? And if it's the second one, what the fuck kind of powers do phoenixes have?"

Ollie is one of my favorite people. Having been the first one to succumb to our curse, he's the best out of all of us. When we became creatures of the night, our humanity was pieced out and intertwined with shards of barbarity and splinters of wickedness. If we're not careful, more pieces of our mortality slip away and are replaced with increased particles of evil. But Ollie—he's clung to every bit of his humanity and has cradled it with an empathy that normally isn't found in vampires. Granted, he kills for me when I can't. But he is the glue that holds our family together. Darkness has tempered him in some ways and softened him in others.

"In the almost three hundred years I've been on Earth, I've never even heard of this," Dad says, his left leg jittering, making the smoke leave intricate designs in the air. "But I would imagine it is a metaphor for a fire wielder."

"A fire wielder?" I query, quirking my brows up. "Doesn't Mom do that thing with her arms that lights all the candles in a swoosh?"

"I love when she does that!" Ollie exclaims, lightening the mood a tad.

"That's minor fire magick," Dad chides Ollie. "She's not a fire wielder. She can't make flames come out of her fingers or hands or anything. She can only make it come alight with things already prepared for fire."

"Do you know any super old vampires that were around even before Mom's curse we can ask?" I question Dad.

His gray eyes slide to the lake in thought. "After your mom discovered the curse and what had happened," my dad replies, tapping on the cigar so the ash falls to the ground, "she sought out others, as we couldn't be the first vampires to ever grace the Earth."

"And?" I press.

"We found the secret order of vampires, the Nyktorim Syndicate," he answers. "They're very different from us. But this was hundreds of years ago. I've no idea if they are even still around."

"We should ask her," I state, a glimmer of hope igniting in my chest. "If older vampires are around, they should know how to find a phoenix or if there even is one."

"Go ask her," Dad says, stubbing the cigar out in the ashtray. "We need to do something; this shit is getting bad. I saw eighteen cases in the ER before lunch yesterday."

"What are you doing for the blowback on that?" I ask, sliding the glass door open and entering, the smells of pot roast and gravy tantalizing my senses.

"Veilweaving them to believe they have the flu," Dad answers as he trails in behind us. "But the only thing we can do for them once they're bitten is kill them. We can't let them wander out in the world as those zombies. The world will fall even faster if we let it get out of control."

Sliding onto one of the barstools, I ask, "What do the warlocks even want with that many grims?"

"What any arch nemesis is after: Power and immortality," Dad answers, whisking his arms around my mom's waist and kissing her neck. "The more a grimspawn eats, the more youthful and powerful the warlock controlling them will be. One warlock could control over a hundred grimspawn. We need to wonder why there are so many warlocks. If they're making so many, the fae must be gearing up for something huge."

"And you went to the Neverdusk Dominion to see if you could get any information?" Mom asks, standing by the island holding the stem of her elegant wine glass filled with blood.

"We did. The fae said Tallyn and Trystan haven't been around in months," Ollie answers. "They didn't know what to tell us."

"There's got to be somebody who knows something," Jasantha adds. "They know we're on the brink of a pandemic, right? I mean, someone has to want to stop this from happening."

"Maybe that's what the fae king and queen want," Hattie says dismally. "Maybe they want total destruction."

"How long do we have?" Scarlet queries. "Before the world is overrun?"

"That's nearly impossible to determine accurately," Dad responds, scratching his beard, the sounds intermingling with the crackling fire in the attached living room. Leaning on the kitchen island, he says, "They've multiplied rapidly in the last few months. I would imagine at this rate, if something isn't done to stop them, in six months the world will look like a much different place."

Hattie bites her nails nervously. "Just go into the Neverdusk and raise hell. Start ripping heads and wings off until someone starts talking."

"Hattie, for fuck's sake," Scarlet chides. "That's just going to start a war with the fae that we don't want."

"What the fuck do you suggest then, *Scarlet*?"

"Just shut the fuck up and let the adults talk," Scarlet scoffs, darting her gaze to Hattie.

Hattie lets out a sharp exhale. Ollie's look quells her outburst.

Even though Hattie loves to play the part of the bratty teen, she still embodies a vicious woman who gets what she wants. Being the youngest one, we are ferociously protective of her, but she often gets the brunt of everyone's short tempers. Not that she doesn't bring it on herself most times, but Jasantha and Scarlet are hard on her. That could quite possibly be why she acts out toward our parents most of the time.

"What about the Nyktorim Syndicate you discovered after you learned about our curse?" I ask Mom, getting the attention off Hattie.

"Gods, I don't know where to find them; it's been so long," Mom answers, taking a sip of her blood. "I can research, check the census, and see if I can track them down. The leaders' names were Blackwood and Ravenscroft. Shouldn't be too hard to find out what happened to them."

"You do that, and maybe tomorrow after dark, Ollie and I will go back to Neverdusk. We can't veilweave fae, but maybe someone will fall for Ollie's charms and give him information."

Ollie smiles and pours himself some of the blood my mom had put in a wine bottle. "You're a good-looking vampire, too, brother. Shouldn't be too hard for us."

His smile does not ease the doubt and hesitation that creep up my spine at the thought of returning to the Neverdusk Dominion.

7

DESTRUCTIVE BLUE EYES

SAYAH

"What about this spell you were saying we should do earlier?" I ask, setting my 'Yes' pile aside and taking a drink of my tea.

"Ah, yes," Hilda says, setting her pictures down. "Safe passage spell, and a healing one for us."

I walk to my spell cabinet and open it. "What do we need?"

"Three white candles," Maggie answers, "quartz crystal and rose oil for the healing. For the safe passage, we need a piece of white cloth, bay leaves, sea salt, tiger's eye stone, white sage incense, white candles, and some dirt."

I look at my aunt imploringly. "And you know this off the top of your head?"

"I've done it a time or two." She sniggers, a knowing smile hiding behind the laugh.

"I've done a few myself and still need to check books for reference." I laugh. "Okay, I think I have all the supplies. The bay leaves would be in the kitchen, though, in the spice's cabinet."

Hilda grabs it while I gather the other things she needs for the spells, picking up Mama's wand for good measure. There's a power in it that I don't quite understand. It's light but heavy, if that makes any sense. The wood feels alive, like touching a live tree and feeling it breathe. There's a slight sound of high-pitched ringing every time I bring it near me, and it smells like earth, soil, and magick. The base of the wand is dark brown and ombres into a very light, almost blonde color.

When I return, we huddle in a circle in front of my altar by the window.

"Okay," Maggie resumes, her face steadying in concentration. "First, set the candles out and put the picture of your folks in the middle. Now, hold the stones, and put all your energy into them, thinking with all you have for the safe passage of Fran and Dan and for us, healing from this pain. We'll pass the rocks around to each of us and do this."

I take the quartz and hold it in my hand. Imagining the crystal's power has accumulated from all the world's wonders, I ask that power to help guide my mom's spirit into the next realm. The warmth of my hand is pressing into the rock, and I give it all the strength I have left. When it feels like all I am and will ever be drains into it, I pass it to Hilda, taking the tiger's eye stone in return from Maggie.

I do the same with this one.

"Now put the rocks next to the picture," Hilda instructs after the crystals have been anointed with our magick.

I place them on the altar concentrically, next to the picture of my parents that I used in my spell last night.

"We shall now anoint the candles with the rose oil and light them," Maggie says, twisting the top off the rose oil.

It's a tiny bottle. Mama had gotten it for my last birthday. It smells divine, like the most potent rose I've ever smelled, bottled up and sealed to preserve the heavenly nectar. I use it sparingly and only for significant life events. A new job. A spell for a friend to get pregnant. A death.

We each take a candle and anoint it with the rose oil from base to wick, the saccharine smell enveloping us with the decadent aroma. After rubbing the excess oil on my pulse points, I take the orange lighter and light the candle.

"As they burn," Maggie adds, "take the white cloth and put the bay leaves, sea salt, and dirt in it—"

I add the ingredients to the fabric in my hand.

"—and then light the incense."

I twist the material so the ingredients are tucked neatly inside and set it on the altar. Hilda lights the incense with the fire from the candle and then holds out her hand for Maggie and I to take on each side.

Maggie sets her jaw.

"It is with love in our hearts that we call on all the forces we've come to know," Hilda chants, "water, fire, earth, and air. Gods and Goddesses. Powers within we three. The power within Fran and Dan. Help them find their way to the light, peace, and garden of daffodils. Help us heal from this pain and help Sayah and Gauge find peace and move on. Protect them with our love even when we aren't near her. And protect us from missing our sister and her husband. This is our will, so mote it be."

"So mote it be," Maggie and I repeat in unison.

Letting go of my hand, Hilda dangles the cloth in the smoking incense. She holds it there for a few seconds, her lips mumbling inaudible incantations.

I watch as the smoke billows up and wraps around the satchel. The smoke is the intention, a palpable representation of our inner desires. The herbs inside the satchel are our wishes—what we want from the energy we manipulate. When the smoke binds to the satchel, our dreams and objectives collide, setting a force into the energy around us, a silent plea to the world to help us heal.

Hilda grasps my hand and sets the little package of magick into it. I close my fist around it and picture healing as a tangible thing, something you could pick up, put in your pocket, and save for later, drawing on it when you need to borrow some strength.

I will cradle my grief tenderly, letting this spell ease some of the burn while I get used to the way it settles into my bones.

I hold the satchel tightly and put it to my heart.

The energy in the room is peaceful, and the heaviness from the day lightens a bit. I watch the candles burn for a few minutes with my aunts doing the same. I picture my mom in that white dress, flowing through the field of flowers, touching them with her delicate hands. The light is backlighting her, setting her blonde wildly curly hair alight, beckoning her to come toward it. She looks in my direction, smiling like she is in the picture, light and full of happiness—no curses, no darkness, just light, love, and weightlessness. As the light gets brighter, Mama looks toward it, then back to me, and mouths, 'I love you,' then walks toward the blinding light. It becomes so bright I can't see anymore, and when I open my eyes, I'm shocked that it's dark. I expected the sun to be outdoors by how bright the vision got, but alas, it's night.

We're still standing before the candles, and my aunts are by my side, their eyes opening with a softness on their faces as though they, too, feel the peace.

He's standing on the deck of a lake house overlooking the dark crystal water with his back to me. I know it's him because his black hair looks wind-kissed at the tips that curl around his ears, and the black jacket has the collar flicked up to mingle with the black tresses. His toxic beauty swirls around him, even from behind.

My heart is racing. It feels like a strange dream with the mist around us—which I know it is.

Why am I dreaming of him again?

My heart is pounding so hard he probably hears it because he senses that he's no longer alone and turns. My body quivers, and my knees shake.

As soon as I meet those crystal blue eyes, I won't be able to refuse him anything.

When his eyes meet mine, I freeze. My breath catches in my

throat, tying knots around my ribs. There's a blackness about his aura, so dark it's like light itself has curled up to him and died.

I feel the terror radiating off him in waves, and it shivers in delight while his bright eyes illuminate even the most unforgiving dark.

I should run.

But where?

I'm surrounded by dense forest, its dark gnarled trees offering no escape. With no sense of direction, running seems futile—I could easily get lost in this labyrinth of shadows. Yet staying here is a guaranteed life sentence.

No matter how hard I try, I cannot lift my feet from the deck floor. They're so heavy. I can't move, let alone run.

His destructive blue eyes search my face, glittering with darkness, and he gives me a wistful smile that's laced with fatality. He's tall and spare and deadly elegant.

Something in his gait changes, his body softens, muscles relax, and as he enters my space, the terror I felt before slides off me and into the water below. I fall in love with him the moment he lets the terror ebb, like a tangible force he can wax and wane at his whim. I love him so much, and I don't know why. I don't even know who *he* is.

He walks toward me, and I steel myself, knowing the fire comes next. Anticipating the warmth that sweeps up my body when he gets too close, I clench my teeth to brace it.

He's almost upon me.

It's as though his lips were designed to unhinge me.

I want him to pick me up so I can run my fingers through his hair and feel that fire take over my body. I want him all over me—in any capacity.

In movements faster than I can see, he's in front of me, his hands on my neck, pulling me toward those lips. I want this more than the air to fill my lungs. There's a soothing reassurance in his eyes that speaks to the depths of my soul; something ancient and older than civilization floating between us.

When his lips meet mine, I forget how to breathe. He feels like the rush of jumping off a waterfall, invigorating and fatal, exhilaration and destruction colliding in the mist. His tongue enters my mouth, and I lick the darkness from him. He tastes like magick and shadows.

He gives a martyred sigh, his breath erratic; his darkness drinks from my light. He pulls back, and I miss his lips instantly; the features of his face cracking as though he's in pain like he knows what he's about to do and doesn't want to do it.

An otherworldly white leeches the blue from his irises, contracting them vertically as he opens his jaw wide with a growl. The fangs protrude, and panic hemorrhages from my skin, but I can't move; I'm captivated by the ferocious elegance of his fury.

I can't breathe; he's so beautiful in his darkest form. I don't care if the world burns down around us as long as I get to look at him while I burn.

In a mesmerizing tempered fury, he pushes my head to the side and bites my neck. Along with the crunching sound of my skin breaking open, the fire engulfs me again.

He falls back into the night, his darkness. I watch him through a ferociously burning veil, contorted with a saddened fury, as I burn alive in front of him once again.

The following day, when I open my eyes, the cut-out holes shaped like stars make my dark curtains look like a constellation, morning light lancing through them like they're glowing.

The color of the drapes is reminiscent of the fathomless blue of his eyes.

I jolt up.

Touching my fingers to my lips, the impression of him still burns there. If I press hard enough, I can almost feel him there again when I close my eyes. I yearn for him, feeling my core light up when I think of him draping over me on this bed, licking at his darkness as he laps at mine.

Fuck.

Why can't he be real?

Swinging my feet to the side of the bed, they dangle in the air a few seconds before I hop down and throw on some sweats and a tank top.

As I descend the stairs, I twirl my long hair into a messy bun, careful not to trip on my black cat, who is always lurking in the shadows.

Nox rushes past me as I enter the kitchen and perches on the table. He meows as I scratch behind his ears.

"Good morning, handsome boy," I say as he purrs. I kiss him on the top of his head.

The dream still dangles in my vision as I try to focus on making coffee, thinking about that sexy vampire haunting my dreams.

He's addicting.

As I sit at the table, drinking my coffee, I look through one of the old grimoires from the box, losing myself in the magickal words and enchantments within it.

The book is old and fragile, the pages crisp and yellow with age. A delicate cloisonné decorates the front. My grandmother's elegant script is mesmerizing; instead of reading what the words are saying, I'm paying more attention to the loops of her Gs and the swirl of her Ts.

I am so lost in thought, it's not until I hear the floorboards creak that I realize my aunts are up and coming into the room behind me.

"Oh, wow," Hilda coos, peeking over my shoulder at the grimoire, "I haven't seen that in ages."

"There's a bunch of them in that box. Some of Mama's, some of Grandma's," I say.

Hilda and Maggie each pick a book. They each slide into a chair around me and open their own journals to explore.

The brittle sound of old pages crinkling as they turn, weathered to sepia, and the smell of ancient trees and magick spells taunts the air as I'm pulled into a fleeting memory: My mother, seated at the kitchen table, surrounded by flickering candles, engrossed in one of these books.

"This is interesting," says Hilda, pulling me out of the memory.

I lean over and peek.

There are old drawings of magickal herbs and plants, notes and spells marking the margins.

"What is that about?" I ask, absorbing the colors of the beautiful illustrations.

"Some writings on plants and their uses," Hilda says, glasses poised delicately on the bridge of her nose.

"And that?" I say, pointing to a word that looks like *vampire*.

"It says, *One of the most potent magickal herbs known to witches and warlocks alike is Nightshade. Along with its sister plant, Latana, Vetana, or Nightshade, they are sacred plants used in several ancient civilizations, including ancient Egypt*. It goes on and on."

Why was Grandma so obsessed with this herb?

"There's more," she continues. "*Nightshade can be used for protection against demons, vampires, sirens, and fae*. Then, in the margin, she wrote, *Does not work against formweavers or grimspawns*."

My nose wrinkles in confusion. "What the hell is a grimspawn?"

"Someone controlled by death magick," Maggie says, not looking up from the book she's studying. "Reanimated dead people and whatnot."

"Um . . . what?" I hedge, letting out an uncomfortable laugh. "That's not real, right?"

Maggie looks at me pointedly. She sets the book down, switching the glasses to her head. "Well, like any myth, I guess there may be little truth to it. We'll never know for sure."

"Mmm-hmm," I say sarcastically, and I get the feeling she knows more than she will admit.

Her resolve is steel; she pulls the glasses back down to her nose and lifts the book.

Returning to my own, I see an entry my grandma made next to a color-pencil drawing of a beautiful woman with purple eyes.

"Oh, listen to this," I exclaim after reading a few lines. "It says, *I saw her again. This time, she spoke to me. I knew she was not a ghost, but she was something not of this world we know. I wasn't supposed to see her, though, and that is why she spoke to me. I thought she was a vampire or something . . . maybe fae. But she was not. She was of the sea."*

Hilda and Maggie exchange looks.

Hilda starts picking at her fingernail. "When was that written?"

"Nineteen thirty-four," I say.

"Before we were born," Maggie states.

"What does it mean, do you think?" I say, trying to press them. "Of the sea?"

"A siren, probably," Hilda admits, though her voice is unreliable.

"A siren?" I repeat. "Like, a mermaid?"

"Well, yes." Hilda rises and moves over to the coffee pot, getting herself a cup from the cupboard. "Probably not what you imagine a mermaid to look like, though. These are magickal, immortal beings doomed to the sea to lure sailors to their deaths and drink their blood."

Oh, so grandma was a little coo-coo then?

"She did have a vivid imagination," Hilda counters, as though my inner thoughts crawled out of my brain and crept into hers.

"Yeah, she did," Maggie agrees, winking at me with a suspicious grin. "I wonder if this was for a book she was working on."

"Does it say anything else?" Hilda asks, returning to the table with her coffee. "About that woman she saw?"

"No, the page is torn out where there should be more to the entry," I reply sadly, touching the frayed edges sticking out from the crevice. "I want to know more."

"I'll look through the other boxes at home," Hilda says, opening another book. "Maybe the other page is in there. We have a lot of her old journals."

"Yeah, that would be great, Hilda, thanks," I say, returning to the page about mermaids.

After a few slow moments of only the pages turning, making the only sound, I chew on the inside of my cheek hesitantly. "What do you guys know of vampires?" I say timidly.

Maggie looks up from her book, her wild hair backlit by the morning sun steeping in through the window. "They're said to have powers to compel you to do what they want you to without speaking."

"I've heard that in movies before," I agree.

"Yes, but it is ancient knowledge, too," Hilda says. "Everyone knows they are strong and fast; that sunlight, stakes, garlic, and silver kills them."

"They're also said to have individual powers, too," says Maggie, the look she gets when she's about to drop her useless knowledge on us sweeping over her face. "Like their own special power depending on the person who turned them, their blood type, and the time of year they were born into vampirism. Things of that sort."

I glance at her sideways. "Well, don't you know a lot about vampires."

"Oh, Maggie was obsessed with them back in the day," Hilda replies almost condescendingly. "She did papers on them in college."

Maggie tends to go overboard with things she gets fascinated with. She often bores Hilda to tears when she has random eruptions of her knowledge, wringing eye rolls and harsh sighs from Hilda every time she brings up a topic.

That's why there's a teenage-level wall in their bedroom with a collage of the Moodiest Blues band she 'toured' with in college, or why she claims she knows Italian and is fascinated by Italy but has never set foot there yet talks like she has.

It's funny listening to the two of them banter. They still fight like siblings even in their seventies.

I almost spill my dream of the mysterious vampire who has been haunting me, but then I think better of it and shut my mouth.

I'll keep him as my dirty little secret.

For now.

"Why are you interested in vampires all of a sudden?" Hilda queries, as though she senses my impure thoughts of ungodly creatures.

"Oh, I don't know," I lie, trying to tighten my voice. "Maybe because of *Twilight*."

A chuckle ripples through us before we settle back into our quiet.

Flipping through the pages nonchalantly, I keep looking for more words to tell me anything about vampires.

Why would grandma have a book that mentioned herbs that could kill them if she didn't know more about them?

I'm going crazy. They're not real. *Why am I obsessing about this?*

Letting it go for now, I continue to read through the pages for the beauty of the writing and the magick within them.

There are so many spells within the book. Spells for prosperity, wealth, love, a new job, mourning a loved one, recovering from a divorce, and so on. Each has its own set of ingredients and magickal instructions on how to carry out the spell.

I have my own spell books. I've made them look oddly like a few of these, as though a self-help guide of *How to be a Witch* was passed down through my DNA. It's as though the ancestors before us lit a trail of magick in our veins for us to follow back to the craft long after they're gone.

It doesn't feel like I just chose to go down this path.

It's as though I'm being led there.

8

ELDERTIDE APOTHECARY

DOM

The entrance to the Neverdusk Dominion can usually be found by some sort of running water—fountains, lakes, oceans, rivers; but one has to know where to look to find it, and it's different for every city. The barriers stop anything that's not supernatural or magickal from crossing.

I've been to the Neverdusk Dominion a few times in my two centuries on Earth, and it's usually to get blood and other things. Their collection of exotic drugs is to die for. In my earlier years, I dabbled with Eldertide Moss, similar to potent marijuana, and Feyfire Crystals, which are reminiscent of cocaine.

I also dated a few fae ladies before, a couple from Neverdusk and a few from Luminara Domain. The Neverdusk fairies are darker, and the beings that live there are generally dark creatures. Luminara fae are more on the lighter side, but still, never trust the fae.

I made it out each time with my blood and sanity intact, but Ollie had not been so lucky.

He's hesitant to return.

I feel bad to drag him back here, but he can control all the elements, and that is something we need to get past the barriers.

"They're all just going to say the same thing," Ollie says as we near the fountain we have to enter.

"We have to try. Mom is tracking down the older vampires, and we can do our part."

Ollie makes a noncommittal noise as we approach the entrance.

He puts his hands up and the vibration that emits looks like a glass of water sitting on a guitar as the strings are strummed. The water vibrates and connects with Ollie, then listens to his silent command and parts like curtains opening to a new day. As the water divides, a staircase is revealed inside.

As we pass through the barrier, it feels solid and liquid simultaneously, yet it isn't wet.

The mortals stand no chance of finding it. Fae magick means they see nothing out of the ordinary even while the passage is being used. When we pass through, we simply disappear once all eyes are off us.

The tunnel leading down to the fae realm is hewn from dirt and rough stone for stairs. The corridor is wide enough for two people to walk side by side, and tall enough that someone with mine and Ollie's height still has ease of passage. It is eerily quiet, the kind of quiet to drown in as the darkness unspools. The crooked shadows feel more sinister as we descend. A portion of the stairs swirl around, so it seems we're walking on the ceiling, but that is also part of the magick—the Neverdusk Dominion is below the Earth like upside-down cities underneath every major city in the world. Even though it's hard to tell when we make the switch, the incline of the tunnel is felt, even if ever so slightly.

The narrow corridor is lit by torches, and everything is so silent, nothing but the clip of our boots echoes on the dirt floors. The end comes without any warning; we exit out of the same fountain, ushering us into a whole new world.

The sky here is a velvety blue, and two moons are swollen with silver light. The clouds are bruised with purple ink, and stars and planets seem bigger.

I've always liked it here, but that also comes with a dislike.

It's terminally night here, which works for those who can't venture into the sunshine, but it's *forever* night here. People never sleep, the city never rests, and that means those dark and unruly creatures of the night are at home here.

Ollie and I make our way through the city; there are no cars, only cobblestone streets filled with different variations of hooved beings—centaurs and horses with twisted horns, bulls with five eyes, and eagles with horses' bodies and eagle talons.

Vampires are also abounding down here; there is a wicked blood market at shops similar to head shops where the other drugs are sold.

That's where we're heading.

Passing by fae of every color imaginable, we find the Eldertide Apothecary.

Slipping in through the glass doors, a sexy fairy with long dark hair, pointy ears, and amber eyes greets us. She's wearing thorns that hold up leaves that barely cover her nipples, her soft purple skin shining in the false light.

"You again?" she states flippantly.

Ollie approaches, "Yes, well, I just wanted to see your beautiful face."

A sigh escapes her lips, and I can't tell if it's spun from annoyance or longing.

"We have got to figure out where all these grimspawn are coming from," Ollie pleas with her, "and we know the fae king and queen are the ones who make the warlocks. We would be most grateful if you have any information to help us."

She opens her mouth like she's about to say something and then closes it again.

"Please," Ollie says, reaching for her hand, which she retracts. "What is your name?"

"Nyxaria."

"Please, Nyxaria. The situation is getting dire. They are taking over New York, and if we don't get a handle on them, they will spread their illness like a pandemic. And not one that has a cure."

Her amber eyes have golden rings, almost as if the sun itself lives inside them. "I can't..."

"Nyxaria, please," I plead. "We're running out of options, and it's getting so bad that we'll have to relocate."

Her eyes pointedly flick to the camera on the ceiling then back to us. "All I can say is seek out the witches. They help the fae with warlocks. I don't know how else to help you. King Trystan hasn't been to this part of the realm in months, and Queen Tallyn is in Feylight. They've had a falling out again, and I don't know what's going on."

"All right. Thank you," I say, grabbing Ollie by the arm. She's being watched; we aren't getting anything else from her.

His rigid posture and the tension in his arm tell me he doesn't want to go yet, but I insist, pulling him harder. I'm older and stronger than he is and he knows it, so he doesn't resist.

Once outside, he glares at me, the tick in his jaw clenched tight. "What was that?" he snipes, throwing his arm up.

"Someone is watching her on that camera in there. Whomever it is doesn't want her to disclose any information about this which means she most definitely knows something about it."

"So what do we do?" he asks as we meander further down the line of shops.

"We find someone who isn't being watched."

9

PAIN THAT CHANGES YOU

SAYAH

Sitting outside the school in my car, the steering wheel keeps going out of focus as I run through things I will say to Gauge to save him from his grief.

Having to tell him over the phone that both his grandparents died was quite possibly hell on earth. Not being able to hold him while his ten-year-old heart shattered cut into me in ways no blade ever could. I wanted to wait to tell him in person, but he knew something was wrong by the sound of my voice when I called him to say goodnight. I have a thing about honesty—given how his father and I ended up—lying is the number one thing someone can do to break a relationship. Being truthful with the people you love is something I drill into him, and who would I be if I didn't uphold that?

I'm happy that now I can hold him.

As soon as the school bell sounds, I see his bright green wheelchair emerge from the maroon double doors, ahead of all the other kids.

His sweet cherub face is fractured by sadness, and the puffy red circles under his brown eyes tell me he has been crying all day.

I get out of the car to help him with his crutches and backpack.

Gauge almost died when he was born. At a year and a half old, he was diagnosed with Congenital Myopathy, which is just a fancy word for muscle weakness. He's in a wheelchair but can use his legs and walk with crutches; he's just a little less strong than other kids.

I tell him he's differently abled. Never disabled. It's not that there's anything wrong with the word. I know that some people prefer being called disabled or people with disabilities, which is fine, but he doesn't identify that way. I never want him to feel like it defines him

"Hey, baby," I say as I meet him, taking the crutches and backpack from his lap. "How are you?"

His eyes catch mine, and he immediately begins to cry.

Wheeling him to the car and kneeling, I throw my arms around him and let him sob into my shoulders. Mama and Gauge had the kind of relationship I'd always been envious of. She was his best friend, too.

"It's okay, baby. Be sad. Scream, cry, punch things—do whatever you need to, but get it out. Don't bury it."

Gauge sobs so loudly that other kids twist their heads, trying to see what he's crying about. This does not hinder me, and I just hold him and let him sob into my shoulder until he's done getting his sadness out.

Once his sobs abate, I help him into the car and then clamber in myself. "Did you get lots of snuggles yesterday?"

"Yeah," he says, wiping his face. "Are the aunts at the house?"

"They are. They're waiting to snuggle you up."

His little lips curl up at the ends and his smile nearly reaches his eyes. That's all I need right now. He is the reason I live and breathe, and it kills me when he's sad.

On our trip home, I look in the rearview often, ensuring he's doing okay. He picks up his iPad from the floor and watches the weird videos he loves.

"Why her, Mama?" he asks, the sound of his innocent voice wobbly.

"What, baby?"

"Why did she have to be taken from us?"

The question I need help with. He's always asking me questions that I can bullshit my way through. But this one.

How the fuck do I answer this one?

"I don't know, baby. It seems the goddesses always want to take the good people first."

Gauge knows I don't believe in a god like most people do. To me, god is a goddess *and* a god. It's the higher power at work: the breeze in the trees and the juice in the apple. It's the things you can't explain. But I still talk of a god with Gauge to give him something to believe in.

"It's not fair," he bawls.

"I know it isn't, love," I strain to say through my tears like a breath in the universe.

I'm concerned how this death could change him.

Grief is a heavy burden to carry, and while time makes it so that the grief lessens and isn't as large and strangling as the day it happened, there's still a portion of it that knits away a little crevice in your soul that remains there for life.

The shape of that person and their death molds the pain so it's tolerable but not diminished. It shifts from hurting you to changing you.

I do not know how to navigate these treacherous waters, throw him a lifeboat, and rescue him.

The last thing I want it to do is change him, but with every death, change is inevitable.

Somewhere deep down, I feel the guilt of my mother's tragic death flip on its side and turn to rage. It's as if the grief and rage are now twining together, bubbling up beneath a thin sheet of ice that's on the brink of shattering.

10

A WITCH'S AURA

DOM

So far, everyone we've talked to knows nothing of where the warlocks are hiding, nor who is responsible for the influx of the grims.

"It's not looking too good," Ollie states as we exit the twelfth establishment we've entered, trying to get answers.

"Should we just head back?" I ask, looking at my watch.

It's going on 11 PM.

"Let's just try one more place," he says, crossing the cobblestone street to one last hut in the corner of town.

The building is a patchwork of weathered wood adorned with hanging herbs, dried plants, and mystical symbols that sway gently in the breeze. It looks more like a witch's hut than a place of commerce or business, like it would meld seamlessly with an enchanted wood, but the sign on the door reads *Evernight Elixirs* so we stride toward it. The entrance is marked by a crooked door carved from gnarled branches that creak open to reveal a dimly lit interior.

Inside, the air is infused with the earthly aroma of herbs and potions. Shelves line the walls, holding jars filled with colorful powders, roots, and mystical artifacts. A crackling fireplace casts a warm glow, illuminating a cluttered but organized workspace with cauldrons, spell books, and curious trinkets.

The witch's presence is palpable, leaving a lingering sense of enchantment permeating the air around the hut. The silence stretches before us, and the air feels heavy, like we're encroaching on someone's private space rather than a business.

"Hello?" Ollie calls out to the seemingly empty house.

"We should go," I say, turning to leave.

"Hi, can I help you?" says a soft yet angelic voice.

When I turn around, a gorgeous woman with long red hair and piercing green eyes emerges from the back room.

"Hi, yes. Hello, ma'am," I stutter. She looks to be only in her twenties, so I don't know why I'm calling her ma'am. "We were just looking for someone to answer some questions for us. It's a matter of . . ."

"Life and death," Ollie finishes for me.

The witch's eyes soften as they narrow on us. "Oh, shit, is everything okay?"

"Well . . . No," I say bluntly. "An infestation of grimspawn is taking over the city above. My family and I, well, we're . . ."

"Vampires," she finishes for us.

"Yes, and these awful things are infecting our food supply."

When she wrinkles her nose, Ollie says, "We're not the only ones in danger. If not managed, it can turn into a pandemic, and then the world itself is screwed."

The witch takes a whistling pot off the stove and pours some into a cup. "I know of these creatures," she says, taking the cup and walking over to a table to sit. "Please, have a seat. Would you like some tea?"

I look at Ollie, who only looks back at me questioningly.

"Oh, shit, sorry," she says, wrinkling her nose. "You guys are vampires; you probably don't drink tea, do you?"

"Well, no, but not because we're vampires. It's because it's gross," I state, sitting with her.

She laughs. "I'm Shayde Cleary. And you are?"

"Nice to meet you, Shayde. I'm Dominic, and this is Ollie. We're sorry to bother you; we hoped to find someone down here with any answers."

She unravels her tea bag and dips it into the steaming tea, the steam swirling in the air. "You're looking for the warlocks that create them, right?"

"Yes," Ollie says, crossing his legs. "That is correct."

"We've been hearing things," Shayde says, wrapping her hands around the brown mug. "Several vampires also reached out to our family in the Salem area. My mom has been doing some spells to see what we can find out. We have an energy spirit, her name is Aura—long story and no time to explain. But she did find something that may be helpful."

I want to know more about the energy spirit, but based on how her gaze intensifies, how the tendon in her neck contracts as though she's uncomfortable, whatever she's about to tell us has significant weight. Ollie and I hang on to her every word. The energy in the room is palpable and intense.

"What is it?" Ollie asks, leaning forward on his knees.

Shayde reclines back in her chair, her long red hair flowing over both shoulders and down to her waist as she clasps her tea on her lap. "It's very vague and doesn't make much sense to me. It's a prophecy. There is a woman in Colorado. Her name is Sayah Thorne. I don't know much else about her, but I do know that for balance to remain in the world, Sayah . . ." she hesitates; a look of pain washes over her face as though a deep sadness has her steeping in sorrow.

"Sayah what?" Ollie presses.

Her gaze collides with mine as though the information will affect me the most. "Sayah has to die."

"So a random woman in Colorado has to die?" I ask, confused. "What will that do to stop this problem?"

"I don't know the specifics," Shayde answers, shaking her head. "And believe me, I've been very blatant in my dislike for this resolution, but Aura would never come to this conclusion lightly. She just said the balance is off, and for it to be restored, Sayah must die. She was chosen. It's out of our control."

"And once she dies, all the grimspawn will disappear?" Ollie asks, his tone edging on confusion paired with disbelief.

"I don't think it's that simple," Shayde answers, eyeing him pensively. "I think her dying would be the catalyst that causes the downfall of the warlocks. That's all I know."

The information oscillates around me for a few seconds. Shayde's words radiate jangling tension, and it leaks out into the air they punctured, causing my muscles to tense.

I lean forward, interlacing my hands on the table. "We have to kill an innocent woman for balance to be restored?"

Her green eyes go cold, the information unspooling something within them. "I'm afraid so."

"So we'll have to track this chick down," Ollie says to our mom once we've arrived back at the cabin. She is reclined on the couch in the living room, her feet propped up on my dad's lap. "You can do your locator spell, and then I'll go out there and kill her."

Ollie usually hates killing as much as I do but knows the last time I drained someone inadvertently, I was in a very dark place for a long time afterward. His volunteering to do this saves me from that dark.

"Why do we have to kill her at all?" I say, trying to find the more logical side to this. "Maybe 'die' is a metaphor for something. Why can't we go out there, find her, and get to know her? See why she is the catalyst?"

"I say kill her," Scarlet agrees.

She and Hattie are sitting on the other couch, Scarlet with her laptop on her lap and Hattie squinting, pointing the remote at the TV.

"I second that," Hattie adds, finding something to watch and setting the remote down.

"I also think that if a wise witch of Salem and her energy spirit says it's the only way, then we must listen and act," my mom concurs with Dad, rubbing one of her feet.

So, everyone in the room wants this stranger dead but me.

"I get what you're saying, guys, I really do," I say, sitting on the arm of the recliner Ollie is in. "But hear me out. Let's do some research first. Maybe there's something else that can solve this. Maybe she's just a symbol for something."

"Says here on her Facebook profile that she's single," Scarlet expands, her fingers flicking over the trackpad. "Looks like she just lost her mom. Tear." She feigns wiping a tear away and gives me a fake sad face.

"See, she's single," I exclaim, looking at my mom. "I can go out there and pretend to run into her somewhere and find out what she's about. Figure out why she may be the catalyst."

"Looks like she's marked that she's going to a concert at this place called the Gothic Theater on Friday," Scarlet adds, her face aglow from the computer screen. "Now you know a time and place she'll be."

"Well, at least I didn't need to get my hands dirty doing those blasted locator spells," Mom says, smacking my dad on the shoulder playfully.

"So you'll let me go out there and try to get answers from her before killing her?" I inquire, looking at my mom and sisters.

My dad has only observed the conversation and hasn't put his two cents in. Normally he's never opposed to a good old-fashioned murder, but the cold stare he's giving the air in front of him is enough to give me chills.

I hate when he's *this* quiet.

"You have two weeks to get us any information," Mom states grimly. "If you don't find anything out by then, we'll come to kill her."

11

WITCH'S BLOOD

DOM

"I know, Mom, I will," I say into the phone, the Gothic Theater looming to my right out the rental car's window. "I'll let you know what happens."

"Just don't dottle," my mom's stern voice fills the interior of the car, her accent lilting through the slanted light from the streetlamp. "Hattie was almost attacked by a grim."

"I'm trying!" I snap, my exhaustion and hunger getting the better of me.

"Odin's Ghost, Dom," she scolds.

I kill the engine of the car. "Sorry," I say, sighing, pinching the bridge of my nose. "I've had a long day of travel and I'm exhausted. Have you had any luck tracking down the Nyktorim Syndicate?"

"No. The trail went cold. I found them all the way until 1851, and then nothing. Dad and I may fly there to see if we can proceed with it. They have a census in the archives."

"Damn. I wonder why their records just stop at 1851?"

"Vampires," she offers. "Sometimes, while moving around and starting over when people start to notice we don't age, we have to start *all* over. New names and everything."

"And you're thinking the census in England will help trace a name change maybe?" I ask, watching a younger woman emerge from a restaurant by herself, looking deliciously like a snack.

"That's what we're thinking, yeah."

The woman walks down the dark street alone; now is my time to get a quick meal. "All right, Mom, sounds good. Gotta go."

"Wait, Dom—"

Closing the call, I press the red button on the car's main screen and disembark to catch my dinner.

The atmosphere in the establishment is pulsating with diverse energies as people mingle, drink, and watch the band play. The venue is alive with a fusion of vampires and mortals, a cacophony of blood mixing in the air and creating a dangerous space for prey; as these places are often where predators lurk. The aesthetic matches the vibe—gothic and dark. People are writhing to the music, the purple and blue lights eerily cascading over them as they dance.

The vampires are effortlessly discernible to me. They abound in every direction, typically possessing alluring and handsome features; devilishly good looks that stand out amidst the ordinary crowd. Our skin is soft and smooth, our features are striking and bright, voices melodic and enticing. Our beauty is that otherworldly, knock-your-breath-out, keep-you-awake kind of beauty, making you question yourself on how something so fucking perfect could possibly be.

Weaving my way through the crowd, different smells arouse my senses as I make my way toward a bar in the back. The humans smell like the products they use—soap and lotion and conditioners—but that only masks the tangy scent of their blood. Vampires—we smell like nature. Woodsy and earthen. There's almost a cinnamon scent, as well as pine needles and damp bark. I believe it's because our hearts have been pumping our blood for so long it's as though they've coalesced with the Earth and made an oath with the soil, solidifying her wish to keep us bound to her for eternity.

Arriving at the bar with a full view of the establishment, a beautiful vampire with striking eyes and porcine white skin stops. “Get you anything, handsome?”

“I’ll just take a beer, thanks,” I say, giving her a flirtatious smile.

She nods and grabs a beer from the cooler, pops the top, and hands it to me. “There ya go, sweetheart. That’ll be five fifty.”

“Put it on my tab, Laney,” an equally alluring woman to my left says.

Laney nods and walks off.

“Um, thank you . . .” I say, holding out my hand.

“Mara. And you are?” She takes my hand and firmly shakes it.

The way her skin is cold but hot and smooth yet rigid tells me she’s a vampire. That and her devastatingly gorgeous green eyes. They shimmer in the purple light but also have a depth that ordinary mortals don’t.

“Dominic.”

“Nice to meet you, Dominic. Not from around here, are you?”

Her eyes track to the silver thimble claw I wear on my left thumb. It’s a defense mechanism I never leave home without these days. Not only does it protect me against the grims, but vampires have a lethal allergy to silver as well.

Double-edged coin.

“No. I’m new,” I respond, quickly slipping the lethal jewelry into my pocket. “I’ve heard this is a good place to come for people like us, though.”

“Yes, this place is where many of us meet, chill, and hang out. There are donor rooms in the back, too, with the mortals who know about us. I’m actually in a band playing tonight called Immortal Echo.”

“No way, really?” I gape at her, leaning on the bar.

She smiles. “Yeah I sing and play the electric guitar.”

“That’s sexy,” I reply, holding my beer up to cheers her.

She accepts my cheers and knocks her beer into mine, taking a drink after.

I take a drink as well. "Can I ask you something, Mara?"

"Sure," she says, lending me a flirtatious smile.

I lean in close to her neck to whisper, "Is Denver experiencing problems with the grimspawn?"

Her eyes turn sad for a split second. "Oh. Yeah, it seems to be happening more frequently from what I noticed. I have friends in other areas where it's worse. Why? Is that what brings you to these parts?"

"Something like that," I state, letting my gaze sweep over the crowd.

My eyes are tracking the movements of the different types of people—humans moving more laboriously and bumbling and the vampires more lithe and precise—when my gaze is pulled by an otherworldly force and I zero in on the woman I've come for.

The world stops, hers the only face in focus in the amalgamation of people.

Sayah.

A shiver traces my bones as she walks in my direction.

The presence of her aura staggers me. It is the brightest aura I've ever seen, bounding around her in a kaleidoscope of colors that aren't even on the spectrum. I blink rapidly just to sway myself from my mesmerization of her.

I know Mara said something but I can't respond. She's all I see, all I hear.

She is why I exist.

So she's a witch?

Witches have brighter auras about them than ordinary mortals. The more powerful the witch, the brighter the aura. With the way hers is glimmering, she's got to be the strongest witch I've ever encountered.

She gets to the bar I'm at and her blonde friend, linked to her via elbow, leans in and orders a drink from Laney. Sayah hangs back and looks around. I can't take my eyes off her when she catches my gaze, I'm immediately flustered and tongue-tied.

She. Is. Flawless. Her body is a celebration of curves, a departure from the bony thinness that characterizes some other women in the room. The way she stands with authority in her skin, commanding attention by just the strength of her stance, I immediately want to bow down and worship her. The dark hue of her long hair complements the sun-kissed tan of her skin, creating a mesmerizing contrast. Tattoos slither down her arms, peeking out from the plunging shirt she wears, revealing the most delicious cleavage.

Oh, and that nose ring. She's got a fucking hot septum piercing marked by a tiny ring of braided gold that's barely noticeable. Between that and her dark eyes painted with black liner, I think I'm falling in love.

She holds herself with a threateningly untamed ease.

The most beautiful woman I've ever seen stands before me, and her death is to come at my hands?

Emotions I don't even have a name for war within my chest, causing my jaw to clench and my grip around my beer to tighten. As feelings akin to frustration and hopelessness tangle within my heart, asphyxiating my lungs, the bottle shatters in my hands as the churning of emotions flares up inside me.

"Shit!" Mara exclaims. "Are you all right? You're bleeding."

I nod at her, still unable to peel my eyes away from Sayah. The way the curve of her body dips before expanding outward to her hips, accentuating her hourglass figure, I picture how perfectly my hands would fit there. Every thought I've ever had moves out of the way to make room for her in my mind, and everyone in the establishment disappears.

I barely notice Laney coming around to sweep up my broken glass; I can't remove my eyes from Sayah, no matter how hard I try. It's as though I'm seeing a piece of myself I've been missing for a very long time, and lo and behold, here it is, in a city a thousand miles from home.

Mara glances at me, questioning in her eyes, as her gaze tracks mine to the witch.

Sayah's attention is on her friend, who's handing her a glass of water.

My heart rate quickens—or maybe it's been beating this fast since I saw her, and I just now noticed. Other vampires near me perk their heads up as though they can hear it, too.

Sucking in a breath and holding it to try and gain my composure, I lean my hip against the bar to relieve my unstable legs.

Someone moves into my line of sight of her.

It's as if the sun went behind the clouds, and I immediately feel her absence from my life. It's dark and cold; she was my light—even for those twenty seconds. Choosing to stand on shaky legs, I brace myself and shift my weight to see her again.

The next person to stand between her and me again will lose their head.

She looks at me. The flush to her cheeks is nearly immediate as she gives me a smile that reaches her eyes. The feeling is mutual. Gravity assembles around her; we all swirl around in her orbit, as though she swallowed the sun and moon and all the stars in the sky.

An imperceptible breeze sweeps through the crowd, blowing the witch's hair against her cheek, her scent accompanying it.

Witches blood is very sweet and very addicting.

I'm not the only one that smells her.

A vampire behind her and across the bar shoots his gaze to her. His black pea-coat and scarf accentuate his murderous black eyes.

My predatory vision zooms in on him and I watch his movements. His eyes go white for a split second and then he shifts them back to black, squaring his shoulders as he walks in her direction.

Instead of panicking, the killer inside steadies my nerves, setting my resolve to the beat of the bass.

Slipping the claw onto my thumb, I excuse myself from Mara and race—without looking supernatural—into the crowd.

He's using the same faster-than-normal pace to reach Sayah without drawing attention, and he is moving fast. But he doesn't notice that I see him.

Before he can reach her, I intercept his path. I jab the silver claw into his neck, causing instantaneous paralyzation. His body falls to the floor with a thud. Nobody on the dance floor even notices.

I need to get him out of here without looking obvious. Veil-weaving a crowd this size would be too time consuming.

"Oh, shit! Brenden!" I laugh, concocting a cover as quickly as it comes to my head. "Can't hold your liquor like you used to, dumbass!"

Some people look at me and smile, shrugging their shoulders.

A guy claps me on the back. "Some of us just want to stay young forever." He laughs.

I bend down to grab the vampire by his shoulders. "You have no idea." I grin, yanking him backward toward the side of the stage.

The vampire is heavy, but I manage to get him off the dance floor and to a dark corner of the building. He's wide-eyed and pale, his gloved hands grasping his neck. He can still see me, the poke wasn't enough to kill him instantly. He's just paralyzed from head down.

The silver's poison is a slow death when it's in small amounts. Straight to the heart would be better. Instant kill.

Fuck a slow death.

Throwing some tablecloths over the mummified vampire, I walk to the edge of the concert still in the shadows, scanning the back bar to see if Sayah is still there.

She is not.

It's not hard to find her though, her aura bounds around her like headlights on a foggy highway. She's returning to her table with her friend in tow.

I watch them for a few minutes and then my gaze slides to where I was, where Mara is still at the bar, talking closely to Laney. I'll catch up with her later and provide an explanation.

Wiping my thimble claw on the dark curtain of the stage, I stick it back in my pocket and straighten out my shirt, wiping any dust and debris from my jeans. Looking one more time before departing my secluded hiding spot, I peek again and see that her friends have left her alone at the table.

It's time to approach her for a conversation.

12

THE DARK STRANGER

SAYAH

I'm scrolling through my phone at the table, waiting for my friends to return from the bathroom, when a blur of colors on a cool gust of wind startles me into looking up.

Not expecting the handsome man I'd seen at the bar to be sitting at my table, I jump.

"Sorry, I didn't mean to frighten you!" he yells over the pounding music.

His voice is strangely dangerous, inciting fear and unease. Little bubbles of excitement swell up inside me and intermingle with the fear, concocting emotions I'm unfamiliar with.

He. Is. Gorgeous.

He's tall with short dark hair and bright hazel-green eyes. Muscles jump under tattoos covering his arms and peeking out from under his V-neck tee. The energy around him is a strange mixture of excitement and intrigue mixed with a little danger. He smells delicious, like Earthy musk and cedar wood bathed in a winter-spring.

"It's okay," I answer, flicking my phone off and setting it on the table. "I just wasn't expecting anyone to be there."

"I'm Dominic." He holds out his hand for me to shake.

I take it. "Lasayah."

"What?" he shouts.

"La-say-ah!" I yell at him.

"Oh, beautiful name." He leans in to kiss my hand.

I can feel the warmth of his breath; the scents of fresh linen and pine needles engulf me.

"Nice to meet you, Lasayah."

"My friends all call me Sayah."

"And mine call me Dom."

Through my disbelief at having this handsome man sitting across from me, I offer him a smile that consists of charm and a little bit of a don't-fuck-with-me sparkle in my eyes.

He gets up and moves chairs to sit next to me. The minute his hazel eyes bore into mine, any unease slips off me like oil.

"I'm sorry to be so forward, but I noticed your tattoos. I love it when women have sleeves."

"Thank you," I say, twisting my arm out to see the backside of the fairy. "I love ink."

He pulls my wrist toward him, examining the artwork. "Very nice detail."

"You got some pretty badass ink yourself," I return, nodding toward his arms.

"Thanks," he says, rolling up his sleeves. "It's the story of my life."

I admire them. They seem to have the theme of light and dark—angels and demons, flowers and skulls, the moon and sun. Latin words and Roman numerals are interspersed throughout the pictures. I'm about to ask him what they represent when the girls arrive.

"Hey," they both say, wry smiles painted upon their drunken faces as they slide into the chairs across from us.

"Dominic, this is Claire, and this is Anna. Guys, this is Dominic."

"Hi, Dominic," Claire says, holding out her hand. "Nice to meet you."

Dominic takes each hand and presses his lips to the top, like someone from another time. Even the way he moves is lithe and calculated.

Claire blushes, taking a swig of her beer. "So, where are you from, Dominic?"

He scoots his tall bar chair closer to the table, leaning his ink-clad arms on the surface. "Originally, I was born in Florence, but I came to the U.S. pretty young. I lived in New York for a long time and just moved out this way a few months ago for work."

Even though he's yelling over the music, his deep voice is soothing, the kind of sound that could make anyone feel better even if they were dying.

"Wow, Italy?" Anna says, leaning in, interested.

"Yes," he smiles. "I haven't been back in a long time, though."

"What do you do for work?" I ask, my interest in this dark stranger growing thicker with every syllable he speaks.

"I am a data analyst for a software engineering company."

"Oh, nice," I respond, sipping my water.

"And you're here in the Denver area?" Claire asks, tonguing the thin black straw of her rum and coke into her mouth and sucking.

He shifts in his seat, his black shirt tight around his biceps. "I work in LoDo, but live in Windsor."

"Dang, commuting to Denver daily must be rough, huh?" I ask.

"It's not too bad," he tells me, his straight white teeth glimmering. "I work nights, so I leave to work after rush hour is over, and I get home before it starts."

"Yeah, that would make it better, I guess," I concede, adjusting my seat so our knees are touching.

"Where are you from, and what do you do?" Leaning toward me more, he offers me a smile.

My heart flutters. His dark eyes look lethal, but then again, they are as poignant as a ballet dancer.

"I'm from here. Born and raised. And I'm in customer relations for a technology firm."

"In Denver?"

"No, in Fort Collins."

"Ah, so not far from me." The way his smile dispenses with this information and his posture hold assignment, like there's something he intends to do and now is in range to do it.

"Nope, not far," I reply, his green eyes like gunmetal, quick-witted, sharp, *and lethal.* "I bought a house north of there a few years back since it was cheaper to buy there than to rent in Fort Collins."

"Homeowner, huh?" His brows kick up in intrigue. "Boss bitch."

A nervous laugh fights its way off my lips as I play with the condensation on the glass.

He leans in. "And are you single?"

The words, those lips—sensual yet commanding. "Yes. Divorced. With a child. Single mom."

"Oh, okay, cool. Independent, strong single mother lady. I like that," he states and waves the waiter over. "What would you like to drink? It's on me."

"Oh, I don't drink. But thanks."

"You drink no liquids whatsoever?" he says teasingly.

"Well, I drink virgin daiquiris."

"There you go. I'll take a Bourbon, top shelf, rocks, and this fine woman will take a virgin strawberry daiquiri."

The waiter nods and scampers off.

I peek over at the girls. They are talking amongst themselves, probably realizing I'm smitten with this gorgeous dark stranger who seems interested in only me and are allowing me to flirt with him. Either that, or they're too drunk to realize anything else happening around them.

"So, no booze then?" he asks, shifting his weight to face me better.

"Nope. I gave it up a year and a half ago."

"Any reason you care to disclose with a handsome stranger?" He winks behind the smile.

I can't help but feel drawn to him like he's pulling me into some gravitational pull around just him.

"Let's just say I had a rough patch. I beat cancer and was miserable in my marriage and then divorced him. He had a new family right away over Christmas. Booze became a way to numb, and it got out of hand.

"I was driving home drunk from Denver during the day and had an epiphany. I had already lost so much and I was about to lose the rest. If I got pulled over, I'd lose my license, which would cost me my job, followed by my home, and then ultimately, my son. So I quit. I got to the point where I wanted to feel everything again, even the bad." I don't know why I'm sharing this with him. It usually takes me a few dates to tell men about my personal story. Still, there is something about how he's looking at me, making me want to tell him like the words are being pulled from me rather than me choosing to say them.

"Wow. Cancer? You okay now?"

"Yeah, I'm okay now. Just hit five years post-treatment, so I was deemed cured."

"Congrats," he says, taking the bourbon from the waiter and handing me the daiquiri.

"Thank you."

"Not a problem. So,"—he takes a slow sip of his whiskey, the ice chinking against the glass—"now that you're in the clear, what are your goals and dreams?"

A man that's interested in my dreams and goals? That's unique.

"I am a writer and in school. Trying to get my book published and a degree. But," I pause and look around, bracing for the impact of the words I'm about to say, "my parents just passed away last week, and so I'm trying to get through that right now."

"Your parents just died?"

The way his attention is anchored on me is disarming.

"Yes," I say solemnly. "We had their balloon release earlier today."

His manscaped brows pull together. "That is so tragic. I would say I am sorry, but I know how old that can get. I've lost people too. I hope you're doing all right."

"Thank you for not saying sorry. I don't know how to respond to that."

"Right," he says, shrugging his shoulders and holding up his palms. "People don't know what else to say, but responding can be hard."

"Who did you lose, if you don't mind my asking?"

"Not at all. I've lost many people." He pauses, and his mountain-colored eyes drift away as though chastened by loss and electing it to return to him. "All my grandparents. Aunts. Uncles. Cousins. A few friends."

"That's a lot."

"Yeah, but more about you. Why're you here?"

Taking a sip of my daiquiri, I glance at Claire and Anna. They're clumsily dancing with one another, each shot making them tipsier.

"Because these two wanted to get me out of the house and away from the sadness. I'm trying to do what my mom would want and find the light in the dark."

"Good for you. That's all you can do."

"And you? Are you single? Divorced? Didn't I see you with a pretty blonde by the bar earlier?"

He lifts the glass to his lips, and I can't help but notice the sensualism of his mouth again, his upper lip exquisitely sculpted. The kind of mouth that would keep me up at night.

"I am single. Almost married once. And that blonde was trying to flirt. Blondes aren't really my type."

"No? And what is your type?"

"Sexy, strong, independent brunettes with curves for days and as many tattoos as me."

The delicate flickering in my stomach is making it entirely too difficult to stifle the giggles I'm suppressing. His astute gaze devours my every word, beseeching and bewildered, calming my heart and making me feel safe.

"Would you like to dance?"

"To this?" I say, inclining my head toward the band; the music is upbeat and funky. "I can't dance like this unless I'm drunk. I probably suck at it then too, but at least when I was drunk, I didn't care how bad I looked." I give him a cheeky smile.

Suddenly, as if on cue, the music changes to something slower.

"How about now?" he asks, his eyes returning to mine, a devious smile playing at the corners of his mouth.

He stands and offers me his hand. Taking it, I feel a slight buzz. He doesn't seem to notice, but I do.

The girls wink at me and say something I can't quite hear as I follow him to the dance floor before the stage.

Holding me in the classic dance stance, he places my hand on his shoulder and holds my other one. We sway to the music, the lights dim, and for a moment, it seems as though we're the only ones in the room. It's easy to get lost for a fragment of time with this sexy man holding me.

As the song continues, he inches closer to me, the sweet smell of earth magick and spiced fire stirred into his fragrance. I breathe it in, letting him sway me to the beat of a soft rock song with a violin. Violin music has always spoken directly to my soul.

While we dance, I feel comforted, almost drunk-like. It's been so long since I've felt the soft bubble of drunkenness, and I almost panic that my virgin daiquiri had booze in it. But I know I'm not drunk; it must be just the atmosphere. Or the man.

Suddenly, he dips me, and I'm not ready for it. I scream as I fall, the ground rising fast to get me. But he's here, holding me, his perfect face above me. I laugh as he grins, pulling me back up.

"I'm awkward," I say apologetically.

"Not at all," he purrs, pulling me in closer. "Just relax. Let me move you."

And I let him move me. He moves me in more ways than he knows.

When the song ends, he holds me still, his lips inches from mine. My breathing ceases, and suddenly, I'm nervous again.

"I like you," he says, whiskey lingering on his breath.

"I like you too," I return, unblinking.

"I'm taking you to dinner tomorrow night."

"Okay," I answer quickly, with little thought, and how easily I agree surprises me. Something fascinating about Dominic draws me in, and I want to get to know him more when we aren't screaming words at each other.

"Let's go back to the table and exchange numbers."

Nodding, I let him lead me. As he pulls me by the hand, I realize how badly I had wanted him to kiss me on the dance floor now that the nerves have slipped away.

When we return to the table, the girls are all tipsy smiles.

"Have a nice dance?" Claire says, tipping her beer to her lips.

I can tell from the glitter in her eyes that she's feeling mighty fine at the moment.

Knowing that my blushing is giving me away, I nod. "It was fantastic."

"Okay, what's your number?" Dominic asks, taking out his phone.

I take it, putting in my information, even spelling my name in case he forgot. When I return the phone to him, he types something, and I feel mine vibrating in my back pocket.

"Just making sure you gave me the right number," he says, smiling, stowing his phone away again.

"Of course I did," I say, saving his number under *Dominic*.

"Good," he adds, taking another sip of his bourbon. "Well, I will let you spend time with your girls. I'll text you tomorrow for the details of our date, okay?"

I nod with disappointment, brought up short that our little reverie is over.

He stands and pulls me to him, sliding his arms around my waist and wrapping me in a hug. I take a deep breath, inhaling his glorious scents as they unspool into the air around us. I close my eyes and allow his smell to soothe me; I feel at peace.

"It was nice to meet you, Sayah," he whispers to the shell of my ear.

The hairs on the back of my neck stand, sending chills down my spine.

"I can't wait to see you again." He kisses me on the cheek and then is gone.

"Are you gonna see him again?" Claire tries to ask as I slide into my seat again, although the words are jumbled and slurred.

I giggle. "Yeah, he's taking me out tomorrow night."

"That's so awesome, Say. I'm glad," Anna says.

"Me too."

Things like this don't happen to me. Especially when I'm with beauties like Claire and Anna; guys usually flock to them, not to me.

I cannot wait to see that man again.

After Dominic's departure, I try to keep having a good time, but the rounds of beers and shots keep coming. When groping commences—a solid squeeze to my right boob by Claire—I decide it's time to go.

Going out with the girls is always fun; however, it's different now that I'm sober. I used to be the life of the party, laughing and being dumb, dancing and making an utter fool of myself. The last few times I went out with them, the more drunk they got, the more I felt out of place. It's like being an outcast. Alcohol is the only drug people make you explain why you don't use it, and having everyone ask why I'm not drinking is starting to get old. It's why Claire is closer to Anna now.

Claire and I had been inseparable when we were each other's drinking buddies, and Anna is that to her now.

On our way home, I feel my phone vibrate and pull it out of my pocket at the next stoplight.

> It was so lovely to meet you. You are gorgeous.
> Can't wait to see you tomorrow.

Because both girls had passed out after merging onto the highway, I have no one to share my schoolgirl giddiness with, so I set the phone down at my side.

Pulling to a stop in Claire's driveway, I finally text him back.

> It was nice to meet you, too. I can't wait either!

I help the girls into the house, make sure they're lying on their sides on the couches, and head back to my car when my phone vibrates again.

> Let me know when you make it home safe,
> okay?

He is so sweet and handsome. The butterflies in my stomach excite me. But on the other hand, whenever I consider dating again, I worry about someone coming into my space with my child, which always tugs against those feelings of sweet new beginnings.

And there is something dark about Dominic I can't quite put my finger on. The further I get from him, the more that coat of euphoria slides off, and I feel the darkness seeping in.

13

EMBERS OF THE BROKEN

DOM

Something about Sayah speaks to me on a different level than other women. She seems familiar, and I know she's in her thirties, but she has an aura about her that's as old as time. There's also someone in my past who she's very reminiscent of.

I couldn't find out much about her in our short encounter. She seems to know she's a witch, as she carries that with an effortless grace, but I'll need to spend more time with her to glean much else, or what she knows of grimspawn and vampires or supernatural characters.

I need to find out more information about Sayah, and if I don't get that information, my family will come to kill her. But for now, I'm enjoying getting to know her.

I tracked down Mara when I left Sayah's table and talked to her some more about the local haunts in LoDo. She told me the location of the Denver entrance to Neverdusk, so tonight, before my date with Sayah, I plan to go there and search for any additional information.

I've spent the day texting Sayah, getting to know her while I shopped around for a house to rent in Windsor. I needed to make my lies to her believable. I hate lying to her, and I tried to pepper my lies with truth to ease some of the sting—I actually am a data analyst, just not in Colorado.

Under normal circumstances, she would be someone I'd be interested in dating.

After parking at the 16th Street Mall, I search for the fountain that looks like a bunch of stacked blocks, as Mara had said.

Approaching the fountain, I place my hand on the smooth surface, and like a silent symphony, the water in the fountain obediently parts.

Emerging from the other side of the fountain into an inverted Denver, the skyline and cobblestone streets are devoid of cars. The graceful-hooved beings traversing the walkways and the vividly colored fairies fluttering about paint a picture of a world distinctly apart from the one I left behind. The towering structures remain recognizable, yet the two large moons casting a metallic glow against a rosy sky confirm I've crossed into a different realm.

Mara told me to look for a crystal shop called Whispering Willow Potions.

Making my way through the hustle and bustle of Neverdusk, I find the store on the street she'd said it would be on.

The shop, ensconced within the verdant embrace of the concrete jungle around it, emanates an enchantment that draws seekers of magickal remedies. Adorned with winding vines and bioluminescent flowers, the exterior adds to the ethereal charm.

Pulling the handle on the wooden door, a bell chimes, alerting the keepers of the shop that I've entered.

The interior is bathed in a soft, ambient glow emanating from alluring crystals suspended from the ceiling. The air is rich with the heady fragrance of rare herbs and magickal ingredients. Shelves adorned with intricately labeled jars line the walls with powders, roots, and exotic flora. The polished, worn wooden floor creaks beneath my feet as I move through the shop, and the gentle sound of bubbling wafts from a hidden chamber. There are corners filled with beguiling trinkets, charms, spell books, and parchment scrolls bearing handwritten ancient recipes. The space feels both intimate and expansive.

The proprietor, a slender man wearing a dark blue cloak, moves gracefully among the shelves. His demeanor stiffens when he catches sight of me. His skin, the color of milk chocolate, flushes and takes on a darker hue. "Oh. The blood donors are down the way; I have none here," he says in an accent I can't place, his blueish-gray eyes sweeping over me with disdain.

"I'm not here for that," I say hesitantly, not wanting to scare him. "I was hoping to ask you some questions."

"I see." He blinks owlishly. "I may not have the answers you seek, but I can try. Please, come with me."

Nodding, I follow him to a back room beyond a layer of beaded curtains.

When we arrive at what looks to be his office, he sits amongst the clutter on his desk, and I take a seat in the chair opposite.

"I'm wondering if you have any information on the witches helping the fae king and queen make warlocks? Or maybe have any information on how to find the warlocks creating the inundation of grimspawn we've been having above."

Like everyone else we've talked to, except Shayde, he pauses and rubs his brows. "I don't think anyone in this area will have that information. But the Velvet Moonrise Coven in Vegas may have some answers."

"The Velvet Moonrise Coven?" I repeat, setting the name to memory.

"Yes. They are a very large organization out there, shouldn't be hard to find them."

"So you are unaware of the grimspawn or the rise in their numbers or anything?"

He shakes his head, the blonde locs swaying with the movement. "They don't come here, and I don't make it up there often. If I hear anything, I can let you know somehow."

"Yes, please, if you don't mind."

He retrieves a pad of paper and a pen from the drawer and hands them to me. I scribble my name and number and then offer the pad back to him.

"Also," I add as he rips the top page off with my number and places the pad back in the drawer, "have you ever heard of a phoenix?"

His eyes narrow to crinkled slits. "The bird that rises from the ashes?"

"Well, yes, but in this case, I feel it would be a supernatural being. It's mentioned in one of my mother's grimoires as to how to defeat these grimspawns."

He inventories his surroundings, his gaze sweeping over his bookshelves that take up one wall. "I may have seen something," he says, rising and going to them. Pulling out a sizable burgundy book, he sits back down and flips through the pages. "Ah, yes. There." He points to the page he's opened up to, flipping the book around so that I can see better.

The drawing shows a woman floating in midair, naked, encased by flames. Her arms are outstretched, her head is tilted back. She seems to enjoy the fire rather than being burned by it.

He turns the book back around and leans in. "It says, *The Phoenix will come when grimspawn ravage the earth. When times are detrimental, the only outcome is total annihilation. Look for them in the burning embers of the broken. Watch for them in the sorrows of the dismayed. They are conditioned for this; their souls are put through a series of tests to withstand the fire. For them to rise, they first must die.*

"The margins here say, *Last recorded phoenix was in sixteen ninety-two.* That was around the time of the witch craze."

"What does that mean?" I ask him, my voice thready with wonder.

"It means the phoenix will come when times get too dire."

"And if I've found the potential phoenix, does that mean I have to light her on fire?"

His expression is inscrutable. "I would not advise that, but I am not the one to ask."

"Who do you recommend I ask?"

"That would be a question for Tallyn. The Luminara Queen."

"And how do I find her Royal Highness?"

"You don't," he says, slamming the book closed causing dust motes to explode in the air. "She finds you."

14

NEW BEGINNINGS

SAYAH

The blue-eyed man revisited my dreams.

As I lay in bed staring at my ceiling, I try to grasp at the dream like smoke that's fading away from me.

All I can remember is that he'd been at that lakehouse and those flames, which frustrates me. I feel like whatever it is, it's trying to tell me something.

This is starting to get weird.

Taking a deep breath and letting it go, I rise out of bed and get dressed, grabbing my phone from the bedside table on my way out.

There's already a message from Dom.

Who is the guy, and what planet is he from?

Thoughts of Dominic pull my thoughts away from my nighttime mystery man.

Good morning, beautiful. Text when you awake
so we can plan our date.=)

As I descend the stairs, I smile at the message.

Good morning.

Wondering what our date will be like, I amble toward the kitchen to make myself some coffee.

My phone buzzes.

Hoping you slept well. What do you like to eat?

I like all the food. What do you like?

I like all the food as well. What are some places up your way?

There is a great Mexican place in Fort Collins that has the best surf and turf. Wanna go there?

As I wait for him to respond, I make a cup of coffee and head into the living room.

Sounds excellent. I'll pick you up at 7.

You don't have to come up here to get me. I can meet you there.

I really don't mind. It is my pleasure. I'm kinda old school. Just shoot me your address, and I'll be there at 7 sharp.

Even though I have very real and scary good feelings about Dominic from last night, I'm still leery about sending strangers my address. I'm very protective of my child, and it's his home I'm guarding. But I have guns and alarms and can hold my own should he try anything shady.

Something inside me tells me it's all right for Dominic to know where I live.

I send my address and begin my chores for the day.

Around six, I shower and prepare for the date, choosing a lower-cut dress with flowers.

At 6:55 PM, the doorbell rings.

I spritz myself with perfume once more and bound down the stairs.

He's there with lilies—my favorite flower—when I open the door. His chest hair and tattoos can be seen through the top two undone buttons on his white shirt. He has on black slacks and shiny shoes and looks fantastic. His scent stirs on the breeze; pine needles and rich soil, like walking through a forest at midnight.

"Hey," I say, a little breathless from the stairs, or maybe it's him.

"Hello, beautiful. You look amazing. These are for you," he says, extending the flowers to me.

"Thank you. Lilies are my favorite."

"I was hoping they were. And this is for your child." He presents a candy bar on the other hand.

"Awe." I gasp, taking the chocolate bar from him. "You are so sweet, thank you. He loves chocolate almost as much as I do."

Dominic grins and shifts his weight from one foot to the other.

"Would you like to come in a minute while I put these flowers in water?"

"Sure," he says, stepping inside. His eyes dart around, taking in the scenery.

My house is medium-sized in the suburbs with tall ceilings and large windows. The stairs leading up are right by the front door, in the living room, and the kitchen and dining room are at the back of the house. All over the walls are pictures of Gauge and me; not an inch of wall space is wasted. I've considered redecorating and taking down old pictures, for many of the frames are from my marriage. The pictures just changed.

"Your home is lovely," he says, walking me to the kitchen through an arched doorway.

Intermingled throughout the house among the trinkets and pictures are plants. They're everywhere, it's a chore to water them all weekly.

"Thank you. It's not much, but it's our home."

"It's lovely," he says again, looking at a picture on the wall. "Your son looks like you. What's his name?"

"His name is Gauge. You think he looks like me?" I ask as I fill a vase with water. "A lot of people say he looks like his dad."

"I have never met the man, so I wouldn't know, but he looks like his mama," he says, inspecting the picture closely, then turning to me. "The eyes. Almond-shaped like yours."

"Yeah, except his are brown. They were blue when he was a baby but turned brown early on."

"Brown is a nice color," he states as Nox comes barreling out his cat door to the basement, stopping in his tracks and hissing at Dom.

"Nox!" I scold, turning the water off.

Nox runs off, the sound of the cat door swinging in the hallway.

"It's all right," Dom says casually, leaning on the bar-height kitchen table. "Pets sometimes don't like new people."

Setting the vase of flowers on the tabletop, I say, "He's normally very sweet. So sorry he did that."

"I'm not worried about it," he says as I lead him into the living room.

"Okay," I say, wiggling into my light winter coat and collecting my purse from the banister at the foot of the stairs.

"Ready?" he asks, his dark lashes sweeping down my body as he checks me out.

"Ready," I say with a smirk as he leads outside.

His hand is strong and comforting against the small of my back as he whisks me to the passenger side of the sleek-looking black Mercedes in my driveway. He pulls open the door for me and waits until I'm all the way in before securing the door closed.

New car scents tickle my senses as the cool leather of the tan seats greets any bare flesh that touches it. I sit in the seat, stowing my purse below me, and fasten the seatbelt around my lap.

"So," he says as he clamors in, pressing the glowing button that ignites the engine, "which way? I followed GPS to get here. I need you to get me to the restaurant."

"Sure, just go that way until the stop sign and then take a left."

He does as I say, pulling his seatbelt on as he backs down the driveway.

Billie Holiday serenades us from the stereo. He flicks the music down by a button on the steering wheel.

"So, you're a witch?" he asks nonchalantly.

"What?" I ask incredulously, the flush to my cheeks making it hot in the car. "Go straight at the stop sign."

He passed right by my spell cabinet. And the altar by the window.

"It's okay. I don't judge."

"Well," I say hesitantly.

It's hard to talk about this with people who don't know me. I watch as the car's headlights illuminate the fields of corn and sod farms that pepper Highway One, searching the amber waves for words to say. Highway One is the back country road that connects the big city of Fort Collins to the small farm town of Wellington.

"I saw your cabinet," his voice severs the silence. "And some other things."

"Oh," I say, the words and explanations all lost on me like the shadows that scamper back into the darkness as the light from the car shines on them.

"It's all right. My sister is Wiccan. She practices magick. I've known a few other witches in my day as well."

"I haven't been practicing for long. I'm still learning."

"Oh, yeah? Who's teaching you?"

"Myself. My mom and grandma were witches, too, but I didn't learn much from them when they were alive. So, I'm reading the books they left behind."

"Books? Like grimoires?"

"Yes, exactly. Not too many people these days know what a grimoire is."

"Like I said, witches in the family," he says, and his lip quirks upward in the corner as he looks at me. "So, tell me about your witchy ways? That intrigues me."

"Does it?" I tilt my head, eyes grazing sideways to meet his.

A subtle pallor washes over me, my skin reacting to how I intrigue him. His gaze remains fixed on the road ahead, yet the curiosity that emanates is palpable, seeping from his eyes and enveloping me. It's like the interest is a tangible force dissolving into my being.

"Not much to tell yet," I utter, almost embarrassed. "I just do random spells here and there. I believe in the goddess as much as the god, and I believe in karma; you get back what you put into the universe. I don't believe in hurting anyone."

"I feel that. What kind of spells?"

"Um, I do spells for luck, healing, and prosperity. That sort of thing."

"And does it work?"

"So far, I think so. It's nothing immediate, but I feel that it helps. Lately, I've been doing spells to help my parents into the afterlife and for my heart to heal eventually."

"Do you feel any better? Your heart anyway?"

"I'm not sure," I answer honestly. I'm not aware if the magick is helping anything except the strange dreams I've been having.

"Well, I'm a believer in magick. I say you keep doing it until your heart feels better."

I smile at him. "I hope so."

We switch to small talk for the rest of the drive.

When we arrive, he runs to my side of the car again and opens the door for me.

"Such a gentleman," I say as I take his hand to help me out.

"I try to be the exception. It's insane to me how men treat ladies these days."

"I know, right? I find it hard to believe men like you still exist."

"Such a shame, really," he responds, holding my hand to the door, where he opens it for me.

I nod in thanks and walk in.

"Hi, welcome to Blue Agave," the blonde hostess addresses us as we enter. "Do you have a reservation?"

"Yes, under Sangravelli," Dominic replies nicely.

Dominic Sangravelli. Has a nice ring to it.

"Right this way, Mr. Sangravelli." The young hostess leads us to a table in the back.

The restaurant's ambiance is dark and quiet; all the tables are adorned with candlelit vases that sit on tables clad in white linen. Scents of carne asada and the sounds of fajitas sizzling make my stomach grumble.

When we arrive at our table, Dominic holds the chair out for me. I nod, sit, and slip out of my coat.

As he sits across from me, our waitress takes our drink orders.

"I'll take a bourbon on the rocks, top shelf. And she'll take a virgin daiquiri."

The waitress smiles and is on her way to fetch them.

"So, my sexy witchy lady, tell me all about you."

"What would you like to know?"

"I want to know it all." He grins. His stormy eyes are dark green with flecks of Baltic amber. They are on me, and I feel that pull again like I'm being drawn into his force field.

I smile back, wondering where to start.

As if he reads my mind, he says, "You can start with if you have siblings and your parents."

I eye him curiously. "I have one sister, but I don't lay claim to her at all. We had a falling out years ago, and since then, I haven't spoken to her."

"Oh, okay. What happened?"

"She has always hated me. Growing up, we were never close. She wasn't close to my parents either, but when they divorced, she chose to live with my dad, and I lived with my mom. She fell hard into drugs in her teens and just spiraled from there. She's never met my son and didn't even come around when I was sick."

"That's terrible. She sounds like a lost soul."

"Absolutely. I think she was born with a dark, dark soul. I cannot describe her. She emanates darkness. When I'm around her, I feel drained, as though she's sucking the very life force from me. We shouldn't talk."

"And your other parents aren't close to her?"

"She was closer to my dad. When they divorced, I lived with my mom and stepdad. She moved to Kansas with my dad fifteen years ago or so. But even he has lost touch with her since she has gotten addicted to meth."

The waitress returns with our drinks.

"Did you need a few more minutes before you order dinner?" the waitress inquires.

"Yes, please," Dominic answers. "I haven't even looked. I will, though, promise." His hazel eyes glance up at her and smile, and she blushes at the gesture. "No problem, take your time," she says, then saunters off.

"Meth? That's some pretty bad stuff, yeah?"

"Oh my gods, yes. It does bad things to good people. Can you imagine what it does to bad people? She's the darkest dark there ever was."

Why am I telling him all this? The words are pouring from me with no second thought.

"That's too bad," Dominic says, picking up his menu and perusing the items on it.

I follow suit. "So, what about you? Any siblings?"

"A few," he says, his lips quirking up as he laughs, and it lets the sweetest dimple on his left side go free. His eyes are still looking through the menu. "I have three sisters and two brothers."

"Wow, you have lots of siblings. That must be nice. I always wanted more siblings. Or at least one I was close with."

"Yeah, they're great. I'm pretty close with all of them except one."

"Which one?"

"One of my brothers. He's kind of like your sister minus the drugs. We were close growing up, but he has gone off the deep end the last few years. Just a lost cause and I haven't spoken with him in decades."

"Decades? Aren't you like thirty?"

"Oh," he says, shaking his head like he's said something he didn't mean. "Yeah, I mean . . . I mean, it has felt like decades."

"I feel that," I say.

His face seems to relax.

"It feels like decades since I've spoken to her, too. But you're close with the others?"

"Yeah, for the most part. They all live in New York, so I don't get to see them as much. If I had to pick one I'm close with, it would be Scarlet. We're twins, so she and I have that whole twin psychic connection."

"I just love that name, Scarlet. So pretty." I figure out what I want to eat and set my menu down.

"She's just as pretty as her name, too. Broke many hearts in her day."

"I bet you have tons of nieces and nephews then?"

"No, actually, I don't," he says, setting the menu down as the waitress approaches.

"Did I give you enough time?" she asks.

"I think so," he says, looking at me for agreement.

"Yes. I'll have the surf and turf, please. Medium for the steak."

"Okay," says the waitress as she jots down my order. "And for you?"

"I'll take the same, please, but make my steak rare. Thanks," he says, handing her the menus.

"Be right up," the waitress responds with a flirtatious smile and grabs his menu.

"Rare, huh?" I query.

"Yes. I don't like it when it's chewy. Rare just melts in the mouth." He smiles.

"So," I continue, "none of your siblings have children?"

"No, Scar and I are the second oldest. My oldest brother has never married nor has any children. And my younger siblings haven't yet, either. I think they all want some one day, but so far nothing."

"Interesting. And you're how old?"

"I'm thirty-six. My oldest brother is thirty-nine, and the younger siblings are thirty-two, twenty-nine, and twenty-five. So, still young. Plenty of time to find someone and settle down. How old are you?"

"Same age as you," I reply, sipping my daiquiri.

"And you have been married once?"

"Yes. We were married for about four years, together for eight."

"Do you guys get along okay?"

"We're better now. It got better once the dust settled. I didn't like the woman he was with first after me at all. The one he's married to now, however, I like."

"You've been divorced for how long?"

"About three years now."

"So, he's married and had a girlfriend before that, all in the span of three years?"

"Well, the first one overlapped a bit. But that's neither here nor there. Tell me about this 'almost married' thing." I smirk, remembering his comment about almost being married at the bar last night.

"Ah, that. It's a somewhat complicated story. It concerns why I don't speak to my oldest brother."

I eye him imploringly, willing him to go on without me having to pry. He seems hesitant to talk of this brother that he doesn't speak to.

"I was with a girl," he goes on hesitantly. "Very much in love and would've gone to the ends of the Earth for her. Everything was as it should be, and I asked her to marry me. Had the ring and everything. Then he appeared out of the blue and fell for her, too. She, in turn, fell for him, and they ran away together."

My heart feels a pang of guilt for him. I shouldn't have brought it up. It still seems very raw.

An awkward silence hangs between us, and I don't know whether to go on with the topic or change the subject.

"Did they end up marrying?" I say, finally.

"No," he says, playing with a frayed string on the linen napkin. "She died."

"Oh my gods. How?"

"Let's just say it was mysterious circumstances, and they never concluded how she was killed."

"Killed? Do you know who did it?"

When he looks at me, I see the pain in the depth of those hazel eyes. There seems to be a darkness that befalls him, and something sinister, giving me the chills that are not from the drafty restaurant.

The waitress appears with dinner. She sets the plates down gently, first in front of Dominic and then me. "Anything else I can get you at the moment?"

"Sayah?" he asks me, as the waitress is paying no mind to me.

"I'm okay, thanks."

"I think we're good, love, thank you." He gives her a courteous smile. "Looks delicious," he says, picking up the A1 and unscrewing the lid.

I can sense he doesn't want to talk anymore about the mysterious death of the girl he once loved.

Deciding to brush past it, I say, "And your parents? Are they still married?"

"They are. They've been together for eons, it seems. Still happy and all that, too."

"Wow. That's so unheard of these days."

"How's the steak?" he asks, pointing at mine with his knife.

"It's delicious. How's yours?"

"Wonderful," he says, forking some lobster. "Well, now that you heard a bit of my darkness, can I bring up a bit of yours?"

"Yeah, that's okay," I reply tenderly, chewing on a bite of lobster. "Which dark are you referring to?"

"Cancer."

"Ah, that. It's a bit of a long, sad story."

"I've got time," he says, smiling.

I can't get over how easy it is to talk to him. I go on to explain everything—the chemo, the awful bone marrow biopsies, blood transfusions that took all day that Mama would accompany me to, the spinal taps, being hospitalized three times—all of it.

"Where was the ex?" Dominic asks.

"He had to work. Or he was home with Gauge. He only came to the bone marrow biopsies because those were my worst fear."

"He should have been there for you for all of it," Dominic retorts, his voice drawing a bit of anger behind it. "I would have been."

"That's so sweet of you to say. It was hard, though. We had to keep the roof over our heads since I couldn't work. And Gauge couldn't come with me to much of it, so he would have to stay with him."

"I would have found a way. That's all I'm saying."

"It was okay. I had my mom," I say, and the sting in the memory bites at me more than I like at this dinner.

"I'm glad you had your mama," he says, plucking the word from my mind.

"Me too," I reply, cutting a bite of the steak, putting it in my mouth, and chewing slowly.

"I'm sorry for bringing that up. When you mentioned you had cancer last night, I was curious about it. I knew it would dredge up hard memories for you. I am sorry."

"Don't be. I don't mind talking about my mom. Or my cancer."

"Did you lose your hair?"

"Yep. Full-on baldie. But I rocked that shit." I laugh at the memory.

"I bet you did," he responds, smiling back. "So much pain you carry."

"I'm so sorry I have been going on and on; you are probably bored to death."

"On the contrary, I think you are one of the most fascinating women I have ever been to dinner with," he replies with a reflective smile.

My heart flutters again at this.

The sensation lingers like a dream hanging on the edge of my consciousness, ready to dissipate with waking. This handsome man leans in, his genuine interest in me evident as he savors every word of my story.

"Well, thank you."

"You have been through some unimaginable pain, and yet you have this aura about you—you're stunningly beautiful and able to shine through it all. You don't have this poor-me attitude; you have a let-me-tell-you-how-my-story-makes-me-stronger vibe. I dig it. Very much."

"I'm so glad you think so. Sometimes I feel as if I'm not strong at all."

"Sometimes strength isn't always depicted in muscles, steely words, and inerrant resolves. Sometimes it shows itself within the softer corners of you—the way you weaken with other people's pain or sit and laugh with the beautifully broken. The way you show up each time the world knocks you down or by the way you feel so deeply for people who you hurt when they do. That is strength. You're one of the strongest people I know, Sayah. And I have known a lot of people."

I offer him the sweetest smile I can muster.

"I'm so glad you decided to come out with me," he utters, his eyes blazing like torches in a medieval castle. "I'm having a great time."

"Me too."

"So,"—he grins, taking a sip of his bourbon—"what do you like to do for fun?"

The rest of the dinner is spent laughing about lighter topics, balancing out the dark that had taken over the first half of our date.

We talked of Gauge's first word being shit and how he said "gonkies" and "warsies" instead of monkeys and horsies. He told me anecdotes about growing up with so many siblings and the pranks they all used to play on each other. We laughed more in the second half of the date than we did all evening.

Outside, after dinner, the sky is midnight purple with bright stars scattered across the heavens. The moon shines like a broken ornament in the sky, casting a silver luster over the world. Christmas lights hang in all the trees, making the square feel magical.

"Wanna walk with me?" he asks as we climb the stairs from the basement restaurant.

"Sure," I answer, taking his hand as he leads me toward the square.

"It's pretty here," he says, his eyes alight with the city's beauty.

"It is. I love how they leave the Christmas lights up til spring. It just makes it magickal."

"Fitting for a magickal being such as yourself."

Again, my heart flutters. The rhythmic sound of his voice is alluring to me, and even though it's an American accent, the way he makes it sound is sexy. Every syllable he uses seems to draw me into him, enticing me into this force field that emanates around him.

As we walk, I take in the magical allure of the city and just enjoy holding hands with another human again. The place where he touches my hand is warm and has a slight buzzing, but I'm not sure if that's from it being a little chilly outside and my hands cold.

We stop in the square and watch the band playing some jazzy little tune, the people dancing and smiling, and the city's ambiance decorates us entirely.

He turns to face me. "I want to see you again," he whispers softly, his face edging closer to me with every breath.

I usually don't kiss men on first dates, but he would be an exception.

"I want to see you again, too."

"And again, after that. And again, after that. And again." He is pulling me closer to him, his fingers interlacing with mine. He pulls my palm up to his lips and kisses it, not letting go of our eye contact.

The beat of my heart is racing, and these magical little butterflies are surfacing to gather around my throat. I'm scared to kiss him because first kisses are usually awkward, but I try not to overthink it too much.

He's just about to my lips when his head cocks sideways as though he hears someone say his name in the distance.

"What is . . ."

"Hold on," he mutters, listening for whatever he'd heard.

Suddenly, his eyes are on mine, and a feeling of dread spreads over me, then it's gone.

Minutes later, and I don't know when we got here because I don't remember walking this far, we're sitting on a bench in a small park on the outskirts of the square. It's like waking up from a dream where you're trying to grasp at the fading memory of it, but that only makes it disappear faster.

Dominic is next to me on the bench. "Are you all right?" he asks, his dark brows knitted together in a combination of concern and guilt.

"Uh," I mumble, looking around. "I don't know how we got here," I tell him honestly.

I didn't drink any alcohol.

"You fainted. I carried you here. Are you sure you're all right?"

Panic sets my limbs on fire at the word faint.

The fear that the leukemia will come back is a constant dread that lingers in the back of my mind. I felt fine the entire night, so the fact that I fainted is worrisome.

"Hey," he whispers, turning my chin to look at him. "You're okay. You must have just eaten something that didn't agree with you."

"Yeah, well, I'm always worried about the cancer coming back. What if it was a symptom of that?"

"Oh, darling, don't you worry about that. I'm sure you're just fine."

Looking into his eyes, I believe him. Something strange in his hazel irises seeps into me, comforting me, making the worry melt away. At the same time, it's edged with being tangled like an uneasy comfort. There's still a bit of dizziness, not understanding why I shouldn't be worried, but I'm not anymore. Now I'm just tired, and there's a haze around my consciousness as if I had drunk twelve tequila shots, although I hadn't.

"Come on, I'll take you home."

When we return to my house, I let him open my car door and take his hand as he offers it.

He walks me to the stoop, where we stop in the pale light of the porch.

"I had a really good time tonight," he says softly, sliding his arms around my waist and pulling me to him.

Still foggy from the night's end, I let him and put my arms around his neck. "I did, too. Thank you for dinner."

"You are most welcome."

His face inches toward mine, and my heart thunders in my chest. I lick my lips right before he reaches them.

It is the sweetest, most subtle kiss that I have ever felt. Like ice on a summer's day, I melt into his arms. At first, he lightly brushes my lips with his. And then, he parts them, inviting me to taste his mouth. I do, and as I lick his tongue with mine, my blood rushes thick to the very surface of me, and I teeter on some edge I didn't know existed until this moment.

His breathing becomes heavier, and he pulls away just when I think I'll burst from emotions. His brows are pinched together like it pained him to kiss me, and his eyes have taken an almost white hue. He turns his head from me, hiding his face, and I'm embarrassed and confused.

Does my breath stink?

"I'm sorry," he utters, his head still turned from me. "I just . . ."

"No. It's okay. I understand," I say, beginning to leave him and go inside.

"No, wait," he states, grabbing my hand. When I turn back around, his eyes are back to normal. "I'm sorry, it's just.... I'm finding resisting you harder than I thought it would be."

"To resist me?" I question. The fogginess from the night returns, and I feel like I'm lost in a dark field, trying to find my way back home.

"You're incredibly sexy. You're smart, intriguing, strong . . . enchanting. Honestly, you're everything I've been looking for in a woman for a long time. My adrenaline got the best of me, and I felt that if I didn't stop kissing you now, I'm likely to tear your clothes off of you and take you here on this porch."

It's a very alluring thought.

"And," he expands, "I know that I won't be your first of anything, but you're the kind of person I'd want to be my last of everything."

The words hang in the air and pierce every inch of me. I know that

I find him attractive, and there's something about him that calls to me, that draws me in and makes me want to stay, but I don't know if he's *the one*.

"I see," I reply, the words lost on me like rain in a waterfall.

"*And* I've said too much," he answers, hanging his head in embarrassment, stepping down from the porch.

"No, wait," I say, taking my turn to pull him back. "I'm sorry. You just caught me off guard with that. It's our first date, and I didn't know how to respond."

"I know," he says, his eyes searching my face. "Look, I was trying to say that I like you. I don't want to mess this up by going too fast. I want to keep seeing you, see where it goes, and let nature take its course."

"Me too."

The panicky feeling begins to ebb, and I feel a bit better.

"So," he answers, stepping up to join me again on the porch. "I am going to kiss you goodnight and leave. And I want you to think of where you would like to go for our second date on the next night you are free."

"Okay," I say, the word tasting ashen in my mouth.

His lips meet mine again; this time, it's swift and sweet.

"Goodnight," he says when he lets my lips go.

"Goodnight, Dominic."

He punctuates his smile with a soft wink, turns on his heel, and heads down the sidewalk path.

15

WHISPERING LEAF

DOM

My mind is a swirling rush of emotions and energy, thoughts and musings, fear and excitement violently compounding against each other, ruining and restoring me simultaneously. As my car escalates down Sayah's street and away from her, I think back on everything that went awry.

The date itself was excellent. I find myself much more attracted to Sayah than I ever thought possible. Getting to know her personally makes all those feelings that were stuttering me at the bar magnified with her up close.

Typically, we can take emotions and flick them off like a switch, steeling ourselves to any mortal sentiments or obligations of social constructs. But with her, my ability to flip it off is not only disabled; it's intensified. I feel her in my bones and nestling into my skin; the sharp wit of hers is piercing through my own resolve.

She is something else entirely.

The dizziness in my brain is making me feel like I'm buzzing, like I'd drunk a hundred shots of whiskey that were laced with Feyfire crystals. Being in her presence is like getting out of the shower. That million-dollar, fresh skin, clean feeling that only comes after being cleansed in hot water. She douses me with something tangible on my skin; a layer of her still rests all over me even after I've left her.

Having to veilweave her to forget we saw those grims is grating on me. I don't like that I'm already lying to her, and now I had to take away some of her memories. The look on her face when I told her she had fainted was enough to wrench my heart free from my chest and toss it into a garbage disposal.

Seeing those grims in the alley of a smaller town like Fort Collins tells me they *are* getting worse everywhere though, not just in the major cities.

Oh. And the other thing.

As I was kissing her, I could smell her sweat and perfume and shampoo mixed with the agonizing scent of her blood, and I got caught up. When the kiss turned into that heated rush, I couldn't help myself. My fangs almost came out, and I about bit her before I even knew what I was doing. Luckily, I'd been able to turn around and gain my composure.

I'm more worried than ever about my family wanting her dead. I don't know how, but I have to try to keep them from killing her. I have to help her find her magick.

"Siri, call mom," I say to my car as I merge onto the highway, pressing the pedal to the metal, and the car roars in response.

The line rings three times.

"Hello?" comes my mom's steely voice over the car speakers.

"Mom."

"Hi, Dom!" Scarlett echoes from the background.

"I have you on speaker phone," Mom says, even though I deduced that myself.

"Yeah, mom. Got it."

"So, what did you find out?"

"Just mostly about her life up until this point. She's been through a lot. Also, I went to Never again earlier and talked to a shaman. He found something about phoenixes in an old grimoire—I guess the last known one happened to be around the witch trial era. He mentioned a coven in Vegas that may know more about the warlocks and grimspawn, so I'm thinking of going there soon." I'm intentionally alluding to my severe attraction to this woman.

"And what of her powers did you discover?" Even over the phone, my mom is hard as stone.

"Nothing yet. I'm the one who brought up that she's a witch. She was almost embarrassed about it. But then I could tell her guard came down, and she opened up more."

"So essentially, she's a new witch." My mom's tone skates on the edge of boredom, telling me she is unenthused.

"Yes. Learning her power. Her main teacher just died, and her aunts aren't local, so she's having to teach herself."

"And you think the prophecy has something to do with her powers?"

"I do."

"What if I send you that bracelet, Dominic?" Scarlet asks, which is surprising because usually Scarlet would be all about the murder.

"What bracelet?"

"You know, the moonstone one Mom gave me when I came into my power? It will enhance Sayah's powers."

"Yeah, that may work. But how will you get it to me?"

"You brought your mirror with you, right?"

"Of course."

"I'll send it through the mirror."

"And once she has the bracelet and has had a chance to harness her power, what then?"

"I gave you two weeks to figure this out, Dominic," my mom chides. "If it isn't resolved in that time, we'll take matters into our own hands."

"I'm going to need more time."

"Dominic," mom starts.

"Mom, just give me 'til the end of the month. It will take some time for me to help her with her powers and go to Vegas to talk to that coven."

"What is that going to do, Dominic? What do you think the coven in Vegas will really help with?"

"I don't know, Mom, maybe coming up with another way to get to the bottom of the grimspawn problem or help us find the warlocks *or* learn the meaning behind this phoenix prophecy without killing an innocent woman." I can't help the heat in my voice.

"Ooh, sounds like Domie has a crush!"

"Scarlet," I say, exasperation coating her name like honey.

"You and your hopeless heart for humans is going to get you in trouble one day, Dom," Mom says, though her tempered intonation tells her own hopeless heart is to blame for many things as well.

"Whatever, just. . . can I have the time?"

"You have a month, Dominic," Mom says, and the tempered tone is again jagged. "If you don't figure it out by then, we will come to kill her."

Arriving back at the house I'm now renting in Windsor—where I fabricated that I lived because it was between the town she lives in and Denver—I park my Mercedes in the garage and close the door.

I was lucky enough to find an Air B&B with what I needed for the time I'll be here—and the area I picked is very upscale and suave, costing me a cool $500 a night to rent this fully furnished home.

I also picked this place because it is on a lake, and while I don't know how long I'll be here, I want it to feel as close to home as possible.

Pulling my brown leather suitcase onto the large Cal-king bed, I'm rifling through my things to find the mirror when a large maple leaf with colors of bright orange and yellow and burnt sienna falls right from the ceiling and lands on the bed. As I pick it up, it morphs into a scroll made of papyrus, with a hand-written note in elegant script on the page.

A Whispering Leaf.

Whispering Leaves are the method of communication that fae of the Neverdusk and Luminara use to send messages. It's been a long time since I've received one. The last one I got was when I was dating that lady from Luminara, and she would send me Whispering Leaves to let me know where our next clandestine meeting would be.

Luminara Fae are not supposed to mingle with dark things like me.

Meet me at the docks at Pelican Lakes at 11PM sharp.

—Tallyn

Wonderful.

A meeting with the Luminara Queen.

I've never met her, but I know my family members have.

Dealings with fae are never advised.

I up my ornate and antique mirror—it's just a simple handheld mirror made of bronze—but what's unique about it is that it's my spelled mirror.

Vampires cannot look into mirrors, otherwise we will see our true reflection, our actual age. Hattie has the power to make anyone see what she wants them to see. So she cast a spell on eight different mirrors, one for each of us that only allows us to see ourselves as we looked the year we turned. As long as they remain in our vicinity, i.e. within the same state, we can look into any mirror and not revert back to our true age.

Hattie apparently already cast her spell for me to see the bracelet in the mirror, for when I retrieve it out of my bag, there is no reflection of myself, only the bracelet.

Carefully, I pluck the jewelry from the mirror and place it safely in my pocket.

The mirror dissipates to its shiny reflection, showing me the face I've known for two hundred years.

The path to where Tallyn wants me to meet her is quiet this time of night. Still cold from winter's kiss—as spring is fighting its way to the surface with all her might—all the trees remain suspended, as if in remembrance of the wind, and the night is spun about in a cool mist.

Minutes seem to bloom and molt like seasons as long as it seems it takes her to arrive when I finally hear the sound of a branch breaking.

Turning toward the noise, I find Tallyn behind me.

Her mystic beauty is spellbinding, her long black tendrils half caught up in a braided crown with branches and sticks, her pointy ears sticking out of the dark tresses adorned by silver dangling jewels. Eyes the color of a coral orange reminiscent of a Caribbean sunset, they exude both power and danger at the same time. Her voluptuous body is barely contained in the gown of leaves and flowers; her iridescent wings flutter behind her in a delicate rush.

"You must be Dominic," she says, floating herself to the ground where the boundary of air and Earth collide.

"And you must be Tallyn," I say, holding out my hand.

Her shrewd eyes lance down to my hand and then back up to my face, her brows drawn together in contempt.

Am I supposed to bow to her?

As I lower my hand, she says, "You've been poking around the Neverdusk Dominion looking for answers, so I hear." Her winsome voice replicates the winding rush of rivers through a ravine and being struck by a summer typhoon.

"Yes, Your Majesty," I say, and the terseness of her formal name in my mouth shocks me. "We have a problem. The grims are infecting our food supply. It's getting dire. We need help to contain it."

Her sensuous pink lips downturn into a frown and she crosses her arms over her chest, the silver bangles jangling. "That would be my brother Trystan's domain. I cannot help you with that."

"We think we found the answer, a phoenix, but we don't know what that means or how to achieve it. Would you know anything about that?"

Shaking her head, her soft wings flutter on her back, picking her body up easily and gliding her toward the water. "I haven't heard of a phoenix in this realm or any others in many years."

"Well, we think we might have found one," I say, following her to the lakeside, "but we just need her powers to come to light. Can you help with that?"

Her iridescent wings gleam in the moonlight as they set her down on the sandy soil of the beach. The wind lifts her raven hair ever so slightly as she turns to face me, her orange eyes tapering towards my mouth. "And who is the woman you believe has this power?"

I don't know why, but I feel my body constrict with her question. Maybe it's the way she's asking it, or maybe it's the suspicious nature of her energy. I get the feeling that she isn't just asking to help us but has a darker agenda for what she wants the information for.

"A local witch. Lasayah Thorne," I say carefully but still notice how her name softens on the tip of my tongue. "She comes from a long line of witches, and a prophecy has been spun that she is the next phoenix. But that also may have a double meaning or be just a metaphor for a power she comes into. We are just trying to figure out how to help her come into this power."

"Bring her here, to this place," Tallyn says as she kneels. Her long pointer finger, be-ringed with black and silver jewels, stirs the dirt, swirling it around in a small circle. As she stirs the Earth, a small tornado of dust kicks up and twirls around in the air. The wind gathers ever so slightly, grazing me with the smell of magick and fire. "Give her a gift to make her cry. I need a tear to fall to the ground. When it does, I will be below in Luminara and can use it to help push her powers forth."

"What will the tear do?"

She appraises me with a coruscating gaze. "It will assure me that she is being led to her fate."

That sounds subliminal. "I'm trying to keep her alive. My family wants her dead. I need assurance that this is all to keep her alive."

"If her destiny is to be a fire wielder, we need to push her to that destiny," she says, still stirring the wind. Flicking her finger, a tiny flame emerges from the tip of her fingernail, and she stirs it into the funnel. "Earth, air, and fire. All you need is water."

After a flash of a little explosion from the miniature tornado, the dust settles back down in a circle of ash on the ground. "And this little spell will activate when her tear falls?"

"It shall. Bring her here tomorrow night," she says, her stoic posture rigid and refined. Bending down once again, she palms the surface of the lake, and ripples expand outward, the water parting in two and folding over each way. Below the waterline is a dark staircase leading down to Luminara.

As she descends without even a goodbye, I call after her, "But how do I make her cry?"

Without turning around, she tells me, "Give her something that makes her think of her mom." And then the water folds back over, erasing the fact that a staircase was ever there.

How does the Luminara Queen know about the death of Sayah's mom?

16

THOSE EYES, THOUGH

SAYAH

The fog from the night is still thick within me as I climb the stairs to bed. Even though I'm not worried about the fainting—which I think I should be—it's more so the uneasy feeling I'm getting that surrounds the night.

Dominic is a seemingly perfect package. He's sexy and strong, tall and tattooed, and radiates independence. He's funny and sweet, as evident with his gestures of chivalry and all that encompassed our date tonight. Buying Gauge a candy bar was the cherry on top of a perfect evening. But there is something in his eyes that has me feeling as though I should run - and far.

Escaping out of my heels and slipping into my nightclothes, I try to grasp at something that I think should be there as part of our date, something that has me shaky and uneasy and the energy all around me shifts.

Something happened and I feel it like a lost thought that I can't quite grasp.

Eyes.

That's all my brain will tell me.

Was it his eyes?

The way they had looked after we kissed, it was as though all the hazel had drained out of them and they were just white, like Halloween contacts.

The phone dings as I flip the switch in the bathroom while opening the message.

> Thank you for escorting me out tonight. It was as wondrous as you are. I can't wait to see you again.

The feelings he gives me are such a weird mixture of what I'm used to. I'm used to either butterflies, or hesitation and the red-flag feeling I get when I'm about to ghost a guy from Tinder. This is a perfect mixture of the two. On one hand, I'm attracted to this guy, and in any other circumstance, I could see a future bloom with him. On the other, something awkward and strange is niggling at the back of my mind. I don't know if it's just me being scared of new relationships, but it feels deeper than that. There's something that I can't put my finger on. Something happened on our date that gives me the terrors. Like something I lost and can't find but need and yet don't remember what it is. I fight the feeling of blocking his number and ghosting him right now.

It makes me sad, and I ponder what to do; if I should walk away now and not speak to him again, or to give him a chance and see where it goes.

Climbing into bed, I open the message again and look at the letters, fighting something within myself on what the answer is.

Finally, I text back.

> I had a really good time tonight too. Sorry if I seemed distant at the end, I'm just worried that I fainted. I can't wait to see you again, either.

A few minutes later, he responds.

> Please don't be worried about that. I feel that you are fine and just got lightheaded. When is your next free night? I want to take you some place special.

This is my weekend that's free, so my next free night is actually tomorrow night.

Well, I am free tomorrow night and then not again til Wednesday.

Okay. Tomorrow it is! I'll pick you up at 7.

Okay. Can't wait!

The two contradictions of feelings are still swarming my mind as I plug the phone in on the nightstand and turn to go to sleep.

As I drift, the excited feeling wins.

The mist is thick this time, and I can't see in front of me. I'm walking, although I don't know where I am. The fog is so thick, it's as if the clouds have landed on earth, and I'm walking among them. I may even be up in the clouds, but then I can feel the soft soil of the Earth beneath my bare feet.

I feel him, even before I see him. His presence drenches me and the energy around me shifts again, I feel him like you would feel the wind.

But where is he?

The danger's present, I know it's life or death if he finds me, and yet all the same I begin looking for him, wanting to find him, wanting to know more about him and why he's haunting my dreams.

Those blue eyes pierce through the fog, and they're all I see at first. The black hair comes next, and then his handsome face.

He's wearing all black in the sea of white mist, although it's twilight and the clouds themselves have an effervescent glow.

The danger grows worse as he approaches me. I stand still, knowing I should run, knowing that his bite will kill me every time and not caring all the same.

"Who are you?" I ask, frozen in place as he draws nearer.

"I told you. I'm Sebastian."

"But why are you haunting my dreams?"

"Who said I'm in your dreams? I think you're the one who is in mine, princess."

Chills run up my spine and down to my fingertips, yet my blood runs hot against the surface of my skin. "Regardless, why are we in each other's dreams?"

"I don't know," he responds. His enhancing gait has me edging to a type of cliff in my being, knowing I'm doomed but wanting despite it.

Those blue eyes.

Bright with something else. They're something not of this world. Even though he's to be the death of me, I still need him more than I need the sustenance my existence relies upon.

He smiles a crooked smile, the left side of his mouth curling up as the right side stays flat. I want to bottle that wicked grin and drink it down like an elixir.

There's something about that smile that yanks at me, something about his world that I need to be in, regardless of what it costs.

He's inches from me now and I still don't move, knowing it's gonna hurt like hell when he bites me but wanting the rush, his lips, those eyes, that smile, all of him. I will take every part of his damned existence if it means I get to feel those poisonous lips on mine.

"Why do I burn each time you touch me?"

"I don't know that either," he replies, reaching me as a look of desire tinged with menace passes over his expression. "All I know is that I need you. And when I can't resist you anymore, you burn and it kills me. I don't know who you are, but I need you in my life. Your blood calls to me, makes me completely helpless to the thirst and blinded by passion. Every time I see you, I must drink from you. It's programmed into my mind."

"You're a vampire?" I utter, although I know the answer already.

"I am," he states, his voice silky with peril that settles into my bones.

The beat of my heart is rhythmic against the black backdrop of our reverie. The pulsating begins dancing down my sternum and as he inches closer and closer, it moves further south—between my legs. His face is inches from mine, and I can smell the midnight and ruin on him mixed with winter. Fresh and dark. The heat from him being so close to me nearly makes me moan in anticipation, and the exquisite torture of not having him all over me almost pushes me off that edge that is surely behind me. His breath is hot; he's almost to me and his breathing intermingles with mine, tangling our breath together, causing a stressed exhale that's I've been holding back to escape. It comes out as a whimper that I can no longer control and that sends him over that same edge.

His sultry soft lips suddenly land on mine and It. Is. Magick.

The danger mixed with magick and paired with an all-consuming love has me feeling like an avalanche, gaining momentum and strength as it topples me to my doom. Even though I feel it down to my bones that I should run. . . I cannot. There's something keeping me here locked with him that I can't ignore.

Knowing what's going to come next is something that should frighten me to my core, but I welcome it and will him to bite me.

I want to feel that fire, I like the way it burns.

His breath on my face is hot and the heat between us is intense on its own, without the flames. He kisses me with his whole body, and it feels like falling off a cliff. He offers his tongue to me and I embrace it, deeper into my own mouth he goes, and it isn't close enough for me. I need to feel him inside me. He is searching my body with his hands and I welcome it, my own fingers wandering up to his black locks, entangling them within the short silky tresses.

He kisses my cheeks, down the front of my throat, to my cleavage as he caresses one of my breasts. Another moan escapes at the pleasure it incites. This makes him fiercer in his expedition of me and something sparks that rage within him; for he looks at me while his eyes go icy white, his lip curls up, revealing the blinding glint of sharp ivory as they elongate out of his cuspids.

As the sharp pricks of his fangs pierce my carotid artery, the fire engulfs me. The sensation of him sucking my blood, draining me yet filling me up at the same time as the fire spreads from where he bit, explodes outward from my clit to the tips of my fingers and toes. The intensity of the fire consumes me and I continue to want him, the taste of him lingering on my lips.

This time he burns with me and is still drinking from me as the flames consume us both.

My phone dings, waking me.

I roll over and grab at the cord.

Good morning, beautiful. I hope you slept well.

Smiling to myself, I write back.

Good morning to you, handsome. I slept well. I hope you did too.

The dream covers me and I remember the way I'd felt with Sebastian, my midnight mystery vampire, all over me. My clit is still tingly at the thought of him.

The way he makes me feel in my dreams is something that I want to feel in real life. Granted, he's a bad kind of good, a dangerous sort of love. But whatever the reason he's infecting my dreams, I don't mind it and welcome him to keep visiting me. I crave it.

As I meander throughout my productive Sunday—cleaning the house, doing my homework, and some light yard chores—Dominic is in constant contact with me via text about my day and what I'm up to. I like that he's interested in me and regardless of the weird feelings I get with him, I keep up with the excited butterflies that I also feel with hesitation. It keeps the sad memories of my parents from plaguing me.

During my shower, I wonder what Dominic has planned for the

night and begin to feel hot flutters surrounding the date and what it's going to bring.

Running a brush through my hair one last time, the doorbell sounds, and I spray a spritz of one of my many perfumes as I leave the bathroom.

Dominic is looking dapper as ever, even if he is only wearing a t-shirt and some jeans. His hair looks nice, spiked in the front as usual and his eyes are bright and hazel green this evening.

"Hey you," he says, kissing me on the cheek as I open the door to greet him.

"Hey," I answer, moving aside to let him enter.

"Did you get all your stuff done, beautiful?" His arms are around me, sliding around my waist and pulling me to him. I let him move me again, just like he did on the dance floor.

"I did, thank you."

His lips are on mine and the quivers are soft and feathery. I kiss him back but before it can get as heated as it did last night, he lets my lips go.

"Ready?" he asks softly.

"Yes," I answer.

He grabs my hand and I let him pull me to the car.

Of course he opens the door for me, helping me in, and then we're off, heading toward the highway.

"Where are we going?"

"It's a surprise," he responds, the sly glint shining in his eyes.

Surprisingly, we drive to the Windsor exit, which is where he mentioned he lived the first night we met.

"Are we going to your house?" I ask.

He looks at me almost deviantly and says, "No" with a smile.

I'm leaning back in the passenger side, admiring the city of Windsor pass us by through the closed car window. The streets are crowded and bustling, people meandering from shop to shop or from restaurant to the square. Dominic seems at ease as he drives us this way and that, to the twisty roads on the outskirts of town that lead to the richer neighborhoods. As we turn into Pelican Lakes, a gated community on a golf course with a beautiful lake that's popular for weddings, I take in the sights. Having been here a few times for company picnics, I love this area and hope to one day live here—when one of my books makes me millions, that is.

Massive houses sprawl along the road we linger on, each covered in ivy and divided by expansive lawns and wrought-iron gates. I know if I were to open my window here in the summer, I would smell the oleander, lilac, and honeysuckle come from the sprays of trees and bushes spotting the scenery.

"Is this your neighborhood?" I ask as we continue to the end of one street and then turn onto a dirt road.

"If I said 'yes,' would you judge me?" he asks and his tone has a playful hue, but I'm still not sure if he's serious. I watch as the tendon in his hand flinches a bit as he grabs the black steering wheel, nervous.

"Of course not," I answer honestly.

He lets out a small laugh, relaxing somewhat, and continues down the dirt road until we come to a small parking lot on the edge of the beach.

"Here we are," he says, pressing the button to kill the engine and escaping out of the driver's side.

First he lets me out of the passenger side and then, as I look around, he runs to get something from the back.

The sun has set already, but the sky's in its vanilla stage, where it's not dark yet and not quite light. The moon is just a sliver in the sky, a sky that reminds me of cotton candy. A rainbow of melted colors sits on the lake, looking like a box of crayons has tipped over and melted into the water. The trees surrounding the lake are just beginning to get their leaves, so they are a bright color green, and the light makes them seem like they're glowing neon.

I love this time of year; when the grass is starting to come back from the long winter and is as green as you could imagine it should be, still healthy and not burnt yet by the summer sun. It reminds me of a fairytale land. Some magickal place between winter and summer where everything is fresh and new and ready to be awakened from their slumber. Even though it just snowed a week earlier, it's nearly spring in Colorado and so the seasons often blend together.

Dominic appears with a picnic basket and a bottle of sparkling cider with two champagne glasses.

"A picnic in my favorite place in the world right now."

"That's amazing. It's beautiful here."

"It's where I come to find peace in this place. The only place I've found that remotely lives up to where I'm from in New York."

"This reminds of you of New York?" I ask, scrutinizing the gorgeous scenery. "This is not what I would picture when thinking of New York."

I follow him down by one of the boat docks, and along a path that lines the lake.

He sniggers a bit. "I am from Upstate New York. It's called Lake George."

"Oh my gods! I love Lake George!" I exclaim as he stops and sets the picnic basket down.

Opening it and retrieving a checkered blanket, he looks at me with a surprise. "You know the area?"

"Oh yeah! Well, I was there a few times when I was a kid. My family was from New Jersey, and we used to drive to Lake George in the fall and stay in some cabins there."

"Wow, what a small world," he says, sitting down on top of the blanket and patting the place beside him.

"I know, right?" I respond, obliging him.

Pulling out a few votive candles, he lights them and sets them up around us.

After the candles are lit, he gathers the food from the basket and hands me a sandwich in a clear sandwich baggy.

"I didn't know what you liked, so I made peanut butter and jelly sandwiches, with chips."

I let out a small laugh. "That's perfect. I actually have a new found affinity for them now that I'm a mom."

"I was hoping that you wouldn't be sick of them."

"Gods no! PB&J is amazing! Gauge loves them."

Dominic chuckles and hands me a bag of Lay's.

"So, I noticed in one of your pictures that he's in a wheelchair. Can I ask why—if you don't mind me asking."

"Not at all," I say, finishing my bite of sandwich before continuing. "He has a rare muscle condition called Congenital Myopathy. No one knew what it was until he was a year and a half. Nearly killed him at birth."

"And what is it exactly?" Dominic asks, the sounds of a bag of chips opening pierces the moment.

"It's in the same family as muscular dystrophy, but it doesn't get worse over time. He just has muscles that work differently from ours. What is five pounds to you is thirty to him."

"So he will be able to walk one day?"

"I did some research while getting my associate's degree. It seems the kind he has can get better with hard work. He just has to work out every day if he wants it. And if he's anything like me, one day that fire in him will consume him and he will get what he wants."

As I talk of my son, I cannot get over how he's looking at me. He hangs on every word that I say and he wants to know all about me and my child.

That's one of the hard parts about dating for me. Before, it was just me. Now that I'm back in that world, I'm dating for two. Every guy that I meet I have to do a screening of and make sure that they like kids, that they're cool with kids, that they understand that my child will always come first.

It's exhausting.

My ex didn't seem to have taken the same caution of who was around Gauge at first and was just not wanting to be alone, no matter the cost.

On the other hand, I am doing everything I can to make sure that whomever I decide to bring home and introduce to him is going to treat him as though he's theirs. That they're going to be good to him and make sure that he's safe and loved and never put second.

It's why I haven't brought anyone home to meet him yet.

No one has leveled up that far.

We talk of life and home and places as we eat the sandwiches and once they are gone, Dominic eagerly digs in the basket for something else.

"Here." He hands me an envelope with a red seal on the front. "This is for you."

Wondering what's inside, I look at him questioningly.

My fingernails are just about to tear it open when he says, "Wait. First, I want you to lie back with me."

Nothing in his eyes tells me to worry. I lie back with him and look at the sky that's starting to show twinkling stars through the clearing clouds.

"Okay, now open it."

As I tear the envelope open, inside is a card that says:

Be it known that star number HIP 53043 with the Celestial Address of 10 hrs. 36 min. 49.0 sec and Declination of + 52° 15'23.0" Epoch 2000, in the constellation Ursa Major shall henceforth be known by the name of

Frances Cartwright

To the one star that shines so bright in my eyes, I give you this one in the heavens.

My nose burns as tears sting my eyes. I'm blown away that someone would be so sweet as to dedicate a star to my mother.

That's the reason he had asked Mama's full name during our texting earlier.

He looks at me and his green eyes soften. The corners of his mouth quirk up and he reaches out, wiping a tear that stubbornly escapes with his thumb.

"On the map in there," he replies, unfolding the accordion paper, "if you look, it shows you how to find the star."

Looking on the map, I see the constellations that will help me find the location.

My chest tightens and hot tears keep stumbling down my face.

He's pulling me to lay in the crook of his arm, where I clutch the certificate and sob quietly. It's not like me to cry in front of people, especially in front of a man I've just begun dating, but this is something else entirely.

It's so fitting to me that Mama has a star and this man, who barely knows me, did something so incredibly sweet and charming that truly touches the depths of my soul.

In this moment, he becomes something more to me and whatever hesitation I'd been having, melts away with the tears flowing down my cheek onto his shirt and into the ground.

"Thank you, Dominic. This is amazing." I sniffle. "Sorry about your shirt."

There are little tear stains on the front and going down the side. "Hey. It's okay. I didn't mean to make you cry."

"It's just so sweet."

He wipes more of my tears. "I just had a feeling that this would be the perfect thing to get your mom. I didn't know her, obviously, but I can feel from you how special she was. And, witches like nature," he chuckles softly, and it's an easy laugh. I like the way it sounds—it's soothing and comforts me deep within my bones.

I bend my head upward to look at him and he strokes the side of my face gently, his hands soft and strong at the same time.

He pulls my chin toward him.

There's nothing rushed or erratic about this kiss. It's genuine, loving, and romantic.

The butterflies erupt from my stomach and flutter to the tips of my toes.

He changed the game.

"There's more," he whispers, once he lets my lips go.

"More?" I wonder, letting him sit us up.

"Yeah, something small. I found this—" he digs out one more thing from the basket.

It's a small box, one that jewelry would come in, and my mind begins to wander.

He passes me the gold box, and I eye him questioningly.

"Don't worry, it's not a ring." He smirks.

Something in me relaxes a bit. Although I knew that it couldn't possibly be an engagement ring, as we'd only been on two dates, there's something in his eyes that tells me it's still something very special.

"Remember when I told you that my sister is a witch?"

"Yes, I remember."

"This was hers. She has been practicing a long time and this is thought to be enchanted. I thought it would help you with your own magick."

I open it, revealing a bracelet.

The gold bracelet, though shimmering, still looks very old with darker age spots. There are intricate designs in the metal and the stone that's at the front is a gorgeous moonstone. It's iridescent and pearly, taking up the whole front of the bracelet and looks like there's another galaxy within it.

"Oh, Dominic, it's gorgeous."

He takes the bracelet out of the box and puts it on my wrist, making sure the clasp is secured.

"The bracelet is very old. I have no idea where Scarlet got it from. But she put her own special magick in it as well, and then gave it to me for protection when I moved out here."

"I can't accept this, Dominic. It's a gift from your sister, to protect you."

"I have other things she gave me," he says with a smile. "I think that this will help you with your own magick."

I admire the bracelet on my wrist. The place where it touches my skin seems to glow a little, and although I know it's a trick of the moonlight, something dances up the back of my spine saying that I'm about to see more magick in myself than I ever thought possible.

It chills me.

I kiss him this time.

The whole night has affected me so strongly, the thought and detail he put into the gift for my mom and giving me the bracelet.

I'm swooning.

We spend the rest of the night talking and laughing and, quite simply, falling for each other. It's around four in the morning when the birds begin to sing, that I realize the time and that I have to work in three hours.

As he kisses me goodbye on the porch, I want nothing more than to invite him in, get twisted up with him in the sheets, but I know I'm already going to hate life all day tomorrow.

He leaves me, and as he drives away, he also leaves me with the lingering sense that there's something so incredibly special about him that I need to become more familiar with.

I cannot wait to see him again.

"All right baby," I say to Gauge the next evening as I tuck the blankets up around his chin, "sleep good." I kiss his forehead and close the book we've been reading, setting it on the nightstand by his bed.

"You too, Mama."

"See you in the morning. Love you."

"Love you," he says, and I close the door behind me.

It has been a long sleepy day at work, but I still feel compelled to try something with this new bracelet.

I pull down one of my mom's grimoires from my spell cabinet.

I'm unsure of what I want to do with the bracelet, but I can feel its power and want to add to it, add a piece of my own magick to it and see what it would do.

There's a spell of gathering power, and what harm can come from that?

Collecting the ingredients it calls for, I move over to the altar and set them up one by one.

A few herbs, some stones, a candle or two, and my small cauldron that's the size of a little bowl.

After lighting the candles, I sprinkle the herbs into the cauldron.

Whispering words of magick from the book, I close my eyes and recite them repeatedly.

There's a rush of heat that encompasses me like a shower. I feel it start from the top of my head to the tip of my toes. Keeping my eyes closed, I can still see through my lids that the bracelet begins to glow, as if whatever power within it escapes and enters into me. It swims through my veins and gathers my own essence, and pools somewhere in the deepest, darkest parts of myself. The new power finds a lock within me, a cloak that has been draped over me, and like the feeling of something clicking into place, the lock snaps open and the cloak dissolves.

For a long time, I'm unsure how long, I recite the magick words, with my arms outstretched, willing the power to take over me. I feel it like one would feel a powerful drug taking over, pooling warm in my extremities, almost hot in the crook of my arms and backs of my knees. It pulsates throughout my entire body. Then I shift the energy and push it back into the bracelet, commanding it to take whatever part of myself that's magick and enter this stone.

The stone lights up as brightly as the sun, and though my eyes are still closed, I feel the power, the heat. It's the most powerful spell I've ever created.

As the stone dims and takes on its normal hue once more, I open my eyes and stare at it.

There's something new and powerful lingering in me. I can feel the shift more than I know anything else at the moment.

I want to try something.

Arising from the ground and walking over to the cabinet, I gather petals from a dried rose that I put in there a long time ago.

Walking them back over to the altar, I set them neatly in front of me on the floor.

Concentrating as hard as I can, I hover my palm over the petals and will them to rise.

Something that's stirring deep within me heightens and the buzzing I feel in my soul reverberates into my bones. Power that I've never known before gushes out of me, almost as though I am sweating, but I'm not hot.

That's power.

The petals shift and shake, each one rising from the ground one at a time.

I remain hovering above the petals and lift my hand further and further away, until all the petals are six inches from the floor.

Arising from the ground again, I pull the petals up, higher and higher, until they are level with my eyes. In utter dumbfounded amazement, I watch as the petals float in front of my eyes.

Thoughts clutter my mind in an overwhelming, thunderous uproar. The power that I behold is only in its infancy and thinking of what will unravel from it staggers me.

Walking away from the petals and letting them float there, I glide over to my phone on the table and snap a picture to send to Dominic.

The power is still dripping off me as I sit on the couch, eyeing my nascency and try to wrap my mind around what the hell is happening.

The sound of the phone dinging wakes me out of my trance.

> I knew you would be able to harness that power!

The magnificent pride succinctly wraps around me as I look at the message along with my new bracelet that's now blazoned with my power. Not only am I dating an ostensibly charming new man, but one that is wending me to build on my magick.

This has to be some sort of dream.

17

TASTE THE SHAPE OF HER

DOM

How I managed to get wrapped up in a grimspawn crisis on the brink of a pandemic and find myself in a budding romance is beyond me.

I'm a fucking idiot.

That's how.

Going into this, I never knew I'd fall for the witch. But here I am, thinking of her non-stop and counting the minutes until I see her again. The memory of her scent lingers with me even now—a hint of strawberries and wildflowers mixed with summer rain and springtime thunder. I can taste the shape of her; I can hear her in my bones. Thinking of the way her thick thighs bounce when she walks and how succulent her ass looked in those jeans.

Fuck.

I could bite right into her.

I salivate at the thought, my eyes trying to switch to their predatory white, but I push back at it and steel myself, solidifying my core while taking a deep breath.

I need to eat.

Even though we can eat human food, it does nothing for us. We don't feel full after eating it, and it doesn't do anything to our bodies. It doesn't even come back out; it just…turns into blood.

Sitting on a bench in the middle of Windsor, watching people for someone who will be susceptible to my charms, my phone vibrates in my pocket.

Pulling it out, I see a picture of rose petals floating mid-air from Sayah.

She has entered my veins and is becoming inescapable. I'm proud of her for making new strides with the bracelet I gave her.

Now I just gotta keep my family from killing her.

Hopefully, the tear did the trick for Tallyn.

I haven't received another Whispering Leaf, so perhaps that's helping her summon more power.

Who knows.

A biting breeze blows the scents of so many different flavors of people my way. To a mortal human, it would be chilly, but because our blood is different, we don't feel temperature the same way they do.

There's a scent on the breeze that smells like jasmine and strawberries. I spot a young girl stumbling out of a bar, lighting a cigarette, and teetering down the narrow passageway between two buildings.

Standing, I follow her slowly, delicately maneuvering fast between glances of bar patrons.

Up ahead of me, she takes a drag of her cigarette and trips over her own feet, falling down ungracefully on her knees.

"Fuck!" she spews.

Flashing up to her, I catch her eyes and hold her gaze; before she can startle I begin my veilweave.

You are not afraid. I'm not going to hurt you. You will let me drink from you, and then you will go home, forgetting you ever saw me.

Her green eyes gloss over stonily, and she robotically tilts her head toward the sky, her fingers lifting the cigarette toward her red lips. Pulling smoke from the filter, the tendons in her neck flex, and my mouth waters. My fangs slither out from my gums, and my eyes compress into vertical slits, the dryness indicating the white has siphoned all the green from them.

Her skin is salty and tastes like bathtub jungle juice, but as soon as my teeth pierce her skin and the delectable nectar hits my tongue and slides down my throat, I am soothed. Blood is like a balm to a burn, soothing a deep and unyielding hunger.

As I drink from her, I feel the presence before I see it.

Before I can race away, the creature jumps on my back and tries to gnaw at me. Dodging the first attempt, I duck right and try to grab its arm, catching the sight of the grotesque being before me. The features of her face have melted together, skin covers her eyes, and her nose is flattened; only a gaping mouth with rows of razor-sharp teeth remain.

The only weapon that I have on me is my thimble, and I know they aren't as reactive to silver as we are, but I jab up anyway and slice cleanly across the grim's face, brownish-black blood gushing out.

The creature shrieks and comes at me faster, almost taking a chunk out of my arm. Narrowly escaping the attempted carnage, I flee to the left as it clings to my pant leg, dropping me to my knees.

Drawing all my power, I whisk upright just in time to see her razor-sharp teeth directly in my face.

Her breath is hot and sour, the smell of rotting flesh and body odor ripple through me, and I think of Sayah before I'm ripped apart. Her ocean blue eyes are like a salve for my damned soul, a calming thought before the end…

A silver machete pulverizes through the top of her skull, halving her face. The top half falls off and lands on the ground with a thud as her lifeless body collapses onto mine. The acrid stench of the rotten blood is enough to make me gag as I heave her off me and corral the retching feeling, stumbling to the side.

"That one nearly got ya there," a female voice says to my right.

Raising my gaze, I notice a buxom, brown-haired individual with a button nose and full, crimson lips. She gives off the vibe of someone heading to a college kegger rather than resembling a typical vampire, her maroon leather jacket contrasting her pale white skin.

"Yeah," I respond, hoisting myself off the ground and dusting my pants. Not that it's going to get the awful grim guts off them. I need a shower. "Thanks."

"No problem," she replies, bending down and wiping the machete blade clean on the grim's pants.

"Do you just always carry your machete on you, or?"

She rises, her prominent chest bouncing with laughter. "No. I live up there—" she inclines her head at the metal fire escape scaffolding lining the east side of the building we're under. "I heard the bastard shriek. They're getting worse."

"You're telling me. My family and I are looking for ways to get a handle on the influx in New York, but it's leading us nowhere fast."

"Yeah, I don't know anything about that," she says, offering me a bemused smile. "I just kill 'em when I see 'em. You've gotten no leads?"

"Maybe a coven in Vegas can give us insight on the warlocks. But that's all so far." I don't know this broad from Adam; I'm not about to tell her anything more than that. Even though her energy is tingly, like she's very upbeat and positive, I don't trust any old vampire I meet on the street.

"I've got friends in Vegas that can show you around. They may know more than I do. My friend Jesse. You got a phone?"

Retrieving the phone from my back pocket, I hold it to my face to unlock the screen and hand it to her.

"There," she says after plugging her friend's number in. "Just hit him up when you're there, and they can help you."

"Thank you, um. . ."

"Cora," she says, offering me her hand.

Shaking it, I reply, "Dom."

"Well." She lets my palm go and leans her machete against the brick wall. "You gonna finish her, or?" she asks of the still veilweaved human, lighting another cigarette and staring into space.

"Uh, no, I don't do that. You're welcome to if you'd like; I just don't want to witness it."

A sinister grin splits her face, her irises contracting and flaring white. “Oh, one of those vamps, huh?” she teases, the ivory of her fangs glinting off the amber light of the streetlamp above.

“Yeah, something like that. Want me to toss this thing in the dumpster?” I ask, kicking the grim’s side.

She kneels before the human and slips the girl’s hair all to one side, gripping her neck. “Nah, I got em. I’ll toss them both out in the dumpster.”

“You sure?”

“Yeah. Go. Get out of here. And be safe out there.”

“Hey, thanks again,” I say, turning to leave the way I came.

The resonant sound of skin being punctured and slurping follows me as I track back down the alleyway.

Almost getting my face chewed off has a purpose, I think as I rush towards the direction of my car.

It led me to someone who may know how to find the entrance to Never in Vegas.

18

AN EPIC LOVE IS STIRRING

SAYAH

The soothing air of Vegas envelops me as we walk from the Uber that picked us up at the airport to our hotel.

The last time I saw Dom, he surprised me with three plane tickets—for Claire, Anna, and me—for an all-expenses-paid trip to Vegas.

He has a convention to attend while we're out here, so he'll be in business meetings all day.

As the bellhop opens the double doors to the immaculate suite, we follow the cart in and our jaws drop.

"Wow," breathes Anna, meandering about the gigantic suite that's basically an apartment in the sky.

The room is lavishly furnished, with a living room, a kitchen, and a private balcony pool. Two bedrooms are attached to the main room, with private balconies, double walk-in showers and jacuzzi tubs.

Meandering over to the bedroom on the right, I see Dominic has already set his belongings down on the king-sized bed. His brown leather suitcase is neatly packed, the top open to show many white shirts, boxers, socks, and other things.

His suits are hanging in the closet.

We've barely seen each other these last few weeks because of my custody schedule, and since he works nights, my time with Dom has been limited.

"I guess this is our room," I say as I deposit my purse on the dresser.

Smells of fresh linen and coconut explore my senses as I whisk my eyes around the extravagant rooms. I have never stayed in anything so beautiful. Growing up poor, being in a lower-class bracket with my ex-husband and now a struggling single mom, my idea of getaways always involves lower-priced Air B&Bs, motels, and double twin beds at the Marriott.

This is next level.

Dominic is already in Vegas, having arrived late last night, as he has all-day meetings for the rest of the weekend. He will be joining me later this evening. From the looks of things, he didn't sleep, or the maid had already been in here to freshen up, as our bed is made with the white towel twisted into a swan on our bed. All the towels, soaps, and lotions are in the bathroom. His black shaving kit is open but still packed with his things on the counter. The smell of him hangs in the air; his scents of summer fire and earthy musk cling to the bathroom walls.

Entering the living room, I watch Anna and Claire do the same, eyeing the décor, the fully stocked mini fridge, and the cute little towel designs on both beds.

"What is it that Mr. Romantic does for a living?" Claire inquires, eyes wide with wonder and awe.

"He's a data analyst for a software engineering company, but that's all I know," I hedge. I have no idea what he actually does when he goes to work.

The bellhop finishes taking our luggage off the cart and is about to leave when I grab a folded ten-dollar bill.

"Thank you so much," I tell him, slipping him the money.

He bows his head in thanks and closes the double doors to the suite behind him, leaving us to our wonderland.

Returning to the main room, I walk over to the double sliding doors to the balcony pool.

"Shall we go for a swim?" I ask as Claire and Anna join me.

"Absolutely!" Claire answers, slipping the black straps of her dress off her shoulders and wiggling it to the floor.

We've come prepared, as Dominic messaged me when he arrived last night and sent a picture of the private pool lit up at night against the backdrop of the city of lights.

"I'm gonna make a drink," Anna announces, walking over to the mini-fridge.

"Make me one too, babe?" Claire asks as she and I walk toward the pool.

I flick off my flip-flops and unbutton my jean shorts, writhing my hips to escape out of them. My moss green bikini with gold dangling stars is underneath as I shimmy out of my gray tank top.

The Vegas May heat is in full effect, and it's around seventy-nine degrees at noon. I dip my toes in the water first. It's bathwater warm. I enter the pool with Claire, who's clad in her coral orange swimming suit; her flat tummy, which I'm infinitely jealous of, glistens as she dips it into the water.

Claire is a rare beauty, hailing exotic looks that she received from her Native American mother and her French father. She has short, jet-black hair that she often wears straight and eyes that are the color of sea moss on a dark rock. Not very tall, she is only around five feet-three inches, but is as strong as an ox.

Our view is the fountain below and the entire city of Vegas. I can't wait to see the city lights and my handsome man when the night comes.

"So, are you two official yet?" Claire asks from beside me.

"Close enough, I think. We haven't said 'boyfriend' and 'girlfriend' yet, but that may change this weekend." I'm all giggles at the thought of this.

"Oh, Sayah has a boyfriend?" Anna adds, eagerly setting the drinks down on the pool's edge. She swoops her floral dress over her head, revealing her purple tankini beneath it.

Anna is also a shorter girl like Claire, but whereas Claire has jet-black hair and an exotic look, Anna's hair is white-blonde and gives off more of a Viking vibe. She has a long face like me, and her eyes are a bright baby blue, the kind of blue that feels like you're being sucked into her soul.

"Pretty much." I blush, unable to hide my giddiness from the girls.

"I feel like we haven't even seen you since you met him at that mixer," Claire says, taking a drink of her cocktail.

"I have just been working, doing school, and being a mom. I haven't really hung out with him too much; he works nights, so our schedules are opposite."

My phone dings from my bag in the apartment.

"That's probably him," I say, sweeping through the water to exit the pool.

Water drips from my body as I open the entrance to our room from the pool; I stride to the dresser and retrieve my purse.

Digging my phone out, I open the message.

Just got out of one meeting, on to another.
Hope you like the room =)

The room is fantastic! You are amazing! Can't
wait to see you later!

Closing the message, I return to the girls in the pool.

"So, what's he like?" Claire asks with a sparkle in her eye as I submerge myself again, stowing the phone on the side of the pool.

"He's amazing. He's polite and charming. On our second date, he got my mom a star."

"Awe," both girls coo, the glint in their eyes reflecting a sincere empathy for me, but Claire's face falls slightly as though she's a bit jealous. It's a good jealousy, though. My friends are genuinely happy for me, considering what they saw me go through after my divorce.

"I know! I really can't even believe that I found someone like him. He brought me flowers and a candy bar for Gauge on the first date. He's like the sweetest guy."

"Does he have any single friends?" Anna inquires, her brown

sunglasses reflecting the aqua of the pool and blue sky that has hardly any interruptions of wispy white clouds.

"He has a few brothers," I answer. "One that he doesn't speak to. But the other I believe he is on good terms with."

"Why doesn't he talk to his brother?" Claire asks.

"Something about a girl." There's no need to disclose the mysterious death associated with the strange story behind it. I don't need their opinions of the man footing the entire bill for our vacation swayed.

"Ah. That'll do it," Claire says, setting her drink down and diving into the water.

"What else?" Anna asks. "What does he like to do for fun?"

"I'm not sure of that yet," I respond honestly. "I only see him at night. We haven't talked about what we do in the summer or anything. I really don't know him all that well."

A realization dawns on me that I really don't know too much about him.

That will change.

"That's okay, babe," Claire says, resurfacing, slicking the water off her black hair. "You're in the beginning stages of a relationship. You'll get to know him more and more each time you hang out."

"This is true," Anna answers, taking her turn to dive into the water.

"Have you guys fucked yet?" Claire asks, situating her sunglasses again and retrieving her drink from the side of the pool.

"Not yet. Really, not even close. We've just hung out in public places. Once, he kissed me on the porch passionately and turned away. I thought I had bad breath, but he told me I'm the kind of girl he wants to be his last of everything, and he didn't wanna ruin it by going too fast."

"Oh my god, he said that?!" Claire exclaims, her mouth agape.

"Yeah, on our *first* date!" I respond, twirling my hair up into a messy bun. "It totally threw me off."

"Why would it throw you off? I think it's wonderful," Claire retorts.

"I don't know, 'cause I didn't get that feeling around him. I just felt it was too soon to tell something like that."

"I get that," Claire says. "You're being careful with your heart, as you should."

"The more time I spend with him, the more I feel it. I mean, I don't think he's the one or anything. He doesn't give me that 'soulmate' vibe. But I can see him becoming an epic love. That's all I get for now."

"Epic loves are the best," says Anna, swimming over to us from the side.

"I agree," Claire adds. "Even if it's not something that lasts forever, it'll be something you remember forever and ever."

I take my turn diving underneath the water. When I resurface, the girls are chuckling about something one of them had said.

"What are you two whispering about?" I ask, swimming over to them.

"We were just saying tonight will probably be the night you two get it on." Claire laughs.

"It's the first time we'll spend the night together," I concur.

"Oh, about to lose your virginity," Anna jokes.

"That is true!" I laugh. "It's been so long; I think it grew back."

Peals of laughter echo, and I find myself smiling and giggling harder than I have in a long time.

Little black dresses have nothing on us; we each have one on, Claire with a tightly clung black, floor-length dress that hugs her curves and accentuates her breasts, and Anna has a flowing black dress with lace peek-a-boos all over, from neckline to knee. My dress hangs off my shoulders and plunges down the front, is lower in the back to the floor but comes to a halt pick-up above my knees.

The mixture of our floral perfumes lingers in the elevator with us.

Pressing the button for the lobby, we each take turns checking our makeup in the mirror-laden walls of the lift. Soft melodic music serenades us as we descend from the top floor, finally dinging to alert our arrival at the lobby where the restaurant we're meeting Dominic is located.

Dominic is already at the table that the host leads us to.

Dressed in a suit and tie, he looks as stunning as ever as he stands to greet us. The white shirt is unbuttoned, revealing those tattoos and his tie hangs loosely around his neck.

"Well, hello there, sexy," he says, sweeping me up into a hug and a luscious kiss. That earthy smell of cologne is still clinging to him; however, it has dissipated throughout the long day of meetings.

Before the other two girls can sit down, he speeds over to their chairs and pulls them out, scooting them in as they sit.

I'm last.

"Enjoying your time so far?" Dominic asks as he sits down himself.

"Oh my god, yes," answers Claire. "Thank you for this, all of it. The penthouse suite is amazing. I've never seen anything like this."

"I could get used to this life," Anna states.

"So, you are just here for meetings?" Claire asks as the waiter comes over and hands us menus.

"Drinks for the ladies?" he asks.

Claire's eyes light up with a captivating sparkle upon spotting the waiter, and this luminosity dances across her expression. Her face's sultry softness and flirty transformation reveal themselves, a telltale sign that she has spotted something she desires.

"I'll take a tequila sunrise, please," she says seductively.

"Make that two," Anna seconds, lighter.

"I'll just have iced tea, please," I put in.

"I'll get those going," replies the waiter, gliding his smile toward Claire. "Any appetizers while you decide on supper?"

"I'll have to look," answers Claire, showing off her perfect teeth in a smile, her Marilyn Monroe piercing glinting in the light. "Thanks, though."

"Sure thing," the waiter replies and saunters off.

"So," Dominic continues, "my company attends a trade show here twice or thrice a year to gain clients. They send some of us to come and spread our name as much as possible. They always assign me because the first time I came, I garnered a couple million-dollar clients for them."

"A couple?" Claire inquires a look of shock in her eyes. "Wow, that's a lot of money."

"Yeah. My company is recognized worldwide because of the merger. So, I get to come every time. It's a free trip for me." His smile is smug but not arrogant. He never seems to boast about his wealth, but it's clear he's very wealthy.

"That's so cool," Anna responds. "Where else do you get to go?"

"I've been all over," Dominic answers as the waiter drops off our drinks. "I've been to Tokyo, Cork, England, Italy, Spain. All over the states. I haven't worked for this branch for very long, so this is my first time out here for them, but I know that'll soon change when I work my magick here this weekend."

Hopefully, he works his magic on me, too.

"That's all I want from this life," Claire says, fixing the strap of her dress. "To travel the world."

"You haven't lived until you've seen it," Dominic answers, taking a drink of his bourbon.

"Where have you been so far?" Dominic asks Claire.

"Oh, just to Mexico—" she stirs her drink, mixing all the sunrise colors. "But I love that place so much. Other than that, just the states."

"That's more than me," Anna says dejectedly, her eyes sloped down at the corners. "I have only ever been out of Colorado. I have never been out of the country."

"You will get to someday," Dominic encourages her as she pops the cherry from the drink into her mouth. "What about you, gorgeous?" he asks me, his dark eyelashes fluttering toward me, the mysterious curtains of mystery guarding his chartreuse eyes.

"I've been to Mexico and the Virgin Islands. Went on a cruise once and stopped by Venezuela, Curaçao, and Puerto Rico. That's really it, though. Nothing big like Europe."

"Well, maybe I can change that," he whispers, kissing me on the tip of my nose.

Those flutters arise like a bird in the wind, as if a hummingbird creates a monsoon in my stomach. The subtle thunder that awoke in me once has risen again, chasing away all the clouds of doubt I once had before with him.

Maybe the hesitation I initially felt was just me guarding my heart and keeping him at arm's length. Because right now, there's nothing that I want more than to go on adventures with this man.

The sun's heat from the afternoon still clings to the humidity of the evening long after the sun finishes its descent. Standing guard of the glorious city, the moon's imperial watch has just begun. Interlocking patterns of blinking lights illuminate the metropolis, buzzing and alive with activity. Down below, the fountain dances its balletic gait to the music that plays; however, we are too high up to hear the song.

I sit on the patio couch by the pool, slipping out of my heels and rubbing my feet. I don't wear heels often, and this is the reason.

Claire had successfully flirted with the waiter at dinner and got herself and Anna invited to a staff party after his shift, which gave Dominic and me the evening alone at the suite.

Dominic is fixing himself a drink before he joins me.

"Can I get you anything, love?" he calls from inside the hotel suite.

"Just some ice water, please. Thanks."

"I really like your friends," he says as he joins me on the balcony a few minutes later, handing me the ice water.

"Yeah, they're amazing. Especially Claire. I've known Anna a long time, but not as well as I do Claire. But they're really getting close lately."

He appraises my eyes. "Does that bother you at all?"

I swallow my drink of water. "No, Claire and I have always had a relationship like that. We're inseparable, close for a few years, and then we drift but never apart. Just to new, everyday kind of friends. It's hard to explain."

"I get it. I'm the same with my brother Ollie," Dominic says as he sips his drink, the ice chinking along the side. Setting it down on the table, he continues. "He and I are in that 'we don't talk every day' phase, but we're still there for each other."

His fingers interlace with mine, and I feel that strange magic at his touch. I lose focus on the conversation as he does, looking at his manly wide and not-so-calloused fingers, the longing for them to touch me in *places* extinguishing the desire to keep talking.

His commanding gaze deploys a heated rush that devours our words with a seductive silence. His green eyes turn hungry; I want to ruin his body with mine and have him taste my darkness.

"I just have to tell you," he breathes, the scent of whiskey flirting with the earthfire smell of him, "you look so good in that dress." Inching closer to me, he whispers, "Good enough to eat," to the shell of my ear, erupting pinpricks of goosebumps all over me.

"So do you," I answer as his fingertips trace a path down my right leg.

It almost feels like we're about to have our first kiss again; the nervousness paired with excitement has me feeling woozy. He's slow, methodic, edging closer to me, and I want him to kiss me, feeling my body respond to him immediately. Anticipating his lips on mine, I wet my bottom lip, but he doesn't kiss my lips at first. He tilts my head sideways by my neck, diminishing the space between us.

His breath is hot against the curve of my neck where it meets my shoulder, chilling me yet heating where he kisses. Fire flushes to my face and spreads down between my legs as he sucks my skin. My clit tingles in response as he nibbles along my jawline and chin, claiming my lips at the end of his expedition.

It's been so long since I have been with a man. I'm drenched wet the instant his tongue glides into my mouth. His rhythmic kisses match his movements. The heat is so intense on my lips—the lips on my face and those that hide beneath the surface of my panties. His hands wander slowly to make sure I'm okay with the touches, and when I release a low, tortured breath, he removes the straps from my shoulders and takes hold of my plump, bare breast. Feeling myself slipping off a ledge, I fear I may cum the moment he pinches my pebbled nipple. His mouth moves down my neck again, and when he takes my breast in his mouth and bites down softly, I'm brought to the very boundary of that ledge.

"Harder," I breathe, the tingle of the bite traveling from my nipple to my clit in a glorious and torturous electric shock.

Arching my back so he takes my breast deeper into his mouth, the glass slips from my hand, and I can't bring myself to catch it. It falls from and crashes to the cement below, shattering. The sound should've awoken us from our lustful encounter, but it does not. We need to feel each other so much that nothing can cause us to abandon this moment.

His left hand brushes the sensitive skin of my inner thigh, ascending higher until he reaches my panties, the wetness proof of my arousal. He claims my lips while he gently plays with my clit the way he had my nipple, and the sensation electrifies me down to my toe tips. He gently rolls the swell of my clit back and forth, flicking his finger side to side until I'm about to scream with pleasure.

His breathing is erratic and urgent. I let my hand wander to his shirt, pulling at the buttons and accidentally snapping a few of them off as I set the ripples of his abs free.

The corded muscles of his stomach greet my hand, and I grow even wetter at the feel of him. I need him inside of me, and when his finger plunges into me, I moan, but it isn't enough. It makes me hungrier.

He leans back from me, his wanton eyes pools of desire and lust, maybe even a little hunger. He watches me in awe as he immerses his finger deeper, curling the tip of it to massage my inner wall. I tilt my head back and close my eyes, gripping the cushion as euphoria consumes me.

I cry out in ecstasy, and he swallows my scream in a greedy rush, tasting like mountain air—fresh, clean, and crisp. I widen my legs for him, and he swoops my right leg over him so it's draping over his lap.

Being pleasured by him is like drinking a cold glass of lemonade on a warm summer day, the breeze cooling the sweat accumulated from the sun's scorching kiss. He's satisfying an urge that's been lurking in my darkness for a long time, quenching a thirst my vibrator at home could never, and he's not even inside me yet.

The outline of his erection in his pants is enticing me; I skim his rippling muscles down to the zipper and slide it down. His giant cock springs to attention once freed, and like a magnet, my hands are all over it, coercing animalistic groans from him as I stroke. Feeling the length of him, the rugged ridges of his dick, the soft skin of the mushroom tip gorgeously glides in and out of my hand. I'm near to that edge with just the feel of his hardness.

"I want you," he breathes into my neck, and I try to pull him on top of me. I don't even care if we don't make it to the bed.

With my tits hanging out, his kisses growing hungrier, he suddenly stands, pulling me into a straddle as he continues to taste my mouth. My dress rises up, and I can feel his cock teasing my entrance as he walks us into the bedroom. As he throws me on the bed and leans into me, I grip his sides, feeling the need to anchor myself as I am about to lose all control with just the thought of him entering me.

My head is light as he lets up on the kisses and pulls my dress all the way off, ripping the panties so they're just shreds of fabric on the floor. I lock my hand around his neck as he keeps his mouth on mine, sucking my bottom lip in between his teeth, biting a little but with no sting.

I kinda want a little pain.

When he bites down hard enough to cause a cresting of that resplendent torment, I rock my hips in response, letting out a long and breathy moan. The tortured groan he releases lets me know that he's burning as hot as I am. He needs me as much as I need him.

It's intoxicating, the intense whirlwind of sensations flooding me all at once. My pussy is sweltering with passion, and I'm a drenched mess. For a split second, I think it's a little embarrassing, but he lets out a sexy groan when he touches me there. I know it's a welcome reaction to how he's making me feel.

My breathing is shallow, and there's a chance that as soon as he puts his cock inside of me, I'll cum faster than I want to. Still, I fasten myself to the intoxication, letting the exquisite passion temper me.

His hardness is rubbing on my swollen clit; I may hyperventilate, overwhelmed, given my hindered breath. I move my hips up and down, making him moan with anticipation, arching my back, practically begging him to put himself inside of me, but he won't.

I continue to sway my hips under him, sliding myself over the backside of his dick, hoping that I can catch the tip and capture him inside of me. Still, he keeps teasing, keeps kissing, keeps licking until I feel I'll go mad from not having him.

Finding the waistline of his pants in a fumbling lust, I shove them off his hips.

The penetrating green of his predatory eyes slice me to my bone as he admires me, leaning up to wiggle out of his pants. His abs coil as he rolls his body out of the shirt, making the tattoos flex. I arch my back, imploring him to bring his mouth to my breasts. Instead, he takes my legs over his shoulders and slides down, slipping his tongue over my clit.

Gripping the comforter of the bed to moor my writhing body, I find a pillow with the other hand and moan loudly, the sensations blinding me, tunneling my vision and almost causing me to black out.

The feeling of his tongue wiggling over my clit, sucking and kissing, and devouring every inch of my pussy, cause shattered stars to grace my vision as I climax.

Twitching as he slows down, I want him inside me desperately.

He whispers kisses to my navel, tugging on my piercing with his teeth. Cresting at the peak of my breasts, he teases each nipple, tracing patterns with his tongue up the column of my neck. There is no part of me left undiscovered; his destructive mouth is a sanctuary for my corrosive desires.

As he kisses me, he pins my hands above my head and slides his hard dick inside me without even having to guide it. With ease, it enters from being so wet. I cry out with the pleasure it brings me, the depth of him matching me perfectly as he submerges himself inside of me slowly, burying himself as deep as he can go. The tip of his cock presses against my G-spot with ease, and again, I moan, grabbing the pillow to muffle my screams.

With him deep inside me, he removes the pillow and turns my chin to face him, staying inside of me and not moving.

"No," he growls, his baritone voice echoing in the room; the fact that he's commanding me makes my body clench around his gorgeous cock. "I want to hear you scream."

Leveling me with a look of desire, a dizzying haze takes over me, and I feel drunk; everything is heightened, and I can barely move. I writhe up and down, trying to get him to move in and out of me, and when he does, It. Is. Paralyzing.

He swirls his hips, pulling in and out of me, deeper and harder with each thrust. I can't contain the moans; every time I let one escape, it makes him harder and hungrier for me. He lifts my legs over his broad, muscular shoulders, and I watch the ink dance beneath his skin as he thrusts.

Feeling myself climb higher and higher, it's almost too much for me to handle, and I wish he would flip me over and take me from behind.

He pulls out of me, grabs my waist, and forcibly flips me around so that my knees are on the bed and my ass is in the air.

What the hell? Did I just say that thought out loud?

Oh well, I continue to let him move me, and it is pure ecstasy.

He wraps my long hair around his fists, his other anchored on my hip and pulls as he enters me, slamming into me as hard as he can.

Never in my life have I met anyone that meets my needs as he does. It's as if he's reading my thoughts and pushing the right buttons at all the right times, depths, and paces.

The sound of his pleasure pulls me to the brink, the wave of my orgasm weakening my knees. As I fall to the bed when they give out, I want him to keep going, to make me cum again and again.

Chasing my orgasm with his hungry dick, he flips me so I'm sideways, grabbing my breast as he continues to rock his body inside and out of me.

I want him to take control, to fuck me as hard as he can.

Fuck me til the bed breaks.

Fuck me to destruction.

His pace picks up, and his plunges deepen, answering my un-beckoned plea.

"Oh," I groan, rolling my head back.

The plunges become so deep and hard that the bed's wooden frame collapses, sending us both slanting to the floor.

"Fuck," he says as I crawl off the bed; he's holding my hips as he follows me.

Once we're level, I push him back with my ass so that he's lying down, and I'm on top of him backward.

Spreading his legs, I slide my legs underneath his knees and bury his dick within me.

The position of his dick inside me from this angle brings me back to that ledge, and I moan, rocking back and forth until I start bouncing. Feeling my large breasts bounce with each recoil makes me hotter; I brace my hands on his knees and concentrate on moving my ass up and down on top of him. The sound of his moans light me up, and he grabs my hair again, making me look at the ceiling as I ride him.

"Cum for me," he commands, and I continue to bounce on him, feeling the depth of him pierce me and cause me to explode again.

With a primitive growl, he grabs my hips and pulls me to the floor, his animalistic nature brimming as he feeds from my lips while he climbs on top of me. I swallow his kiss, drinking in this sexy fucking man and his pleasure.

"Fuck, Sayah, you're so gods damned wet," he says into my mouth without breaking his ravenous kiss. "I'm gonna cum."

"Cum for me," I command.

In the inhale of his drunken words, and with him, I began that climb once again.

Lifting my legs above his shoulders, he pretzels me, dipping into my world and pulling out, causing a detonation of the most luscious torment I've ever experienced. The height of this orgasm begins slowly, my entire body going liquid hot and tingly, starting in the middle and ricocheting outwards. Like the explosion of an atom bomb in slow motion, it scorches through me to my ends, growing in momentum as it pierces outward.

Pulling his dick out to the tip, he plunges in one last and final time, as deep as he can go, and the detonation of his own orgasm ignites with mine, causing the fiery combustion to destroy me.

The feeling of him letting go inside me is something out of another world. It feels like euphoria becomes hot little butterflies that release into my veins, and every pore feels numb and tingly.

He collapses on top of me, his chest heaving, the remnants of my orgasm cementing me to the floor.

"What the fuck?" he breathes, laying his head on my bare breasts. We both lay breathless, letting the feeling of euphoria consume us.

"Yeah," I say on an exhale, twisting my fingers in his brown hair. "What the fuck is right."

"I've never. . ." The sentence is unfinished, but the unspoken words say more than I could ever say.

"Mmm-hmm," I reply breathlessly, the stars still shooting across my vision.

"You are amazing," he says into my nipple, cupping my breast and kissing it. "And so are these."

Feeling his chest rise as he laughs, I return the giggle. "Thank you."

"Mmm, you are most welcome."

"You are really good at that," I rasp through an exhale. "It's like you were reading my mind."

"That was nothing," he returns, propping his head on his elbow to look at me. "I'm a bit out of practice. Wait until next time, I'll go all night long."

If that was him out of practice . . .

Holy fuck.

"I'm down for that anytime," I say, tracing my fingernails down his biceps, teasing little goosebumps out of his skin.

"Good," he says as his breathing levels out. He softly strokes the side of my face. "I believe you have me falling for you, Lasayah Thorne."

His soft lips brush mine.

Butterflies rush to my stomach as the sensuous kiss spills his secrets, receiving my confessions. At the same time, the stars and moons become our priests to bear witness.

An epic love is stirring.

19

VAMPIRES OF VEGAS

DOM

Laying here next to Sayah, listening to her breath come and go from her lungs, the peacefulness of her sleep tangles with emotions that are warring inside me.

Sex with her was absolutely mind-boggling—never in my life have I ever climaxed that hard with someone. It was as though my soul departed my body, entered a new realm, and dined on the blood of angels.

Even though I cannot read her thoughts, I can *feel* them. It's part of my power, feeling a person's intentions. Occasionally, I can see a person's thoughts if they let me. But people are often so guarded that it's hard to do, and they can feel the intrusion.

Feeling her chest rise and fall under my arm, a little snore escapes her mouth and makes me smile. I love how imperfectly perfect she is. Every curve, every line of her, every wrinkle, and every scar. I trace the freckles on her back, her skin velvet under my touch. Goosebumps rise as I memorize her every bend, following the curve of her spine to the gorgeous mountain of her hip, beautifully decorated with trapped lightning beneath her skin.

My thoughts spiral out of my head and mingle with her lightning, eating up all other rational thoughts that bound around in my head.

Without rousing her awake, I roll onto my other side away from her and use my speed to rush me to the door. Quietly sliding the patio doors open, I slither through them and up to the balcony.

I draw an intense breath of air and let it sink to the bottom of my lungs before releasing it, trying to capture my spiraling thoughts.

I like this girl.

This witch.

This *woman.*

I am definitely falling for her.

These past few weeks, I've watched her come into power as flawless and seamless as I've ever seen. I've been around witches my whole life, and never have I seen power as strong as hers not only come to rest at home in her but is brimming, almost exploding out of her, just waiting to be unleashed. I don't know if it was the spell Tallyn spun on her, the bracelet I gave her, or her own magick igniting—maybe it's all three—but it has been fascinating to watch.

During our time together, I've helped her hone her magick by going through spells my mom had sent us. Sayah's taken every spell and bonded with it, letting them enchant her bones and make a home under her skin. Each one except fire. The other three were like watching a reunion of old friends, pieces and parts of her returning home to lay and rest until they all may be ignited one day. Fire has been the only that has so far evaded her.

Her determination is contagious. Granted, her power is volatile and unpredictable, but how she leans into her struggles and uses them to improve herself is awe-inspiring. Instead of giving up on something hard to grasp, she sits in the uncomfortable and wallows in the way it bends her. Once she learns how the power works and interlocks within her, she grasps it. Then she grows with it, not letting it overpower or define her, nor does she let it abandon her.

My eyes chase the lights of the city, tracking down to the shimmering fountain, dancing to a song I cannot hear, but this mist of memory from earlier today visits me.

Earlier, I walked down to that fountain stealthily in the shade of the buildings and met with Jesse. He's a tall, scrawny fellow with amber eyes and flaxen hair. He was mingling in Vegas's shadows with four or five other vamps.

He walked me to an entrance where the underground tunnels lurk, the intricate tunnel system below the city of Vegas that's a sanctuary for the unhoused and provides a community for less desirable souls of Sin City. A below-ground cardboard suburb, the fort-like structures were all lined up against the cement walls of the town, reminiscent of a different version of Vegas in another realm.

Perfect for vampires.

Jesse and his crew introduced me to more vampires and a section of the cardboard city where the donors dwelled. The only problem with that was all of the donors were drug addicts, and that means when you feed from them, you're also feeding on laced blood. Some vampires like that sort of thing since it produces the same euphoria that comes with killing someone, but because I'm an addict, I cannot risk that. I declined the opportunity to feed.

That, and they charged money, and I had no cash on me at the time.

They congregated in a makeshift lounge area, ripped and stained couches and chaise lounges strewn about haphazardly, candles of every color burning for the light. The vampires I was with paid a few to get their fill; a skinny blonde girl with pock-marks all over her offered her neck and let the rotund vampire feed.

The smell was not great—smelling like old milk, body odor, and burning medicine. In one corner was where donors waited, charging anywhere from $20-$80 for a drink, depending on how long the vampire wanted to feed. The eerie candlelight threw obscure shadows onto the donors' faces, most of them skin and bone with greasy hair and moldy clothes.

On the other side was the drug den, where multiple people crouched in the corner holding spoons and cooking dope, others driving needles into their arms for their fix.

I always hate going to places like that, as it wreaks havoc on my conscience. I wouldn't say I like seeing people powerless over things that are beyond their control, as it reminds me of the times I've been lost inside my own addiction.

On the way out, Jesse showed me the entrance to the Neverdusk Dominion.

It is below the Bellagio Fountain.

Later today, as Sayah and her friends explore the city, I will continue my quest to find anyone to help the grimspawn infestation.

The only thing I have to worry about—one more thing I have to worry about to add to my pile of worries—is that I think Sayah is starting to suspect something different about me.

20

A WARNING

SAYAH

When I open my eyes, the room's dark as the sun's still asleep, yet the city lights twinkle wildly outside.

We'd fallen asleep on the floor since the bed's broken and a little tilted.

His arm drapes over my side, holding me from behind, and his soft snore hums in between my shoulder blades.

My right hip has gone numb from the hard floor, and although he had covered us at some point during the night with the white comforter, I'm still a little chilly being naked and on the floor. I try to shift my weight to get the throbbing pain digging into my hip to go away, but when I do, I rouse him awake.

He suddenly jolts up.

"What time is it?" he asks, jumping up to find his pants where he had deposited them in the throes of our passion. His bare ass is cute and round and has a nice, hard shape. Bubble butts on men are the best. "Oh, thank gods. It's only four. I have to get in the shower."

I try not to notice his gorgeous penis, which is still large when it's soft. I tingle again, wanting to feel him all up in me again.

"What time do you have to be there?" I ask, sitting up and pulling the comforter to cover my boobs.

"Before the sun comes up," he says, bending down and kissing me, pulling the comforter away.

"Mmm," I moan against his lips.

He pulls me up and escorts me into the shower with him, and I scuttle behind him on eager feet.

Turning on the hot water, the room fills with steam as he kisses me hungrily, shoving me gently into the shower as his soft penis begins to grow while he cups my breasts.

This time was not as long as last night, but I still climaxed hard as he had me pinned against the shower wall and fucked me from behind, standing up.

After the shower, he dresses for work as I climb into the crooked bed, hair wet and dripping, closing my eyes while feeling completely satisfied.

With life. In my situation. My *man.*

Drifting back to sleep, I feel him kiss my forehead before he leaves.

When I awake again, the sun is blazing in the room, causing all the white things within to glow. I draw up from the broken bed and head to the bathroom to grab a robe.

Entering the main room, Claire and Anna are awake, snacking on some room service.

"Hello there, sex hair," Anna says, tossing a piece of Danish at me.

Snatching it out of the air and popping it into my mouth, I ask, "Is it bad?"

"Was it good?" Claire asks, her eyes squinting. "Cause your hair says it was."

"Oh my gods. The best sex I think I've ever had. We broke the bed."

"Lucky," chides Anna, ripping off a piece of her blueberry muffin. "I want some of that."

"You guys didn't get lucky with any of the wait staff?"

"No," Claire says almost sadly.

"Got a few numbers, though," Anna adds. "We may go back there tonight. Depending on what you and Dominic have planned."

"I don't know if we have anything planned," I state, plopping down next to them. "What do you guys wanna do today?"

"I say walk the strip. Maybe check out that psychic. Do lunch somewhere. Check out the Chippendales," Claire chronicles our day in ten seconds, handing me a plastic cup of coffee with a lid.

"Chippendales, huh?" I say, opening the lid and pouring in some creamer, watching the coffee pale.

"Why not? Just because you're not single anymore doesn't mean we aren't."

"And besides," adds Anna, "you can always look."

"This is true," I smile, taking a drink of my coffee. "Never hurts to look."

As we walk the strip, the sun's leaving brilliant, dappled patterns on the ground beneath my feet. We stop in front of the psychic Anna had seen on our way in.

Because this is Vegas and the psychics are as commercialized as getting your nails done in a salon, we go in and see our own psychic at the same time.

I walk into my medium's domain, which is a dark room with crystals and other things that line the walls. The psychic does not sit at a table with a crystal ball in front of her. Instead, she lounges on a recliner, sipping a cup of tea, her curls being held back by a colorful bandana.

I'm practical about psychics, knowing that not all of them are honest and have gifts. Still, I tend to go into any readings with an open mind, giving them the benefit of the doubt. If they are full of shit, I don't tell them. I play along and then leave better known for it.

"Come in," the psychic says warmly, smiling. "Please. Have a seat."

I oblige her and sweep my purse off my shoulder, stowing it underneath my chair as I sit.

Holding out her hand, she says, "My name is Quinlyn. You are?

Taking it, I reply, "Lasayah. But friends call me Sayah."

"Nice to meet you, Sayah," she replies, crisscrossing her legs underneath her. "Have you ever had your cards read before?" she asks, unwrapping her tarot cards and shuffling them.

"A few times, yes," I say, crossing my legs.

"Okay, awesome. So, I ask that you not tell me anything, okay? Just think to yourself what questions you want the cards to answer as you shuffle the deck."

She holds out the thick cards that are beautifully illustrated. I project my questions deep within my well of energy to the point where I envision them entering the cards. Then I hand them back to Quinlyn.

Taking the deck, she cuts it, laying three cards before her face down.

"This first one is your past, where you have been that has led to where you are," she says as she flips it over and examines the card. "Mmm, hmm. Five of cups."

She picks it up and shows it to me.

There is a figure gazing at three spilled cups while two remain standing.

"This card typically represents sorrow or regret," Quinlyn explains, setting the card back down. "You have great sorrow around you and have suffered plenty in your short time here. Not just broken hearts, but shattered and torn by many beings, not just men. The universe seemed out to get you for a time." Her gray eyes appraise me, her expression softening.

Hit the nail on the head with that one.

"This next card is your present," she says, flipping the next card over and examining it. "The Ten of Swords."

Showing it to me, I see a figure lying face down with ten swords piercing their back.

"This card could represent a period of intense difficulty, betrayal, or being surrounded by darkness," her voice takes on a more serious tone. "There are many things at work in your energy. There are new people, some dark and dangerous. Others you've let go of, and that's a good thing. I see a lot of toxicity leaving your life. But there are choices that you're making that are letting other darkness in. Something is swirling around your aura. You are coming to terms with who you are, and you'll become powerful, but at the cost of something, and I don't know what. What you're playing with now can change your life in many ways. Be careful of the power you wield."

My goosebumps react to her words.

"The last card is your future. What is going to happen in times to come."

With the last one, she takes careful caution, flipping it over and narrowing her eyes on me as she does. "The Lovers."

Holding it up for me to see, two skeletons embrace each other. "This card usually represents a choice," she continues, setting the card back down.

There is a few seconds of silence as she braces her arms on each side of the chair, tilting her head back and closing her eyes.

She leans forward again and says, "Whatever you are doing now is awakening something ancient and powerful. There's a threat on the horizon that you'll soon come to terms with. Choosing to imbibe this power may have dire consequences. This card can sometimes be called the Gemini card. It shows that there are two people, two of every kind of person, one bad and the other good. Your darkest desires will want you to choose the darkness, to revel in the deep dark instead of playing with the feeble twilight. Regardless of your choice, someone will get hurt; there will be pain, and part of that pain will be yours to own as well. It's up to you who you wish to hurt less, as one will hurt extremely less than the other."

None of this makes any sense to me, but somewhere inside, I know I need to remember it. Something in my future will cause me to look back at this and delve deeper into what this psychic says.

"Even though your choice will hurt you," Quinlyn continues, "you have something in you that will save a lot of people. Your pain will end others' suffering, and so this path you're on is one that you're meant to be on. Others before you could not rise from the ashes as you have, and you will have to keep rising out of those ashes. For you are like a phoenix. And your blood is potent. There's a reason that you've been dealt the things you have. Your pain and suffering will not go unrepented. You have a magick within you that is unlike any other kind of magick the world has ever seen. Please take caution when honing your power, but hone it all the same. Conquer it. And seek the advice of others who walk your path, for they will guide you where you need to be."

"And what of love?" I ask, and instantly feel silly for saying it.

"One love will rise you from those ashes. And one will put you in them. Your heart will want the pain. The burn. The fire. That is the love that will consume you. The other is safe. It won't take you to the ends of the earth, but it will protect you and keep you safe. When the time comes, you must choose which love you want. The love that ends you. Or the love that revives you."

"And what if I choose the love that ends me? What then?"

"That is your choice to make. You will know when the time comes which you must choose."

There are so many questions that I want to ask, but I know that Quinlyn won't know the answers to these.

It's up to me to find them on my own and in due time.

"I know you have lots of questions," Quinlyn says as though she's read my mind; the features of her face are severe, her mouth a firm line while she talks, "but I read the energy on you and the cards. All I can tell you is to be careful. The magick you're playing with is stirring something ancient and powerful. Your eyes tell me you know exactly what I'm talking about. Just be careful with it. The energy around you contains darkness, which is seeping into your soul, attaching to and leaking into you. Careful if that's the darkness that will consume you."

I nod again as all the words I can think to say flutter out the window.

There's something about Dominic that has a dark tinge to it. But I don't want to let him go. I want to see where it goes.

"Thank you, Quinlyn," I say, standing.

"You're welcome."

My mind floods with thoughts as I retrieve my purse and head toward the exit.

Who the hell is going to ruin me? It can't be Dominic, can it? Sure, there's that darkness in his eyes, but he's fantastic. He's sweet, sexy, kind. And if Dominic is the one that will ruin me, who's the one that will save me?

If Dominic is the darkness, I want to be in darkness with him. There's always something in his eyes that's unfathomable, that tells me he knows grief beyond my comprehension. He has an agony playing at something in his aura, and I feel it sometimes when I'm near him. Something about him is unnatural, disarming. Haunting even. Like a weeping willow tree growing in the middle of a desert. Something that's rare and shouldn't be yet is. To behold him tells you a story. He's unyielding. Indestructible. But dangerous? No.

Well. Maybe a little.

I leave the room and meet with my girls on the other side.

"So?" Claire says as we gather in the foyer and walk out.

"Interesting," I say, not wanting to go into detail. "Yours?"

"Oh, apparently, I am going to meet the love of my life this summer," Anna responds, her voice dripping with sarcasm.

"You don't believe her?" I ask, pulling my sunglasses down over my eyes as the blast of Vegas heat stuns me.

"God no," Anna says, pulling her glasses again. "I'll believe it when I see it," she laughs.

"I believe mine," Claire adds, unwrapping a piece of gum and popping it in her mouth. "She said I will be showered with love and affection in the future."

"Yeah, by us," Anna responds, putting her arm around her and kissing her cheek.

"Awesome," Claire says, and now her voice is wet with the same sarcasm.

As our day on the strip winds down, we eat dinner at a little pub on Fremont.

The sun has set already, and the lights are coming alive in the city, lighting all of Fremont ablaze with neon.

"Sorry I'm so late," Dominic says, joining us as we finish dinner.

"No worries, babe," I say, trying the name 'babe' on him for the first time. It felt right. He doesn't even flinch and kisses my lips. "Are you hungry?"

He grins. "Famished," he says, pulling the strap of my tank top off my shoulder.

"For food." I giggle, pulling it back up.

"Oh, well . . . then no," he laughs and leans back. "Did you guys have fun today?"

"Oh, yeah," Claire answers, wiping her face with the linen napkin. "We saw a psychic, had lunch, then caught a show."

"What show?" he asks, his gaze dipping to me.

"Naked men. NBD," I answer honestly. I have nothing to hide from him.

"Nice," he replies without a stutter. "How was that?"

Anna's face flushes. "Great," she answers, grinning.

"Yeah, she has a date with one of the strippers later," Claire teases her, nudging into her shoulder.

"Sure do," Anna smiles, throwing her napkin on the plate.

"What are you going to do?" Dominic asks Claire.

She looks at Anna and smirks. "I'm gonna be the third wheel, of course."

"Well, that sounds . . . fun?" Dominic says questioningly.

"He's bringing a friend for her," Anna states, touching her lipstick up in her compact mirror.

"Oh, good," Dominic replies, waving the waiter over.

"Well, I think we're gonna head back to the hotel and get ready for our date," Anna says, gathering her things.

"Okay," I say, "will you guys let me know where you are so I don't have to worry that much?"

"Yes, Mom, we will," Claire retorts and stands up, kissing me on the head. "Take care of our girl."

"You know I will," Dominic replies and the two are off to hail an Uber.

"What would you like to do this evening?"

"I think walking on the strip with you would be fine," I answer and kiss him softly.

After three years of being single and being so picky that I didn't think I'd ever find love again. And here I am, in Vegas, with this hot guy I'm falling for.

And I think he's falling for me too.

We're walking hand in hand down the strip after dinner, enjoying the grandeur that is this city. City of sin. City of lights.

Just looking at the size of the buildings has me in awe. There's so much money in this city. So much money that I could never dream of having.

He stops me in front of the Bellagio fountain to watch the water dance.

From behind me, he begins to sway.

All is right with the world again.

"You know what I was thinking?" he whispers to the shell of my ear.

"What?"

"I think I want you to come to Lake George with me over the Fourth of July. Meet my family."

I'm shook. "Really?" I turn to look at him. "You want me to meet your parents and siblings?"

The look on his face tells me he's serious, and there's a wonder in his eyes that questions why I would even doubt it. "Of course."

"Well, maybe it's time you meet my little man then."

"Really?" His look now is skeptical; however, the color of his eyes is still darker than I've grown used to.

"Of course. I think it's time."

"Sayah, I would love that."

"And I would love to go with you to meet your family."

He smiles at me and kisses me softly.

My phone buzzes in my back pocket.

Claire is calling me.

"Hello?"

"Sayah, can you get here now? Something's wrong with Anna. These guys are creepers, and I'm scared."

"Where are you?"

"At some apartment. I'll text you the address."

"Do you need to call the police?"

"No, nothing like that. I think they drugged her. I've got her now; she's sluggish but can still walk."

"We're on our way."

I hang up, and Dom's look tells me he already knows something's wrong.

He pulls me toward the parking garage.

"They—"

"I know," he cuts me off.

"But how?"

"I heard. Her voice carried. Let's go," he demands, leading me quickly to the luxury car he's renting while here.

Together, we drive to the address Claire had texted and see the two girls hobbling down the stairs.

Scrambling out of the car, I bound over to Claire and help support Anna, who seems drugged and drunk and incoherent, yet she can walk on her own.

In a breathless rush, Dominic passes us, his eyes cold and fierce, the features of his face contorted in a fury I've never seen on him.

He's kinda scary.

"Dom!" I yell as he stomps up the stairs, but he either doesn't hear me or he doesn't care.

Claire and I help Anna stagger to the car, where I open the door and help Anna in. Claire climbs in next to Anna, lying down on Claire's lap.

"What the fuck happened?" I ask as soon as I'm in the passenger side.

"I don't know, dude," Claire says, her face still pale in shock. "We were there, chilling. I was talking to a boy named Logan. Anna was doing shots in the kitchen. I went to the bathroom and came back and saw fuckface try to spike my drink.

"I fucking yelled, and he pretended like he didn't know what I was talking about. I was fucking pissed; I went looking for Anna 'cause we were gonna leave, but she wasn't in the kitchen anymore." Claire lovingly looks down at Anna and strokes her white-blonde hair. "There was a locked door at the end of the hallway, and I knocked on it. All I heard were shushes and laughs, but then I heard Anna say, *'No, don't!'* I was about to kick the door in when Logan grabbed me from behind.

"I head-butted him and fucking screamed, making a scene. Someone finally opened the door, and Anna was on the bed, just like now. There were like three guys in there. Sayah—they were . . . about to gang rape her." Claire's chin trembles and she begins to weep.

I can't stand to see Claire cry; when she does, it breaks anyone who witnesses it; her anguish is so profound.

"I don't know what came over me; I started punching and screaming and pulled out my phone and told them I was gonna call the cops. The guys scattered, I grabbed her and ran, calling you on the way out."

"Oh my gods, Claire," I say, holding her hand. "I am so sorry."

She grabs it as we share a silent moment of understanding.

"Do we need to take her to the hospital?" I ask, still holding her hand.

"No," she says muzzily, letting go of my hand. "I think she needs to sleep it off. I'm ready to go back home tomorrow."

"Me too."

She looks out her dark window. "Where do you think Dom went?"

"I have no idea," I say, but my mind wanders.

What's he doing up there?

As if my question wandered up those stairs and summoned him itself, I see him coming down the stairs, taking two at a time. It's almost inhuman how fast he moves.

As he gets closer, I can see that he's covered in blood.

My heart falls.

He climbs in the car, and there's a gash on his eyebrow an inch long, and horror hangs on his features.

"Oh my gods, Dominic! What the fuck happened up there?"

Throwing the car into reverse, the tires screech as he speeds us off. "Let's just say they won't be drugging women anymore."

That's all he says; the air in the car and the tension in his voice tell me he has no desire to speak of it now—or ever.

Turning to look at Claire, she shrugs her shoulders, and I turn and watch the road.

Back at the hotel suite, Dominic carries Anna to her bed and lays her gently on top of the covers. We sit in the living room when he emerges, awaiting an explanation.

Remembering the large gash on his forehead, I dash to the kitchen to grab a towel. After wetting it with cold water, I return to the living room, where he sits silently with Claire, staring absentmindedly into the dark television on the wall.

When I sit down next to him, towel in hand, the large gash on his face has disappeared, and all that's left is the remnants of blood.

I take in his bedraggled figure, his clothes soaked in blood, the wound that I'm sure was there but isn't anymore.

"Don't worry, it's not my blood," he answers my unspoken thoughts.

Maybe it'd been a play on the light when he had entered the car.

"Then whose blood is it?"

"Theirs."

"Whose?"

"The ones who drugged the girl."

"How did you know which one it was?"

"I just did." He sits up, agitated. "Imma go take a shower."

He walks off and leaves Claire and me alone in the room.

His demeanor is different. His gait, the way he moves, his energy, shit, even his eyes have changed. It's like we're in a room with a complete stranger.

"I don't know what to say," I mumble when I hear the door to our bathroom close, and the unmistakable sound of the lock clicking follows.

Claire looks at me with quiet eyes. She's either unsure of Dominic or utterly cool with it. It's hard to tell with her.

"What do you think he did to them?" I ask.

"I'm not sure, but I hope he hurt them. That's all."

Leaning closer to her so I can whisper, I say, "What if he killed them?"

"I don't think he killed them. Say, that party was crowded. Think about that."

"True," I say haltingly.

Everything that the psychic had said to me comes to a resounding halt and I have to confront it. What had Dominic done to those guys? Sure, they deserved it, but why is he covered in blood? Whose blood is it? And how did he know which one of the guys to pummel?

The questions are mounting when the sound of the door opening dishevels the silence in the room, and he comes out, dressed in basketball shorts and a white tank top, drying his dark hair with a towel.

"Hey," he says, and his anger inside seems to have diminished; his eyes are back to their standard emerald green.

"Hey," I answer shortly, my annoyance sitting on the edge is bubbling.

"I know how bad that looked," he starts, his deep voice a simmering hollow. "And it wasn't as bad as it seemed, okay? I asked them where the two guys that came with the hot girls went. They pointed to a back room. I kicked the door in, and they were about to do it to another girl. I smashed some guy's face in with a lamp; he fell over and bled all over me. It was enough to get the other two to run in the other direction. I picked the girl up, got her out, and called the police. Then I left in a hurry."

His story sort of makes sense, but there are some holes in it. And I'm still annoyed.

"Well. Thank you for that," Claire says, crossing her legs on the couch. "I was about to do the same thing."

"I can't stand when pansy ass men do that to women."

"It doesn't make sense!" Claire responds, shrugging. "I mean, they were good-looking. We probably would've hooked up with them if we had gotten drunk enough. *What* is that?"

"It's part of their prowl," Dom answers, pulling a thread on the couch cushion. "They like the hunt. They live for that rush. It's what men like them do. They have women throwing themselves at them all the time. Getting girls is easy for them. It's the ones that are passed out, and they can do whatever they want with that turn them on. I've known guys like that. I've kil—" he stops himself.

I look at him with a frayed sense of curiosity at what the end of that sentence would be.

"I've beat up guys like that before. I have sisters."

Okay. He almost said kill, but he means he would have killed them if they had messed with his sisters.

Right?

Fear needles at the back of my neck.

"I know my brothers would've killed them tonight," Claire says quietly. It seems the two of them are on the same page.

I don't know what page I'm on. I'm all for justice. Eye for an eye. A bully to the bullies. But there had been so much blood. And so much strange fog surrounding the night and the events that I keep returning to what Quinlyn said.

There's a darkness about him. When he stormed off to take a shower, there was an affronted dignity in that gait, something that tells me he was tortured by what he had just done but had done it all the same. A shade of emotion hangs on him that doesn't exist in this reality.

Claire stands and straightens her dress. "I think I'm going to bed."

"Goodnight, babe," I say as she bends to hug me.

"Night," says Dominic, extending his hand out for her.

She takes it and squeezes. "Thanks again, Dom. I know that Anna will be appreciative in the morning."

He nods, and I shift, pulling my legs under me and grabbing a throw pillow.

"Are you angry?" he asks when Claire's gone.

"Not angry, just—surprised, I guess."

His eyes linger on mine for a moment and then drift off someplace, I know not where. There's such a haunting look on his face, a look that tells me he's adrift somewhere in his misery, and in that moment I want to hold him. I want to be drifting with him in that vast dark ocean, should it mean he doesn't have to drift alone.

"Hey," I say and rub his back.

The tortured, brooding look in his eyes reveals to my soul that he wants to share something with me; he wants to reveal a secret so big that it may change the way I look at him.

"Sayah, you are my everything," he says.

I did not expect that. I can tell what it cost him to admit that to me at such a moment.

"You are my everything, too, Dom."

He is becoming much more than I ever thought he would become. Maybe now he'll be able to share his secret with me.

This may be the beginning of that story that the medium had begun to tell.

With that, the last of my anger folds within itself and disappears.

I stand up and walk him to the bedroom, where we collide passionately and break the bed even more.

In the middle of the night, I awake to Dom not being in the bed next to me. When I sit up to look around, I see him on the balcony in the moonlight, admiring the city.

He's shirtless and has on only his boxers. The tattoos that cover his arms and chest are also covering his back. His legs, too, are sleeved.

It's fucking sexy.

But there's something about his aura tonight that makes me worry for him. Something has unsettled him, and I need to be by him, to make sure he's all right.

Before I open the sliding screen door, he turns around.

His eyes are revelatory and achingly guileless.

"Hey," he murmurs softly, and turns quickly, wiping his face.

I wrap my arms around him, holding him, kissing his shoulders.

It's not clear as to what's making him so sad, but there's something about his sadness that's resounding, and he's wearing it like armor. It's like the sadness I carry for mama. It cracks me open, revealing a part of me that resonates with his agony.

"What's the matter?" I ask him softly.

There's a slight sniffle and then he speaks. "There are some things in my past that you don't know, Say. Things I don't wanna talk about right now. I will one day, I promise. But not right now." The way he's talking is controlled, as though it's taking great effort to keep it steady.

There's a secret he's keeping from me, that's a definite. I can feel that he doesn't want to discuss it any further, and the least I can do is hold him and let him know I'm here for him.

As I slither around to slink under his arms and hold him from the front, there's a sharp pain in my foot.

"Ouch," I cry out and lift my leg to see that the bottom of my foot has been sliced open by the piece of glass that fell last night when I dropped before we fucked.

At the sight of blood, I become faint. It's not the blood; it's the gash. I did okay with all the cancer shit I'd gone through, but gashes, no. I don't do well with gashes.

I hobble over to the chairs and sit, feeling faint.

"Oh, jesus, Sayah, here. Let me grab something."

He runs into the room and is out again within seconds.

How the hell did he do that so fast?

As he's wrapping a towel around me, I swear his eyes grow a catlike shape, and his face contorts a bit before he turns away from me.

"Are you okay?" I ask as I hear him take a sharp intake of breath.

Steadily he replies, "Yes. Just squeamish."

It takes a few lingering moments until he gathers composure enough to turn back around.

His face is back to normal, although he does seem a little pale.

Everything's starting to feel like some weird dream I'll wake from at any moment.

"You're probably going to need stitches."

"Nah, I'll be fine. I'm sure there's a first aid kit in this penthouse somewhere. Wrap it up and call it good."

Chuckling a bit he says, "Okay, tough girl."

He scoops me up in his arms and deposits me inside on the crooked bed. He leaves me and rummages around the bathroom for a first aid kit.

"Ah-ha," he shouts and runs back with gauze and Neosporin. "Dr. Sangravelli to the rescue."

"Well hello there, doctor. I'm in need of medical attention."

With our giggles, the mood immediately lightens, and I almost forget about his sadness.

I do not, however, forget the look that was in his eyes at the sight of blood.

21

VELVET MOONRISE

DOM

The residual effects of killing those cunts still hang over me like a veil. Though taking lives is a risk of me going dark and never coming back from it, the fact that those twats nearly raped that girl created an anger in me that mitigated the pull of darkness. If it wasn't for that, killing three people damn near yanked me there. I took on that fuck-wads personality for an hour after I ended him and still feel his death being stitched into my soul.

Taking human life is often threefold.

When you diminish the life force of human beings, it produces toxins in their bloodstream that act as a drug to us. As their humanity drains from them, it melts into their blood and enters us, which coats our bones like honey. As their death evaporates into us, not only do we feel high, but everything about them enters us as well, making us become them for minutes, sometimes hours after they die.

Pieces of them never leave.

We are a walking jigsaw puzzle of all the people we've killed; little bits of our victims take up residence in our shallows, shifting and molding the personalities we own.

So not only do we get high, but we gain a new piece of our personality, and we get fed all in one fell swoop.

This is why most vampires love killing.

This is why I hate it.

I don't like the high. I don't like becoming someone else, and I don't like the demise of a human settling into my existence. Each and every time it occurs, the agony I feel is inescapable. I drown in it.

I tried not to let Sayah see it, and I thought I was alone when I left the bed last night and crept out onto the balcony.

But she saw it.

That and when she bled I damn near came; the scent of her blood is so intoxicating, unlike anything I've ever smelled before.

There's something different about her, something special, and I feel it thawing me, melting me down inside and coating my bones.

I'm going to have to tell her about me soon. I have to tell her my secret without revealing to her the fact that my family and, quite possibly, the warlocks all want her dead.

My trip into Never proved unsuccessful.

Everyone in the Neverdusk Dominion appears to be protecting the warlocks and the fae who create them.

I came up with nothing on them.

I am meeting with the Velvet Moonrise Coven today in their sanctuary below the city.

While going down to the tunnels, my phone vibrates with a call from my mom.

"Yeah?" I answer, quickly ducking under an awning to avoid the sunlight.

"Time's running out, Dom. It's getting worse here," Mom says somberly. "Dad and I found the Nyktorim Syndicate. They've advised to end it."

"End what?" I ask though I know her answer before she says it.

"The witch. They believe the prophecy is true and that she needs to die to regain control. They will send someone for her if you don't get her powers to ignite by the next full moon."

"Fuck," I seethe, the walls feeling like they're closing in on me.

Desperation is a hallowing feeling. Sometimes it feels like anger, but I know right now as the desperation hallows out every once of who I am, that this is what hopelessness feels like and it fucking pisses me off. I hate feeling this way."

"I'm getting there," I voice, trying to convince myself as much as her that I am, "I know she's on the verge of awakening her fire. I'm meeting with a coven today to see if they can help. Did you come up with anything?"

"Dom, I know you are falling for this woman and don't want her to die, but maybe you need to think about the greater good here—"

"The greater good would be for her to find her fire and stay alive so that we will have her around to keep them from respawning, Mom!"

"Dom, don't yell at me, I'm only trying—"

"No! I know what you're trying to do. Just chill the fuck out and let me handle this. I'll get her to find it, please. I need more time."

"There's nothing I can do, Dom. They know where she lives now. If she doesn't find her magick by that moon, they will come to kill her."

Pulling the phone from my ear, I click the red disconnect button and hang up on her.

I can't even with her right now.

I'm sure I can figure this out before anyone comes to kill her. I've already invited her over to the lake house to meet my parents, so if I can keep her alive until then, they'll see for themselves what a powerful being she is. Then, I can force them to help me.

Steeling myself, I calm my racing nerves as I enter the tunnel below a bridge by the shade cover and find my way to their hiding place.

Their sanctuary is exactly where Jesse said it would be, and as I duck under a fort made of boxes, the mixture of opium and weed swirls around me. The far end of the little house opens up to another tunnel, and beyond this, magick occurs. The barrier that keeps mortals out senses the magick in my blood, and instead of hitting a wall, I walk through it.

As I step through the threshold, leaving Vegas's grit and neon glare behind, I am enveloped in an otherworldly atmosphere. The architecture of the building echoes the grandeur of a Gothic cathedral, with towering arches and ribbed vaults reaching toward the heavens. The stone pillars are adorned with twisting vines and carved with arcane symbols, and gargoyles take the form of fantastical creatures—half-human, half-beast, frozen in eternal vigilance over the sacred space. The air is heavy with the scent of ancient incense, and a dim, ethereal light filters through the stained glass windows, casting kaleidoscopic patterns on the stone floor.

Instead of the traditional scenes of saints and biblical narratives, the windows are adorned with intricate depictions of witches in various states of power and enchantment. Their figures are rendered in vivid hues of emerald green, deep purple, and midnight black; their faces etched with determination or masked in mystery. Each pane tells a story of magic and mysticism, capturing moments of spellcasting, flight on broomsticks, and communion with the natural world.

The flickering candlelight dances across the walls, casting eerie shadows that seem to come alive in the corners of my vision. The atmosphere is charged with a palpable energy, a potent mix of reverence and foreboding. It's as if the stones of the building hum with ancient power, whispering secrets of forgotten spells and lost rituals.

Laughter comes from a back room, and I find my way there. When I open the door, I am greeted by the pungent aroma of cookies, witches happily laughing at a table playing cards, and an atmosphere thick with happiness and contentment.

"Hi," says a witch with amber eyes and blonde hair. "Can we help you?"

"Yes, I'm Dominic Sangravelli. I was hoping I could ask you some questions about the grims infecting our cities."

"Come join us, Dominic," Blondie says.

She's a gorgeous older witch sporting a colorful bandana around her head and a plethora of silver bangles, every finger decorated with colorful rings. She has kind eyes and a bright aura.

"We'll answer what we can."

Sliding into one of their chairs, four alluring beauties surround me, all with different hair colors and glimmering bright auras. Spinning my tale for them, I explain what I've learned so far and how I came to be here.

"It seems like you're looking in the wrong places, Dom," the witch named Emma states as I finish my story.

"You mean the Neverdusk?" I inquire, it dawning on me that I've been searching the wrong realm.

She nods and takes a joint that's being passed around. "They are not going to give you answers because their king, Trystan, is causing this for his own means. You need to look in the Luminara—the light fairy realm."

"How do I get there?"

"Unfortunately, you can't," Krystal says, her brown eyes sparkling into mine. "Because of the feud between Trystan and Tallyn, all access points to Luminara have been closed. You can only go there via invitation."

"I met with Tallyn herself. She said nothing of this. She seemed like she was new to the information that I was giving her," I say, inhaling the scent of marijuana lingering with the other scents of patchouli and elderberry incense.

"Never trust the fae," Nicole states, her onyx brows that rival her hair and pierced with several rings tighten in severity.

"You probably gave her the information she needed to go after Sayah," Emma adds dismally.

My eyes widen. "What do you mean?"

"If she and her brother are feuding again, and he is making the warlocks, then she will want them gone as much as your family and the Nyktorim Syndicate do. She will want Sayah's death as well."

Fuck.

This is getting out of hand.

The hard wood of the chair suddenly feels uncomfortable and I adjust in my seat. "Is there anything you can give me to help her find her fire?" Gazing into each of the witches' eyes, their glare softens when they sense I am falling for this girl. The desire to save her drenches my aura and I can't hide the desperation in my voice. "I believe that is all she has to do. She has magick that can help defeat these things, and I have to help her ignite it."

"Reveal your true nature to her," Nicole expands, blowing out the smoke dappled by candles into the air. "You can let her come into this knowledge on her own, or you can tell her, but in doing so, it will open her mind up to the supernatural. Do not tell her about the prophecy or that you think she will end the grims. That will alter her path and may taint her ability to ignite that fire within her. Tell her what you can and watch her power blossom."

"You feel that telling her about the supernatural realm and revealing my nature will help unlock something in her brain that will unleash her fire?"

"If she is to be the one to put an end to the grims," blondie says, her hair turning silver in the light from the sconces, "by using her fire, fire that she cannot access yet, then you must draw it out of her. Opening her mind to the notion that things beyond her wildest dreams exist will open more doors to her powers. This is one way to do that."

"And what is the other way?" I ask though I am not sure I want to know the answer.

A shiver reaches my skin at the way Blondie's gaze intensifies. "Putting everyone she loves, including herself, in danger."

22

A SHOCKING REVELATION

SAYAH

The flight home had been a quiet one.

Anna slept the whole time, having awakened the morning after the assault feeling as though she had drunk one too many fireball shots. Claire was melancholy and quiet, holding Anna close all the way to the airport and on the plane as well. I said goodbye to Dom at the hotel. He had been supportive of the girls' silence, knowing words are not enough to quell the awful feelings that being drugged and almost raped dredge up.

The only words Anna had spoken were to thank Dom followed by a hug for saving her.

It wasn't until I got home and turned on the T.V. that I learned of the three men who had been found dead in a Las Vegas apartment complex.

They offered no details as to the circumstances of the deaths, only that they were suspicious and being investigated as a homicide.

It has to be a coincidence, right?

I try to put it as far back in the corners of my mind as I can, but something isn't adding up.

"So when's he coming over?" Gauge asks, wheeling into the

kitchen where I'm cooking dinner, jolting me momentarily out of my addled fog.

"Um . . ." I wipe my hands on the dishtowel and fling it over my shoulder, tugging the phone out of my back pocket. "He should be here any minute. Are you excited?"

"Yeah," he replies giddily. "I'm glad you won't be alone when I'm not here."

Gauge has been wanting me to find someone for a long time.

As I stir the spaghetti sauce, my mind goes back to him.

More and more details about Dominic are confusing to me. There's that feeling that he has something big to tell me about himself and I'm not going to let him leave tonight until I find out what it is. Part of being an empath is that I'm able to read people. I know when they're angry or sad or have something burning inside them that they need to get out. It's why I'm always drained after concerts or crowded places. I'm an energy sponge and I soak up other people's energy like rainwater on grass.

But what can it be?

That's when the doorbell chimes.

"I'll get it," Gauge sings.

"Well, hello there, sir," I hear Dom's deep voice billowing into our little house. "I'm Dominic. You must be Master Gauge."

I walk into the living room to see Dominic shaking Gauge's little hand. "Nice to meet you too. But I'm not a master."

Dom laughs and hands him something. "These are for you."

"What is it?" he asks, peering into the paper bag he hands him.

"Shh," he says, putting his finger to his pursed lips. He bends down and whispers something to Gauge that makes him giggle.

"And what is it?" I query as Dominic slips out of his shoes.

"It's our secret," he says, pulling his hand out from behind his back and handing me a paper bag as well. "This one's yours."

I peek into the bag and see candy and scratch tickets. "Thank you," I say, smiling. "Hungry?"

"Ravenous," he answers with a smirk.

"All right, dinner is almost ready. You two can help set the table.

Gauge, check your blood sugar. Dinner is going to be around seventy-five carbs."

"Okay Mama," Gauge says, wheeling over to the coffee table to deposit the paper bag before heading over to the kitchen.

"How long have you had diabetes?" Dominic asks Gauge as he grabs the pile of napkins I hand him.

"I was diagnosed at four, right, Mama?"

"That's right," I answer, removing the boiling water from the stove.

"Wow, that's a long time. How are you doing with it?"

"Pretty good," Gauge responds, taking the forks from the pile on the counter and putting them on the napkins Dom is setting out.

"He's good with it. He keeps control of his numbers and his A1C has come down to 7.8. Which probably is Greek to you." I laugh.

"No, I know quite a bit about it. My dad's a doctor."

"Really?" Gauge asks, intrigued. "That's cool."

"Pretty cool, huh?" Dominic asks and hands him a napkin to set on the other side of the table. "So, you're on a pump?"

"Yeah. See," Gauge says, pulling the pump out from his pocket.

"Way cool," Dom answers, walking around the table to check it out.

"I can do the site changes all by myself. I've done my CGM once, but I usually have Mom do that. That one hurts."

"I bet. Wow, you are so, so cool. Way cooler than me! I can't stand needles, I faint."

Gauge laughs, his chubby cheeks getting rosy. "You do?"

"I do. I'm a big pansy. You are so much stronger than me."

"I tell him that all the time," I say, taking the garlic bread out of the oven. "I could not do what he does. He doesn't flinch when he has to check his blood or change his sites."

"Oh, man. Maybe you can teach me how you are so brave. Or lend me some of your bravery."

Gauge giggles, putting his pump back in his pocket. "You can't teach bravery, silly. You have to just *be* brave. It's easy when that's all you have."

Sometimes the words that come out of him amaze me.

I feel the smile spread from ear to ear looking at the way my child and my man are getting on. This is something that I've yearned for, for a long time.

I hope that whatever he has to tell me doesn't change this.

No matter what, I'm not letting him leave the house tonight without telling me, though.

"That was delicious Sayah, thank you," Dom says when dinner is done, helping me bring the dishes to the sink. "Need some help?"

"No, I'm good here, thanks. I think you have a Mario Kart date with a ten-year-old." I smile, placing a rinsed dish in the dishwasher.

"All right, holler if you need me."

He kisses me swiftly on the cheek and retreats.

Within minutes, there is laughter and happy screams coming from the living room. As I grin to myself about how the whole night is going down, I'm debating on how to bring up this thing I want him to tell me.

Is he a secret agent?

I feel silly.

If he is though, that does explain some of his strange behavior. But not all.

Superhero?

Magician?

Witch?

That's it! He's a witch like me and that's how he knew I was and gave me the bracelet. He's a witch.

But if he is, then why has he not come right out and say it?

So many things swim through my mind, all while putting dishes away, cleaning up dinner, and watching the boys try beating each other in Mario Kart for a few rounds.

It's still plaguing my mind as I follow behind Gauge while he crawls up the stairs to go to bed.

"It was so nice to meet you," Gauge calls down to Dom through the banisters as he lands on the top stair. "Sorry for kicking your butt so hard in Mario Kart."

"Nice to meet you too buddy! And I demand a rematch. Next time I come over, it's on!"

"Okay, but that's your butt!"

"Okay, head to bed," I instruct, helping him up into the wheelchair we keep upstairs for him to get around up here.

"So, what do you think?" I ask Gauge after he has plopped himself into bed, making sure to keep my voice low. The way the house is built, sounds carry.

"I like him, Mama," Gauge says through a yawn. "He's good to you."

"He is good to *you*," I say, booping him on the nose. "And that is all that matters to me."

"Well, I think you should keep him. He's nice."

I sure hope I can.

"Sweet dreams, my love. I love you."

"Love you too, Mama. Goodnight."

"Night-night," I say, turning out the light and closing the door.

As I descend the stairs, I can see Dom sitting on the couch scrolling through his phone.

Nervousness bubbles up inside of me and I don't know how I'm going to bring this up. I figure I'll sit down and let it all spill out.

He glances at me as I make my way to the couch and sit next to him.

"Thank you for dinner tonight," he says. "Your son is truly an amazing little man."

"Thank you," I respond. "He's my whole world."

"I can see that. You're a great mom."

I press my forehead to his and take a deep breath. Here goes nothing. "I want you to tell me whatever you've been wanting to tell me for some time."

The way his hazel eyes question mine is perplexing. Like a cross between being utterly terrified and also there's some relief lingering in the golden flecks of his green irises.

"What?" he asks, backing his head away, and I immediately shake mine.

"Dom." I pull his chin toward me when he tries to deflect. "You can tell me. I will not judge you, whatever it is. I promise."

"Sayah, I can't—"

"Dom, please. You can tell me."

"I'm a vampire," he says bluntly, as though telling me he's a mechanic.

"Ha!" I blurt out, but it's automatic. I can't help it.

I don't know what I'd been expecting, but that sure as hell wasn't it.

"Sayah, I'm serious."

I feel my eyes grow wide.

The words hang in the air like smoke between us, and I freeze. His eyes remain on mine, unmoving, and suddenly a fear larger than life itself rises in the back of my throat like bile. Fear that he's a psychopath and in my home where my child sleeps.

"Vampire?" I ask dubiously.

Is he a serial killer?

Oh my gods, he's in my house and the nearest gun is in my car.

I look toward the garage, thinking if I move fast enough I can get to the garage door, slam it in his face, tip over the dog food bin to slow him down, and jump over the handicapped railing to my car to grab my gun.

"Sayah, listen, I know that it's a lot to take in," he says, grabbing my hand.

I try to pull it away. "You're crazy!"

"No, please, listen to me," he pleads as I slip out of his grip and quickly stand. "I'm not going to hurt you, please believe me."

"Vampires don't exist!"

Even though I'm terrified, there's a lingering softness in his eyes that comforts me. I remember reading about vampires in my grandmother's grimoires.

They can exist, can't they?

Maybe he's telling me the truth; it makes all that strange shit that has been happening make more sense.

I mean, I'm a witch who practices real magick.

"Sayah, please. Look," he says, standing with me as the jangling tension of an impending battle rages on in my mind.

His eyes change to a cat-eye shape and the irises drain of all hazel leaving only the color of white with black rims remaining. His skin goes pale, his touch grows cold, and the incisors shoot out from his gums.

Even though I should be scared, I'm not.

He is stunningly beautiful.

The angles of his face sharpen, as though I am watching someone live photo-shop their picture. The subtle wrinkles by his eyes iron out, his hair smoothes where it was rustled, and every facet of his being becomes perfect, not one flaw visible.

The energy in the room shifts, and I can feel that he's fearing my reaction to this more than he's afraid I'll fear him.

"See?" he says as his fangs melt away and his eyes return to normal. His voice is controlled, steady; his green eyes still fixed on mine. "I'm not going to hurt you."

"I don't know what to say," I finally utter, and though everything within me tells me I should be terrified, I'm not. It all melts off the minute he shows me his true self.

"Sayah," he says almost in tears. He looks to me for my approval which disarms me.

"I need a minute," I say, trying to process the new information. His eyes are smoldering and there's a subtle fracture in them, spilling nothing but fear of losing me because of what he just told me.

I walk away from him, and he doesn't follow me. Over at the window, I gaze out and up to the sky, as though the stars hold the answers. I think about the last few weeks with him, all those crazy and unexplainable things.

Can he read my thoughts?

He remains still on the couch, head in his hands, silent and contemplative.

I turn back to the stars.

Thoughts slice into my mind all at once. The fact that we've never met up during the day and how sometimes he moves so fast I can barely see him. The night of our first date is still shrouded in mystery. He has, a few times, talked as though he's a lot older than he says he is. There's a haunting mystery about him, a tortured look in his eyes at times that I can feel the sorrow undulating around him. Times when I swear he seems to reach into my mind and pluck thoughts right out of it. And most recently, Vegas. The gash that seemingly vanished. Those men. That blood. The agonized look in his eyes after we got back to the hotel room. And my senses are always telling me there's something he's burning to tell me, a secret so deep that he fears it will change the way I feel about him.

Dominic Sangravelli is a vampire.

A very old one at that.

I have no idea how old he is, but I'm guessing somewhere in the 18th century.

That's just a guess, but one that I'd likely bet on.

His soul tells me so.

And I do believe he still has a soul.

It's drenched all over him that he doesn't enjoy being a vampire; he doesn't like killing and only does it when he must, taking the lives of those who would do other people wrong. His sufferings unmitigated by promise of any alleviation soaks him like rainwater.

That sort of makes sense to me. I've always been a bully to the bullies, and will defend the people that others mock and ridicule. I can only imagine that if I had been a vampire, I would be the same way.

Wait!

Dom can't be a vampire!

This is the real world and things like that don't exist.

My mind wanders back to the three men in Vegas who died.

Is this really happening? Mama, what do I do?

There is light in the dark, I hear on a whisper. I don't know if it's my mother's voice or my own, but all I know is that I'm not afraid of him.

I turn around and walk back up to him.

"Did you kill those men in Vegas?"

"Yes," he replies solemnly, his face contorting into guilt and shame. "But I only kill people who deserve it. I don't kill innocent people." The admission is soaked in rage and filled with sorrow.

"I know you won't hurt me," I say finally. "But I need to know your story. All of it. I need to know that you're safe to be around. You just met my son, my world. I have to know if you're safe."

He nods and stands. "What do you want to ask me?" he asks, and there seems to be a lightness about him now. His handsome features have softened somehow, as though a huge and heavy weight had rewired the expressions on his face and is finally returning to normal.

"I want to know your story. The whole story."

He takes a deep breath as though borrowing the strength from the air, embracing the tale he's about to tell.

23

VAMPIRES ARE SEXY

SAYAH

Although the past several minutes have been unreal and blurry, as though I'm living in a dream state, I'm now fascinated with this man and his story, determined to know everything.

Vampires exist. One is sitting in my living room.

And I have fucked him.

I have to know everything about him now.

"So, how old are you, really?" I ask as we sit on the couch, drinking my non-alcoholic wine from swirling blue glasses.

"Two hundred and eighty-six. I was born in 1737 and made a Vampire in 1773. I celebrated my fortieth with a beer during the American Revolution." He grins as though he's making it up. Still, I know that he's telling the truth.

"And you were born in Italy?"

"Yes." He smiles, taking a sip of his wine. "I was raised in Florence with my two sisters and two brothers."

"And how? How did you come to be a vampire?"

Dom rearranges his legs to face me better, setting the wine glass on the white-washed barn-door coffee table. "My mom is a powerful witch. She had lost a few kids before my oldest brother was born, so when she became pregnant with him, she put a spell on him, thinking it would protect him in the womb. When he survived, she did the same for all of us kids, and each one of us was born with this spell in us.

"We were all at Ollie's bedside when he died at twenty-nine, leaning over him, crying. He was still maybe ten seconds, then he gasped, shot up, and grabbed Hattie by her neck. His eyes were white, those long pointy teeth coming out of him, almost killing my sister; blood was fucking everywhere. We hadn't ever heard of vampires. We didn't know what the fuck this was. He would've killed Hattie if my dad hadn't socked him in his face, knocking him out. When he came to, his eyes were normal, his skin was peach again after being gray from being sick for so long, and the broken nose from my dad—healed. Then he started walking around," he says, animating his arms around with the story. "Like nothing had ever happened. We were baffled."

"So what did you do?" I ask, leaning in, picturing the first one of them turning for the first time and thinking how scary that would be.

"We didn't know what to do! My mom felt it had something to do with her spell, so she returned to that shaman. He told her what was to be our protection in birth made us immortal in death. The shaman had heard of creatures like us. He said that because the spell was done with blood and the moon, those became our slavers. But that didn't sink into my mom until Ollie went outside in the middle of the day and nearly burned to death. We got the fire out in time before it left any real bad scars, but you can still see them on his arms, legs, and stomach. Stark reminders of why we can't go into the sun."

"I can't imagine being without the sun." I tilt my head, trying to imagine a life in the dark. It bristles me to no end. I feel so bad that Dom can't go in the sun.

"Who cares about eternal life if you have to live in darkness for the rest of eternity?" he responds solemnly. The way his posture crumbles, his eyes glisten, and his mouth turns down lets me know he misses the sun as much as one would miss the rain if they couldn't have it anymore. "Scarlet has tried a few things over the years, trying to spell amulets and talismans to try and help us meet the light again. Nothing's ever worked."

"No? What happened."

He rolls his sleeve and points to the swirly and beautiful skin under his ink. "Got burned real bad. It's not fun. You burn from within. Then it bubbles up into flames if you stay in it too long."

"Holy fuck. That's awful."

His face is reflective like he is reminiscing on the last time he tried entering sunlight.

"What's it like to be a vampire? You said you don't like killing, so do you eat animal blood like in *Twilight*?"

"You know, I've never seen that movie." He chuckles, the slight wrinkles on the side of his eyes scrunching together. "I heard they sparkle, and I couldn't handle that."

The image of this handsome man in front of me glittering in the sunlight is enough to cause me to laugh out loud. "Same," I reply, setting my fake wine down as I shovel my feet under me on the couch, hugging a pillow.

"But to answer your question, yes and no. It isn't sustaining, so it's like eating a few grapes for you. Human blood is satisfying and filling; we don't have to kill to get fed. The only time I kill, it's people like those guys in Vegas. I choose the bad ones, those who don't deserve to live. Other times, I get by with animal blood or feeding on someone enough to sustain me. Then I veilweave them to forget, and it's as though they never met me."

"Veilweave? What's that?"

"We have magick in our voices that enchant people to do what we say. They can't refuse; they are spellbound."

"So, like casting a spell on someone with your voice?"

"Exactly."

"Wouldn't everyone within earshot be hexed then?" I ask, wrinkling my brows.

"Not exactly," he responds, leaning in closer to me. His eyes bore into mine and again I feel calm, like I'm falling into them. I want to do anything this man wants me to do. Anything. "We pull you in real close like this. Then unlock our magick, like clicking a lock open. Because of our eye contact, you feel drawn to me when I whisper to you. Like you would do anything I asked of you. I would then say, 'Raise your arms,'"—my arms shoot up above my head of their own accord—"and voila. You are veilweaved."

"That's fascinating," I reply, looking up at my arms chilling in the air.

"You can put them down now," he says, releasing me from my compulsion.

"What other powers do you have?"

"Like all vamps," he smirks, leaning back into the couch cushions and propping his arm over the one between us, "I can heal fast. I'm strong; I have a wicked sense of smell and hearing. I can veilweave people and manipulate memories." His eyes pinch as though he's trying to remember everything. "We all have that way of making you feel completely at ease, not scared. Making you easy prey."

The way his gaze turns sinister toward me is sexy.

Come eat me up, Mr. Vampire Man.

Frigid feathery kisses dance along my spine as I scoot closer to him. "What's the difference between the blood?"

The green of his irises retracts and compounds into a vertical shape as he tracks something across the room. "Human blood is more sustainable. I can go twice as long without blood when I drink it. It's because of a person's life force. Their memories. Sometimes, I see them when I drink their blood. And if I drain them completely, I can take on their traits."

The memory of him being utterly different in Vegas after he killed those guys shoots through me. Even his walk was different. "Is that what happened in Vegas? After. . . ?"

His expression turns sad and discouraged. "Partly," he replies softly. "And also partly because I don't like taking human lives. I detest it."

"So you veilweaved the people at the party to tell you who the guys were? And then again to forget you were there?"

He nods.

"How could you veilweave so many people at once then?"

He shifts a bit, cocking his head to the side. "With larger groups, we can expand our magick. Directing it to a larger crowd is harder since it's both the eye contact and the voice. I turned the music off, stood on a chair, and projected my veilweave outward. It, like, covers them like a net. Then I said to forget I was here and that a fight broke out, and the dudes turned on each other."

"So you could totally rob banks if you wanted?"

He laughs, the features of his face softening. "I could. Definitely."

"Well," I say, leaning into him more. "If you ever need a partner in crime, I'm your girl."

Pulling me into him, he kisses the top of my head. "I'll keep that in mind."

Laying my head on his chest, I can hear his heartbeat. His skin is warm. He smells delicious. I want to kiss more answers out of him. I unbutton his shirt and kiss his chest. "Have you ever veilweaved me?" I ask in between my kisses.

I feel his heart rate pick up. When he doesn't answer, I look up at him.

The nod he gives me is riddled with shame.

My own heart drops. "When?"

"The night of our first date," he confesses, his voice shaky. "There had been an attack. Grimspawn. They were eating a woman. I was able to save her and divert them, but you saw things you shouldn't have. So I veilweaved you to forget the altercation."

I lean back from him, scratching my head and swirling my hair into a messy bun. Having someone you are falling for being able to fuck with your mind whenever they want is disarming. Having that power over someone is unsettling. And the fact that he altered my memory to think that I had fainted bristles me.

"Can you give memories back?" I ask, trying to hide the hurt in my voice.

"I can," he replies.

"I'd like to relearn it."

"Are you sure?"

Taking a deep breath I nod. "Yes. I don't want there to be any secrets between us."

"Okay. Hold still."

He draws closer to me, his eyes focusing on mine, and I feel I'll fall within them. As his razor-sharp focus dials in on something profound in my soul, the lost memory of the night comes rushing back. I remember him almost kissing me, us running to the alley . . .

I teetered behind him on unsure feet, following him to where he heard the noise. Finally, we reached a place where four buildings met, and the alleyway was dark. There was a woman on the ground and a hooded man standing over her. I couldn't tell exactly what he was doing because three other men and one woman were blocking my view, watching whatever was happening on the ground.

Dominic moved so fast I didn't know he had released my hand. The hooded figure who was standing over the woman on the ground was flying. It landed hard against a giant metal dumpster.

The three hooded men acted as though they were as bewildered as I was and went to make a move on Dominic. Stealthy, he thwarted all three as they came at him, punching one so hard he fell to the ground and hit his head on the pavement with an offensive crack. Dominic's body moved so fast I couldn't see him connect with the other two; as they barreled at him. He used a roundhouse kick to one of the assailant's faces, who went flying in one direction, and the other soared toward the back door of another establishment.

My mind was racing a million miles a minute, and all I could think about was going after the girl.

Watching this go down, the woman backed away and headed toward the alley exit. While Dom was fighting the one man who had gotten up from the doorway and was coming at him again, I went for the female.

My heels were rhythmically clicking on the ground, and when the woman turned to look at me, I swore her eyes were glowing red.

It must have been the light, but I would never know because the woman was on me, pinning me to the ground.

I scrambled under her weight and blocked her punches to the face, trying to get back up and get the upper hand.

All I saw was the woman shooting up and away from me, falling upward into the dark of the night.

I had yet to learn where the woman landed or if she even did.

Dom was there, holding out a hand to help me up.

As I got to my feet, Dominic was gone again, and I thought I must have hit my head on the pavement, for when I looked, he was over at the woman on the ground.

I gained my bearings and walked over to them when I was pulled in the other direction.

My hair flew before my face, and I couldn't see. I think I screamed, but when I gained my vision back, I saw that it was Dominic who was pulling me away from the scene.

Minutes later, we were sitting on a park bench. Dominic held my face, speaking into my mind, veilweaving me to forget everything I saw.

I've been gazing at nothing in particular during the resurfacing of the memory. It's so odd to have a memory you don't remember doing in your head. It's fuzzy and crumpled around the edges and almost seems like a memory of a movie I'd once seen rather than something I lived through.

I slide my gaze back over to Dom, who's waiting, anticipating my relearning the memory.

"So weird," I say.

"Isn't it? My siblings have done it to me a time or two."

"Can I ask you something?" I say, putting his hand in mine.

"Anything," he replies.

"Please don't ever take a memory from me again without asking me first, okay?"

All levity diminishes and he holds my stare sternly. "I promise."

"Thank you. So, who was the woman with the red eyes?" I ask, pulling my hair from the messy bun and flinging it over my shoulders.

"She was the warlock controlling the grimspawns."

Letting this uneasy, tangled feeling wash over me, I say, "Grimspawn?" That word is flickering in my memory. I remember reading it in my grandmother and Mama's grimoires.

"Fucked up creatures that are basically reanimated dead things, sorta like zombies," Dom answers and almost shudders at their memory. He pulls me back to him so I'm leaning on his chest. "They eat people and take on youth and memories of those they eat, ultimately changing into the person they fed on. Eventually, though, those faces melt off, and they're just like these faceless creatures with sharp-ass teeth."

"That sounds awful." Thinking of these awful things, knowing they're out there lurking, sits uneasily in my bones. I don't like thinking about evil monsters roaming the world my kid lives in. "Who the fuck makes these things?"

"Warlocks," he says, playing with my hair, twirling a long tendril around his finger. "Dark warlocks. Behind every monster is a witch or warlock."

"Why would anyone want to make something so evil and deranged?"

"I know it's linked to an ancient curse. But I don't know what that is. We've been fighting grimspawn all our lives. But we don't know much more about them. We feel the warlocks use the grimspawns to live forever without having to do any of the killings. Their life forces are connected somehow."

"How do you kill them?" I ask, unbuttoning another one of his buttons and feeling his soft skin.

"Grimspawns can be killed in the way you'd kill a vampire. But the warlocks keep making them and we don't know how to kill *them* yet. They have magick too powerful to get near them," he answers. His voice steels, frustration lingering in the inflections—as though he's tried hundreds of ways to kill them before and has come up with nothing.

"And how do you kill vampires?" I don't mean for the octaves in my throat to go up a few notches, like I need the information for nefarious reasons. But. I'm cuddling with a vampire. A girl needs to know how to defend herself.

He puffs his chest out to get a better look at my face and grins suspiciously, his perfect white teeth gleaming. "And why, pray tell, would I tell you that information?"

He tickles me, and I squirm.

"You know, in case you decide to get wild. Ya girl's gotta know what to do in that situation." I laugh as his tickles abate. "No, but for real. Just in case I run into another vampire that isn't as charming and fucking sexy as you."

"Mmm-hmm," he says.

I lean my head on his chest again.

"Pretty much everything you heard is false—except the sun. Sunfire projectiles—weapons infused with sunlight can kill us. We can be killed by silver-laced anything because it fucks with our regenerative powers, and some vamps have lethal allergies to it. Cut off our heads, and we're fucked. We can't look into mirrors that aren't spelled."

"What?"

"Yeah, mirrors!" He laughs. "I don't know why that's a thing. But if we look into a mirror that isn't spelled, we'll see our actual age and become it."

"No way!" I say back. "So, like, is there some vampire you made that didn't know and is walking around all ancient and decrepit?"

His chest heaves with laughter. "I would imagine so, yes."

"OMG, I would totally do that to someone who fucked with me. Like not tell them about the mirror thing and have them get all old and ugly!" I'm laughing so hard my stomach cramps.

"Next time some bitch crosses you, I'll turn her into a vampire for you, and we won't tell her!"

"What? I have a few people in mind right now." We let our laughs hold us captive for a few seconds. "So what do you do to stop it? I mean, you look fine as hell for a two-hundred-and-eighty-six-year-old. I, myself, don't feel a day older than thirty, and you're over here making two hundred look good."

The sly smile and stricken gaze he gives me flickers butterflies to life in my stomach. "Hattie. She can make people see what she wants them to see. So she spelled mirrors for each of us. In spelling these mirrors, we only see what she wants us to see when we look into *any* mirror—so long as our spellbound ones are near us."

"Wow, that's fascinating."

He takes my neck gently and tugs my face toward his. "You're fascinating," he growls and lights me up inside.

Taking my lips into his own, my core tingles and his charisma floods me. He's so fucking sexy, and being a killer, a predator who could end me with a flick of his wrist, excites me to no end. I feel his tongue slither onto mine, and I moan, his lovely mouth destroying me.

He's still grasping my neck, and his other hand wanders down my shirt and pinches my nipple, sending charged little ripples right to my clit.

Arching my back, he finds his way into my pants and slides his finger from my opening to my clit, swirling his fingertip gently at its center.

The hand that was around my neck reaches into my shirt and pinches the other nipple, causing exquisite pain to send my vision to the stars.

Writhing in pleasure, he covers my breast with his mouth, biting and gripping firmer to get a better mouthful.

I almost cry out but remember how sound carries and stifle my scream.

Coming back up to me, he slows down, pulling my lower lip into his.

"Mmm," he says, his sultry lips still wrecking me. "I could eat you right now."

Peppering kisses down his neck and reaching over to feel his cock, I say, "Please do."

Growling, he takes my lips hungrily for a few seconds before he lets go. Holding my face in his hand he pulls me away. "Not here. Not yet. I don't trust myself with you just yet."

Slipping my hands down his pants to feel his erection I reply, "You've already had me. You can handle it."

Laying his head back and closing his eyes as my hand rubs down his length, he moans. "Yeah but now you know who I am. And I want your blood. I want us to wait until I get used to you knowing and can fuck you without killing you." He looks at me as I drop my lips around his dick and make his throat rumble in response. "Fuck," he hisses, arching his hips so I can take him deeper.

I hold his eyes with mine as I slide my tongue down the backside of his dick and then take him deep again.

Back up to the tip, I say, "What were you saying?" as I play with him, my lips brushing against his sensitive skin.

"Sayah, fuck," he moans, holding my head while he thrusts upwards.

Looking at him again, I wiggle my tongue at the tip of his head to hear that sexy growl again.

He retains my eye contact as he bites his lower lip, pushing my head back down.

I grab onto his hips and fuck him with my face until I bring him to the brink of cumming and stop, pecking kisses up his stomach to his lips. He grabs my face and kisses me hungrily, wildly bucking up and flying us to the other end of the couch.

The sensation is terrifying and tantalizing at the same time and he ravages me with kisses, breathing deeply and desperately at the same time.

I wrap my leg around him and pull him closer to me, his hardness rubbing the seam of my jeans right against my clit. I quiver violently as he rips off my shirt and devours my tit with tongue and teeth.

I am about to pull his pants off when he suddenly pulls his head up and looks at me, his eyes white and his fangs out.

I jump violently.

Realizing this, he flashes off me to the other side of the couch.

Sitting up quickly, I watch as he hangs his head, runs his fingers through his hair, and collects his breath.

"Dom?" I ask quietly. "Are you okay?"

"I'm so sorry, Sayah. I knew this was a bad idea," he admits, pulling his head up and looking at me. "I was afraid the beast would take over."

"Oh, honey," I say, covering my boobs up and scooting in closer to him. "Your beast is fucking sexy. I'm here for it."

He looks at me like no one has ever seen his darkness as beautiful. "Really?"

"Oh my gods, yes. Dom, your darkness is what makes you you. I adore everything about you. I see your beast as an extension of you and he is sexy as fuck. Albeit, it is a little scary when caught off guard, but, honey, you can bring that sexy motherfucker to my bed anytime."

His face shatters with levity as he chuckles at me. "Sayah, you're one sick fuck, you know that?"

"You adore me and you know it," I reply grinning, laying us back against the couch again.

Granted, it was pretty fucking terrifying seeing him like that up close and personal, but I'm more than a little turned on by it.

I want to know what fucking a vampire is like now that I know he's a vampire.

24

TRAIL OF MOONLIGHT

DOM

That was close.

I didn't even feel the change take over. I was so caught up, being turned on by her and wanting to bite her tangled together too fast. Seeing her lips slide over my dick was too much for me to handle. I wanted to fuck her and end her, and those two feelings can never mix.

Not ever again.

When she said I was sexy as the vampire, it staggered me. I don't think anyone has ever told me I was sexy as that monster. It's comforting and jangling at the same time.

When I'm that person, I'm a monster. Even my thinking is different. It's like the demon that lives in us takes over and controls us. Things I do as a vampire, I would never do as a mortal.

We've migrated from the brown couches to her oversized, fluffy reader's nook chair. A daybed wide enough for two people.

"So, do your siblings all think like you do?" she asks., interrupting my self-loathing.

"No, not really," I say, dragging my fingers slowly over her legs that drape over mine. "They all like killing. Hattie didn't want it initially but realized how much she loved being the villain, so she took to it.

My oldest brother is the only one who sought out his own death to make it come faster. He wanted it."

"This is the brother you don't talk to because of a girl, right?"

I feel my muscles constrict at the mention of him. I don't like talking about him. "Sort of. There's more to it than that. That one is the most fucked up thing he's done."

I feel her tense up. "What did he do?"

"He's the reason I died. He killed me. He's the reason I turned vampire at thirty-six."

"What! Why the fuck would he do that?"

"Cause we fell for the same girl," I admit, though I'm still hesitant to bring her up. Sadie's memory haunts me still, even though it's been hundreds of years since I've seen her face. Before Sayah, she was the last one I had these strong feelings for. "Her name was Sadie. I loved her. Was going to propose."

"And it never happened?"

"No. The night I was going to, he showed up. I found out then that they had been fooling around and were in love with each other. He and I got in a fight, and he broke my neck. He knew I would turn, so it made it a little better, but he knew I didn't want to be a vampire. So it was cruel. He fled with her after killing me."

She lets out a rough exhale. "That fucking sucks. I'm sorry that happened to you. Why would he do that to you?"

"We've always had that love-hate relationship," I say, feeling the tension in my neck at having to talk about him.

"But she ended up dying, right?"

"Right."

"What? Did he kill her too?"

I nod, grabbing her hand and interlacing my fingers through them. "He sure did. But that's what Ollie tells me."

"What did Ollie say?"

"Just that Bash loved her and wanted to turn her. She didn't want it. That pissed him off, so he killed her."

"Bash?"

"Yes," I respond. "My oldest brother. His name becomes him, as he's known for bashing heads in."

"Wow, that's nice," she replies sarcastically. "And is that how he killed her?"

"From what I gather from Ollie, they got drunk one night, and he drained her to her death and then fed her his blood, forcing her into being a vampire. See, when you make a new vampire, you have to drain them, feed them, kill them, and then feed them again. But before he could kill her, she ran."

"I'm guessing he found her and killed her anyway?"

"Yep. You guessed it. He killed her in a fit of rage. But she knew she had to feed to turn, so when she arose, she hit him over the head with a cast-iron skillet and ran again instead of feeding to turn."

"What happens when you don't feed?"

"You basically desiccate. Your body shrivels up, and you become stone. Still alive but not really."

"So that is how she died? She desiccated?"

"No," I laugh at this story's twists and turns. "Apparently, he found her and forced her to drink from him. When she did and changed, she hated him for what he did and left him once more. When he found her again, she was with someone else. So he drove a silver-laced wooden stake through her heart. And killed the man she was with as well."

"Jesus fuck. What a psychopath."

"Yeah, he can be."

"And you haven't talked to him since?

"I didn't let a girl keep me hating him for centuries. We have an on-again-off-again relationship. I let him back in, and he does something monstrous; we fight, and then we don't talk again. It's a pattern."

"I see." She stops her questions for a second and looks at our interlaced fingers. "Didn't you say you had three sisters? Not two?"

"Yes. Part of Bash's evil ways," I say, shifting our weight a bit so we're more on the pillow. "After he killed Sadie, he lost his mind. He killed a dozen more people and made half of them new vampires. One of them happened to be a siren."

"Oh, shit! A siren?" She sits up to look in my eyes.

"Yep. Half siren now. Half vampire."

"I remember my grandma's grimoires had a note about sirens. She mentioned someone who was 'of the sea,' but I hadn't known what she meant until now. She must have met one."

"Crazy, right! She's pretty badass. She's dangerous and moody but has gotten control over herself in the last one hundred and fifty years. I don't trust her like I don't trust Bash."

Pulling out my phone, I scroll through my pictures until I find a picture of Jasantha.

My gorgeous sister, with midnight-black, smooth skin, blood-red hair, and bright green eyes, stares at us through the phone screen.

"She's beautiful," Sayah responds. "And what are her powers?"

"She has octaves in her voice, her siren's song, that can lull anyone into a trance. She has done it to me a few times. You wake up not remembering anything that just happened. I woke up a few times in public in just my underwear after pissing her off. She finds that funny."

Sayah laughs, picturing it. "How does that work then? The whole hybrid thing?"

"She can live either in the water or on land. Because of her hybrid blood, she can walk in the sunshine. She has offered her blood to me a few times to see if it would help me walk in the sun."

"And it didn't?"

"No," I respond sadly, clicking my phone off and setting it on the arm of the chair. "Nothing has ever worked. The spell my mom put on us is powerful. The moon rules over the sun, every time."

Lingering thoughts of sadness pull at me, remembering the last time I felt the sun warm my skin. Missing the sun is akin to missing a limb. You're not the same without it.

"So, you haven't seen the sun in over two hundred years?"

"Right. Only in movies. Gods, I miss it."

Her eyes are reflective, as though she is trying to borrow my feelings of deprived sunlight to see how it feels in her skin. "I'm so sorry, Dom. That must be so awful. I don't know what I'd do if I couldn't be in the sun. I wonder . . ." she trails off, as though her ideas are too big for words.

"What?" I ask, sliding to the side of her to see her face.

"I'm wondering if I should try something."

"Like what?"

"I'm not quite sure. But I wondered if I could try it on a piece of jewelry. Pull the moon's energy to protect you in the sun?"

I look at her incredulously. "You think you could do that?"

"One way to find out," she says, wiggling out from under my arm.

Rising, she goes to the spell cabinet.

I follow her to her beautiful wooden secretary. The smells that waft from it are woodsy and earthy incense, like a witch's den.

She's handing me things, things I don't know what the fuck they are or why they'll help, but fuck is it sexy seeing her in her element.

After she's done handing me shit, she pulls out a gorgeous Lapis Lazuli that's attached to a chain. Raveling it into her hand, she grabs the rowan wand. "All right, let's go out on the back porch."

I follow her lead, instantly hard when she puts her witch hat on.

Figuratively. She's not wearing a witch hat.

But fuck me, that would be hot too.

"Okay," she says after setting her rocks on the railing. "While I consult the moon, I want you to hear my words and hold those crystals tight in your left hand. In your right, hold this—" She hands me the Lapis Lazuli—"while I speak, pull the words into those stones and believe it with your whole soul, okay?"

I nod, hanging out in a state of intrigue and disbelief.

Sayah tilts her head back and finds the moon, her astute beauty piercing the dark with her light.

"Goddess of the moon," she speaks, giving breath to the words, "give upon us your energy to heal Dominic from your darkness. Gods of death, Gods of the sun in my state where he burns, let this item protect him and shield him from your rays as long as he wears the Lapis Lazuli. No more should he burn. Lend me your energy to imbue in this stone, and when you are not present, let it radiate around him and protect him."

I hitch my thoughts to hers and read the energy surrounding her.

The palpitating breath of power gives her conviction, and with that, she shoves her energy to the moon, commanding it to give its light to the wand. Every ounce of concentration is pushed out. I push it out with her, gazing up at the moon and imagining it thawing to liquid, seeping into the black sky.

As if the moon is listening to us, it shakes and shivers, and a shockwave ripples through the blanket of stars around it. The moon is melting, the lustrous irradiance seeping from the velvet sky and flowing like a river to the deck at our feet.

The trail of moonlight is indeed lighting up the dark and gliding into the tip of Sayah's wand, which in turn takes on an austere glow. It gracefully glissades down from the dark sky into the wand like a phosphorescent waterfall, glittering as something would in a black-lit room. All sound seems to have ceased in respect for the magnificent occurrence, as though Mother Earth and all her creatures are in reverent awe.

As the moonlight dissipates into the wood, she holds it before her, her face aglow in the luminescence.

She shifts her gaze to me, mouth agape, and I'm just as staggered as she is.

"Okay," she stammers, still trying to grasp the magick she caused, "Hold out the Lapis Lazuli in the palm of your hand."

I do as I'm told and hold out the stone.

Slowly, she presses the wand's tip to the stone and we watch the glowing wonder leave the wood and enter the rock, creating a bright glow our faces light up with. It's almost blinding. Once the brightness subsides into the wand, the rock glows before us until I clasp my fist around it and close out the light. Holding my hand out in front of me, it's alight like I have a fistful of fireflies. Our shadows dance in the rhythmic glow akin to torchlight.

Holding my fist to my heart, I talk to the moon. I ask things of her that I've asked her millions of times. I've screamed this to her on my knees in desperation. She's never listened.

Please set me free.

I beg of you.

I will worship you more fiercely if you let me worship the sun, too. I love you both. You're both my girls. I can be shared. But please let me feel the warmth of the sun again. My bones are so cold. Being warmed by the sun is like being embraced by a gentle, unseen force. She creeps into every pore of my being. She lays down a sensation of vitality and comfort like the universe herself is breathing life into me.

Your embrace is just as extraordinary. The tendrils of your darkness beckon me home, and my demons are at peace in your dark.

But I am part witch. And that side of me . . . that side needs the whisper of summer's embrace. I have two sides, and they both need to live.

Please.

I'm begging you.

As my whispers subside, the glow simmers to a sparkle, returning us to the darkness again.

When I'm done, I clasp the chain around my neck and tuck the stone safely into my shirt. A new trinket from my lady love that may be the key to my salvation.

Frosty touches like a ghost's caress sink down my spine.

"Do you think it worked?" she asks as we stand together on the deck again bathed in darkness.

"I think it did. But . . . I'll put my hand in the sun first to make sure."

"I think it did, too; I can feel its power. It's palpable. I just . . . I don't know what I'd do if it didn't work."

I stop her and lift her chin. "The thought alone that you'd make me something that would free me from the dark means the world to me." I pull her lips to mine and kiss her gently; she slithers her arm around my neck and caresses my face with her other hand. She feels so good on me. I pull away, interlacing my fingers behind her back. "If anyone can free me from the dark, it's you. The problem with Scarlet's spell was that she has the same blood as me, so she's controlled by the night. If anyone is going to spell something that will take power away from the moon, it'll be someone who's ruled by light. Your warmth is so powerful; you are driven by light and love, and you have a bond with the sun. Since we have a bond with the dark, it would be hard for us to take that power away from it. You are bonded with light. It should be easy to take the power away from the dark."

"Can we try it tomorrow morning?" Her ocean eyes sparkle as she gazes up at me.

"We can. If it doesn't work, I'll have to stay inside all day until I can go outside again."

"No problem," she says, kissing me. "Gauge loves lazy pajama days."

"And if it does work, it may help your case with my family."

Her expression withers and her eyes look into mine, but they go beyond me like she's fallen into a void.

"Hey, where did you go?" I ask, wiggling her hips.

"Oh, hi," she says quickly. "I was panicking thinking about meeting your family. What will that be like? Will you tell them I know? Will we act like I don't know? What—"

"Stop," I shush her and kiss her cute little nose. "My mom and dad are fine with people knowing as long as they know you won't spread our secret. My mom is nurturing. My dad is kind, but he has a hard temper. He can be scary, but only to me. And to Bash. Hattie, you don't have to worry about. She's sweet. Scar will be hard to win over, but that's because we're twins. Jasantha, she's like a perfect mixture between Bash and me; she can be kind and humanly, or she can be hard and murder-y. I think that's the siren in her. And Ollie, he's a kind soul. He hates being a vampire as much as I do."

"I thought you said your middle sister Hattie is all murder and mayhem?"

"She can be. You have to keep in mind that we're all vampires. We can all be murder and mayhem when it comes down to it."

"Great. So, little ol' me walks into this house full of vampires that are all, in your words, murder-y, and I'm gonna be like, 'Hi. I'm Sayah. I'm with your son and brother. Please don't eat me.'"

I laugh and put her arms around my neck. "Nobody's gonna eat you. They just may want a little taste." I snort a growl and nibble the shell of her ear.

"You're not making me feel any better with your jokes."

Pulling her in, I wrap my arms around her head and kiss her lips. "I'm so glad that you know."

"Me too. But—so, they're all gonna be there?" she says, nervousness still intertwined in her words.

"All but Bash," I reply shortly.

"They don't talk to him either?"

"Nobody but Ollie does, and that's only once every fifty years or so."

"Okay. So, just the one crazy sibling will be there. Oh, wait—no, make that two 'cause Hattie."

"We're all crazy, darling, we're vampires."

Her chest rises and falls, but the energy about her tells me she's terrified about going to my parent's house.

I can't blame her. Something is unnerving about walking into a den of vampires being a mortal and the primary source of their food. One of us takes some getting used to, but the seven of us at once would be terrifying to someone just learning about all this.

I have to make sure to put her mind at ease.

"Besides," I say softly, "if this talisman works, I'm dating a witch who can take away their darkness which may win you millions of brownie points with the vamps."

25

A BOND WITH THE DARK

SAYAH

The following day, I wake to the sounds of pans banging around and no Dom in my bed.

Rising from the sheets as my heart rate quickens in a soft panic, the sound of Gauge's giggle echoing up the stairs eases my fears immediately.

I dress and head down there to join them.

"Oh, hey, good morning," Dominic says as I enter the dining room. "Sorry if we woke you. Little man woke up and wanted pancakes, so I got up and started making some."

"That's fine." I smile, taking a seat on the barstool. "How did you sleep, love?" I ask Gauge.

He's in the kitchen, helping Dom prepare the pancakes. He has flour on his cute chubby cheeks and is stirring the batter in a bowl on the top of his lap, clad in SpongeBob pajamas. "Good. How did you sleep, Mama?"

"I slept good, baby. Thanks."

I'm totally in love with the sight of my man and son making pancakes together in the kitchen. Then it dawns on me that this is the first time I've ever seen Dom in natural light.

Even though the sun isn't blazing into the windows yet, as my house is dark in the kitchen, I still wonder how he can stay out of the sunlight completely.

His perfectly sculpted jawline, his chiseled core, wearing nothing but his jeans and muscle shirt as he flips the pancakes. The tattoos that snake his body, his dark, spiky hair, the eyes that are green—for now. The secret that he was burdened with for so long used to drape him like a cloak, and now that I know his secret, his aura is lighter, and his eyes pick up on things that they used to linger on with sadness.

"All right, buddy, here, let me take that," Dom says, taking the whisk from him and setting it in the sink. "Okay, now, carefully pour a small circle right here."

Gauge obliges and carefully pours the mixture onto the hot griddle. "Like this?"

"Yes, that is perfect. You're an amazing sous chef."

Gauge smiles while pouring another circle, then wrinkles his nose. "What is a sous chef?"

"A sous chef is basically a chef's assistant. The second in command."

"Oh, cool, I like that."

"Yeah, you're an important pancake maker." He leans down to whisper in Gauge's ear, but I can hear him. "Your mom will be the final judge of our pancakes, though."

Gauge sniggers and continues to pour the fluffy mix.

When the pancakes are done, I sit at the table, Gauge setting my plate down for me that beholds two fluffy golden pancakes with a perfect square of butter.

"Syrup, Mama?" Gauge asks, handing me the bottle.

"Yes, please, thank you, love. These look wonderful."

"All him," Dominic says, sitting down across from me.

Gauge remains in his chair.

"How are they?" Gauge asks as I take the first bite.

"Delicious! Perfect, love."

Gauge smiles and cuts into his pancakes.

Watching Dom slice into his food, I realize that is one question I never asked him.

How is he able to eat real food?

Also, what *does* he think about when he's around humans? Is the scent of blood always lingering, and when it is, how hard is it to fight?

I think there's a section of me that will always be worried about him being so close to my innocent child. But the witchy sense in me tells me he's safe. Although he's ruled by dark and blood and danger, he has spent hundreds of years managing it and keeping it under control. From what he told me and what I have already come to realize, he punishes the people who are not worthy of human life, and that's only when he'll get his fill of the sweet nectar that gives him life, even though it means he takes it from someone else.

And, like he told me, he doesn't have to kill to get his nourishment. He needs only to drain enough and veilweave them so he doesn't have to take it.

After breakfast, I send Gauge upstairs to take a bath, which takes him longer than normal kids as he can't walk, and it takes some time to get up the stairs.

I draw the bath for him, and when he's in it, I bound down the stairs to try out the necklace we created.

Dom is ready in wait, still in the house's shadows but staring out the window in longing.

"So how can you be in a house lit by the sun and not burn?"

"Direct sunlight is what does it. My car has tinted windows, and my house has tapered doubled panes, so the UV light doesn't get in."

"Ah. Gotcha. Okay, so how do you wanna do this?"

He caresses the necklace as though it's his lifeline, his oxygen in an air-stricken environment. "I will have you open the front door, and then I'll put my hand in. If we see smoke, shut it."

"Okay. Ready?"

Inhaling deeply, he says, "Yeah, go!"

I put my hand on the door handle, hesitate, then turn and pull. The sunlight spills in and drenches me in its warmth. He walks up, stands behind me, and cautiously pulls up his hand, inching closer to the streak of sun. The tops of his fingers touch the light and don't burn, then his fingers, then the back of his hand.

No smoke.

"Is it working?" I ask, not knowing what to expect.

Straight flames?

Smoldering?

Explosion?

Slow burning like a marshmallow on a campfire?

When nothing happens, he uses his other hand to move me and steps into the sunlight, one foot at a time.

Nothing.

He looks at me with childlike wonder in his eyes that I have never seen before. Something light and airy that reminds me of a deer in a clearing, eyeing a stream that hasn't seen water in an eternity.

He puts his hand on the screen door handle and opens it.

Fresh air flows in and kisses us both, but to him, it's as though the wind has kissed the sweat away after dying in a desert for ages. I can feel that from him, being the empath that I am.

I follow him calmly into the outdoors and watch as he steps into the sunlight for the first time in over two hundred and thirty-six years.

It's as though I'm watching someone emerging from a dungeon they've been in for their entire lives. His eyes squint at first, not being able to handle the light. Although it's a chilly morning, the apricity touches his skin and caresses it like saying hello to a friend one hasn't seen after decades apart. At the start, he shields his eyes with his palm, takes his hand away, and looks up at the pale blue sky that's still dusky with morning. His arms outstretch and he pulls the sunshine into him, the bond with the dark shattering before my eyes.

Pride is brimming within me, and although I haven't known him for long, my love for him has grown in the past twenty-four hours. What should have made me hate him, leave him behind, and never look back is the very thing that pulls me to him as he's pulling the sunlight. I am the sunlight in his dark, and while I was willing to be in darkness with him, I'm also willing to fight the darkness in his honor.

I want to defend the sun and protect his soul against the moon, even if his soul is drenched with gloom.

Now that I know his secret and know that the entire time I felt the hesitation, the feeling that I was being drawn to him is now known that it's part of his vampire power; the power to keep me calm, make me feel at ease and take away my worry. But there's more to it than that. Something deeper draws me to him that's stronger than hypnotic, but it isn't him who's bewitching me. It's as if the very fibers of my being are pulling him to me instead of his alluring nature drawing me to him. The more I get to know and fall for him, the harder it is to fight, even if there is still an aching doubt that tells me there's something dangerous about him.

As he basks in the daylight and reunites with the incandescence, I interlace his fingers with mine and share it with him. Even though some of my neighbors are out and about for their morning walks with their dogs, and we probably look pretty strange standing in the morning with our arms out, none of that matters to me.

What matters to me is that he's embracing the radiant morning with all of him; every ounce of his flesh is reeling in it, and I hope it's seeping into his soul. The dark clusters of evil circulating about him for hundreds of years are being chased away, and he will leave this moment feeling as refreshed as he could have ever imagined.

"What are you thinking?" I ask him as I turn him to face me.

The soft features of his face that had once been hardened and sad are now relieved with ease; soaking in the sun, he bends down so that he's at eye level with me. He looks at me like I have brought him water in the desert. "I am thinking that I adore you, Sayah. More than I can explain. You have given me back the light. I cannot tell you what this means to me. You have no idea how many years I've spent in shadows."

"I can't imagine, Dom. I cannot fathom being without the sunlight."

"So," he breathes, taking a step back but still clutching my hands, "The first thing you thought of instead of running for your life was to help me meet the light again? You thought nothing of your life, the danger you are in now, or any of that?"

"I mean, it was all swirling around in there, but mostly, I wanted to help you."

"You are something that is not of this world, Lasayah Thorne. I do believe you have angel blood mixed with the witch's."

The sound of my name on his lips makes it sound surreal. Within seconds, those lips are on mine, and I feel myself fall a little harder for him, a little deeper, even if there is an echo of a doubt that he is my *one*.

Despite the slight nagging feeling deep within my bones, he will still be an epic love.

26

A TINY FLAME

DOM

I'm relatively certain I've met the woman I'm destined to spend my life with. I cannot get over the way Sayah lives; her life and magick and blood and resilience stagger me. They're all attached to a string threaded through me, and the more I pull at it, the more it unwinds something within me.

Instead of running from the monster I am and the family that wants her dead—albeit she doesn't know that part—she took that terror within herself and still found a way to help me.

Making me a sun talisman.

Meeting the sun for the first time after centuries solidified that she's a powerful being with the magick to conquer anything. We still have yet to get her to find her fire, but we're working on that tonight as we prepare for her parents' celebration of life.

She wants to do some magick for the celebration without telling people it's real magick.

"While we're thinking of things we can do," I say as we sit at the patio table on her deck, basking in the remnants of the afternoon sun, "why don't you grab that spell I got from my mom, and we can work on fire some more?"

"All right," she says, scooting the chair to bound into the house.

When she returns, she hands me the spell Mom had sent me. "I don't see how I will do fire magick at the celebration."

"You're not. But while we think, do those exercises I told you about. Open your mind. Feel that fire. Listen to your blood and bones and magick. It's in there; we just have to draw it out."

"Why are you so adamant that I learn fire magick?" she says thoughtfully, though her tone suggests she's playing.

"I think it'll help to have all four elements. Once you unlock fire, you will unlock many other powers."

She smiles at me and closes her eyes, holding a red tapered candle before her.

I chant the words of my mother's spell and watch as she concentrates on pulling up her powers, chanting the words with me.

"Good," I respond as the aura around her gets brighter. "Now, blow that candle to life."

Her eyes still closed, she sets her breath free on the wick.

Nothing happens.

"Ugh!" she growls.

"I think it's cause you're trying too hard, love."

"Why won't fire listen to me? All the other elements are behaving!"

"Think of it like writer's block. Something is blocking you from that fire, and you have to get to it. Imagine it is yours—or, better yet, your son's. Someone took it from him, and now you're trying to get it back. Picture it in your mind, igniting your insides and coming to life at your fingertips. Visually see it happening in your mind."

Listening to me, she closes her eyes once again and mumbles something with her lips. I know she's having a silent conversation with her powers, so I remain quiet and watch her. In a fleeting second, everything stills, like the Earth is listening to her request. The wind suspends, the birds quiet, and even the distant sound of the highway muffles. She leans forward and exhales once more, this time, the tiniest flame ignites on the tip of the candle.

"That's it!"

"Oh my gods!" she exclaims with excitement. "I did it!"

"You did it!"

A profound relief washes over me. Even though it is the tiniest of flames, like a miniature version of an actual one, it means she's tapped into that power.

It may be enough to save her life.

For now.

The next day, I'm meeting Sayah and her family at the little art studio nestled in the foothills that she chose for the celebration of life.

As I wait for the cars to arrive—as I am the first one here—I text my mom about all the magick that Sayah and I have been doing lately.

But is that enough, Dom? A tiny flame is a little to work with.

It's a start. We'll keep working on it. Please tell the Nyktorim to hold off.

I will let them know. But that isn't enough to stop them or anyone wanting more significant results. That tiny flame did nothing to suppress the grims taking over our city.

I get that. But like I told you before, the spell she made for me with the moon and helping me walk in sunlight—that's huge. It should show for something,

I know Dom. I do. And I know you love her for it. I'll do what I can from my end.

That is all I am asking. Thank you.

I close my messages and turn the car off when Sayah's vehicle pulls up.

Sayah disembarks the vehicle first, followed by her dad and stepmom.

Her dad is easily six foot, has a head full of hair that's graying, a gray mustache, and square glasses that frame his eyes. He stands firm and proud as I approach him, extending my hand.

"Hello, sir. I'm Dominic."

"Dominic. I'm David. Nice to meet you."

His grip is firm; I can tell by the tension he is measuring what kind of man I am by the firmness of my hold. "Pleased to make your acquaintance, sir. And you, madam?" I hold my hand out in a gentler manner to meet her stepmom.

"Lydia," she says, offering me her hand. I take it gently and kiss the top of it in a bow.

Lydia is about as tall as Sayah, wearing white hair in a short pixie cut. She also has glasses that accentuate her pretty brown eyes. She is skinny and wears a lovely flowery dress with a jean jacket.

My eyes track back to David to see if he's impressed with my other-timely charm, but he doesn't seem phased. In fact, a glint in his eye is almost sinister.

After meeting her aunts and also the ex-husband who brought her son, I help Sayah through most of the day, lending her strength as she reads the eulogy she wrote to her family and friends.

While working on our magick last night, we devised a spell to bring a storm with no clouds while she played the slide show she made for her parents.

The picture slide show is twelve minutes long, and as she sits next to me in tears, watching her mom and stepdad's life on the screen, she squeezes my hand when the song *Hurricane* comes on.

We're sitting in the back row of the big room, next to the floor-length windows that line the east side of the gallery.

Moving like a cloud at the mercy of wind, I slip out the doors Sayah'd left open and spill the spelled water onto the mountain soil, returning to her side before anyone could know I left.

As the video subsides, there's a flash of lightning and a rumble of thunder that causes a collective jump within the group.

A tumultuous rain follows and beckons the ceremony goers from their seats to hover over by the windows.

The funny thing about this rain is that there are no clouds directly above us. There's a dusty blue sky and clouds all around, but nothing to explain the rain falling straight down from the sky from nowhere.

Commotion and chatter arise as her aunts, eyes agape and filled with tears, look at Sayah knowingly and open the doors to the patio.

Sayah, Gauge, her parents, and I join them on the deck to observe the phantom storm. I hold her as we all watch the rain fall on the lake, the ground, and the mountains and over the covered balcony of the art studio.

As we're watching the rain, I hear whispers of the celebration goers how coincidental it is that rain falls after all the mention of storms in the eulogy.

For the rest of the celebration, we go around to everyone who has come, snacking on the food and drinking our sparkling cider.

When all but close family remain, I take Sayah for a walk down by the water to soak up the scenery.

The rain has ceased, and the sun is bright and welcoming, especially to me. I am still in wonder of the sun and being drenched in it. I have her sunglasses on—as I have yet to buy my own.

"You did well today," I say as I hold her close, sitting on the stone bench at the water's edge.

"Did I?" she asks.

"Your words to your mother were beautiful. I didn't know you could write like that."

"It's my gift," she whispers, laying her head on my shoulder. "Thank you for being here. And for helping me with my spells. You have no idea what it means to me."

"Anything for you. I hope that your family likes me."

"I think they do. I really do. Especially my dad. He's old school, so he appreciates a good, firm handshake and being called 'sir'. I think you won him over with that."

"Well," I say, shifting my weight a bit with pride, "it's from the time that I'm from. People don't treat people as they used to. I try to change that still."

"I like it. Vampire or not, that shit's dope."

"Dope," I repeat. "I think that word is outdated now. I heard a youngin' the other day use the word 'rizz'. Rizz is what we're saying now."

"Nope," she laughs, snuggling in close to me. "Not happening."

27

THE DARK HERO

SAYAH

"Bye, baby," I say, crouching to hug Gauge. "Text me later, okay?"

"Okay, Mama." Gauge kisses me on the cheek before I stand.

"Thank you for coming. Truly," I say, embracing Derek's wife, Chrissy, in a hug.

"Oh, goodness, you are welcome, honey. So sorry for your loss," Chrissy replies, hugging me back.

"Thank you," I answer.

Derek gives me a side hug, and I lean in quickly and then move away. "So sorry for your loss, Sayah."

"Thank you," I say while Dom finishes his hug with Chrissy.

"It was nice to meet you both," Dom says, holding his hand out to Derek, who takes it and shakes. "And you," he says toward Gauge. "You and I still have our Mario Kart rematch to do!"

Gauge laughs as Dom squats to hug him. "Okay!"

"Drive safe," I tell them, wrapping an arm around Dom as they head to their car.

Hilda's loading a crock pot into the back of their car, so Dom lets me go to run and help.

"Why don't you come over for dinner tonight, Dominic? So, we can get to know you better," Hilda says, shutting the trunk after Maggie adds the empty food trays.

Dom's green eyes brush mine for a passing moment, and in them, I can tell he's asking for my acceptance.

"Yeah," I say, "come over for dinner. I'll make something."

"Okay," he smiles, and it's settled.

I hope my aunts won't pry too hard.

I see some rustling in the bushes off to the side that causes me to branch my look sideways. What appears to be a skinny white girl with long red hair, brown boots, and blue jeans is skulking behind a tree. I'm almost sure it's my sister Laureya.

Shaking it off as my imagination, I open the door to my vehicle and get in, though I watch the place I think I saw her for any movement.

Nothing but a big black crow flies away.

Later on, back at my house, after putting everything away from the celebration, I'm pulling things out of the fridge to make nachos and handing them to Lydia. She loves to cook and is fantastic at it, so I always give her free reign in the kitchen.

"So, where are you from, Dom?" Maggie asks him as she and Hilda sit down at the kitchen table.

I listen intently, excited to see how fast he can tell his human story.

"I was born in Florence," Dom says easily as he moves to sit with them, "but I was raised in New York."

"Oh, Florence?" Maggie swoons. She's the aunt who loves all things Italian.

"Yes," he replies, pouring some water from the pitcher I'd put out on the table, "but I was so young I don't remember much of it."

"Do you still have family there?" Hilda asks, propping her elbow on the table.

Dom's gaze flickers to mine as I grab a knife from the drawer.

I know what he's thinking.

Not for a very long time.

"Most of my family is in the Lake George area."

Hilda's jaw drops and her eyes blow wide. "Lake George?" She turns to look at me.

"Yes, Aunt Hilda," I say, tossing the lettuce into the sink. "We found we had that in common right away."

"That's so amazing," Hilda says, returning her attention to Dom. "We used to go every year when Sayah was a tot. So many fond memories of that lake."

"And what do your parents do, Dom?" Lydia asks, starting the hamburger meat as I finish with the lettuce and wash the tomatoes.

"My dad is a trauma surgeon, and my mom runs an online boutique," Dom replies, fidgeting with his paper napkin.

"Oooh, a boutique!" Maggie exclaims, "What sort of things does she make?"

"Oh, she makes jewelry, some gift boxes, bookish stuff, things like that." His green eyes retrace back to mine.

In our conversations, since I learned he was a vampire, he told me his mom runs an online witch shop selling spells, trinkets, and tarot cards.

I had mentioned to him earlier that I hoped nobody would bring up anything witch or Wiccan.

My dad and Lydia aren't too keen on my witchy ways. My dad's not a churchgoer, and neither is Lydia. Still, I know they believe in the same god the Christians do, and my dad has mentioned me not believing in the same god with contempt before. It's not something that I want to get into today.

"And what is it that *you* do?" interjects my dad, sipping a beer in the archway to the kitchen. His tone is brutal and indifferent—per usual for Dad.

"I am a data analyst for a software engineering company," Dom replies, turning to face my dad better. "Basically, I translate numbers into plain English for everyday businessmen. My job is to take data and use it to help my company make better business decisions."

"Interesting," Lydia replies, slicing the tomatoes.

Hamburger sizzling in the pan, I join Dom, Hilda, and Maggie at the table, getting out of Lydia's way. My dad wanders into the living room to watch golf.

As Lydia dices, she turns and says, "Have any children, Dom?" her penetrating gaze probing Dom.

He lowers his eyes to the table slightly. "I don't have any kids, no." His voice is controlled again, reliable, and the sober smile on his face still reflects a tinge of pain in his eyes. "Maybe one day," he adds, acting out a normal human conversation, winking at me. I give him a smile. "Where are you all from, originally?"

"Oh, we all grew up in Pennsylvania," Maggie answers, doing something on her phone. "We moved to New Jersey when we were all teens, and then Hilda and I lived in the same house we grew up in until about five years ago when we moved to Washington state."

"And there were five of you, yes?"

"Yes. Now there are three," Maggie says solemnly, setting her phone on the table.

"Speaking of sisters," Lydia asks nonchalantly, peeking her head toward the living room to ensure my dad doesn't hear her. "Sayah, you haven't heard anything from Laureya, have you?"

Being caught off guard by the question, I linger on my stepmom for a few seconds, wondering why she's bringing her up.

Did she see her at the celebration, too?

"I called her to tell her mom died," I reply, putting my hand on Dom's lap. "She hung up on me. You haven't either, I'm assuming."

"No, but that's what's weird," she replies, adjusting the glasses on her face. "She usually comes around occasionally to get money from your dad. We haven't heard from her in over a year."

"Huh," I say, wondering if I should mention that I swear I saw her earlier. "Must be way into the meth now, then."

Lydia looks at me and squints at my snide indifference toward my sister.

When she returns her attention to the sizzling pan, I retrieve my phone and unlock it, pulling up the message thread that's just messages to her from me.

All unanswered.

> Hey, were you at the celebration today? I swear I saw you.

Hitting send, I return my attention to the group, setting my phone on the table.

"So, Sayah tells me that the house you lived in as girls was haunted," Dominic says to the aunts, changing the subject.

"It was," Maggie replies, eyeing him demurely.

"What sort of stuff happened?" Dom asks, intrigued. He leans closer to the table. "I had a house once that was haunted, too. I love ghost stories."

"Oh, we would see lights on the hill thinking it was my dad coming home, and it wasn't," Hilda says seriously. She's the best at telling ghost stories. Her face is always so grim when she tells them; her brows draw into a tense line, and her expression doesn't waiver.

"They lived in an old house on the grounds of this park," I explain. "My grandpa was the caretaker. Since they lived on the grounds, Grandpa would walk to work and back."

"Oh, wow. That's cool," Dom says, propping his head on hand. "What else would happen?"

"Our book bags used to sit in a corner, and one night, a rubber band shot across the room, and they fell over," Hilda says, looking to Maggie.

"Sayah's mom and her Aunt Janet shared a room," Maggie continues, "One night, they heard breathing in the vent and chains on the stairs, so they pulled the covers over their heads. Something burst into the room and started thrashing all the perfumes and things off the dresser top. They realized it wasn't a dream when they woke up in the morning."

Chills climb my arms and the back of my neck.

Their ghost stories never get old.

Lydia stops cooking for a moment and leaves to grab something from the living room.

"What about you, Dom?" Hilda asks. "What happened to you?"

"Oh, this old house we had when I was a kid had a singing ghost," he says, reclining back. "She was gentle and liked to turn the lights on and run the faucet, but nothing too major."

Suddenly we hear a scream. *"David?"* comes Lydia's panicked voice from the other room.

Chairs scraping against faux wood echo as Dom and I scamper into the other room, quickly followed by Hilda and Maggie.

My dad is lying on the couch, gray as a sidewalk, dripping sweat, and talking nonsense.

"Daddy?" I exclaim in a tone of wild panic, running and skidding to my knees at his side. "Daddy, what's wrong?"

"I'm gonna die tonight," he slurs; his voice is high-pitched, and it's clear that he's not himself.

"Lydia, what is it? What's wrong?" I look at her, my eyes burning frantically into hers.

"I don't know," she breathes, kneeling on the floor beside me. "I came out here to get my water, and he was like this. He asked if I thought his eyes were dilated, and then he started telling me goodbye, that I was the love of his life, and he doesn't know what he would have done without me." Tears are streaming down her face, and hysteria taints her voice.

"Does it have anything to do with his heart?" I inquire, holding my dad's clammy hand.

Six years ago, my dad suffered from cardiac arrest and had a defibrillator implanted.

"I don't know," she says, stroking his hair, her eyes bulging with fright.

"I love you, Sayah. You're my one and only," my dad stutters, and I can tell from his eyes that something is seriously wrong. All I can think about is that I just lost my mom a month ago, and now, I'm going to lose my dad, too.

Dom pulls me up by my arm and into the hallway. "It's his blood pressure," he says quickly, the dark mystery of his eyes penetrating. "I can help him, but I have to move fast, and we can veilweave them later to forget."

I nod urgently as his fangs protrude and his eyes whiten. Following him back into the living room, a grotesque crunch echoes as he bites into his arm, deep enough to draw blood. He squeezes it so the pool of crimson is thick and dripping and shoves his arm onto my dad's mouth before he can even protest.

Lydia gasps and freezes in horror.

Hilda and Maggie keep unreadable expressions, watching Dom as though he was doing CPR. As strange as that is, I return my focus to Lydia.

Dad's eyes are fixed on the ceiling, absentmindedly blank as he grasps Dom's bleeding arm with both hands, suckling at the wound like a baby cow at a bottle. As he drinks, the gray begins to fade, his color returning.

"What's he doing?" Hilda asks, seemingly incapable of looking away.

I put my arm around her, not knowing what else to do.

"What are you doing?" Lydia screams, scrambling to her feet and retreating from Dom. "You fucking psychopath! We need to call nine-one-one!"

Panic blows her eyes wide, making my heart race.

I hope Dom hurries to veilweave her first so that she stops panicking.

Satisfied that my dad has gotten enough, he jumps over the couch and grabs Lydia by her shoulders like he reads my thoughts.

At first, she puts her arms up in defense, trying to slip out of his grip, but the moment she catches his eyes, her thrashing stops. Whatever his mind tells her, it's enough to calm her as her eyes go blank, her arms limp at her sides, and she nods.

She stands silently when he lets her go, as though in a trance.

"What the hell is happening?" Hilda demands, tense and shaking in my arms.

With no visible movement, Dom grabs Hilda's face. I watch his eyes narrow, and Hilda relaxes in my arms; her shoulders and neck tension eases.

Maggie, bewildered by all that's happening, says nothing as Dom moves to her, taking her face in his hands and veilweaving his silent coercion.

My dad, whose color has returned to normal and his hair has dried from sweat, sits up looking perplexed. Dom is a whiz of colors as he flashes over to him, sitting in front of him on the coffee table, putting his hands on his shoulders, and the dazed look melts away.

Lydia snaps out of her trance and goes back to the kitchen. My two aunts return to their seats at the table, and Dad resumes drinking his beer and watching his golf.

It's as though nothing happened at all. Mystified and perplexed, I grab Dom's hand and pull him to the front patio.

"That . . . was amazing. How did you know what to do?"

He clasps my hands in his. "I could hear his heartbeat had slowed. The way he was sweating and with what Lydia said, he asked about his eyes being dilated; the light from the window must have gotten bright. Being around a surgeon my whole life, you learn a thing or two about blood pressure."

"And what about your blood helping him?"

"My dad has been studying our blood for centuries. We are still unsure how many things it can cure. Still, because of our rapid healing ability, it has healing agents, unlike human blood. We learned long ago that people heal by feeding someone our blood."

"Will he turn into a vampire?"

"If he dies in the next twenty-four hours. Just keep a close watch on him. I veilweaved them to forget I fed him blood or that they saw that part at all, but they will still have a memory of him having an episode."

"Can your blood cure cancer?" I can feel the question burning all over my face.

"No," he answers quickly, letting go of my hand to stroke my face. "My dad, being a surgeon and all, does things when he has to while at work. A few of those things have been tried on cancer patients. Let's say that it didn't go at all how he was hoping it would."

"How can your dad stand being a trauma surgeon?"

Dom contemplates the question, and I don't know if he's finally tiring of my inquiries. "He made a choice when he had Scarlet turn him—him and my mom—that they would not be monsters. He was going to help people, to atone for what he does when he needs to feed. But working at a hospital also gets him unlimited access to blood. So, because of that, he and my mom don't have to feed on people that often. Once or twice a year, if that."

"Oh, well, that makes sense." My heart swells for him and the relentless beauty of his face—this tragically dark and brooding hero. "Thank you for saving my dad, Dom. I—I don't know what I would do if I lost him, too."

Although the vampire in him hinders him from having an easy grace, he's still as soft and delicate as dusted soot. I feel him beginning to take up residence in my brain and bones and base of my spine and thread through me like nerves. Looking deeply into his hazel eyes, I lean my forehead against his and whisper, "I love you, Dom."

His eyes narrow on mine, and it looks like he's letting go of fighting something, sharing bits and pieces of his protected softness. "I love you too, Sayah." He sighs. "More than I have ever loved anyone."

He lowers his lips to mine and unglues something within me. Whatever wall I had been holding up for him came undone, and now this love for him is like a deluge through my soul.

"We should get back in," he says, letting me go. "I want to make sure everyone is doing okay."

I nod and let him pull me from the porch.

As we enter the house, my dad sits on the couch with his beer in a koozie, watching golf, his cheeks the perfect pale peach they were before the incident. He smiles at us as we pass by, nodding to Dom as we approach the kitchen.

Lydia's busily cooking at the stove, listening to one of her podcasts. Hilda and Maggie are flicking through something on their Kindles at the table.

"Oh, good, you're back!" Hilda exclaims, setting her Kindle down. "You have to finish telling us about your haunted house experience."

And it seems all is forgotten. My dad had been healed.

By vampire blood.

As I drift off to sleep later that night, I think of all that has happened in the last few months.

Losing my parents, meeting my love, and learning his secret. Sometimes, I feel overwhelmed by what I'm doing with my magick. But what tugs me into sleep tonight is not Dom, the celebration, or anything else that happened today.

It's Sebastian.

I see him as clearly as if he's in my room at the foot of my bed with an announced purpose.

I sit straight up.

He's wearing all black, and there's no light in my room except for the tiny nightlight in my bathroom.

His blue eyes, haunting in the darkness, filled with sweltering passion and intense longing, hold me transfixed and stop my breathing until I force myself to take in the air.

"What are you doing here?" I ask, clutching the sheets up to my chest, aware that I'm only wearing a thin tank top and no bra.

"I don't know," he answers, his voice sexy and deep. "I haven't seen you in my dreams lately. I guess I missed you."

"What is it that you want from me? Every time you visit my dreams, you kill me, or both of us. I don't know what this dream is trying to tell me."

"I don't have any answers for you." He steps toward me, and the urge to run screams at me. "All I know is that when I dream of you, I breathe a little easier the next day, the burden a little lighter. Your light feeds me, and every time I breathe you, living is simpler and a little less painful the next day."

"Well, every time I dream of you, I wake up confused as hell," I spit out, my voice querulous and demanding.

The all-consuming passion and love for him is dwindling, and I wonder if that has anything to do with the fact that I have now found love.

He takes another step toward me, and as soon as he does, something about his gaze disassembles me. It divests that wall that had started to build up, and again, I feel immured by him like I need him to live. As he grows closer, my limbs weaken, and that hot rush tingles in my toes.

He's at my bedside within a second, and his gaze is greedy; those eyes are burning into me.

His angry mouth, which seems like it has turned cruel at my words, softens, and I need it on mine. I want his fire. I need it.

His rough hands suddenly brace the back of my neck and pull me up to him, his lips careening against mine as though one more second without them would indeed rip him apart. I feel his tongue, the fire begins, and the invisible agony of burning starts at my toes.

The surrendering sanctity of my neck is under his fangs again, and the sound of the flames engulfing us both is all I hear, along with the feeling of that extemporaneous fire.

When I open my eyes, I swear there's smoke swirling in the sunlight.

The fact that the dream has returned puts me on edge and makes me curious as to why this strange man is revisiting my dreams.

I know he's a vampire.

Playing with the thought of if I should tell Dom catches in my mind a few times, but there's a lingering feeling of guilt as if I'd cheated on him.

I'm an honest and sincere person. I have no need to dissemble.

But even though it *was* just a dream—I couldn't have cheated on him—the feelings that arise whenever Sebastian enters my world make my feelings for Dom pale in comparison. I wish that I had those feelings for him.

Feelings that the world stops moving and changes its rotation to pull the two of us together. A force of nature that's incomprehensible but tangible and real and downright impossible to ignore.

I remember the way I first felt those feelings for him fading, not as intense as my first couple of dreams. But then, as he got closer, I felt them come flooding back.

This scares me because it tells me that this vampire is real and is infecting my dreams and making me feel real feelings. He can control my emotions and the Earth he stands on.

Last night's dream might have been real; he could have been in my room with me and then veilweaved me to make me think it was a dream.

It was too real.

There was smoke.

But then why am I not burnt?

Laying in bed still, I extend my arms to check for burns, and nothing is there.

Not a hair singed, not a parcel of skin burned. There's no need to tell Dom about the dream.

Right?

28

OUT OF TIME

DOM

"Dom, I'm sorry, there's nothing I can do," my mother's British cadence echoes through my cell phone.

"Fuck! Mom!" I'm pacing around the living room of my rented house, wearing a path on the hardwood that matches the worn path in my patience.

"It's been three weeks since you helped her with her tiny flame and nothing with fire since."

"I've been working with her with the other elements; the fire doesn't want to come out. I need a seasoned witch to help her; I've been doing it alone. Her aunts aren't helping. I need you to come here, meet, and help her."

"Dominic, we are out of time. The leader of the Nyktorim lost a daughter to the grims. It's personal now. They're sending someone to her as we speak."

"Fuck," I say again, kicking a basket with magazines in it. The basket goes flying, magazines sailing across the room. "How much time do I have?"

"A few days. They're consulting the witch you saw in Never. Shayde?"

"Yeah, Shayde."

"They want to consult her energy spirit, Aura, first to see what the prophecy says, and they are in Salem. If she tells them, they will journey to Colorado to carry out the rest of their mission."

"Their mission? Their mission is to *kill* the woman I lo—" I cut myself off. I can't say the words. I can't breathe to life what flits around on broken wings inside me. I am desperate, feeling it slipping into my voice and spilling through the phone.

I can't lose her. Losing her would be like losing the one person who breathes life into your broken pieces and still looks at you as though you are whole. Losing that unfathomable existence, the only one who not only welcomes your demons to her table, but she learns their names and introduces them to her own. Like how autumn dies for winter to let spring live.

"Oh, Dom," her motherly tone is strident. "You knew the risk. The entire reason we sent you out there was to try and see if we could avoid her dying. You *knew* better than to fall in love with her son!"

"You know what? Fuck it. I'll handle it myself."

"Dom--"

I hang the phone up and throw it onto the couch.

The sun beaming outside is warm and comforting, yet my desperation swallows the light and makes me yearn for the dark.

Salvation is a reckless companion to a tender heart.

The phone rings again, and I pick it up.

Ollie's name is across the screen.

"Hello?" I answer.

"Hey," Ollie quips, his brotherly voice always steady. "You doing okay?"

"I don't know what else to do," I say despondently, walking over to the window and picking at the peeling paint on the sill. "I should have brought Mom here sooner to help with the fire spell. After seeing everything else that she was capable of, I thought she'd get it by now. I—"

"Why don't you have Scar or Hattie come help you?"

"Are you kidding me? You know they wouldn't help me with this.

They're all about killing her. If I brought them near her, they'd snap her neck."

"Doesn't she have to die by fire or something?"

"Is that a witch joke?"

Ollie laughs, but it's hallowed. "No, the whole 'phoenix' prophecy thing. There is someone else you can call that likes murder and mayhem that may help you with the blokes coming to kill her."

"I'm not calling him Ollie. No."

"Just saying."

"Got any other ideas?"

"Well. What was your plan thus far?"

"Keep helping her with her magick and wait for Tallyn to send another Whispering Leaf so I can get more information from her."

"And there's no way to get Tallyn to contact you otherwise?"

Going over to the couch again, I sit. "No. She has to come to you."

"I guess your only option is to lay in wait at her house and intercept anyone that comes to kill her. Help her with her magick in the meantime."

"You know any strong witches that can help me with that?"

"I may know a few. Give me some time. I'll see what I can come up with."

"Thanks."

"Sure. And Dom . . ."

"Yeah?"

"Try not to die yourself, okay."

I laugh. "I'll try not to."

29

NYKTORIM SYNDICATE

DOM

For the next three days, I'm a complete mess.

Sayah doesn't know, but I've been living in my car across the greenbelt from her house, watching her every moment she is there alone.

The first few days are quiet. There is nothing out of place, and she comes and goes from work. I follow her to work, stake out in the parking lot, and watch for any nefarious movement in the bushes or surrounding areas.

After she gets off, I follow her home and wait in my car until the early morning hours, when I creep into her house. I pretend to just get off work and lay with her in bed until she gets up to start her day again.

It isn't until the third day that the Nyktorim show up.

Sayah is in the shower when I hear and feel the magick with which they enter.

Like a breath of lightning, I'm at the basement window where they've entered.

Four of them.

Unlike other groups of leaders, this one is more matriarchal. However, they don't identify as any gender; they are simply nonbinary. They've been around since the dawn of time and quite possibly are even older than the fae. They are like a cross between vampires and warlocks; they drink blood but not to live. They drink it because they love it, and the high they get propels them through any universe they choose to enter.

They are quite possibly what would happen to us if we killed every time.

I never knew they existed before my mom mentioned them, and the only reason I know anything about them now is that they transfer information into my head as I look at them.

I just know now.

Their skin glows as they traipse closer to me, and I feel afraid of them, but I bite down on the terror, knowing I have to do whatever possible to protect the woman I love.

The one closest to me is very tall and fair; long white hair cascades to the floor, and wrinkles as deep as canyons crease their face. Their eyes are milky white with age, and their fingers are long and bony. They all don white robes with sleeves large enough to fit a briefcase in each. Each one of them looks more ancient than the next, and my first thought is that they don't have the luxury of spelt mirrors; they obviously have looked into one and become the very age they all are.

"You can't kill her," I tell them as they hover closer to me, the eerie glow coming off their skin illuminating the dark basement.

We don't need your permission to do anything, youngling.

Their voices are everywhere and nowhere, directly in my mind and around me like whispers.

"WAIT!" I shout as they glide past me, feeling the desperation seep out of my skin and into the air. "Please, wait."

The tallest one stops and turns to face me, their pearlescent eyes drinking in every feature of my face. *What will you have us do, child? Let her live, and everyone else dies because of the grims?*

"But you don't know that killing her will stop these things. Some witch in Salem has an energy spirit that had a prophecy, but I don't believe killing her will make these things disappear. I believe it is a metaphor for her fire magick. I just need more time to get her to ignite it."

They ignore me and turn once again to continue toward the stairs.

I flash in front of them and lay my hand on the being's shoulder. "Please. If I can't get her to find her fire magick by the next full moon. I'll kill her myself."

The silence is deafening.

They are having a silent conversation in their minds.

"So?" I ask after what seems like an ungodly amount of time.

If nothing has been done to quell the grimspawn problem by the next full moon, and she isn't dead... we will eliminate her and your entire family for the trouble.

A knot forms in my throat.

I nod. "You have a deal."

The tall one nods their head, and they silently retreat to the window, where they evaporate like dust and float away on the wind.

Fuck.

Now, not only have I doomed Sayah if she doesn't find her fire magick.

But my entire family is now tied to the doom as well.

30

MARKED

SAYAH

A few weeks later, as I'm driving to work down a farmland highway, the rising sun silhouettes the mountains but in a glorious burnt yellow color. Late in May now, all the green is starting to poke through the brown of the winter, and even though it's starting to warm up, I still have the heat on because I hate being cold. The car smells of the heat, and my little Febreze air fresheners make the cacophony of smells swirl around me. At the same time, I listen to my morning radio show.

I love this drive to and from work as it's my only time to myself when I do not have to cater to all of Gauge's needs, and I can let my mind wander.

The radio hosts are my favorite, and I'm listening to their weekly episode of War of the Roses—a show where the cheated spouse is sneakily calling the cheater via the host with free roses to see whom they send the free flowers to—when they're interrupted with a special news bulletin.

"We interrupt this regular programming to bring you breaking news," comes a news anchor woman's formal voice. "A dangerous and possibly armed criminal has escaped from Kit Carson Correctional Facility and is believed to be hiding in the Denver area.

"Chaco Dominguez was serving a life sentence in prison for violently murdering his four stepchildren. Mr. Dominguez has spent most of his life in and out of prison, serving time for violent acts against women and children. Before the murder of his stepchildren, Dominguez had been released after serving time for attempting to murder his sister after brutally raping her and her fifteen-year-old son. Dominguez is considered armed and dangerous, and we strongly caution all residents of the Denver area to stay alert. If anyone has any information on Dominguez's whereabouts, call the nine-news hotline or nine-one-one. We will post updates on our Facebook page as they come in."

The first thing that comes to my mind is those idiots in Las Vegas and Dom killing them for attempting to rape Anna. This man murdered his own children and raped and tried to murder his sister and her son. This is the type of man who deserves to die, and he's out and about, doing gods know what to gods know who.

Throughout my day at work, I research during my downtime, trying to focus on my daily grind—but this situation bristles me to my core, and I'm bound to kill two birds with one stone.

Literally.

I google Chaco Dominguez's mugshot to find the stories about his crimes and his episode on my favorite true crime podcast, *Sword and Scale*, which is fueling the fire. Barely getting any of my work done, I formulate my entire plan while feigning a productive employee, ending the day by printing a map of the Denver area he is suspected to be in.

The minute I arrive home, I consult my grimoires, searching for the locator spell I'd seen in passing.

Gathering the color of candles I need and a few other ingredients, I sit in my living room in the candlelight and place the map and picture on the floor. Sprinkling some charcoal dust on the map, I hover my hand above the map and close my eyes.

In complete concentration, I summon Lilith.

"Dark goddess of death and madness, guide me to the one who shatters societal norms and embodies sickness itself. Illuminate his whereabouts, so together, we may deliver him unto you and purge the world of his insatiable malevolence."

My vision goes black, drinking the light around me.

There are suddenly flashes of light, like spider silk, spindling a nightmare.

A dusty, dingy hotel room with two twin beds adorned in red floral print from the '80s. A heavy-set Mexican man with a thick Spanish accent is sitting before a rickety round table, snorting a line of cocaine. When he leans back up after snorting the line, I can see he has a thick black handlebar mustache, and his eyes are as hard and cold as night itself.

Two sickly-looking men are with him, speaking in Spanish, and while I do understand the language, I can't make out what they're saying.

The vision splinters, and when I open my eyes again, I'm back in my house, on my living room floor, sitting before my lit candles.

A sinister circle of charcoal dust marks the area around the hotel.

Before blowing out the candles, I take a photo of the map with the circle and plug it into Google Maps.

Dom is going to be at the house later. It has been a habit lately for him to come to my house when he gets off so we can at least see each other for a few moments.

Like ships in the night.

When my head hits the pillow, I'm so worked up with anticipation and rage I can hardly get my mind to shut off.

Sleep interlaces with my mind when I feel the bed shift, Dom climbing into bed beside me. It's still dark in my room, so it must be early. I curl up to him, and he kisses my head.

"Hey," I whisper into the darkness, his scent of Earth and cedar and maybe a little sweat surrounding him.

"Hi, beautiful," he answers sleepily.

I snuggle up to his warm chest and feel that immediate comfort as he wraps me in his strong arms. Counting the breaths coming from his chest, I know he's tired, but the anticipation of telling him my plan is eating away at me.

I have to tell him.

"I have someone for you," I blurt out and feel him crane his neck to see me.

"You *have* someone for me?" His voice is stern.

"For you to kill."

Silence.

Is this okay?

"Oh, you do, do you?" he deadpans.

Maybe he's hesitant to have me be involved in the killer part of his world.

"I did a locator spell on him," I hedge. "He's a bad man, Dom. He's wanted for extremely violent crimes. I know where he is, and I want you to kill him."

The muscles in his arm tense, and I feel him go ridged in my touch.

"So, you're like my pimp now? Except instead of finding people for me to fuck, you find people for me to kill?" I can hear that mocking smile.

I punch him. "Dom, I'm dead ass. You have a duty to kill this man."

"A duty? Wow, Sayah, you're really getting into this."

"Dom. I've thought about this. You need human blood to sustain. And there are bad people in this world. Might as well kill two birds with one stone. No pun intended."

"It was a good pun, though," he says, pulling me closer. "Have I told you lately how much I love you?"

"Nope," I answer, my tone edged with sass.

"I love you so much. I am so lucky to have such a beautiful and caring witch as a girlfriend who helps me be the best vampire I can be."

I laugh. "I love you too. But I'm serious. I will help you in any way I can. You live, they die. Sounds like a good plan to me."

"Me too, babe. Me too. I'm gonna get some sleep now. I'm tired."

"You should switch to the day shift now. Now that you can go in the sun."

"I'm already two steps ahead of you."

I look up at his face, only a suggestion of shadows and planes because of the dusky dawn glow in the room, but his eyes are almost dark black. I can always tell how hungry he is by the color of his eyes, and the last time I'd seen him, they were a mud brown. "Really?"

"Yes. I start next week."

"Oh, that makes my heart so happy. So. When can we go over our plan?"

His weight shifts; his muscles tense. "Our plan?"

"Yeah. To get this guy I found?"

"You're not having anything to do with it," he retorts, his tone imperious. "You're ruled by three-fold. I can't have that coming back on you."

"Dom, it won't. And you need me. I have to help you find him."

"You said you found him already. Say, you're not coming."

"I am. I don't have to go inside. But I want to come with you when you do it."

This time his weight shifts, and he sits up a bit. "Why? Why do you have to come with me when I go to kill someone? Sayah, I don't want you to ever see that side of me."

"I get that. I do. But I don't want anything to happen to you. I want to put a protection spell on you."

"Then do, but you're not coming. That's final."

"Oh." This time, I shift my weight and turn my back to him. "Final, huh?"

"Sayah, don't do that. I don't want you to see that side of me." There's a compunction in his voice and that weighted sadness that had left him when he found the sun comes back again.

I know that's a side of him he isn't proud of and doesn't want to show me. But someday, he will have to.

"Dom," I say softly, turning back around. "I know it's a side of you that you don't want me to see. But you are my love, and I love every part of you. Including the killer part. I'll see that side of you one day."

"No, you won't," he says quickly, defensively.

"Not directed at me. But I am bound to see you in your natural state. We're linked now."

"How are we linked?"

Even though I don't feel we're soul mates, I still feel drawn to him. We're not endgame, but we definitely have an epic middle chapter. A sudden sadness pings in my chest when he doesn't recognize the thing that pulls us together.

But he's a vampire, and I'm supposed to be drawn to him. He's not drawn to me.

"Never mind," I speak defensively now.

Bristling even more, every muscle in my body tenses.

This is the first time he's pissing me off.

"Sayah." He pulls me to him as close as he can. "I feel that too. I'm sorry. I've been working all night, and I'm tired. I feel the bond we have. I'll show you that side of me when the time comes. But that time isn't now, okay?"

Realizing this is a battle I'm bound to lose, I kiss him and let him drift off to sleep.

As dusk approaches the following evening, after Derek has picked up Gauge, Dom and I sit at the dining room table reviewing our plan. It's Friday night, and he doesn't have to work this weekend.

The sun's golden rays delicately lend the room a safe, serene look, a dark juxtaposition for the pernicious things we're planning.

"So this is the motel," I say, pulling the address up on his phone in Google Maps.

He leans into me and peers at the map.

"All right, I'll probably leave my phone in the car when I arrive. I don't want to let them know I'm coming."

There's a sinister softness in the inflections of his voice that gives me chills.

"Yes, and be careful. It looks like this motel is a run-down crack motel in the ghetto of Denver."

He gives me a crooked smile, and his eyes are striking in the ochre color of the sunset. They're muddy brown, tinged with black. He needs to feed soon.

"I'll be careful, my love," he answers, tucking a loose hair behind my ear.

"All right. One more quick thing before you go," I state, hopping out of the chair and bounding to the spell cabinet.

I gather my purple altar cloth, lavender incense, white candle, and the most enormous black tourmaline crystal.

Assembling the candle and incense atop the purple cloth, I close my eyes and blow, lighting the candle as I do with my breath. I use the flame to light the incense.

Dom's looking at me with a coruscating gaze, disarming me. Still, I continue meditatively, smudging his aura and the crystals with the inchoate smoke.

"Gods of strength and power, protect this man on his journey. Usher him through the danger with the grit of light and cunning. Element of Earth, keep his feet protected on the ground. Element of air, surround him in purity and protection. Element of water, wash away the negative energy. And element of fire, burn away the evil." As I speak the last of the spell, I slide the tourmaline through the fire's flame. "So mote it be." I hand him the crystal and say, "Keep this in your pocket for protection, okay?"

He takes the black rock and slides it into his pocket. "I'll text you as much as I can."

Nodding, I hug him and walk him to the door.

"I love you," he says, taking my lips.

"Love you," I respond through the lip lock. "Be safe."

I watch as he descends the front stoop and embarks on his journey to feed.

Anxiety strangulates me an hour later while I wait for the text that it's been done. Everything from:

What if they know what he is, and they staked him with silver?

What if they have Nightshade?

What if he was decapitated?

How else can Vampires die?

Pacing my house for the hundredth time, I recheck the phone.

Still waiting for new messages.

The message screen is pulled up on my phone while I wait for the little bubbles to show that he's texting. The last message is up, saying:

I'm about to go inside. I love you.

Now, I wait for what seems like hours for him to let me know he's okay.

These are dangerous criminals that he's going up against.

But he's a vampire. A killer. With strength and wit and an ability to lull people into calmness. He's seemingly unassailable.

I shouldn't be this worried about him.

As the time ticks by, my heart races faster and faster.

Was the protection spell I did good enough?

Can you protect vampires with magick?

Of course, you can. I answer my own thoughts resolutely. I protect him from the sun with his necklace.

Maybe I didn't do a strong enough one. Maybe I should've spelled some more jewelry, a ring or something.

Time itself has stopped. I don't know why I'm so worried about him anyway; he always does this.

Doesn't he?

The nerves within me feel as though they're mush. Every muscle is tense, and there's a tingling sensation in my arms that I can't shake. Every time I look at the phone, seeing no new messages burns me, dissonance in contention with conviction, reason frayed with doubt.

When my phone rings, it's like an elixir for my burns, a soothing agent to calm the serrated nerves the last hour and a half have caused.

Dom's name flashes on the screen.

Pressing the green answer button, I say, "Hey. You okay? It's been so long."

"I'm good," he says, though the tension in his voice reminds me of a doused star. "I'll be there soon. I wanted to tell you I'm all right."

Feeling that my insides are as thin as a drum, I can sense that whatever it is, he doesn't want to talk about it over the phone.

It must be what he feels after he kills someone.

I let it go for now, knowing it's more than that.

"All right. Drive safe. I'm proud of you."

Silence.

Remembering what he said about sometimes taking on the personality of the person he kills, I figure these rigid and severe vibes I'm getting are from the man he killed and not from him himself.

"I love you?" I say, questioning in my tone.

"Love you."

And the line goes quiet.

When I see his black Mercedes pull up into the driveway, I feel like a constellation of lacerations held together by stitches of uneasiness and fear. It's taking everything I have to hold those stitches of myself together.

In the time that I'd waited for him, so many things have gone through my mind.

More vampires. A siren. He's been bitten by a formweaver.

What scares me the most is that he was bitten by a formweaver.

I run up to the car as he clambers out and check him for bites.

He's wearing all black, so I can't see well, but I can tell that he's covered in blood. It's all over his skin, his face, his neck. He hugs me, and I examine his neck, arms, and anywhere I can. Judging by the desolate look in his eyes, something beyond anything I know has gone wrong.

"Oh my gods," I exclaim. "I've been so worried about you."

"Let's get inside," he says, raking his hands through his hair. "I don't want anyone to see us."

"Who would see us?"

He doesn't answer and pulls me by the hand.

When we're safely inside, he shuts the door and deadbolts it.

"Dom, what—"

"He's dead. I drained his blood and two of his cronies that were with him."

His eyes are green again, meaning he at least got his fill of human blood.

"Well, that's good—"

"They were trackers, Sayah."

"Trackers? What are trackers?"

"They work for the warlocks that spell the grimspawn," he says, and his tone is edged as sharply as a knife. "From what I know, grimspawns and warlocks need each other to thrive. When warlocks create more grimspawns, they create trackers who are marked, people who must go through a series of tests to be spelled by the warlock. They have to endure a life of unbelievable crime and murder to desiccate their soul enough for the warlock to become one with theirs. As they commit their crimes, their mark gets darker and darker until it's all the way filled in. The more heinous the crime, the quicker the mark darkens."

"Why would anyone want to be a grimspawn?"

"They don't want it, Sayah. They are chosen by the warlocks and spelled to believe that's what they want. It's like our veilweaving spell, but much worse."

"So, Chaco Dominguez was a tracker?"

"Worse. His mark was all the way dark. Meaning his next crime was going to turn him into one."

"So? The world has one less grimspawn."

"No, that's not it, Sayah."

There's a terror in his eyes that I've never seen before. And to see terror in the eyes of a killer unnerves me more than anything I could have ever imagined.

"Because he was marked and I killed him, it means the mark was transferred to me. I am now marked."

He pulls up his sleeve and shows me the crescent moon mark that looks like a branding, the skin raised from the surface of his flesh. I graze it with my fingertips, not comprehending what the mark truly means.

The disorientation must have been spilling out of my eyes, for he covers the mark up and turns to me.

"We can figure out a way to spell it off of you," I say and go to the cabinet and grab a grimoire.

"Sayah." He grabs my arm and leads me to the couch. "There's no way to spell this off. It's the magick of a warlock, a power unlike any you've ever seen. The warlock that spelled this mark will not stop until I am hers."

"Hers? How do you know this warlock is a she?"

"As soon as the mark appeared, when Chaco was dead and drained, I saw her. In a flash of my mind. But I saw her as clear as day."

"There has to be a way. What if we track the warlock and kill her?"

"I don't know of a way to kill a warlock, Sayah."

"Drain her of her blood!"

"They're protected by magick."

"So I'll spell your blood and hide you from her."

"I don't think it works that way, my love."

I assume an injured air. Anger is rising like bile in my throat.

What the hell are we supposed to do now?

"What does this mean?"

"Well," he goes on blithely, his dark brows drawing together in contemplation as he looks at the blood on his pants. "Driving home, I had nothing but time to think. My entire life, when we had to fight these things, I have never come across one that was a vampire first. Yes, they drink blood and eat people, but they are driven by this mark to lose their minds to the warlock in control. They feed on people, and sometimes, they can become the people that they feed on if they—"

"If they what?"

"If they eat enough of them." His gaze remains anchored on me. "They were trying to get to us because they wanted vampire blood. Consuming the blood of a vampire would make them immortal and, therefore, make the warlock connected to the grimspawn immortal. It's why they spell grimspawns in the first place—to do their dirty work so they can live forever and not have to do the killing."

"So . . ."

"So whatever warlock spelled this mark now has a vampire who is marked; it's basically like hitting the jackpot. She's not gonna wanna let me go."

"And what will happen to you?"

"I'll be spelled to her forever. Doing her bidding. Basically, she's my sire now, and whatever she wants me to do, I have to do. Be that killing people, eating them—whatever she desires. I'll lose my mind and be a walking zombie. Living forever to eat and consume blood for her."

"What are we going to do?" I waiver. I'm lost in a dizzy dissonance, a dark and nefarious maze, not knowing which way is out. "This is all my fault."

A hot, raw pain plunges me into darkness. I just found him. I love him. And now I'm going to lose him forever.

"Shh, it's not your fault," he says softly, pulling me down to lay on his chest.

Tears seep from my eyes at all the broken possibilities that shatter at my feet. I don't want to lose him. And because this is a world I know nothing about, I don't know how much time I have left with him.

"If I hadn't meddled and tried to find someone for you to kill, you wouldn't be in this predicament."

"You were only trying to help. You couldn't have known, nobody could have."

"How much time do we have until . . . "

"Until I become a mindless zombie?" He smiles limpidly, though fear laces his tone. "I have no idea. I have to call my mom."

"Do you think she'll know of anything to do?"

"She's our best bet," he replies. "It looks like we'll be traveling to New York sooner than I had thought."

Going to New York with a coven full of vampires to talk to a witch-vampire hybrid about her son who was marked to become a grimspawn—nothing to bat an eyelash at.

31

FIND MY RUIN

DOM

The visceral reaction to being marked by a warlock started with pain at the mark, followed by burning goosebumps prickling my skin, rolling into revulsion roiling in my stomach, and leading to everything aching, rejecting the new cursed branding that now decorates my arm.

As I had my fangs deep inside Chaco, the first indication I knew something was off was that I didn't get that sated feeling consuming blood from the vein typically encompasses. That, paired with the feeling of the air being completely drained from the dark hotel room, and a deathly ringing in my ears, precluded the vision.

She came to me in a blast of wind, transcending the boundaries of sheer malice, a living manifestation of shadows. The white spilling of her hair bounded around her as though she was floating, accentuating the darkness of her evil aura. Two massive black horns jutted out from the top of her head and curled up and around to the back. The horns, adorned with intricate black embellishments, added to her ominous allure. Colorless eyes pierced my soul, instilling an indescribable terror that defies earthly language. Cloaked in a black dress, her unnaturally pale skin emitted an otherworldly glow, and her pointed black nails, adorned with dark jewels, scraped along my arm as she drew the mark.

When the mark was drawn, and the blood was drained, the hotel resumed the same air, yet the profound darkness that she embodied soaked the room and everything in it like a thick layer of soot.

The thought alone of being a slave to someone else, losing my mind to a force beyond anything I can comprehend, is enough to ruin me, to wreck me from the inside out. Utter loss and hopelessness swallow my breath and the air in my car feels stale and suffocating.

My heart races as fast as my car moves, returning to the house to pack my suitcase. Traveling with Sayah into a den of vampires who want her dead adds to the million-pound weight sitting on my chest, asphyxiating me from the inside out.

I need to call my mom to tell her I'm bringing Sayah to her, but I can't tell her I've been marked over the phone.

No, that will have to be done in person.

I have no idea how she's going to take that.

"Hello?" Mom says after a few rings.

"Hey, Mom. I'm coming back. Can you pick us up at the airport later?"

"What? Why? What's happened?"

"Nothing. I want to come home."

"Is she dead then?"

"What? No, Mom. She's not dead. I need more help drawing her magick out."

"Oh. You're running then."

"Odin's ghost mom. I know she has fire magick. I've seen it. I need you, Scarlet, and Hattie to help draw it out of her."

The line is quiet for a moment. "All right."

"Really? You'll be nice?"

"I never said anything about being nice."

"Please. Try to be nice. And don't kill her."

"I will try to help you draw her magick out of her. And if we can't get her to wield her fire magick and those fucking warlocks or the Nykorim come for us, I will kill her."

"All right. Don't mention anything about this or that I don't live here in Colorado, okay?"

"Bloody hell, Dominic, you've not told her anything?"

"There hasn't been a chance to. I will. While we're there . . . tell Hattie, J, and Scarlet to behave okay. I don't need them killing her either."

"Why is it that your reckless heart always seems to get us in trouble?"

"You say that to all your kids."

"Yes, well. You all seem to love blindly without thinking of the consequences."

"We get it from you."

"I resent that," she says, but I can also hear the smile behind the words.

"I'll see you later, okay? I'll text you the flight information when we have it."

"Okay. Bye."

Flicking the phone off, I throw it on the passenger seat and watch the headlights whiz by me going the other direction. I think of Sayah and all she's become to me in the short time I've known her.

The danger sitting at the edge of us, always in the periphery, does nothing to stir the magick within her. I know that telling her of this ever-present and imminent fatality would stoke her fire, blow it wide open, and make her come to terms with her own fate. The things I've given her thus far—the bracelet, the information of the supernatural, and whatever else Tallyn's spell did—have helped her to come to terms with her magick and find the well of power deep within her. But I have not indulged her with that information yet, thinking the fire must come to her terms. It's not something that can be forced.

It's something I learned long ago from my trauma, the magick of the dark that was honed by darker moments and tempered by my survival. My aversion to death and killing, leaving me weaker than some other vampires, caused me to learn to wield the magick I have by finding my ruin and building myself up from the wreckage.

I should be honest with her. Maybe doing so will ignite that magick within her and push her to her destiny—whatever that means. But something profound inside me tells me that she must find her ruin for that power to come to light.

Maybe her fire lies in wait in her destruction.

32

THEY'RE ALL MURDER-Y

SAYAH

When we land in New York and make our way to the baggage claim, I look around nervously for the coven of vampires that we're coming to meet.

"Who's picking us up?" I ask as we retrieve our luggage from the spinning carousel.

"My mom. Her name is Adaline. And don't worry. She'll love you. But when in doubt, tell her you'll spell a necklace for her."

"Dom!" a voice calls.

I turn around to see a beautiful blonde woman running up to him.

She's as tall as he is and reminds me of a Viking warrior princess. Her hair is pulled back into two French braids that are bejeweled. Her brown leather jacket matches her thigh high-heel leather boots that allows her to tower over me. She still looks as though she's in her thirties, but in human years Dom said she's in her fifties, being only sixteen when she had Bash. Her eyes are the same color as Dom's, bright hazel green, and there isn't anything about her that screams vampire.

Until she turns and eyes me; only then do I feel her power like evaporating ice.

"Mom, this is my girlfriend Sayah."

"That's a pretty name," she says, holding out her hand for me to shake. "I'm Adaline."

"Thank you. Pleased to meet you."

There's a sinister softness in Adaline's eyes that is a juxtaposition of beauty and danger. She looks as though she would take you to lunch and treat you well, but would also cut your head off in an instant and not smudge her makeup.

My heart's pounding so hard it might kill me before Adaline can.

Or make me faint.

It's hot in here.

Meeting the parents of a boyfriend is unnerving as it is, but meeting a vampire who's a witch, makes it ten times worse.

A man comes up behind her who matches Adaline's Viking vibe. He's taller than her, which puts him at about six-foot-five. He has blonde hair too, that's more on the dirty blonde side and hangs around his shoulders. He's muscular and has bright blue eyes, his arms covered in ink. He's handsome but in a rugged manly way. I can see him chopping wood on the moors of Scotland in a kilt.

"Dominic," he says, his voice hard and unemotional.

"Father," Dom says, shaking his hand. "This is Sayah. Sayah, this is my dad, Everett."

"How do you do, dear?" he asks.

Both he and Adaline have British accents which is weird because I thought they were from Italy.

As we walk to the car, Dom holds my hand and squeezes it.

"Why are they British?" I ask in a whisper, knowing they can probably hear me anyway.

"We moved around a lot. We lived in England for a long time. My mom liked the way they talked, and I think it probably grew on them after a while."

I nod.

Out of all the things that I'd learned these last few months, misplaced accents are the least of my worries.

As the dark scenery of the highway blazes by in city lights and traffic—although it's around midnight—New York is still buzzing with life at this hour. I let my mind drift to the landscape of tall buildings and businesses, lights twinkling all colors, fading into dark country roads with a copse of trees here and there to a full-blown forest of Uncas-Trees. My mother and aunt Janet had dubbed them Uncas-Trees back when I was a kid driving to Lake George, which are forests of Aspen trees jumbled together so much that they could see Uncas from *Last of the Mohicans* running through them. The old Adirondacks appear ahead like guardians of the upstate part of New York from the busy and bedraggled concrete monsters of the city.

I look through the windshield of the Lincoln Everett is driving and see him take his hand off the wheel and gently put it on Adaline's lap and lovingly they twist their fingers.

It's nice to see monsters embrace each other.

It's close to two in the morning when we arrive at our cabin on the lake, which is all but dark along with the rest of the sleeping neighborhood, save for a few old-fashioned lantern street lamps that line the thin road. The lake is big and beautiful from what I can see though; old, rounded mountains surrounding the still water that reflects all the slumbering cabin lights.

The cabin we pull up to is gigantic.

As we enter the massive entryway, even this room has paintings on the walls. I slip out of my shoes and enter a high-ceilinged kitchen with beams and stainless-steel appliances, black marble, oak furniture, and glass windows from ceiling to floor. Beautiful wainscotting travels all along the edges, giving the mansion a rustic cabin-in-the-woods feel with a hint of opulence and money.

"How are there so many windows in here?" I ask myself, but try to project it to Dom.

"Tapered windows. UV lights can't get in," responds a voice that's not my own.

I realize we now have a shared secret. I can let him into my head when I allow him to.

The kitchen empties into the living room which is furnished with large and plush brown couches, a giant stone fireplace, and the same floor-to-ceiling windows.

"I'll show you two to your room," Adaline says, walking to the far wall where a spiral staircase sits.

I follow her up the stairs and down a long hall to a bedroom at the end.

Another large room, same windows but the ceilings aren't as high here. The bed is a California king four-poster bed, and off to one side, I can see a large bathroom. It's dark, but I can also make out a balcony beyond the two French doors.

"I'm sure you two want to get some sleep," Adaline says. "I'll see you in the morning."

"Goodnight, Mom," Dom says, and kisses her cheek.

She smirks at me and leaves, shutting the door behind her.

"Well, even if I hadn't figured out that you were a vampire by now, I would have known something was up by your parents."

"Why's that?" Dom asks, hoisting his suitcase up to the bed and unzipping it.

"Because they're all murder-y," I reply, getting to my suitcase as well.

He chuckles a bit and pulls out his shower bag.

I take my jeans off and slide out of my panties, slipping on my silk pajama top. I don't wear bras anymore so there isn't one to worry about taking off. As I dress for bed, I can't help but notice him staring at me.

"So that was weird what we did down there," I say, taking my shower bag out as well and retrieving my toothbrush and paste.

"I thought so, too," he says, flashing over closer to me and playing with a button on my shirt.

"What do you think that was?" I ask, slithering my arms around his neck.

"I'm not sure," he answers, peppering the column of my neck with soft kisses.

"Can you see my thoughts a lot?" I inquire, finding it harder to concentrate as he trails kisses down the front of my shirt.

"Only when you let me," he replies, his voice muffled under my skin.

Relief washes over me a bit when I know he can't always read my thoughts. Some things happen in my mind I don't want him to know about.

Not yet anyway.

As he continues to kiss me, he pulls up my shirt and kisses the newly uncovered territory, cupping one of my breasts in his strong hand.

Closing my eyes, I picture that wall of protection that I cage my thoughts within turning paper thin and fading just enough to let him in.

"Fuck me hard against the wall," I unvoice my desire to his mind.

His mouth—that mouth that keeps me up at night—curls, his upper lip exquisitely sculpted, a little bit sensitive and a whole lot of dangerous, telling me, *"Just you fucking wait to see how hard I can fuck you now."*

He flashes me to the far wall and the rush of the air is fucking indescribable as we collide with the drywall, the impact rattling the pictures hanging above it. He caresses my hardened nipple and growls in response, my clit tingling and aching for his touch. But he doesn't oblige me, not yet. He braces his hands above my head against the wall, caging me in, his deadly mouth on mine claiming it for his own.

I chase his tongue, the strokes of it as my hands find the ripples of his arms that tower above me. I drink from his hunger and lift his shirt over his head. He pauses the kiss for a millisecond before the shirt is off and he's back on me, devouring me with teeth and tongue. My fingers tangle in his hair as he rips my shirt off. His mouth consumes the peak of my breast into it; his fang pierces my nipple and that delicious pain eviscerates any other thoughts I have other than I want his cock inside me now.

I find that beautiful dick, hard and gorgeous and just fucking perfect as I slither my hands beneath his pants. The sound that escapes his throat causes both my nipples and clit to tingle in such a way, a symphony would blush at the vibration. His pants are gone now and I have no idea what magick he's using, but I'm here for it. I match his energy and the temperature in the room rises.

He grabs the backs of my knees and pulls me up on him, colliding with my mouth as I interlock my legs behind him, feeling the head of him at my entrance. I arch my hips so he slides against my clit and moan in response. He nips my lower lip and I'm mindless with desire. My head falls back and I see the stars through the ceiling.

Is this his magick?

I look at him and ravenous eyes are on me, devouring my soul with one look.

"You don't care that we're about to fuck in your mom's house?" I unvoice to him again.

"I'll fuck you anywhere. Anytime. Any place. I don't care who's watching."

Fuck that's hot.

I bounce on him, wiggling so that his dick slides closer to entering me, but he flashes us to the other wall with a window facing the dark lake. I moan as he pins my hands above my head. He rocks his hips so that the back of his dick is sliding back and forth on my clit.

"Fuck me, Dom."

His penetrating gaze collides with mine and he pushes into me with one long roll of his hips until he's buried to the hilt within me. I cry out and muffle my scream by biting my hand and he whips my hand away.

"I don't care who hears you, I want the gods to hear you scream my name."

Fuck my life.

I'm already fighting the urge to cum the second his thrusts begin. Whatever power he has or he's using must intensify the feelings of euphoria because *fuck me running,* this shit is almost unbearable.

I writhe on top of him against the wall, matching his thrusts, grabbing for anything to anchor me to the Earth as the entire world tilts.

"Harder."

He moves at a pace I can't comprehend, and I don't know how I'm being held up anymore. His hands are everywhere.

They're on my nipples, on my neck, on my ass, and in my hair.

But most deliciously, he is massaging my clit at the same time pummeling me with his hard and glorious dick. The motions can only be described as akin to my vibrator at home—the rabbit with vibrating ears.

Yeah. That's what vampire sex is like.

Holy fucking gods in heaven, this man is now like my own personal dildo. As the wave of my orgasm plummets me into outer space, I see colors that don't exist in this reality; I hear angels singing and volcanoes erupting; shit, the mountains themselves are quaking with envy as this man nearly kills me with pleasure.

"Then I will fucking die with you."

"Cum with me."

"You feel so fucking good," he purrs. The entire room is spinning and I can see nothing but him.

"Oh. Fuck. Dom, yes! *Yes*! Harder! Harder!" I scream, bouncing my ass to meet his hips, the length of him burying deeper and deeper in me each time.

His control snaps and his eyes flare as he catapults us into the ether. The universe responds to our coiled reserves of power as they snap; my orgasm ruining me from the inside out, destroying any other sensation other than pure, cataclysmic ecstasy.

We shudder as we cum together; I'm riding him and the wave of my orgasm, letting myself feel it from crescendo to hush, the magick in the room pulsing with our desire.

When the world stops spinning, I notice that the entire room is in disarray, even though we only fucked against the two walls.

"Um… What?" I ask.

"Your power. It seems I awakened it a bit." He laughs and the sound of it lulls me to my marrow.

"Wow. That's . . . new."

"I'll take it as a compliment." His drugging kiss is on me again, flashing us over to the bed where I fall on top of him, his hard dick still in me as I ride him slowly.

I want more.

33

CROOKED KIND OF COMFORT

DOM

If loving this woman is going to bring us both to ruin, then fucking her will be our absolution. The way her orgasm collided with mine, shattering us both from the inside out, brought her powers to the surface in a way I've never seen before.

Sharing bits of my darkness in such an animalistic way tortured her slowly, loosening something within her and I watched it unfold, spilling out into the space around us.

The dark halves of us like fucking each other, and whichever half ends up winning, I'm afraid the other half won't survive it.

As she sleeps in the bedroom behind me, I look down at my arms resting on the railing. The mark taunts me like a nasty wound festering in my skin, rotting me from the inside out. I pray to fucking Lilith that firstly, my family doesn't kill my girlfriend before we can get her powers to ignite and second, that my mom can figure out how to get me unmarked.

I think when I do tell them I've been marked, it will cause such turmoil that they'll forget about killing Sayah for a little while. I know my mom will want to do anything to keep this mark from killing me, and therefore, her mind will be preoccupied with that.

A star falls across the sky, catching my attention, and I watch it, consumed with the beauty of the night after being a slave to it for so long. It's one of those crooked kind of comforts; like a trauma bond, finding solace in the very thing that kept me broken for so long.

Being here with Sayah, having her meet my family, and knowing my darkness on a personal level should feel relieving, but it's not. I can't help but think of all the lies I've told or the truths I've withheld to keep her safe.

I have to think of a way to tell her the truth without her hating me.

Thinking of what she may do when she learns the truth—that I do not live in Colorado and only came there to hunt her—I feel that will cause the kind of shatter that is beyond repairable.

She has known so much sadness.

So many things have come for her, have broken her down, and ripped her to shreds. The person she is today—this gorgeous, scintillating witch who wears her sorrow like war paint—was built from the moments that brought her to her knees.

Being a vampire, I have known darkness. I've seen evil and stared true fucking terror in the eyes, and yet I cannot fathom what she's gone through.

I'd do anything to keep pain from making a home in her. I'll seek out her demons and give them their names; I'll learn the shape of her grief to cut out of her soul and add it to mine so she may live lighter for even a day.

To taste my deceit and learn what it costs is a wreckage I cannot afford. Even the ghost of the thought of losing her catches my soul in a vice, a spikey and unyielding kind of torture I wouldn't wish on anyone. The weight of that agony is enough to ruin me, to break me beyond all recognition.

Fuck becoming a grim—if I lose her, that is something I'll never recover from.

If anything comes for Sayah—my family, the warlocks, the fae, the Nyktorim—they may as well take me too. I am nothing without her.

I've found the thing my damned soul has longed for, the very thing that beckons me out of the shadows that lost me. The kiss of darkness has been on my breath longer than she's been alive. Yet the second she entered my life, the wind shattered at my feet, fracturing the evil seeping out of my bones.

She is soothing, like silk and honey and rain and the hurricanes of summer will bow to her. Finding her fire means bending the breeze, tilting the rain, and folding the Earth to her command. Broken flames will climb the pyre on which all the things that came for her lay down to die upon.

As my spiraling thoughts touch the moonlight, the Earth begins to tilt toward my resolve. Until I met Sayah, I'd been parched; the drought from an existence so long and lonely even time became raw and tender.

The way she says my name is like a promise. How she looks at her son like he's her salvation. The way she bleeds words that slide into my center and drop an anchor within me. Her tangled magick searches for softness within me to be soothed. I love her for everything and nothing more than the mere fact that she exists.

To keep the darkness from taking us both, I'd gladly give myself over to this warlock; I'll become a mindless grim to let her live.

If that was the bargain, I'd gladly take it.

I'd take a life of darkness to let her live in the light.

34

REPARTEE WITH MOONLIGHT

SAYAH

As I open my eyes the following day, I see his right arm draped over my bare side. We fucked all night long last night. I came probably eight or nine times, and my pussy is raw and sore today. I almost forgot about the whole reason why we came here, but then I see the mark that looks like a brand on his arm. It's bright white against the rest of his skin, which is a light olive color. I want to rouse him awake and get down to business to get that mark off him. Thoughts are pulsing from me like blood from an open wound, their immediacy sluicing through me.

How will Adaline remove it?

Can she break the bond?

What can we do to get him released?

What the hell are we up against?

He stirs as though the cage of protection around my thoughts is still down, and they are coming alive, escaping, and crawling into his mind.

"Morning," he says, his breath hot and ticking to my shoulder blades.

"Morning," I say in a lofty voice, the kind I use to cover up my real emotions.

The sun shines into the room, and I can now see the lake perfectly from my spot on the bed. It's still early enough in the morning that there's fog coming off the lake and sitting atop it like whipped cream on hot cocoa. The balcony outside looks to be a wraparound because I can't see the beginning or end, just the two chairs that sit outside awaiting company.

"I'm going to take a quick shower," he says, rising from the bed. His cheeky bubble butt flexes as he stretches and grabs some clothes from his suitcase on the floor. "Coming?" he asks as he enters the bathroom, his sexy figure semi-hiding behind the pocket door.

Thinking that a shower is just what I need to calm my aching thoughts, I pull myself out of the comfortable bed and skip to the bathroom, the chill from the air outside the blankets making me shiver.

The large double shower is nice and roomy; he turns the nozzle, and the water spray is still cold. He pulls me into his arms and holds me until the stream is scalding hot, easing the chill of my mind and body.

Shower sex and the calming water helped ease my thoughts, though they're waiting for me as I dry off. After dressing, I check the phone for messages and see two from Gauge.

He had responded to my last message of the night prior, our nightly 'Goodnight, I love you. Sweet dreams. Talk to you tomorrow.' text we always send when we aren't with each other, along with a different character making a kissy face.

> Good morning, boo-boo; I love you and miss you. Have a great day!

I'm hitting send as Dom puts his head on my shoulder from

behind, all dressed and clean and freshly smelling of that glorious cologne.

"Ready to get after it?" he asks.

"Yep," I respond, nodding, and stow my phone in the back pocket of my capris.

He grabs me by the hand and pulls me gently toward the door and down the spiral stairs.

Downstairs, his mom makes some eggs at the large spider burner stove, his father holding her from behind and kissing her neck. She's wearing a sweeping red and white blouse, the painterly drips of crimson making her pale skin stand out like a gleaming chaff.

"Good morning," Adaline says as Everett lets her go and grabs the morning paper from the counter.

"Good morning, Mom, Dad," Dom says, scooting a chair out for me at the twelve-person table underneath the crystal chandelier. The legs scraping against the marble floors echo in the large room.

Everett nods, taking a seat at the bar to read his paper.

Bright light saturates the room, covering everything in a shimmering glow of amber and saffron. As I settle into the seat and pull my phone out again, there's a sudden rush of light. Another woman is suddenly at the table with us in an ephemeral movement. The displacement of air makes me look up.

I guess that vampires have beauty going for them, as it's pertinent to being a killer and luring prey.

Attracting someone to them helps them hunt more efficiently.

Hattie is no exception to this.

She's shorter than Dom but has short brown hair shaved on the sides, spiked up into a faux hawk. Her white skin is as delicate as porcelain, her gray eyes are almost silver, and her lips are lush and painted a soft purple-pink. She has high cheekbones and a classical straight nose. Tattoos cover her, including on her neck and fingers.

"Sayah, this is Hattie."

Hattie grins a little but says nothing.

"Nice to meet you," I utter, but even I can hear the terror in my voice.

"Touch her and die," Dom growls, his muscles flexing as his body tenses.

"Hattie, be nice," Adaline says. "Is everyone hungry?"

"Not for eggs," Hattie answers, her moon-silver eyes not lifting from mine. She reminds me of a rapturous bird or sleek carnivore; something large, frightening, and incapable of human emotion.

My heart pumps hot and fast, and it shows in my cheeks.

To run or not to run?

This is a bad idea. And this is only four of them.

"Hattie," Dom says, his green eyes glowing white instantly, the fangs protruding from his cuspids.

I don't care if he's murder-y right now; that shit is fucking sexy.

"I'm just playing. Relax," Hattie says, grabbing the orange juice from the middle of the table.

"Want eggs?" Adaline asks, having flashed over with her pan.

"Yes, please," Dom says, his eyes returning to normal and fangs retreating. "Where are Jasantha, Ollie, and Scar?"

"They'll be over later for dinner," Adaline replies, spooning eggs onto his plate and then to mine.

"Hattie lives here with us again," Everett grumbles, walking to the table to join us. It's like they cradle their tenderness for each other in harsh words and hide their love in the sharp edges of their villainous manners.

"Daddy loves that I am here." Hattie giggles and plays with some of the eggs with her fork.

"So, what brings you here, Dom?" Adaline says, her emerald eyes passing over Dom with ridged seriousness as she sits down.

The look on his face is incredulous.

Vampires know things. He should know that.

"How'd you know?" he asks with a smirk. Adaline gives him a quelling look. "I've been marked," he says quickly.

All the vampires in the room stop, and the air grows thick.

"What?" Adaline says, dropping her fork.

"I went to kill a bad person the other night, and he was marked. I didn't know. So I killed him and then his mark appeared on me. I saw the warlock's face right when it happened."

"Where's your mark?" Hattie asks, peering over at her brother.

Dom lifts his sleeve and shows them the crescent moon brand mark.

Adaline stands in a blur of colors and a swirl of light as she speeds over to him and grabs his arm. "Oh, Dom," she says, her green eyes growing sad.

"What do you know about this, Mom? Is there anything I can do to get away from this?"

Her eyes spill the answer that she does not want to say. Her head shakes solemnly. "I don't know of anyone personally that has been marked."

"That's not true," Hattie puts in.

Their glances dart over to Hattie, awaiting her response.

"This has nothing to do with what happened to Amanda, does it?" Everett asks.

"Who's Amanda?" I query as Dom rolls down his shirt sleeve to cover the mark.

"Amanda was her girlfriend who was bitten by something that wasn't a vampire and ran off," Adaline says quite harshly.

"Amanda," Hattie interjects querulously, extending the syllables of her name as though she's a bratty teenager correcting her parents, "was bitten by a grimspawn, and I told you this. Mom and Dad think she ran off with another woman, but I—"

"Because you have a history of falling for the wrong women, and things like this always happen to you, and each time they do, you run home heartbroken and mopey," offers Everett as he drags his hawkish gaze to Hattie, which rings eye-rolls from her.

"She was marked, too, Dom," Hattie continues, ignoring Everett and looking at Dominic, her unmerited annoyance with her parents obvious. "I'm telling you. A warlock chose her to be a grimspawn and she was bitten one night while we were out partying. I saw the mark. She began to do things that were not like her, and a few days later, she was gone. But a trail of bodies marked her path. I've been researching since it happened, and I think I can break the spell."

"Was she a vampire?" I ask, my voice shaky.

"Not yet," Hattie says. "She wanted me to turn her. I was going to after we were married. She's my one," she says, and her voice is suddenly sullen. The porcelain of her cheeks looks like they'll shatter from sadness.

"How can you break the spell?" Dom inquires, playing with the eggs on his plate with a fork.

"There's an artifact in the museum in New York City that holds the key to breaking the spell. I need to get it."

"And how do you get it?" Dom asks, a hint of hope in his expression.

"A powerful witch and an even more powerful spell." She pauses and looks at her mom. I hear her voice's optimism but see Adaline's doubt. "The druids were the ones that started the grimspawn spell," Hattie continues, "so they have the key to breaking it. The museum has a key that can be used with the moon to break the spell. We only need her blood and the warlock's blood that marked her."

"What is the key?" Dom questions.

"It's an old rock with some writing on it," Hattie offers. I don't know her well, but I get the impression that she's only giving us bits and pieces. "But I need a witch to help me get into the museum and also to get the rock to ignite."

"I can do it," I answer, thinking this may be my chance to get the murder-y vampire to like me.

I can't help it. I'm a chronic people-pleaser.

And vampire-pleaser now, too, apparently.

Adaline looks at me crossly. "So can I," she adds.

"The more witches, the more powerful the spell," answers Hattie.

"How long from when she was marked to when she was doing strange things?" Dom asks, no doubt weighing his own infliction against that of Hattie's girlfriend.

"A few days," Hattie answers.

"It could be different for you, son," Everett says, picking up on Dominic's concern. "You're a vampire. She wasn't."

"Which makes his bond with the warlock even thicker," Adaline says gravely. "She's not going to give him up easily."

"Which means we have to act fast. Tonight," Dom says sternly.

Hattie gives him a hard stare. "We'll have to get her blood somehow, though, Dom. It won't work without it."

"I'll work on figuring that out," says Adaline.

"Sayah can help with that too, Mom," Dom offers. The look that spreads across Adaline's face is doubtful. "She made me this talisman," he adds, pulling the chain from under his shirt.

Adaline makes no motion that she's the least bit impressed.

"It's spelled. I can go in the sunlight."

Now, her face shifts.

Eyeing the Lapis Lazuli with rapt fascination, as though it's a piece of long-forgotten jewelry she hasn't seen in a millennium, she pulls up the chair next to him. She sits down slowly, takes the trinket between her finger and thumb, and caresses it softly. "This . . . makes it so you can be in sunlight?"

"It does," he murmurs and then nods at me.

My heart swells. "I can make one for you if you'd like."

"Why did it work for her and not Scarlet? Or Mom?" Hattie asks defensively, her tone skeptical.

"I think it's because the moon rules Scarlet and Mom. They have the same curse, so it wouldn't work. Sayah's not the same. She's ruled by light. That's why her spell works."

"You'd make one of these for us?" Adaline asks, and in that moment, her hardness shatters.

The look on Dom's face tells me I've done it.

I've won his mom over.

"I will. For all of you."

I know what this moment has cost Adaline, her letting her warrior façade splinter even a fraction. I know what it means to the creatures of the dark to be reintroduced to the light. Witnessing Dom meet the light again was one of my defining magickal moments. There's a great pleasure within me to help my boyfriend's mom, and the urge to giggle bubbles inside me.

Choking it back down, I look to Everett.

He seems unimpressed.

It'll be more challenging to win him over.

After breakfast, Adaline stands at the sink, rinsing the dishes. Dom and Everett are whispering amongst themselves, reviewing the situation and what has happened to bring Dom to where he is now.

"May I help?" I offer Adaline, handing her the plate.

"Sure," she says coldly and lets me take over, the soft sliver from before all gone.

As Adaline disappears down a hallway, I place the black dishes in the sleek dishwasher one by one until they're all nicely stacked within it. Upon shutting the door, the woosh of air signifies someone is standing next to me, and the hairs on the back of my neck prick up.

Slowly, I turn to see Hattie glaring at me.

Terror coils around my stomach, and I hold my breath.

"Follow me," Hattie demands, and by my frozen limbs, I can tell I'd been ordered to.

Robotically, I follow Hattie down the stone hallway toward the stairs that lead to the basement. Even if I tried to resist, it wouldn't sway the veilweaving of my feet to keep carrying me forward.

Damn, I should have kept the Nightshade on me.

Entering a cozy and brilliant room, the vellichor of the room floors me. It's lined with ceiling-to-floor bookshelves—the kind where you need a ladder on rolling casters to get to the books at the top. Books of all ages, colors, and sizes are tucked into them, not a single space wasted, and my bookish heart swells at the sight, immediately wanting to climb that ladder and investigate them. Amongst the other shelves are jars and vials filled with herbs and other substances, canisters, and tins, bundles of dried sage, and other flowers hanging from the walls and the ceiling. It immediately feels like home.

On the west side of this room is an outdoor patio with a little greenhouse in which Adaline grows her herbs. The lovely little space is complete with those rounded tapered glass windows so she can go in there and use it during the day and not burn up. The room has a massive stone fireplace with comfy chairs surrounding it. The room is cozy and quaint, and I am jealous of not having a room for my spells like this one, instead of a little cabinet.

The beautiful and lithe Adaline is already there, peering into her bookcase and pulling down a few of her oldest and most tattered-looking ones. Hattie takes a seat by the fireplace and pulls out her phone.

"So, tell me about you, Sayah," Adaline says, blowing the dust off the green book she chose and taking a seat on one of the chairs by the fireplace.

Mimicking Adaline and sitting down too, nervousness spills up my insides at being alone with her and Hattie. There's a strong urge to get Adaline to like me, to win her over, but it's hard to tell if she already does.

"What would you like to know?"

Her eyes do not look up from scanning the grimoires. "Anything you feel pertinent to tell me, I guess."

"Well. I'm divorced. I have a ten-year-old who's my world. He's in a wheelchair and has diabetes. I'm in college, I work full time, I write, I beat cancer, and my parents just died."

Figuring I'd throw it all out there and let Adaline choose what she wanted to know next, I laid my heart bare before this vampire.

Adaline's eyes draw up to mine, and her face softens, if not entirely but slightly.

"Wow," she says. "You've been through a lot."

"I have."

"But you didn't mention the witch part at all."

Of all the things I mentioned, I'd forgotten the only thing Adaline wanted to know about.

"I guess I didn't." I play with the fringe on the blanket on the chair's edge.

"I'm sorry about your parents."

"Thank you."

"Was your mom a witch, too?"

"She was. My aunts and grandma were too."

"Did they teach you much?"

"No. They didn't. My mom let me pick my own path, and she was happy when I picked hers by utter luck. But I had to learn a lot of it on my own. She would buy me things, like candles and crystals and everything. But for the most part, I forged my own path."

"What can you do? Besides spell necklaces to help vampires walk in daylight?"

"Um." The fringe is all I can concentrate on. I feel Adaline take the measure of me with every breath and every word I speak. "I can do protection charms. I can spell storms. Make things float. I'm honestly just learning as I go."

"Well, I can teach you a few things if you'd like."

The tension depletes a little bit. "I would love that."

"Okay, here's something," Adaline says, sitting up and changing the subject instantly. "This one here is for lycanthropes to break the curse of the moon. I think it'll work in the same way. We can use the artifact that Hattie wants in addition to the crystal it calls for here."

"I remember something from one of my mom's or grandma's grimoires, too, that had how to glamour someone. We can glamour Hattie to be invisible, and then she can get in that way."

"There'll probably be a sensor that the artifact is sitting on. She'll have to put something in its place. I'll keep looking for a glamour spell."

"While you do that, if I could have a piece of your jewelry you wear all the time, or you wouldn't mind wearing all the time. One from Everett and Hattie too, I can get the sun spell on them for you guys."

"Yes. Here," she says, handing me her wedding ring. It's a giant stone set in golden bands with many diamonds around a larger one.

I'm hesitant to touch it.

"Take it," she says, a little short. "I wear it every day. If it's spelled, I can walk in the sun always. I'll get Everett's in a bit."

"I will need the Lapis Lazuli stone."

"Over there. I keep all my stones in the second drawer to the right."

I stand and take stock of the room around me. I find the drawer Adaline had said and dip into it, grabbing the stone.

Looking back, Hattie and Adaline have already forgotten my existence. I scan the room for the nearest exit, as I need to be out in the elements to conduct my spell. I need to make damn sure I do this right. I don't want to kill my boyfriend's mom the first day I meet her.

That would be awkward as hell.

Seeing a door to the outside through the windows of the greenhouse, I open the door to it and softly close it behind me.

The smell of beautiful wet soil and glorious humidity greet me. I long to peek around at all the plants and herbs that Adaline has within here, but time is of the essence, so instead I make my way to the door that leads outside. Clutching the diamonds, I pull the handle and let myself out, tracking to the lake's edge.

At home doing this, I'd been comfortable. I'm nervous now, being in this strange place, not knowing if his mom likes me, and not knowing if the spell would work this time because I don't have the same passion for Adaline as I do for Dom.

I have to try.

Walking down to the water's edge, the morning sun kisses the still water, illuminating it with an amber coat. Little ripples spill up from the wind's touch, branches of trees bending to the wind. Bright yellow, green, orange, and gold colors pierce through the view, early summer air touching everything in sight.

The last time I'd done this spell, the moon was out, and I had used that as energy to imbue in the jewelry to protect Dom from the sun. Here, the sun's in its early ascent into the sky, and I will have to come up with something different.

Sparing glances down the way, early morning fishermen are setting out on their kayaks, and a few people are taking their sunrise walks along the banks of Lake George.

Behind me, Dom is out on the balcony, eyeing me and basking in the morning sun. I beckon him down to me, as the jewelry on his neck may help me.

"Hey," he says when he arrives, whisking his hand around my waist. "What you up to?"

"I need to spell these," I say, holding out the ring and stone in the palm of my hand. "But when I did yours, I used the moon's energy to protect you. The moon is not out right now. What if I fail?"

"You can do this. The moon is out right now, just in another part of the world. Where is it midnight right now?"

Dom pulls out his phone and Googles what time it is across the world.

"It's midnight in Fiji right now. Put yourself there."

Taking a deep breath, I nod and face the lake. Closing my eyes, I envision myself standing on a beach in Fiji. The ocean blue color of the sky at night is peppered with silver and gold clusters of stars, the sleeping water still bright aqua in the moon's pearly glow. The white sand is soft between my toes and still warm from the afternoon sun, the sound of the waves lulling me into my trance. I have my repartee with moonlight, exchanging secrets and gossip like old friends, and once again ask a favor of the moon.

"Please, Luna," I begin, finishing my silent plea, "I need his mom to like me."

As if in response, the moon twinkles a bit and melts.

I hold the wedding ring and Lapis Lazuli up to the heavens and witness the moon melting again, flowing down the trail of stars to the water, turning the whole ocean silver. This time, I bend down and dip the ring and stone into the silver water like melted dimes, and when I pull my hand away, my entire fist is coated with silver.

It drips onto the sand, where it freezes like metallic tears. When I open my palm, the Lapis Lazuli is glowing like a firefly, melting, swirling around the diamond ring, and slowly entering it.

The smell of briny air swells as the wind picks up, swirling my hair around my face in the tropical island atmosphere.

I close my hand over the ring again and shut my eyes, and lightning lights up the sky as the moon returns to normal.

The soft feeling of the sun on my skin causes me to open my eyes, and once again, I'm standing on the lake's edge with Dom, ring in hand, burning my skin with its newfound power.

When I open it, the ring is red-hot, like metal tempered in fire to forge a sword, but my hand is unharmed.

"That's crazy," Dom murmurs, attempting to touch the ring in my hand.

"Don't!" I warn. "It may burn you."

"I heal fast," he quips, smirking.

He grabs the ring, and the red glow dies before returning to normal.

"Do you think it worked?" I ask as he examines the now normal color ring.

"I do. It feels powerful. Like it's heavy and hot, and it doesn't make sense for how light you think it should be."

"All right, I'm going to go give it to her. Wanna come?"

"Yeah, this I gotta see," he says, laughing as I clench my jaw, biting back an annoyed retort.

It's annoying that he's sitting back, letting me try to win over his mother alone.

His fucking *vampire* mother.

Upon reentering the spell room, Adaline's still sitting in her chair, eyes laser-focused on the text within the book that's sprawled out on the table before her.

"It's done," I say hesitantly, not wanting to interrupt her concentration. "I'd like for you to stick a hand out first, to make sure, before . . ."

"Before I burst into flames?" Her cold eyes fall on me, and I'm unsure if this is Adaline's attempt at her son's dry humor.

"Well . . . yeah," I stammer.

Adaline saunters over to me and holds out her hand. "You need to have more confidence in yourself, girl."

I drop the ring into her open palm. "It worked."

"Then you won't begrudge me walking directly into the sunlight?"

"No, ma'am." My voice is even.

She flashes her white teeth, fangs not barred, but I can see where they should be. My heart races.

Adaline's scary.

I've been scared of people before, but never like this. She has an air about her that reaches in and grips my stomach like a vice. The strength in her body is evident in the way her muscles are fine-tuned, not massive like a bodybuilder, but just enough that they're accentuated when she's not flexing. Reminding me of a shield maiden that stepped off the battlefield, I can tell she's stabby as fuck even when she's nowhere near a knife.

Placing the ring back on her finger, she walks to the greenhouse and throws the doors open.

My heart stops.

What if it hadn't worked, and I'm about to kill Dominic's mother?

Adaline looks back one final time before emerging through the doors into the greenhouse and then out into the outside world.

Nothing happens.

Not only does she not burn, but she also doesn't seem to care that she's out in daylight again for the first time in more than 200 years.

It must be that she can enjoy the light in her house with windows that protect her.

Either that, or she's hard and cold.

The woman gives me whiplash with her reactions to things. One second, she's deep in awe at the trinket I'd spelled for Dom; the next, she's not impressed she had stepped outside in sunlight for the first time in hundreds of years. Maybe it's to cover her earlier slip of letting me see a softer side of her at all.

Who knows?

Entering back into the house, she stops in front of me.

"Thank you," she says, no emotion is present in her words.

"You're welcome."

Adaline grabs my hand unexpectedly. The steel of her eyes burns into mine, and I look to Dom for assistance. He gives me a smile that disarms me.

"Do you feel that?" she asks, her voice like the rush of a river, cold and calculating.

Other than her cold hands on my forearm, I feel nothing. I shake my head.

"I've given you a bit of my power. I want you to try it on Dom. It'll hurt him a bit, but the pain isn't real. What you're doing is making them believe their worst fear is happening to them. You'll soon find out what Dom's worst fear is. Being around this many vampires and being as powerful a witch as you are, you need something defensive to use against us. Because you are ruled by the three-fold law—whatever you do comes back at you three-fold, it won't affect that because you're not doing any damage."

Adaline is helping me even though she doesn't seem to like me in the slightest, which confuses me. Somewhere in Adaline's dark heart sparks an affinity for me, I'm sure of it.

"What do I do?"

"Imagine him experiencing his worst fear. Whatever their fear is, it will take over their mind, which will be all they can see. It may cause temporary paralysis or unbearable pain, depending on what that fear is. It may be useful, especially since we must lure this warlock here to get her blood. I don't wanna take any chances."

"And I have to try it on Dom?" I can't hide the hesitation swelling in my voice.

"He'll be fine, I promise."

I look over to my man leaning against a bookshelf, one eyebrow quirked up in a mocking 'come and get me' manner. His dapper demeanor is dripping with confidence, teasing me to try it.

As much as I don't want to hurt him, I have to try my new power on someone before luring a powerful warlock here. He changes his stance, squaring his shoulders, steeling himself for what I'm about to do.

I close my eyes, take a deep breath, and search my mind for my newfound power. Envisioning myself swimming through my blood, I canal through networks of veins and arteries, searching for anything that seems to be newly placed. Deep in between my shoulder blades is where it's located, a bright orange and delicate new power. It's a soft, sizzling sensation that reminds me of being electrocuted, but just slightly. Pulling it to the front of my mind, I push it out from myself and picture it like a net draping over him.

His hazel eyes grow wide; an invisible force we can't see is crawling up his sleeves as he bats at it convulsively like he's on fire. Screaming, the imaginary flames grow worse, and he falls to the floor, trying to snuff out the flames that are engulfing his pants now. I keep my eyes locked on him, and he wails.

Before I can let him go, the displacement of hot air steals my concentration, and Hattie stands before me. Her ivory fangs are barred, her eyes white and cat-shaped, the dexterity with which she arrives at me unbridled. The glacial stare and hiss she emanates at me cause me to almost lose consciousness, but Adaline's sparring grace steps in and shoves Hattie back. Hattie flies and lands on the beam, crashing down to the floor.

"It's an exercise, Hattie," Adaline scolds her as she peels herself off the floor and gives Adaline a mocking stare.

My breath returning to me, I notice I let Dom go in the upheaval, and the make-believe fire has diminished.

He stands and brushes off his pants, looking embarrassed. "All right, not bad," he says in exultation, an embarrassed inflection in his voice.

"I think it's good for her to have a defensive power," Adaline concurs. "Considering we have to get that warlock's blood somehow, and she's a human in a house full of vampires."

"I agree."

The feelings bite at me, not wanting to hurt my love. I stroll up to him and slip my arm into his crook, laying my head on his shoulder as he kisses the top of my head. It's good that Adaline gave me a new power, invigorating even. Seeing Hattie in her full vamp mode scared the shit out of me but also drew a feeling of dangerous excitement as well.

It takes the rest of the afternoon for me to calm down. My nerves are on edge, and I am absolutely terrified. Being here with them isn't supposed to be the vacation of my dreams, but I don't know if Everett and Adaline like me and his sister tried to kill me.

And that isn't even the rest of them.

As Dom and I are outside on the patio, enjoying the setting sun, he sits close to me on the porch swing and strokes my hand.

"So, you did some good bonding with my mom."

"She hates me," I say.

"She doesn't hate you. She's hard to get to sometimes."

"I made her a ring and didn't know if it was gonna work, and she waltzed into the sunlight like it was nothing. She didn't care that it was the first time she'd been in the light in two hundred years. I expected more."

"That's just my mom, Say. She is a hardened warrior woman. She doesn't show a lot of emotions. But when she does, she does that fiercely, too."

"I wish I knew if she liked me or not."

"She shared a gift with you to protect you. She likes you."

"Well, that's good, I guess."

"You'll grow on her, Sayah. I promise."

"Do I make the talismans for the others then, too?"

"Yes. When the time comes. Ollie and Scar will be here soon. Just do all of theirs at once. Make it easier on yourself."

"What about Hattie?"

"Let her suffer," he jokes.

"Dom—" I scold.

"She's a bitch. Always has been."

"You *are* the one that said she was murder-y." I laugh. "I'm making her a ring. She's going to help us break this curse on you."

"We hope."

"Please stay optimistic. Your mom found a spell that helps break the curse of the lycanthrope. We're gonna go with that, and that should work the same."

"Well. Let's hope that I don't turn all murder-y til then."

His head cocks sideways, again like he hears something.

"What is it?" I ask.

"Scar is here."

Glancing through the windows, I can see around five new people entering the house.

"Which one is Scarlet?" I ask as we stand, preparing to go into the house.

"She's the one, right there," he says, pointing to her. She's not quite as tall as he and has long, wavy, bright blonde hair. Her eyes are green, her lips are full, her body curvy, and She. Is. Stunning. The sculpted angles of her face make her seem like she should be on posters for fantasy lovers, as she looks like a vampire. She's too stunning to be a human. She looks photoshopped.

"And I'm assuming the redhead is the siren?" I ghost the sentence out, feeling an uneasy grace seep about me.

It's nerve-racking.

"Yep. Don't worry, babe, you got this. They're gonna love you."

The wind picks up and blows loose strands of hair into my eyes, which I pull away as Dom interlocks his hand with mine and tugs me toward the door.

I'm not sure which of the creatures I'm more afraid of, but the siren is one of them that makes chills of apprehension skim the surface of me. Not to mention the twin, Scarlet. If it isn't going well with Adaline, Everette, or Hattie, I'm sure it's going to hell in a handbasket with Scarlet and Jasantha.

Taking a deep and calming breath to soothe me, I fortify myself as we again enter the house.

"Domie!" Scarlet squeals as he drops my hand and flashes over to his sister. He picks her up and spins her around, her lengthy hair whipping through the air fast enough to make a sound.

"Scar-bar!" he answers as he sits her down.

The breeze from the open door thrashes my hair around again, and when I remove it, I see Jasantha whip her gaze at me like she found my scent on the breeze. She has beautiful dark midnight skin, her eyes are green and cat-like, her lipstick matches her nails, and her hair is a beautiful red-almost-purple color. Her arm candy is human, from what I can tell, a tall, unnaturally muscular man with a short beard.

"Everyone, this is Sayah. Sayah, this is my twin sister, Scarlet; this is Jasantha and her fiancé Joe; my little brother, Ollie, and his girlfriend, Allison."

Ollie is a pretty vampire, shorter than Dom. Still, they're similar in looks, except Ollie has no visible tattoos. He wears his hair a little longer, wavy, dirty-blond, and has green eyes. Allison looks unnaturally beautiful as well. She has a pixie haircut and brown hair, her eyes are blue, and her face is a little rounder and bright with an aquiline nose.

All eyes are on me, and I'm frozen in my steps. *Thinking* about being in a room full of killers and actually *being* in a room full of killers are two totally different things. The acquiescence of such only abates minutely with the thought that at least there's one more human in the room with me.

Joe.

I can tell by the normalcy of his looks, demeanor, and stature.

"Nice to meet you all," I manage, but my voice betrays me, coming out quiet and shaky.

"Pleased to meet you, Sayah," Ollie says, and is here in a wisp to kiss my hand.

At least one of them is pleasant to me.

"So," Scarlet says, ignoring me, "tell us why you're here, Dom."

"I'm gonna start dinner," Adaline announces. She and Everett have been standing in the kitchen prepping the food, Everett handing her things that she asks of him. It's sweet.

The kitchen table is set with elegant black plates atop the giant wooden table, the candlelight gleaming, delicate silverware resting on black serviettes. Thin yet tall wine glasses are resting by every plate—set for ten people—and bottles of unopened wine are lined in the middle, along with a few wine keys. There are also bottles of what I assume can only be blood among them. They're opened and unlabeled, the clear glass showing the thick, dark crimson liquid within.

Dom tugs me with him to the table and pulls out a chair for me to sit, the rest of the group following our lead.

"He was marked," offers Hattie flippantly, scooting a chair out and sitting.

Scarlet turns a lighter shade of pale. "What?" she breathes, taking the chair next to Dom.

The velocity with which he pulls up his sleeve is disarming—like he wants to get this particular part of the visit out of the way. The brand is white and gleaming, still the obdurate mark it's intended to be.

"Oh my god, how did this happen?"

"I killed the wrong person," he culls.

"We're figuring out a way to break the curse," interjects Hattie.

"How are you gonna do that?" asks Ollie.

Hattie rolls her eyes. "I've been researching. There's an artifact I'm gonna steal that will help Mom and Sayah here break his curse. If it works, I'm gonna use it on Amanda."

"*If* it works?" asks Dom, his eyes shading the emotions he wears on his face.

"Well, yeah." Jasantha's fingernail elongates like fangs do, and she uses it to open a bottle of wine, the popping sound of the cork making me jump. "Dom, this is dealing with a warlock. Those things are half-demon. They're impossible to kill."

"We're not killing her," Dom says defensively, "we're breaking the curse that bonds me to her."

"Have you seen her yet?" Jasantha asks, pouring herself a glass of wine, the lug of the liquid entering the glass like a lullaby in the intense conversation.

"I saw her when I first got the mark. But nothing yet."

"How are you gonna break the curse?" asks Allison.

"Using a lycanthrope spell breaker," Adaline says from the stove.

"Using *her* help?" Scarlet says derisively, nodding her head toward me.

"She's a witch," Hattie remarks.

"A good one, too," Dom adds, defending me.

"What makes this normal-looking woman a *good* witch?" Jasantha asks, and my heart faints; the ineffable feeling of running traps me beneath the surface of something, and the air is thin in my lungs. I look to Dom for comfort.

What if I faint right here in front of all these vampires?

What kind of witch would that make me?

"She spelled us jewelry that lets us walk in daylight," Adaline says genially, and I'm surprised it's her that comes to my rescue.

Throwing the gauntlet was a good call, though. Because all eyes are on me again, but they're curious now, searching.

"You can do that?" Scarlet asks, her cold, incredulous eyes now apprise me.

I give her the sweetest smile I can muster. "I can. I'll make you all one if you want. I need a piece of jewelry you wear all the time. Or that you wouldn't mind wearing all the time."

Dom smiles at me.

The sound of the front door slamming shut causes everyone in the room to look over at who entered.

My heart takes a running leap out of my chest, and I'm pretty sure my jaw also hits the floor. For walking in that door is none other than my midnight mystery vampire.

Sebastian.

35

DESTRUCTIVELY DECADENT

SAYAH

My eyes betray me.

They have to be.

He doesn't see me yet, or if he does, he doesn't acknowledge me.

Handsome is too plain a word to describe this man. He's breathtakingly gorgeous. He's tall, and his black hair hangs slightly disheveled around his face. His prominent jawline is so sturdy, it's as if he has been sculpted. Wearing all black—black leather jacket with the collar flicked up, black jeans, black boots—the black makes the blue of his eyes stand out even more, vivid enough to cut through the most unforgiving dark. Although the blue of them is so other-worldly, he doesn't need the sea of black framing them to make them stand out. The edge of his aura is sharp and cool, like fire.

There's a girl at his side, but I barely notice the woman because I'm trying to breathe, trying to figure out why this very real man is entering Dom's parent's house, out of my mind and into my life.

"Bash!" cries Adaline, setting her spatula down to greet him.

I'm sitting at Dom's side at the far end of the table, next to Hattie who's at the head. I hunch down behind Dom's shoulder and focus on breathing, trying not to bring attention to myself that I know Sebastian, who now I know is Bash.

Dom's brother.

"What are you doing here?" Adaline asks, wrapping him up in a hug.

He still hasn't noticed me.

And even if he does, who's to say he'll also know who I am?

"Well..." His voice is exactly the way it had been in my dreams. Cool, calm, deep, like a babbling brook. "A little birdie told me that my little brother was in town. With a girl no less, so I had to stop by and see for myself."

My heart races.

Dom glares at Ollie—the little birdie—and Ollie also greets him.

Scarlet, Jasantha, Hattie, and Dom exchange looks of annoyance, and something unspoken between them all.

The woman at Bash's side is mesmerizing. Although I don't know her—or him, for that matter—I'm jealous of her. Of her looks, of her life, of the man on her arm.

She is breathtaking as well. Her eyes almost glow a pale brown, like an autumn yellow. Her hair is blonde and hangs in waterfall curls to her shoulders, and her large, prominent breasts spill out of her shirt.

I try to hide my head behind Dom, unable to see Bash as he turns around, hoping he won't see me.

Nobody at the table gets up to greet him. They remain seated, and the silence is resounding throughout the house. A disquieted tension.

So many things are running through my mind.

"Hello, siblings," Bash says, and I can hear his boots clunking on the floor as he approaches us.

This is it.

He's about to see me, and I'll know by his reaction if he knows me too.

No one answers him.

Instead of finishing his walk to the table, he turns to his father, sitting at one of the barstools on the island.

"Father," he says casually, indifferent. There's steel in his voice.

"Sebastian," answers Everett. "What brings you to Lake George?"

"I told you. I've come to see my brother." His voice is cold, like a rapier's samba—elegant, deadly, and utterly merciless.

"That's bullshit, and you know it," Dom says defensively, and *now* he's about to turn around and see me.

He turns.

Those blue eyes catch mine, and he stops. I'm immured by his gaze.

Nothing is said. I can't breathe.

"What do you want, Bash?" Dom asks at my side.

His eyes linger on mine momentarily, and I can't tell if he recognizes me. "Why, I don't want anything, baby bro." His eyes leave mine, and he narrows his gaze on Dom. "Just wanted to see your sweet, cherub face is all. Haven't seen you in, what? Eighty years or so. Wanted to see how you are, what you've been up to. Meet your girl."

He sits down at the table across from Dom and me and pours himself a glass of wine.

"Sit, baby," he orders, and the woman flashes over to him and sits.

She's a vampire, too, obviously.

He pours her a glass of wine and hands it to her.

"Siblings, this is Talora. Talora, this is Hattie and Dom. You met Ollie over there, Jasantha, don't know the dude here, Ollie's girl Allison, Scarlet, and Dom's woman...I'm sorry, what's your name, princess?"

My heart's pounding so loud, I'm sure the entire room can feel it like bass in a little car.

"This is Lasayah," Dom answers for me. Hearing him use my full name makes me feel like I'm in trouble.

Maybe he's being formal to hold a point with his brother.

The brother that has been haunting my dreams for months.

Bash holds out his hand for me to take, but I hesitate.

"Lasayah," he whispers, sliding his tongue carefully across each syllable of my name.

A feeling of virulent and noxious love hits me like a tidal wave. I'm sure if I hold out my hand, it'll be shaking. But I do. And it's not.

Bash stands and grasps my hand, pulling it to his lips. "Pleased to meet you, Sayah."

The way his mouth caresses my name holds a viscous potency, a hesitating and murderous curiosity all rolled into that decadent cadence.

Black hair disarrayed, blue eyes brilliant with a glint of danger and rapture as though seeing me is all the joy in his heart, he calls me by the name that only people who know me call me. He knows me. I can see it in those crystal blue eyes.

We've been haunting each other's dreams, and I know that more than anything else.

An imagined chill laps at the nape of my neck, along with a wave of unnervingly intense emotions. I fight to breathe normally; the feeling of asphyxiating sends hot flashes to my cheeks, and I swallow hard, trying to calm myself.

Dom looks at me, and I feel a tickling in my mind like he's trying to get in. I pull my hand back and look at Dom, shaking my head as though telling him I'm all right, fortifying myself against his attempt.

"Why are you here?" Dom asks again, his brows furrowing together as his frown turns grim.

Bash plays with the glass, slipping his fingertip along the top, making it sing. "I told you. I wanted to see you."

His eyes catch mine again, and I fall into them, take a running spill into his darkness, and feel myself falling into a void, unable to return.

I look away.

"That's a fucking lie, and you know it," Dom retorts.

"Quit with the bull shit already," Everett says raucously from the bar. "We can always use Jasantha to get you to spill the truth, so stop beating around the fucking bush."

"All right!" Bash says, and his voice is terrifying. "All right. I need a favor."

"A favor?" Dom asks. "What do you want now?"

"I need a drop of each of your blood. It's for a spell."

"What kind of spell?" Scarlet asks, flaying him with her gaze.

Taking a quick slug of the wine, he says, "I can't say. But just know it's not shady."

"Bash, everything you do is shady," responds Jasantha.

"No, it's not." Bash is indignant. His voice is defensive now, "It's to break a curse. That's all I'm telling you."

"We're kind of in the middle of breaking our own curse," Hattie says.

"What curse do you have?" Bash asks, and suddenly, it dawns on me that this is a typical dinner conversation for vampires.

"Dom was marked," Hattie answers defiantly.

Bash's eyes draw cold indifference initially, then grow a little lighter. "What?"

"A tracker," Dom answers. "I'm marked for necromancy."

"*Ooh*, who's the warlock? She hot?"

"Bash!" Adaline scolds, setting down a big bowl of salad on the table. "Regardless of the long quarrel between you two, you're brothers. You need to stop it."

"So," Bash continues, and his furtive glances at me are not going unnoticed. "How are you gonna break it? From what I understand, they're part demon. Their curses are unbreakable."

"We have a plan," Hattie says. "And speaking of, we better get on that. Who knows how much time we have?"

"Right," Adaline says, "after dinner."

"I'll help," Bash offers, but there's something plaintive about it. "However, I can."

Dom gives him an incredulous look before his eyes wander to mine, shaking his head. "When have you ever done anything that isn't selfish?"

As Bash is about to respond, Adaline sits a heavy plate of meatloaf on the table, the thud against the oak interrupting the siblings.

"Eat," she orders.

Only sounds of plates thudding, utensils scraping, and wine pouring emanate from the large room.

The old myth that vampires only ate blood creeps up again. Since knowing Dom, I know they don't consume human food to fulfill hunger. They use food to suppress it.

"So, can I have your blood?" Bash asks, interrupting the silence. No one answers. "I'll help with this curse, then you help me with mine."

"As long as afterward, I never see you again," replies Dom as he cuts a piece of meat with his fork.

There's a twinge of disbelief on Bash's face, and then it's gone. The warp and weft of old resentments and alliances hanging between them. "Deal."

"All right," Adaline says after eating dinner and cleaning dishes. "We better get a move on and start on that spell. We need to get Hattie ready for her mission."

We're all standing around the island, chatting amongst ourselves and helping Adaline with whatever we can.

Wiping her hands on a dishtowel, Adaline flings it on the counter and walks toward the hallway. Everett subtly places his hand on the small of her back to walk with her.

I let Dom pull me, aware of where Bash is. Even if he isn't in my peripheral, I can feel him as one would feel an electric forcefield.

Upon entering the spell room, Adaline moves her arms in a swooping motion that brings the fire in the fireplace roaring to life. Dom, not going to be part of the spell casting, takes a seat on the chairs by the fire and retrieves his phone.

"Hattie, stand there," Adaline orders, pointing to a place before the fire. Doing as she's told, Hattie takes her place where her mom had instructed. "Now, we make a circle around her."

I fall in line next to Scarlet and Adaline, irresolutely grabbing each woman's hands. They're cold, but it's a bone-deep cold, not just their skin. The feeling and tension in the grip is worse, Scarlet's more so than Adaline's.

"Repeat after me," Adaline instructs. "And while doing so, imagine a blanket of invisibility covering Hattie. Picture her like a ghost, iridescent and able to walk through walls. *'Impero te, impero ti invisibillis. Te astringuo lingua. Impero ti invisibillis.'"*

"Impero te, impero ti invisibillis. Te astringuo lingua. Impero ti invisibillis," we articulate, each time our voices growing in volume.

Doing magick with his mom and sister is unnerving and unreal. Still, I concentrate as hard as possible on Hattie pulling this off.

A crystal passes between us, and when it's my turn to hold it, I pull all my energy from myself, picturing Hattie becoming invisible, and put it into the rock. The crystal burns in my hand, and I hold it before me when it's almost too hot to hold anymore.

It's glowing.

I pass the crystal to Adaline, who then gives it to Hattie.

The glow dies down, as well as the chanting.

"When you're ready," Adaline says, her dark lashes sweeping up as she blinks, "call upon its power, and it will make you invisible."

Hattie nods and tucks the crystal into her bra.

"You'll need this," Adaline adds, handing her a heavy stone. "Put this on the sensor so the alarm doesn't go off."

"I'm coming with you in case anything weird happens," Scarlet says, glancing from Hattie to her mom.

"Dom is going too," says Adaline, moving over to the table. "This is his curse to break, and he should be there."

Hesitation hits my heart, thinking of the last time I sent him to a city on a mission.

That's what got him marked.

This is all my fault.

"So, me, Dom, and Scar?" Hattie asks, walking over to the chair to put on her boots. "Shouldn't Ollie come too? You know, one more male backup in case he and Dom have to veilweave anyone?"

"We can send Ollie, too," Adaline agrees, putting her spell items away.

"It's a four-hour drive," Hattie says, lacing up her other boot. "We better get moving."

Silence again befalls the group as we exit the spell room. Dom's hand in mine is no comfort to what we will experience. Not just him leaving me alone with vampires, but there's something sinister in the air. I can feel it, like coming down with a cold. Nausea pools in me, and aches filter through my bones.

Bash is sitting on the couches with Talora, and Allison is at the table with Jasantha. Joe, Ollie, and Everett are outside puffing on a cigar, the austere smoke of it illuminating in the pale porch light, the dark lake invisible in the background.

Dom beckons Ollie with his finger, and he appears before us on a breath.

"We're going with Hattie to get the artifact," he instructs.

Ollie nods, scratching his chin, the sound of the stubble on his face resounding. "All right. Leaving our girls here then?" he asks.

"Yes," Dom says and looks at me. His green eyes slant a bit. He, too, has the memory of the last time he went away to a city. "It's gonna be okay," he tells me as he reads me. "The spell will work. I know it."

I'm not sure whether it's his vampire allure that makes me believe it or if something surfaces in myself that makes me think it's going to be okay, but suddenly, I feel like it is.

Ollie's next to Allison in that same inhuman movement, explaining what he's going to do. When he's back, we walk the four of them to the vehicles outside, and I let Dom swoop me up into a hug.

"Be careful," I tell him softly.

"I will, love."

He kisses me sweetly and then evaporates into the car.

Sounds of the car doors shutting and the engine roaring to life skim my ears, and I shiver, maybe at the still early spring air or at what they're going to do. The headlights come on, and the echoing of tires on gravel replaces all other sounds.

When they're gone, crickets and a distant owl hum to me.

I'm left alone with his vampire family and the brother who's dangerous and terrifying, whom I'd been in secret assignations with.

At least I get the feeling that Adaline likes me.

I make my way back into the house. As I walk by Bash as he sits with Talora recumbent in his lap, he looks at me, and that fury catches me sideways and hard.

Ignoring it, I walk up the spiral staircase and back into my bedroom.

Walking to the balcony, I lean on the railing and stare at the stars.

The night is calm; there aren't any interruptions of clouds in the sky. The winds are sleeping, and yet the trees still sway. The smell of moist Earth touches my nostrils as I notice how bright and sparkly the night sky is. The moon's coming up, not quite half a moon, but the silver in it puts any silver on Earth to shame.

As I look up and beg the moon to keep my man safe, I feel Sebastian's presence before I know he is there.

Turning slowly, I see him in the doorway.

My lungs forget how to draw air.

"I know you," he says, his dark voice shattering any calm I'd just found.

I don't say anything; I don't know what to say. I let my gaze sweep over him.

If he's here, that means that he's my death. I know death. I've stood on the narrow edge of it before, and it doesn't scare me now.

Though every fiber in me tells me that it should.

Without even so much as a sound, he's next to me. I try to fight looking at him, knowing that with him standing so close, I'll fall into those eyes again, and this time, with him in person, I may never recover.

I remember all the times we'd let go of consciousness together, sharing fits and starts of each other's slumbering worlds.

"You know me, too," he says, his voice drawing shivers from my spine.

The smell of him is dangerous, like cologne and midnight. There's a hurricane in his eyes and a fire in his bones that tempts me, and I know if I get caught up in his allurement, I'll burn in those flames and drown in that storm.

There's no fire this time, but he hasn't bitten me.

At least, not yet.

"Why do I know you?" I ask, fighting the urge I feel surging inside my every limb. The only choice I have is to accept the madness.

"You've been in my dreams for months." There it is. His peerless gaze ensconces me, slowly sweeping up my body, his eyes drinking up every feature of my face.

Does he feel this passion that I feel? The passion that feels like I would go to the ends of the Earth for him? That I would burn in his fire no matter how bad it hurts because I like how he burns me? That every lingering moment in his life has put him on this path that led up to this moment on this balcony right now?

"You are the one that has been in mine," I state when I finally find my voice, not moving an inch toward him because I don't trust him.

Or myself.

"I think you have that backward."

"Regardless, what the hell does this mean? Why have we been dreaming of each other?" The tremble in my voice gives him conviction, and even though this is the first word we're speaking awake to each other, it isn't. It's as though we have spoken to each other millions of times in thousands of different lives. This is not the first time we have spoken.

"I don't know," he says, and the coolness of his voice trudges through my existence one cadence at a time. I get the feeling he knows this part. He knows it well.

He inches closer, and I feel like I'm being pulled, like his lips are magnets that need mine to feel alive, pressed against them to feel his own existence.

Somehow, I pull my gaze away.

"Sayah," Bash says, and when he says my name, it feels like a warm summer venom has glided through my skin. "Dom can't know."

Dom.

I'd forgotten of Dom.

But why can't he know? And why does Bash care?

"What is it that he isn't supposed to know about?" My thoughts are splintering.

He's too beautiful to not look at.

"The dreams. We've been dream-walking to one another."

"What does that even mean?"

"I don't know what it means," he says, inching closer to me once again. He's so close I can count each one of his glorious dark eyelashes.

A knowing deep within his eyes tells me he does know. He's familiar with this, and I cannot shake that feeling.

"You burn me," I say harshly. "In every dream. You kiss me. Then you bite me. Then I burn."

"I know. I'm in them, too." His tone is almost frigid.

"What does that mean?"

"I don't know," he says again, his dark eyebrows dancing above his eyes. "I had to see for myself that you knew who I was, too. That you have been having the same dreams as me. Each one is so real, and the next day, I feel so . . . different. Your light feeds me, and every time I get to breathe you, I live a little easier, and life is a little less painful the next day."

That's precisely what he had told me in my last dream of him.

I'm having déjà vu.

"What about the last one? In my room? Were you really there?"

"Yes." He peers at me through narrowed eyes, a wistfulness passing over his expression.

"How?"

"I don't know. All I know is there's something about you that I need to live."

"I barely know you. I'm with your brother. You're with Talora. This is crazy!"

"I don't care about any of that. The feeling I get when I see you in my dreams is something I have ached for. I don't care how long it takes. I will have you."

"But you burn me. Doesn't that mean anything at all to you? Because it does to me."

"I think that's a metaphor for something."

I bite back an angry retort. "I don't want to try it out" is what I say instead, folding my arms demurely around me.

I can't move again; his lips inch closer to mine, and I'm curious if it is a metaphor. Maybe it's a sign to me that he's that passion, that all-consuming, ineffable love I'm missing in my life, and that's what the fire is for.

The fog grows thick, and I remember there's someone I have feelings for, but I can't think of who that is now.

Then it hits me that this is all his power.

All vampires have a special power; this must be his. To make me feel at ease and to forget that man I came here with.

Fighting against the fog, I push back against it as hard as possible.

My nose wrinkles. I rummage through my soul, trying to find that power, to dredge it up and throw it at him, and there's something in me that doesn't want to know what his worst fear is. Even though he's a monster, his worst fear is probably abysmal.

Backing away from me suddenly, he must've sensed that I was searching for something to divest him of. He folds his arms across his chest protectively.

"Bash?" comes Talora's voice from down the hall.

He looks toward the bedroom and then back toward me.

"Dom can't know," he says again.

Then he's gone.

The further he gets from me, the more and more the fog lifts and the details about the moment that had just happened become clearer.

So many questions are milling through my mind that I almost forgot why we're here.

The curse and the artifact they have left to retrieve.

Putting Bash as far as I can away from my mind, I decide the best thing to do is ignore him and let him fade away.

Maybe there's a spell I can do that will erase him from my mind and stop him from revisiting my dreams.

Wondering if Adaline will mind much if I peruse through her grimoires, I head back out of the bedroom and down the spiral staircase.

The room is quiet; a few others sit on the couches watching something on T.V. Bash is not on this floor, so he must have retired to one of the bedrooms with his lady.

I go around the kitchen and down the stairs to where the spell room is located.

Adaline's not in the room.

There's an eerie feeling in my heart.

This is a vampire's dwelling; her secrets, herbs, and spell books are here. I do not find it within me to try and go through a book, even if it's a simple meandering, looking for a spell.

It's a spell I need to break a bond I have with one of her sons.

The other son.

Maybe it can wait until I get back home to do it.

As I'm leaving, I hear voices from a slightly ajar door down the hall from the spell room.

I remember seeing it in passing when we first came down here.

It's Adaline's office.

Trying not to listen as I walk past, I overhear.

"So that would make him a tribrid then?" comes the voice of someone I don't initially recognize.

"Yes." This is Adaline's voice.

I back myself to the wall to listen and not be seen.

"He's part demon, part witch, part vampire."

"And you think that's the curse he's trying to break?"

I now realize it's Jasantha's voice whom Adaline's talking to.

"It has to be," Adaline replies, her voice full of worry. "I don't know what other curse he could be talking about."

"If he's part demon, wouldn't that make him a warlock then?"

"Yes, but one kept the other at bay because I'd been doing my own magick and made the vampire curse. Until now, it would seem."

"Are you going to talk to him about it?"

"I'm going to try. But not with that Talora woman around."

They stop talking, and my heart stops with them. I shouldn't be hearing this.

Bash is a tribrid? But how?

"Well," Jasantha begins again, and I creep away from the door as quietly as possible.

I return to my bedroom without running into anyone and collapse on the bed.

So, Bash is trying to break his curse, but what curse would that be? The warlock curse? Does it mean he is also marked to become a grimspawn?

So many questions are running through my head again, and I want to talk to Dom to pick his brain and see if he knows what this means.

The new information I'd just acquired—the fact that I now know that Bash is a real person and has been having dreams of me too—everything that has happened in the last forty-eight hours must have wiped me out because the next thing I know, I'm waking up to Dom and Scarlet stumbling into the room.

"Dom!" I exclaim. Scarlet walks him over to the bed, one of his arms draped around her. "What happened?"

"He blacked out," Scarlet says tonelessly as Dom dangles from her arms haggardly, at an unnatural angle. "The warlock has started to come for him."

Scarlet lays him on the bed, and the look of worry that passes over her face dissembles the toneless words she'd spoken.

I sit up and examine him, looking at his face and anything else that may be out of sorts.

"Did you get the artifact?" I ask, getting closer to him.

"Yes. Mom is working on it now; I'm going to go help her. Come when you can. We need to get this done soon."

Scarlet's gone, but Ollie remains in the doorway.

Dom is barely coherent, but I need to know what happened from someone who doesn't look as though he got hit by a truck.

He's pale and sweating. The look of distemper on his face is almost flagrant, as though if he breathed on me it would smell like bourbon.

The depravity of his appearance is disarming.

"We had Scarlet calm him and gave him some bourbon as well," Ollie says, the abeyance of his own voice calm and relaxed. "It's kind of like being drunk for a vampire. He'll recover soon."

"What happened?"

Ollie comes all the way into the room and sits on the chair in the corner. "We got there and got Hattie spelled. She went in, and everything was fine. Suddenly, Dom's eyes went black. He began mumbling, talking to someone who wasn't there, speaking in tongues. I'm a vampire, and it scared me to my core."

His words grate on me and cause a panic that I bite down on as hard as possible. "You have no idea what he was saying?"

He shakes his head. "No. He started acting possessed, trying to get out of the car. I had to use all my strength to get him to stay in the back. Scarlet came round to the back and got him spelled enough to get him to calm down. When he finally came to, the only thing he was saying was that he was supposed to kill . . ." Ollie stops and looks down.

"Supposed to kill who?"

His soft eyes are on mine, and they grow cold quickly. "You."

My heart skips, the rubatosis unmooring me. "Me? Why me?"

"He didn't know. He didn't remember any of it when he was all the way himself again."

I look back to Dom, now asleep, his brown lashes resting on his soft face like a dark curtain of mystery.

"Sayah," Ollie says hesitantly, "For whatever reason, the warlock wants him to kill you first. He won't be able to control himself soon. It'll keep getting worse and worse."

"So, what am I supposed to do?"

"I don't know," he says rigidly, pulling a stick off his pant leg. "Until this curse is broken, you may have to run."

"Run? Run where?"

"Somewhere where he wouldn't know you to go. Go home. Get your child. And run."

This doesn't make any sense. I can't run right now; I need to help fix him. Even if I entertained the thought of running, I have a life back home, and so does Gauge. How am I supposed to just run away? Then there's the split custody thing. If I take Gauge out of the state, Derek will have me arrested and, worse, have Gauge taken from me.

"I can't run yet, Ollie. I need to help them to break this curse."

"Well. Do what you need to do." Ollie stands to leave. "But there may come a time when he can't help what he does. When that happens, run."

He's gone, and I'm alone with Dom, the man who's now cursed to kill me.

Here I am, thousands of miles away from home, in a strange place with a house full of monsters. The only one that I have who's protecting me is my boyfriend, and now he's under some spell that's making him try to kill me.

I want my mom.

What am I going to do?

Ollie told me to run.

Retrieving my phone from my back pocket, I look at the time. It's almost six in the morning. I think about calling Claire and Anna; I miss them and want someone to talk to.

Unbidden tears infiltrate my eyes as I walk out to the balcony.

Time may have stood still. I stare at the water, wishing I had someone I could call. Someone that would help me understand this mess that I got myself into. But what would I say to Claire? She has no idea what has happened since I learned of Dom's dark secret.

There's a hammock swing off to the right of the porch, and I go to it; pulling my knees up to my chest, I cry. I cry for all the things I've been through.

Wondering why the world is always out to get me.

There never seems to be any good in my life. It always leads to evil.

Sitting here for a long time, I watch the sun come up over the water, watch the light kiss the lake, and give the world the first fiery breath of morning.

I know that I should go in and see if Adaline and Scarlet need my help, but there probably isn't much for me to do.

I'm not a strong witch yet. I can't accomplish much. I don't know why I'm here.

There's a hand on my shoulder, and I half-expect to see Bash here again because why not? It's the last thing I need, so it's the first thought in my head.

But it isn't Bash, it's Dom.

"Hey." I sniffle and look up at him for a second, trying to decide if he's himself or under that spell.

"Hey. It's okay. I'm me." The opacity of his skin is unsettling.

Pulling him down, I wrap myself in his arms and let him hold me for a few seconds.

"Do you remember anything about what happened to you?"

I can feel his heart racing. "I am starting to. But when I was sleeping, she came to me again."

"The warlock?"

His chest rises as he nods. "She's awful, Sayah. She terrifies me."

"What did she say? What does she want?"

"She's this awful-looking person with white hair and black eyes. Her lips and nails are black, and her face is so pale white that she looks like a ghost. She's pure evil. And she told me her name is Matrasia. She said that the first person she wants me to kill is you because you are the Phoenix."

"What the hell does that mean?"

"She didn't tell me. All she said was that I must kill you. And there's a desire in my head I'm fighting right now that wants to hurt you. I'm so lost by this, Sayah. I don't know what to do."

"Why does she want me dead? What have I ever done?"

"I don't know. I just know that you're the one I have to kill. If I kill you, my mark will be complete, and I will be hers forever."

A terror rises up in me that frays me. This is a dark I had never imagined. This warlock is part demon and wants me dead; floating petals and making sun talismans are not comparable to a demon's magick. They're not in the same realm. There's nothing I can do to fight this.

"Hey," he says, giving me a weak but hopeful smile, "I trust Hattie, Scarlet, and my mom. They'll be able to break this. I believe that."

"I hope so. I can't imagine what will happen if it doesn't work."

"If it doesn't work," he says, and the tone in his voice dangles in the winds of utter and severe gravity, "you have to kill me."

"No! I will not kill—"

"Sayah, you have to. This mark will change me into someone who is mindless; I'll be dead anyway. And if she wants you dead, there's nothing that will stop me from killing you. You have to keep you and Gauge safe. End me. Take my necklace and throw me in the sun. Or drive a silver stake through my heart. Sayah.." He pulls my chin so that I'm looking at him directly. "You have to."

Tears swim in my eyes and roll down my cheeks.

"Promise me?"

I nod.

If it comes down to it, I am going to have to kill my boyfriend.

36

A TRIBRID

SAYAH

We watch the sun break the horizon and melt the stars, sitting quietly with each other, enjoying our last moments while he's still him. The gentle rocking motion of the hammock lulls me, and his arms are tight against my stomach. His shirt is rolled up to reveal the mark on him, a little more red flecks within the white raised skin. I wonder if that has anything to do with him going dark a few hours ago.

There's no way to tell how much time we have left until the mark ignites him again.

"I overheard your mom and Jasantha discussing something interesting when you were gone." I had almost forgotten the conversation with the unfolding of the latest events.

"What?" he sounds interested.

At least it will keep our minds off our impending doom.

"They were talking about how Bash is a tribrid."

His weight shifts under me, and I can tell by his tone he's surprised at this information. "A tribrid?"

"Yeah," I say, leaning up to look at him. "Your mom thinks that's the curse he's trying to break. She said he's part demon, and since she's a witch, you all are too. And then, of course, the vampire curse she put on all of you. That would make him a tribrid."

"And she thinks that's the curse he is trying to break?"

"I guess so."

"But if he is part demon, that would make him—"

"Not your father's son."

He turns the corners of his mouth down and nods. "That would clear a lot of things up, honestly. About him and about my dad's hatred toward him."

"But how could you all have not known this entire time?"

"My mom is a vault when it comes to things that will protect us." He studies me with piercing scrutiny.

"So why do you think he needs his sibling's blood to break the curse?" I ask, folding my leg up under me.

"I'm not sure," he says, rolling his sleeve down. "And I'm not sure how his way differs from Hattie's."

"Do you think we need to bring this up? To talk about it?"

"I do. But I don't see how."

"Get Bash up here. Ask him. He obviously knows the truth about himself."

"I don't want to hurt my mom."

"I know you don't. But we need information. Maybe this will help the spell they're weaving downstairs. Who knows? But if ever there was a time to get all the skeletons out of the closet, I would say that time is now."

"You're right," he says, and he arises from the hammock. "Let's go."

I take his hand and stand. "I'll be right by your side."

He nods and leads me into the house.

We reach the lower floor. Hattie, Adaline, and Scarlet are busy with the artifact and their spell.

"How's it coming?" Dom asks, and the three women look up.

"It's ancient, and the writing was almost indiscernible," answers Adaline, staring fixedly at the object. "But we're getting there."

"Where's Bash?" Dom questions.

"I don't know," says Hattie, her strange pale eyes skimming over me. "Haven't seen him since before we left. How are you feeling?"

"I'm doing all right," he returns, fidgeting with a button on his sleeve. "Fighting a crazy voice in my head, but I have it under control."

"Keep fighting that," Scarlet swings her restless gaze to him, then back to a book before her. "We're getting there."

I walk up to where the three women are sitting around the table in the spell room. The artifact is on the table before them. It's a large stone that looks like it had fallen from outer space a millennia ago. It's a rusty brown with holes, but it has bright fluorescent blue lines across it. In between the lines is ancient writing, some in characters that look familiar—like runes—and others that look entirely foreign.

"What do you think the writing means?" I ask timidly.

"It's a spell," Adaline responds. "To break a curse. It'll help with the lycanthrope spell."

"Because it's older than any of our spells, it'll be powerful, but it should break a warlock mark. If it breaks a formweaver link with the moon, it can work on a warlock." The conviction in Hattie's voice quells some worry but not all.

"Speaking of warlocks," Dom says, and my heart faints. Should he bring this up now, Adaline will know I told him the information.

"You wanna know why I am asking for your blood?" Bash is in the room with us without us having heard him.

Vampires are slick like that.

"What are you not telling us?" Dom chides.

Bash is lithe about his movements, entering the lair and traipsing around the table the three women sit at, eyeing his mother. "That would be a question for her, I believe."

Her look is unchanging. She keeps her calm Viking demeanor and returns his glare to him.

"What is he talking about, Mom?" Dom asks, a questioning expression lingering on his face.

"There's something you all need to know," Adaline replies, her shoulders never slumping. However, the tone of her voice should have given her an appearance of being bested. "I have kept it from you for a long time to keep you safe. I knew there would be a time when it would come to this, so I shall divulge my secret. In this dark time, the secret I've been living with may help repair a bond between brothers as they face the same darkness."

All eyes look from Bash to Dom. Bash doesn't look at his brother. He merely sits down in a chair by the fireplace.

"How is it that you came to know of this secret Bash?" Adaline asks, her feline eyes scrutinizing him.

"Because the warlock came to me. After this mark appeared."

He pulls down his collar, and there's the same mark on his neck that's on Dom's arm.

"What?" Scarlet says, arising from the chair and looking more closely at the mark. "How are you both marked by the same warlock when living separate lives in different states?"

"There's always a deeper line drawn between things than we realize," remarks Adaline, a pensive expression washing over her face.

"But how were you marked, Bash?" Hattie asks, her dark and pierced brows knitting together in confusion.

"It appeared the other day. And when it did, she came to me in a vision right when it happened, saying that I've always been hers; it took a bloodline getting marked for me to."

"So, because Dom was marked, that is why Bash is too?" Hattie inquires of Adaline. "So, are we next?"

Adaline shakes her head. "No. It's because Bash has always been promised to her. It was a deal I made with her to have children."

There's a palpable wave of shock that reverberates throughout the room.

"What?" Bash questions, leaning forward on his knees and glaring at her again, his face wholly unguarded.

"I couldn't have children," she begins, the truth pouring out of her in a devastating sieve. "So I went to see a Shaman. I was desperate. I saw a few of them. One gave me the spell to keep my babies safe in the womb, which turned into your vampire curse. And the other—" She stops and takes a deep breath as if summoning the strength to say the following words. "The other I had summoned a demon to give me a child.

"The demon was both male and female. The male part offered to give me a seed that would pave the way for other children, but when that child turned twenty-one, I would have to give him over to the female part for a lifetime of servitude. See, me being part witch and him being a hybrid, part witch and part demon, would give them the power they needed for their grimspawn spells. I agreed, knowing I'd do whatever I could to change that.

"Your father didn't know I'd made a deal with the demon, so I didn't tell him at first. But when Bash was born, it was clear he was not a mix of Everett and I. Before we lost Ollie, the first vampire, I did more spells to keep Bash from being marked, and it seemed to be working. I thought I had it beat. He turned twenty-one, and nothing happened all the way until he was thirty-nine, when he died and became a vampire.

"Worried that I was dealing with something beyond my comprehension, I consulted the Shaman again; she told me that the vampire curse, which started as a protection spell, kept him safe from the warlock's magic. She couldn't touch him because he was a tribrid. But she did warn me that vampires are their deepest desires because being linked with a vampire makes them immortal, too, and that one day she will come for Bash. She will find a way, which will come as unexpected as it did. Through a human witch."

Every single pair of predatory eyes falls on me.

What do I have to do with this?

"Even though the warlock didn't have her eyes on Dom or any trackers on him, she used events to bring him to her, mark him, and get to Bash. And now she has them both."

"So, Bash is a witch, a vampire, and a demon?" Hattie examines.

"A tribrid," Adaline explains.

"And that is why Dad hates me and why I don't look like any of you," Bash snarls.

"Or act like any of us," Dom replies curtly.

"Yeah, I'm a monster. Everyone knows."

"He doesn't hate you," Adaline pacifies.

"Why did you want our blood?" Hattie interjects before Bash can argue with Adaline. "What would that do?"

"I thought if I drank your blood under the full moon and chanted some witchy-woo, it would put the protection spell back on me. I didn't have any idea that Dom here had been marked too. When she said bloodline, I assumed it was about you all. Hence why I figured your blood would work to break it."

"Well, that was a nice idea," comments Adaline, her motherly tone breaking through the surface of her guilt. "But this should work for you both. We can get the mark off both of you."

"Who does she want you to kill?" Dom asks, and Bash glares at him, his eyes narrowing.

"Talora," he says.

"Why does she want you to kill Talora?" Dom questions.

"Well, she wants you to kill Sayah," offers Scarlet. "It would seem that she wants them to kill the closest person to them. To get rid of their earthly connections."

"She wants you to kill Sayah?" Bash asks, and his eyes graze mine for a moment.

"Yes," replies Dom, and he looks at me with that same guilt Adaline has on her face in his eyes. "She called her the phoenix."

"The phoenix?" Bash queries.

"Yes," Dom answers. "Why, does that mean anything to you?"

"No. Just wondering why she said that word is all."

But there's a telling in his eyes that says he knows more than he's admitting to.

"So where are we with this mark breaker thing you all got going on?" Bash asks, his night-black hair in disarray.

"We need more time," Hattie answers a little defensively. "And concentration. So, if you guys can just go the fuck away—"

"Hear ya loud and clear, sister," Bash yells, getting up and flashing to the door. "I'll be in my room if anyone wants me."

Clearly abashed, this time he departs with a palpable huff.

"Let us know if you need anything," Dom offers the ladies. "But please, hurry."

"We're hurrying as fast as we can," Adaline replies.

Dom leads me out of the room.

As we enter the main floor, Bash is alone in the living room, sitting with his hands on his chin, a look of disquiet on his face.

I look at Dom to see if he's going to talk to his brother, but he makes no motion like he's going to.

He pulls me up the stairs when Bash speaks to him, halting us.

"I bet you're happy to find out we're not full-blown brothers."

"No," Dom replies despondently, not turning to face him. "I'm not happy about it. I'm not surprised. But I'm not happy."

"Well, it makes it easier to hate me, I'm sure."

"You want us to hate you. Everything you do, you want to be a monster. So, we treat you like one."

"The thing with Sadie, it's not what you think."

"Don't. Ever. Speak. Her. Name. To. Me," Dom says, the imperious quake of his voice jostling.

I can feel the rage catching fire in Dom's bones, and I don't think it's a good idea to tempt that kind of emotional change in him. Who knows how close that curse is, teetering him on the edge, and something—anything—could push him over it, like jostling a leaf.

"I'm just saying, it's not what you think."

"I said, don't speak of it to me."

His voice takes on a rage that I've never heard in him before. I watch the change happen and although it happens fast, it seems it was in slow motion. His eyes grow white with green rims, not black—which tells me it isn't the curse taking hold of him but his vampire rage—his skin turns almost translucent. The cat-like nature of his eyes glower into me, like I'm the target. Quickly, I dive out of the way, and with a speed as I've never seen, he stampedes at Bash in a murderous rush and flies into him, landing them both on top of the glass table and shattering it to bits.

Bash spins back onto his feet and pile-drives Dominic into one of the windows. Luckily, they're the tapered, double-paned windows because they don't break. Dom grunts and punches Bash. It's unlike a normal punch. The house shakes.

Unfazed, Bash's head merely turns a little sideways at the blow, but then he grabs Dom by the throat and, with that same speed, propels him into one of the beams, rumbling the house again. The breath is knocked out of him, and he takes a beat.

He rams Bash into the fireplace, taking the poker and thrusting it into his middle section. Blood seeps everywhere, and when Bash looks at me, his blue eyes are unchanged. He opens his mouth unnaturally wide, and his incisors grow two times their size, revealing the pearlescent ivory daggers in his mouth. He pulls the poker out and then clamps down on Dom's shoulder, more blood spewing from the wound.

Yelling with anguish, Dom yanks free of the bite, Bash has blood staining his white teeth, and it's thick and pooling at the sides of his mouth, dripping down onto the hardwood floor. Dom wrenches Bash's head into the mantle where his skull cracks open, again more blood, bones shining in the shimmering wetness.

The caveman-like grunts coming from the living room, the rumbling of the house as they fight, and the crashes and spills are enough to get Everett to come flying in and separate the two.

When I catch a glimpse of Dom, his incisors, too, are fanged out and gleaming, his eyes blank and scary.

"Enough!" yells Everett with enough force in his voice that the house quakes. "What the fuck is wrong with you two? Get the fuck over it. It was two hundred years ago."

The displacement of air in whooshing gusts lets me know the women are now in the room, no doubt speeding upstairs to the sounds of the commotion.

"Oh, for gods' sake," Adaline quips, the anger in her face like summer lightning. "It's about a girl, you idiots. Get over it. You have women of your own already."

Talora's here too now, as is everyone else in the house.

Neither Bash nor Dom acknowledges this, but their fangs retract, and their eyes return to normal.

Dom walks toward me, grabs my hand, and pulls me up the stairs.

As we're almost to our room, there's a blood-curdling scream, a sound like bones breaking, and all the voices of the people at once in the room we just left.

When we run back into the room, we see Bash hovering over Joe, drinking his blood. His eyes have gone black; the warlock has obviously come for him and has taken over, commanding him to kill Joe. Jasantha is trying to tear him away, screaming, Adaline's trying to keep her from intervening, and the entire room is in chaos.

"What the hell happened?" Dom asks, running to pull Bash from Joe.

"He killed him," Jasantha cries, her voice a mixture of anger and unmitigated devastation. "He's a monster. I'm gonna fucking kill him."

The red of her hair almost darkens, the medallion she wears around her neck glows, and she tilts her head back. Opening her mouth, unnaturally wide, the highest pitch and most ear-piercing wail accosts all my senses, rattling the windows—if they weren't as tough as they are, they'd have shattered.

The sound that emits from her is unlike anything I've experienced. It's like the worst sound I've ever heard—nails on a chalkboard terrible—but ten times worse, that crawls into my skin and sinks into my bones. I'm able to clutch my hands over my ears to muffle the sound. When I look around, all the vampires are doubled over with their hands on their ears or succumbed to their knees with the fatal litany.

Jasantha's eyes turn a beautiful amethyst color, the fangs sprout from the top and bottom of her mouth, and she clambers onto Bash, clamping down on his neck, causing an awful crunching sound that rends through the air. He screams in pain, and his flesh begins to boil at the puncture wounds from the toxic bite, bubbling up all over.

The only one not nearly affected by the siren call is me.

Now's a time more than ever to use the power Adaline gave me.

Extemporaneous rage courses through my veins, and as I think about all the things these people have caused me, I dive through my bones and find that power, scooping it up and thrusting it upon all of them. I don't care. The carcinogenic rush of electrical current leaves my fingers in a fiery orange wave, hitting each vampire with a malignant rush.

A large black cloud flits to blot out the sun, and as it does, each vampire reacts differently to their own worst fears. Dom, Ollie, Allison, and Hattie are engulfed in angry red flames, and I can see them this time. Sounds of fire and flame and screaming cause me to bite back on relinquishing the power, but I do not lessen it. Wailing around, they try to put out the flames but cannot.

Scarlet's body has flipped to a horizontal position in the air. It is frozen there; she's flailing her arms and legs violently and screaming like she's falling to her death. Everett bleeds out of his ears and eyes, toppling to his knees as though struck by some imaginary axe. Jasantha's clutching at her neck, a lariat pulling her from behind, causing her to fall to the floor and be ripped off Bash. Adaline's cradling a baby in her arms, the blue blanket dirty and riddled with holes. She strokes the babe's head as tears roll down her cheeks. Bash's face and neck eschew; he suddenly sees someone lying dead next to him—though no one is there—ineffable sadness controlling his movements as his hands tamp down whoever's hair he's seeing.

Lightning flashes and lights up our dark, as though the universe tells me they've had enough. Calling my power back to me, it evaporates off them and seeps back into me.

Jasantha takes a deep breath and coughs, crawling back and collapsing onto Joe, commencing her mourning. "You killed him," she sobs. "Oh, Joe. Oh, my sweet Joe. You monster!" she shouts at Bash.

Bash crouches on his knees before Joe, blankly looking at the ground.

Something tells me that he's not here anymore. There's a vacant look in his smoldering eyes, and I don't know him well, but even I can tell he's fighting a battle within himself.

He rises slowly from the ground, and I notice that the mark on his neck is a shade darker, his eyes turning as black as the darkest night.

As Bash keeps his slow, monotonous gait toward me, as though he's not controlling his movements, Adaline rushes off toward the basement.

Dom, his eyes turning that vacant black as well, rises from the floor, his eyes locked on mine.

Fear paralyzes me.

Is he gone too now, then?

I summon the power again within me and urge it to come forth, but nothing is coming.

Maybe I used it all up the last time I did it.

As Dom strides toward me, Bash turns his course and goes for Talora. Talora, seeing this, vanishes down the basement steps in a trace of light. Bash follows, but at a slower pace.

I don't have that gift of speed. I turn to run, and before I do, Adaline's back again, holding out the artifact, chanting words I don't understand.

The house shakes again, and there's a peculiar sound of high-pitched ringing. Dom stands still, as does Bash, and the ringing grows louder with the chanting.

A seismic wave explodes from the artifact and hits Dom, then Bash, and they collapse to the ground.

The ringing stops, and Adaline ceases her chanting.

A stillness engulfs the room, and nobody moves, waiting to see what the two brothers will do.

Dom's shark eyes evaporate, his green eyes now locked on mine. "What happened?"

"The curse," I answer on a breath.

"Is it broken?" Hattie asks from where she fell by the table.

"I don't know," Adaline mutters, still grasping the artifact. "We weren't finished with the rest of it. I panicked, and it was the only thing I thought of."

Dom lifts his shirt sleeve. "I don't think it's broken. The mark is still here."

Jasantha resumes her sobbing, cradling the dead Joe's head in her arms. He's lifeless, blood pouring down the side of his neck, pooling on the floor.

Bash is at the basement door. He turns around, a look of confusion taking over his expression as he sees Jasantha rocking Joe.

"You did this," she glowers, shooting him a disgusted glare.

"It wasn't him," offers Adaline, that motherly aura trying to keep the peace with all her children. "It was the curse."

"So it would appear," Scarlet says, sitting up from where she fell and cradling her knees, "as though the curse strengthens when adrenaline runs hot. That's my guess."

"And how do we keep it at bay until we break the curse?" Ollie asks, sitting on the marble floor.

"Keep those two apart," Scarlet scoffs, crossing her legs.

Dom looks at Bash, who's still eyeing Jasantha and Joe.

I can see a look of remorse written all over his face, but I'm the only one who seems to see it. When they all look at him, they see a monster.

Dom makes his way toward me. I'm scared and hate that I'm afraid of him now.

There's no telling what will set him off.

Is it only adrenaline that turns that dark mark on? Or could it be anything that'll turn off his switch and let him walk like a zombie?

Like a grim.

37

YOU ARE MY OCEAN

DOM

The look in Sayah's eyes is enough to crack me open, reach in, and squeeze, making me bleed and break and shatter.

I cannot stand that she's afraid of me now. I can see the way the water of her ocean eyes churn violently against a storm she never expected and struggles to navigate. Hopelessly, she watches this storm as it destroys and tears and steals, and I can't protect her from it.

She's pulled her aura into herself, so no sliver of it is visible to me.

When I reach for her, she flinches, and it burrows so far deep within me that I doubt it'll ever leave.

The unquenchable desire to take her in my arms and comfort her wars with the demon taking over my mind. He wants her death on his lips.

Her blood tastes like his sweetest dreams.

My reality is splintered.

One side of that reality are the parts of me I know the depth of; I can measure it, even though it's as vast as the ocean. My family, the people I protect, my wishes, hopes, and desires, Sayah—they are my ocean, the thing I will protect at all costs, no matter the price.

The other side of that reality is this new darkness I'm unfamiliar with. It's warped and wrong, and the edges of it are fractured, the middle a vast ravine of pitch and morbid black—a darkness beyond the spectrum of any that exists in this reality or any other. The cold of it is a cold that arrests your breath; it freezes your soul and disintegrates your bones.

When the demon takes over, it's to that ravine I go. Time doesn't exist there, and I have no idea what happens around me while I wallow in that murky place. When I come to and see the faces of the people I love looking at me as though *I'm* the monster, it adds to the depth and cold of that ravine.

"Sayah," I say, keeping my voice calm and steady. "Come with me?"

Her perfectly sculpted brows relieve their tension, the lines that bracket the top of her nose relaxing. "Sure," she says.

Interlacing my fingers with hers, I pull her through the house, up the spiral staircase to the second floor. We keep going up to the top floor, winding around the house's long hallways and dark corners. This part isn't used much by anyone.

Dust and cobwebs layer the corners and edges of every window covered with dust and dirt. The smell is ancient; the house was originally built in the late 1800s by a prosperous gin distiller. Since my family has owned it, they've remodeled the lower levels, but the upper ones are relatively untouched. My mom wanted the house strictly for the greenhouse. Dad wanted it for the lower levels built to be a distillery but now are used for more nefarious purposes.

Heavy wooden doors are all closed down this dark hallway, but if one were to open them, they'd see antique furniture covered in sheets and ominous remnants of the ghosts who once lived here.

At the end of the hallway are the ladder steps that lead up to my favorite part of the house—the widow's walk.

Sayah's quiet as she follows me. I'm sure her mind is a million miles away, or maybe in a million places at once.

Up the steeply slanted steps to the door that leads to the roof, I unbolt the hatch and pop it open.

I climb out and bend to help her up as well.

"Wow," she breathes as the wind gusts blow her brown hair around. "This is amazing."

I take her by the hand to the edge of the walk lined with wrought iron fencing twisted into elegant designs. Like an ocean, the lake reaches out as far as the eye can see.

"My favorite part of the house," I say, taking in the calm of the lake, the cool of the wind, the expanse of blue sky.

I haven't been able to take in this view since I broke my bond with the dark.

Although the view is breathtaking, I can't keep my eyes off her.

Watching her take this all in, I see some of the tension melt off her slightly, her soft smile tugging at the corners of her mouth.

I wish I could pluck her worry away, take her in my arms, and tell her everything will be all right, but that's like reaching out to someone in the middle of a hurricane out at sea, and you are on land.

I want to take all the things that threaten her, anything that means her any harm, and destroy it, rip it limb from limb, and toss it into my dark ravine.

But now, because of my mark, the thing most dangerous to her is me.

"I hate this," I fret, watching her worry at a string on her cuff. Taking her hand and pulling her to face me, I say, "Sayah, I can't tell you how much this kills me. I would unhinge the stars and dismantle the moon if it meant it kept you safe, and I am the one you need protection from."

Her wildly frightened eyes behold mine, her thumb stroking over the top of my palm. "I know, Dom. I hate this, too. But we're almost there. We have to keep the faith that your mom will break the spell."

"I know. I wanted you to know that I love you in case she can't. You are my ocean. I've never felt more at peace than on the edge of an ocean, feeling it tug and retreat with pieces of me. It's the only place where I feel the extra particles I've gained from others are quiet and aren't haunting me. And that is how I feel when I'm near you. You are my peace. I will spend the rest of my damned existence trying to bring you that same peace if I make it out of this alive. But if I don't, I wanted to tell you."

Tears well up in her eyes as she slides her body into mine, wrapping her arms around me and laying her head on my chest. "I love you, Dom. More than the stars in the sky."

I kiss her on the top of her head, smelling the sweet aroma of her hair. Leaning my cheek on it, I stare out at the stillness of the lake.

She is the quiet to my loud. Her presence hushes my demons and calms them.

The ravine doesn't seem so scary with her close to me.

It's knowing what that abyss means is what opens another chasm of terror. If I'm in it, that means she is not, and to live in a world where she doesn't exist combines those two abysmal things.

If I'm in that darkness, it means her death.

38

MOMENT IN THE DARK

SAYAH

Dusk is upon us, and the stars are starting to freckle the sky. The sun is almost set, giving that dull yellow light a faint, dreary feeling, keeping everything soft and colorful.

Inside, much of the group is doing our part to clean up the mess that was made. Dom and I are sweeping up the glass, Bash and Talora are putting the furniture back into place, Everett and Ollie are wrapping Joe up in a sheet, and Allison is cleaning up the blood. Adaline, Scarlet, and Hattie have returned to the spell room to commence trying to break the curse.

"What are we going to do with the—with Joe?" asks Ollie, helping Everett to roll him over onto a sheet.

"We need to get rid of it," Everett says, and Jasantha shoots him a look that could probably kill him had she turned her siren powers on. She's still kneeling on the floor next to Joe.

"We'll take him to the lake and sink him," she says solemnly, tears like sparkles on her cheeks. "I can visit him sometimes that way." She makes a low keening sound, as though she's expressing her grief through sound. My heart breaks for her.

It's easy to see how much she loved him by how hard she's grieving.

"I'll take you," Everett says, his stoic features softening toward her. "I need to get out of this place anyway. At least for a minute."

Adaline emerges from the hallway, eyes sharp like tacks and concentration haloed around her as though she's a powerful scientist who has been locked away, discovering the next great equation.

"We need wolfsbane," she announces, tapping her fingernail on the marble island to get the family's attention. "I don't have any left. Didn't know I was going to need it. So, I need someone to go out and get some."

"Where do we find it?" Dom asks as he finishes sweeping the glass into my dustpan.

"There should be some at the local nursery," she says, looking down at me.

"I'll go," Dom offers, setting the broom handle against a barstool.

"I'll go with you," Ollie adds, finishing with rolling Joe up tight.

Everett heaves Joe up and throws him over his shoulder. "Let's go, J," he directs at Jasantha.

Reluctantly, she pulls herself off the floor and follows her dad out the back door.

Dom takes the dustpan from me as I stand. "I'll be right back, okay?" he tells me with the question.

"Okay," I say, unable to hide the despair in my voice. "I'll work on the sun talismans."

He kisses me on the lips. "I'll be right back."

"Ollie, do you have a piece of jewelry you'd like me to spell?" I ask as he walks by.

He appraises me with a look as calm as the sky at sunset and unclasps his necklace, handing it to me. "Thank you," he says, grasping my hand in his. There's a kindness in his voice and a softness in his eyes that isn't like the others. "He's gonna be okay," he says gently for only me to hear.

I nod again and give him a smile before embarking on my journey to gather more jewelry.

They leave out the front door, and Talora and Allison continue cleaning up the blood around the house. Bash is on the floor, picking up the broken bits of glass.

Doing magick and helping the vampires with sun talismans will keep my mind at ease, even if I don't feel like helping some of them. More so the ones that seem to want me dead—like Hattie.

"Hattie, Scarlet?" I ask as she and Scarlet pass to follow their mom to the spell room.

Hattie gawks at me as though I'm her next meal. "What?"

"May I have a piece of your jewelry to spell so you can go in the sun?"

Scarlet looks dubiously over at Hattie and then unclips an earring from her ear, handing it to me.

Hattie looks me up and down, taking that calculated measure of me once again, and lifts her be-ringed, spindly fingers, slipping one off. Plopping it into my hand, she walks off with her sister in silence, not a thank you or a query.

There isn't any desire within me that makes me want to do this for them, but I feel like I have to do something; otherwise, I'm going to go crazy with my thoughts. I feel the dread growing inside me with every passing moment and being here is not doing anything for my soul.

But being outside with the lake and the trees and the wind brings me ease and comforts me. It's only here and now that I feel like someone, or something, is watching over me. Mama's memory bites at me again, and I try to wrap my mind around the fact that my mom is gone and never coming back to help me.

What would she have said about all this?

I can only imagine my mother's reaction to me telling her all about how there are vampires in the world, and sirens, demons, grimspawns, formweavers, and warlocks, and how everything that scared us as little kids is true.

Not realizing it, I reach the water's edge and stop, getting my sneakers right up to taste the water that ebbs and flows to my feet.

I collapse to the ground, not worrying about getting my jeans dirty; I want to feel Mother Earth's soil beneath me.

Putting my hands to the ground, one empty, the other holding the jewelry I collected, I will use my strength to get through this to come to me from that soil. Imploring the dirt to come to my aid and make me strong, to get Dom's curse broken, to get through this weekend alive.

There's a child that needs me as much as I need my mama right now.

How do I know when he's right behind me every time?

It's an extraordinary shift of energy, almost like a buzzing. I feel the danger in the air like one would feel a frost coming.

A shudder skitters down my spine.

"What do you want, Bash?" I ask, not sparing him a glance.

"I wanted to see if you're all right."

"You don't care about me. Cut the shit."

"And you think I'm a monster, just like the rest."

"Isn't that what you want to be, Bash? A monster?"

"I'm a vampire; it's what I am supposed to be!"

"No!" I shout and jump up. "Something inside all of you pushes back that dark as much as the light tries to pull."

"You say this when you have only spent a moment in the dark! I have spent centuries!" he spits back.

His words cut me deep.

"Although my dark is not as long as yours, it's just as black! I have known darkness. Don't come at me with that and say I haven't; you don't even know me." I make sure that the tone of my voice is edged with angry sorrow and not just anger.

"I know you more than you think I do," he responds, drawing closer to me again.

"You are so full of cryptic bull shit, I just watched you kill someone. You don't want Dom to know that I've been in your dreams; I'm about tired of all these crazy, murder-y, psychotic games!"

I walk away, and he teleports right in front of me.

"I couldn't tell you before because Talora always watches me." His eyes tighten on mine. "I've had Scarlet sedate her for me. So I can tell you what I have to say."

"Why? What will that accomplish? I'm in a house full of murderous vampires, as a weak witch who is trying to save my boyfriend, and there is a warlock demon lady who wants me dead! How does what you have to say help me at all?"

"I don't know! But it might; just listen!" He grabs my hand, and that searing feeling sends a shock wave through me. I pull back my arm.

A part of me wants to hear what he has to say, and a part doesn't. I don't know how much of what I feel for him is of my own pound or his allure. Bash is a monster, and I should fear him. But in all of those dreams, there's a look of absolute agony every time he burns and kills me. There are also dreams where he decides to burn *with* me.

"I didn't kill Sadie," he absolves, and instantly, he has my full attention.

"What does that have to do with me?" I ask, crossing my arms over my chest.

"Dom met her first. She was a witch. But I didn't tell him I'd been dreaming of her for years. The same dreams that I've been having of you. And she'd been dreaming of me, too. When he brought her home, I was immediately drawn to her, and she to me. When he discovered that Sadie and I had dreams of each other, we got into one of those fights you witnessed. But, I'd turned and didn't know my own strength yet. I killed him, igniting his vampire curse. I'm the one who turned my brother into a vampire."

The features of his face crack as though this was still fresh like it'd happened last week instead of hundreds of years ago.

"I was overwhelmed with the guilt I felt at this," he continues stonily. "I was going to take my own life. Everything about you becomes heightened when you become a vampire. So, all the guilt I was feeling was tenfold. You learn to control it over time, but I was a new vampire. I decided to leave and sit in my darkness. Sadie was still drawn to me and couldn't let me be alone; she didn't want me to die. So, she fled with me, knowing it would break my brother's heart."

Bash walks along the banks of the lake, and I'm entranced by his tale, picturing what he's telling me in my mind as though it was happening right before me. I follow him quietly, willing him to continue.

"Dom thinks that I wanted to turn Sadie into a vampire because that's what I told Ollie one night, when they thought I was subdued by Jasantha's siren power. But because of my dreams, I knew if I bit her, she'd burn. I refused her time and time again. She was so mad; she didn't care about the burning, she wanted to be with me forever and begged me to turn her. I still refused, so she went out and found another vampire to turn her.

"Because she was born only a witch, her body couldn't handle the vampire curse. To be a hybrid—or tribrid, in my case—you have to be born or die as one. When she returned to me, she was going mad with the mixture of the two bloods, talking of the goddess beckoning her to a forest and telling her she was supposed to be the phoenix, but she messed up by trying to become a vampire. Laying with madness in her mind, drenched in sweat and burning up from the inside, she told me how someone named Freya told her the balance of nature had been thrown off kilter, and she couldn't fulfill the duties she'd been conditioned for. She made me swear I would never tell a soul of this because Freya had told her that the phoenix would rise again one day and it had to restore the balance. She begged me to kill her, saying that since she had failed Freya, the grimspawns had already come for her and marked her, and she didn't want to live like that. She told me she would return to me one day in another life, and that I would know by the dreams."

He pauses here and looks at me.

The vast ocean that opens with this information storms inside me, and I find myself on the precipice of knowledge, trying to wrap my mind around all that Bash is telling me.

"She killed herself, Sayah," he goes on softly. "And if she didn't, she would have gone mad with rage anyway. She drove a silver stake through her own heart and burned. I told them all that I had killed her and the man she had run away with to keep my promise to Sadie. But after she died, that's when I gave myself over to the dark."

I realize we have stopped walking, and my mouth is agape, but my hand is covering it.

Questions lurch and sway like a ship in the storm of my mind; I reach for them as though grasping for light in the dark but none would come to fruition with my voice.

So, I'm supposed to be the phoenix?

What does that mean?

What is the phoenix supposed to do?

Am I Sadie reincarnated?

And then that would mean I was with Dom in another life, and Bash, too?

And Bash isn't the monster they all think he is, yet he still makes them believe that.

"I know so many questions are running through your mind, and I don't have the answers for you. I wanted you to know that I have lived this before and don't want you to suffer the same fate as Sadie. For whatever reason, you were put in our lives to fulfill a destiny bestowed upon you by the goddess. I want you to continue following that path, whatever that may be."

"But what is that path?"

"Sadie said to restore balance. I can only think that so many lines have blurred with us supernatural beings. The hybrids, the tribrids. The grimspawns and the warlocks. I think you may be conditioned to be the undoing of us all."

These last words hang before me and latch onto something deep within me.

The undoing of them all?

I don't want that.

With Dom, even though it has gone awry, I had found a way for him to kill people who deserve to be killed, people who hurt other people and children, and to keep him alive and around for as long as I can.

The luminous part of me found a way to balance his dark with my light, which I found can be done.

With Bash, his darkness pulls at me, and that's another thing that makes no sense with this phoenix thing. If I'm supposed to be the undoing of them all, why do I feel that I could love him wildly and heedlessly, all without fear of it consuming me?

"Just last night, you told me you needed my light and will have me. If you knew that the same thing would happen to me that happened to Sadie, why would you say that? Why would you want that for me? And then to say that I am to be the undoing of you all, none of what you're saying makes any sense."

"Because part of me belongs to you, Sayah, and I don't know how dominant that part of me is." He steps toward me, moving his arm up as though he wants to grab my hand but lets it drop to his side. "There are times, in my dreams, your dreams, that when I am near you, I can't think of anything else in the world other than being next to you forever. When I wake up from them, I need you, and when I was so close to you for the first time last night, I couldn't contain it. It was the same overwhelming feeling I had with Sadie. Even though I knew that we would be the undoing of one another, I couldn't resist. That is the selfish part of me. Now, reliving what happened with Sadie, I've had time to think. That with so much evil in this world, you are meant to undo it all, if not at least some of it. I have to resist you too, so I don't kill you, so you may carry out your destiny."

Contemplating what he's saying to me, there's a part of Bash that wants my death on his lips. But why? The warlock that lives in Dom's mind lives in his, too, and she wants me dead. Now, she has two vampires to carry out her wish.

"Why can't you be subdued by Jasantha?" This is my next question, and I ask this above the others for reasons unbeknownst to me.

"Because I made her," he says simply, his black brows steeply arched. "And so, therefore, she is sired to me. She can't trance me. But they don't know that."

"But if she is a hybrid that was not born of the two bloods, how can she be, and Sadie couldn't?"

"Because Sadie was a witch. She was born with the blood of the phoenix in her, the light. It couldn't mix with the dark. And Jasantha was born with dark blood, as sirens are of the dark. So, the vampire curse could live at home in her. When she died with my blood in her, she died with the hybrid trait. Like I said, you have to be born of one or die as one."

"But if Sadie couldn't handle the two types of blood mixing, how could your mom? She was a witch, too; how could she be a vampire after being a witch?"

"Part of me always wondered that, too, but the dreams of me biting and Sadie burning stopped me from trying. I assumed that because Sadie was supposed to be the phoenix, whatever blood that is, my mom doesn't have that blood within her, and that's why she was able to be a vampire and a witch. That, and she was in cahoots with demons. Her witch blood must have been dampened with darkness, making it easier for the vampire curse to lay at home at ease in her."

"And we can't tell Dom any of this?"

"You can't tell anyone any of this. You have to fulfill your duty now."

"But what if that means killing you?"

"I have this on me now." He pulls down his collar, and the mark there is that one shade darker than it had been. Luckily, it hasn't gotten darker. "I don't want this. And if we can't break it, I don't want to live with what that means. I'm okay with dying by your hand. I've lived for over two hundred years. Maybe next time I come back, you and I can be together as normal humans and have that human life everyone dreams about." He enchants a mischievous smile that somewhat quells my worry for a short time, and then the despair and hushed agony return to us again.

The quiet depths of my soul are churning, a violent tidal wave surging up and crashing into the rocky cliffs of me; my only hope is that the three women inside will find a way to break this curse and put all of this behind us.

But something tells me that not even that mattered.

Even if they do, whatever this phoenix blessing is, I'm sure I'll find out what I'm meant to do.

"Why do you want them to believe you're a monster when you aren't one?"

"Oh, Sayah."

The way my name dances on his lips stutters me.

"I'm the worst fucking kind of monster there is. I'm no fucking good, whatever you wish to believe." He cocks his head to the side as though hearing something that I don't hear. "Shhh, Dom is back. Talk about something else."

"What am I supposed to be talking about with you?" I whisper.

"Here, take this," he says, unclasping the chain around his neck and handing it to me. "Please make one for me too."

"Hey," Dom says as he approaches.

Bash clears his throat. "I was seeing if she was all right. If she needed any help with her light . . . sun-beckony thing." He turns on his heels and walks back toward the house.

As Bash flashes away, Dom stares at me, maybe even into me, and I can see that he's worried about the same thing happening again with me that happened with Sadie and Bash.

"Did I interrupt something?" His tone is drenched in suspicion.

I'm careful in choosing my words. I don't want to ignite that curse and have him wanting to kill me. "I was crying. I came out here to do the sun talisman on these"—I hold out my hands and show him the jewelry—"and I collapsed at the lake's edge. He must have seen me and made sure I was okay."

His nebulous gaze is unreadable. "I find it hard to believe that Bash cared enough about anyone more than himself."

"I don't know what to tell you," I say, my voice gaining more defensiveness. "Did you get the wolfsbane?"

"Yes," he replies, still looking at me hesitantly.

"Hey," I coo, stepping closer and wrapping my arms around him. "Don't be worried, okay? There's nothing to be worried about. I needed a friend, and he was there. That's all it was."

"You don't know him like I do, Say. Be careful, okay?"

"I will."

Kissing me softly, I feel him trying to get into my mind again, like a faint tickling inside my head. "I'm gonna see how they're coming along with the spell. They should be getting close now with the wolfsbane."

"Okay. I'll finish up with these."

He nods and leaves.

While I work on spelling the jewelry in my possession, I let my mind wander to everything Bash told me.

Why doesn't he want Dom to know?

It's almost as though Bash wants this all to end, like he's letting me become what I am to become to save the world or something.

But how am I supposed to know what I'm supposed to do now?

As I spell the objects that rest in my hand, conversing with the moon and deepening my bond with it, I think of my mom again and inwardly beg her to help me, to come save me and let me know what I'm supposed to be doing.

The tears that occlude my eyes make the lake look foggy and warped. I remember being here as a kid with my family, how much Mama had loved it here, and used to paint the fog dancing on the lake in the morning.

A light breeze skitters across the water and brushes over me, and for a fleeting moment, it feels like my mother's hand brushes me softly, telling me that it will be okay.

The sound of the large crash coming from the house draws me from my moment of peace.

My heart drops into my stomach as I run up the hill, knowing it's Dom and Bash fighting again.

As soon as I enter, I quickly stow the newly spelled jewelry on an end table and survey the situation.

There's a collision of forces when Dom rams Bash into a door, the impact of the murderous rush causing the drywall to crack, the filigreed within the wainscoting rattling.

"I told you nothing happened!" Bash manages to get out through forced air; Dom is pressing all his weight into his chest.

Using his elbow to thwart Dom's attempts to break his sternum, Dom stumbles back into Ollie.

"You guys need to chill!" yells Ollie, trying to hold Dom back from running at Bash again.

"That's the same thing you said right before you killed me and then ran off with Sadie," Dom says before he rushes at his brother again.

"Dom!" I shout, hoping to stop them before the curse becomes activated again.

The sound of my voice hits him, and when it does, the mixture of adrenaline and my voice causes him to turn to me and rush at me.

There's no time to run. I have no idea what's happening.

All I know is that the look in his eyes is murderous. He doesn't recognize me.

His green eyes have gone black, his skin is translucent, and the murder in his gait only tells the story of my death. This is all I see before he reaches me in the flash of light.

Then there's a piercing in my neck, kind of like all those times I had been poked and prodded when going through chemo.

The feeling of being depleted of blood is also fresh in my memory. The light-headedness, the bright lights, being able to see my heartbeat in my eyes.

The last thing I see before I lose consciousness is Bash's blue eyes over Dom's shoulder, pulling him off me.

39

THE PHOENIX

SAYAH

Darkness.

That's all there is.

So dark it's as if all the light has been swallowed whole, and not a pinprick of it remains.

When I open my eyes again, I'm on the floor in the main room, still surrounded by vampires. Dom's face has a painted look; pure agony and loss and grief shroud his features like a veil of darkness.

"What happened?" I ask, but I feel light-headed again when I try to sit up. There's the taste of blood in my mouth, and I swallow hard, knowing that one of them fed me their blood to get me back to consciousness.

"The mark," Adaline replies, her voice a quiet sliver of worry and doubt. "We think the mixture of adrenaline and your voice activated it. But Bash pulled him off you on time, and we got him sedated again with Jasantha."

"We have to get this curse broken, now!" Bash seethes through clenched teeth, his face contorted with fury, pacing about the kitchen to my right.

"We're there," Adaline declares, regarding him with a calm interest.

"We need your blood. And his. Then we think we can summon the warlock to get hers."

Bash nods agreeably. "Okay," he says, barring his teeth and ripping into his skin. "Where do you want it?"

"Here," Scarlet offers, handing him a vial.

"Now you, Dom," Jasantha demands, as her voice has to command him while he's vexed by her.

Mindlessly, from where he sits on the ground with his knees pulled up to his chest, he languorously opens his mouth, bares his fangs, and bites into his arm.

Scarlet hands him the vial. The brilliant crimson drips into it while the other vampires watch; some of their faces slack and fascinated, while others have the appearance of blissful unconcern.

As the blood pools into the vial, all the happiness I had felt before this trip has fled. This is bad. And it is only going to get worse.

"Okay, that should do," Adaline states, taking the vial as Bash's wound begins to sew itself up. "All right, girls, let's go."

Scarlet and Hattie, in a whisp of blurred colors, vanish to the basement.

Dom is still heavily sedated, but the look on his face tells me that he's reeling from the guilt he feels in his heart for what he did. He won't make eye contact with me.

Peeling myself off the floor, I go to the kitchen for water.

That's when the dread sets in.

The sensation hits as if all the air has been vacuumed out of the house, leaving an overwhelming surge of despair and sorrow. The sky darkens, the lights flicker within the mansion, and an oppressive silence envelops everything.

We all feel it.

The incursion commences through a veil of clandestinity. I feel them slipping into the location using the artistry of magick; their entrance is silent and elusive. The lights extinguish, plunging the cabin into an eerie darkness that steals away all the warmth from the air. A sudden chill takes over me, evident in the frosty breaths I exhale. I shrink into a cowering position, grappling to make sense of the unfolding events.

There's a harrowing sound of beings rushing into the cabin, displaced air as the nefarious entities void of souls enter—reanimated corpses veilweaved by magick—nine or ten of them at first. They're grotesque looking; some have features, while others have no faces other than rows and rows of sharp fangs, shadows marking the gaunt hollows of their cheekbones. Those with faces have distended veins spiderwebbing across their cheeks and temples, glowing red eyes, and skin as gray as the sky before it snows.

Amidst the chaos, the vampires in the cabin snap to immediate attention. Their white eyes blaze, fangs fully exposed, as the scene transforms into a kaleidoscope of color and a clash of battles unfolds in the blink of an eye. The vampires move with lethal grace, starkly contrasting to the grotesque invaders, their predatory instincts on high alert as they prepare for the impending confrontation.

Allison's subdued from the back of her, the grimspawn biting into her with a loud and sickening crunching sound, and cries of her anger and pain waft over me.

Ollie flashes to her side and seizes the being off her, pulling at the hood of the creature gnawing on her neck. Not only is the being hooked into her by way of its rows of sharp teeth, but it's also ripping pieces and chunks out of her and eating them. Ollie tears it away from her, using his elemental power of air to heave the being to the other side of the room, where it collides with the wall and rumbles the house upon the impact.

As Adaline reenters the room, holding the still un-glowing artifact, the other two sisters crash into the commotion. Hattie collides with the creature about to return to Allison while Scarlet races toward one, closing in on Jasantha. It's apparent that Adaline had vamp flashed away to retrieve the artifact from the spell room, her sudden reappearance marking a pivotal moment in the unfolding chaos.

Hattie unleashes her power of sight to make the grimspawn see things that aren't there, a few swinging and missing beings with no form.

Contemplating what the fuck I can do against these horrid beings, I summon that new power and thrust it at the beings with the hoods. The orange netting falls over them and evaporates, but there's no reaction. None of them seem to be hastened by their fears.

In a terrified state, all that is left for me to do is wait for them to come after me.

Everett pierces the one attacking Ollie through the middle with the fireplace poker, and that gut-wrenching, skin-crunching sound befalls my ears again. He morphs into Ollie, confusing the grimspawn, getting it to chase him a few feet away from the actual Ollie.

Bash has yielded a giant shard of glass from the pile of the remnants of the table that had shattered earlier and slits one's throat, the sight of which causes me to almost vomit. I bite back the bile and watch as the grimspawn falls to the floor, its head wobbling entirely too far back behind himself to recover. Bash then stomps his foot and embraces the Earth's vibrations, using it to shove one with his power across the room and into a wall.

"Dom, up now!" yells Jasantha.

Dom is still in his siren trance, watching nothing but the floor. He lurches up and shoots for one about to bombard Scarlet, but as he does, another grimspawn shoves a long sword through his back, which runs him through to the hilt, dripping blood.

His scream pierces the air, echoing through the cabin, as an intense burst of light engulfs the space, reminiscent of imprisoned lightning breaking free. Concurrent with the grimspawns' unrelenting onslaught, a hiss of smoke begins to snake upward. Amidst the chaos, the thick white smoke swirls, creating a gust that tousles my hair.

A pungent scent of sulfur lingers within the billowing fog, leaving a bitter taste in my mouth. Emerging from the haze, a colossal figure materializes, defying the limitations of mere malevolence. Seven feet tall, at least, she exudes a sinister presence, an embodiment of darkness. Her hair, a river of white, flows down her back, crowned with a dark circlet that frames her foreboding horns jutting from her forehead and adorned with intricate black embellishments. Eyes devoid of color gaze into the depths of me, and a word that doesn't exist in the realm of terror takes over me. Pointed black nails with dark jewels punctuate her eerie presence. Draped in a black dress, her unnaturally pale skin radiates an otherworldly luminescence, surpassing the confines of the ordinary. Describing her as the epitome of evil feels insufficient for the darkness she embodies.

As the smoke dissipates, Bash rushes upon the warlock, jumping on her back and biting down on her neck in such a murderous, animalistic fashion that he looks like a rabid wolf attacking a bear three times his own size. Black blood rushes down her white skin, and yet she makes no motion like she's in any pain or that his bite is hindering her in any way whatsoever.

Abruptly, he stops his rabid attack. The lights flicker, and when they do, black blood covers his face and drips down his neck, and his eyes take on the same hue, drowning the blue completely. As he slides down the warlock and focuses on me, what's beyond his eyes terrifies me more.

My death.

Hattie extracts the sword from Dom, and his blood, saturating his shirt, trickles down his front and pools on the floor in front of him. Pressing his hand over the wound to staunch the bleeding, he limps over to Everett. Three assailants are closing in on Everett, who wields an enormous axe I hadn't seen before, viscously hacking one's head off.

As Adaline chants her magick words, trying to get the artifact to come to life, wind whipping her hair around furiously, Bash arrives at me, and when he kneels down to pull me up, I know it's my turn to die.

I stagger to my feet at his hands, yanking me upward, and the last thing I see before I die is the fragments of his shattered blue eyes in the black depths the warlock summoned in him.

Barring his fangs, he turns my head to the side, bites into my neck, and the agony comes.

The searing blaze starts at my toes and rapidly spreads this time, faster than it ever had in the dreams. Quickly, I'm engulfed in flames, seething up before my eyes. The smell of charred flesh and burnt hair flares up my nose, and the unendurable pain ravages my every pore, every sinew of my life, the very molecules that make me burn. Bash backs away before he burns, too, the fractured blue of his eyes coming back together to form the most agonizing look as he becomes aware of what he did.

"*No!*" Dom's scream echoes as he rushes to me as fast as his injury will allow, the wound made by the grimspawn not yet healing in his chest. The flames have risen so much and are so intense and hot he can't get any closer to me.

The eerie part about it is I make no sounds.

As the flames ravage me, there's a pulling at my soul that lifts me up out of my body. Watching myself burn from above, I can observe the rest of the battle omnisciently.

Feelings of utter sorrow almost plunge me into darkness as I'm being held aloft in that cloud of heat from my own being.

I'm never going to see Gauge grow up.

No pain on Earth can compare to the agonizing thought of not being there for my son. Knowing the loss of a mother to a child, I can't bear the thought of Gauge having to go through that, too. Sadness rips me apart and I feel that more than I feel myself burning.

But why am I not disappearing?

Down below, Everett is pulling the axe out of the grimspawn on the floor and viciously hacking another one, savagely pulling it out and repeating this action a few more times, spattering blood all over the walls and himself. He truly gives his Viking image that barbaric, brutal, and ferocious air he has about him.

Jasantha parts her lips, releasing her wail; that piercing melody reverberates through the air, and two of the other grimspawns crumple to the ground, subdued by the haunting sound. Adaline remains steadfast, continuing her incantation, her gaze locked into the warlock, who observes the unfolding events with a detached fascination.

My body has finished burning and is all but ash when Dom finally gets to me, bleeding onto my ashes from the wound in his chest that has not yet healed. I feel sad, like the wind on the ocean, cold and lost with nobody around to feel me. No one knows I'm still here, floating above the chaos. I wonder if I would soon see my mama. That thought gives me hope.

Unaffected by the siren song, Bash, with black eyes once more, advances toward Talora. Swiftly, he snaps her neck and begins the gruesome task of draining her blood.

That's when the strangest thing happens.

As the drop of blood from Dom's wound descends onto my ashes, an intense pull seizes my soul, drawing my essence back to the charred remnants of my former body. The flames flare back to life, distorting my perception with swirling waves of heat as my body undergoes a mysterious transformation. As my bones and muscles and tissues and fibers sew themselves back together, the swirling notion is euphoric; there is no searing pain; instead, I sense my form expanding, and I find myself standing on my feet once more.

Standing there before them, unharmed and unburned, I examine my hands, my arms, my legs. My skin is glowing, fissures of golden cracks slither all over me, and power is buzzing. It feels like I can shoot my hand out, send lightning into the crowd, and burn everyone within my gaze. I feel drunk, like I drank a hundred margaritas; my body is warm and tingly, my neck feels rubbery, and my head feels like it's still floating above them all. Not only that, but there's now clarity about my thoughts. All fog has been lifted. Memories of everything in my childhood come rushing back, released like birds from the protective cage my mother had placed over me in toddlerhood. Visions of my sister, my mother placing a protective shield on me, Laureya's face, my aunts, and their magick instantly flash through my mind.

I am the phoenix, and power drips off me; I feel it in the molten marrow of my bones.

I know without any shadow of a doubt that I'm the most powerful being in that room.

No one moves, not even the warlock, as I'm more potent than her now.

It's so clear what I have to do. It's as though the thought of it has always lived in me; it was hiding this whole time.

Plunge a heated sword into water, and it'll break, but drench it in blood and fire, and it hardens.

How had I not known before?

The fire that lives in my bones now extends outward from my being in wings of fire, and as I try to grasp this moment and wrap my mind around what this means, time simultaneously moves with urgency and stillness; everyone else in the room but me freezes in place.

It's as though something else entirely is controlling my movements; the alliance I had with gravity to keep me grounded shatters, and I soar into the air, flying up above the fray in the high rafters of the ceiling. Fiery tendrils slither out from the depths of me and extend toward the warlock as the lassos of my fire wrap around her, binding her from the ground up. The ropes tether her arms and extend them outward while another wraps around her neck, pulling her face to the sky—the blackness of her eyes pointed directly at me as I fly above her. They are unfathomable, and yet I feel no fear, even though she stares at me as though she'd devour my soul and harvest every ounce of my being.

There's a slight tingling in my mouth on my gums, and this razor-sharp stinging makes me wince, and yet I know that they are fangs as I feel them elongate from my mouth.

In a movement as fluid as water, I fall downward toward her, like a volcano incarnate, and submerge my new fangs into the warlock's neck; the sound of skin breaking and feeling a crunch is almost satisfying. The taste of her black blood is acrid in my mouth, but I do not drink it. The moment I bite down, the fire in me rushes through me and spews into the warlock, turning her white body black with red fissures of lava. The lava grows so intense that the room's dark is as bright as a forest fire, and the burning body looks like its metal is being melted until it detonates into flames. Ear-piercing screeches like some sort of banshee of the night make even me wince, and I float upward and watch the creature burn.

The flames that shoot out from her become bright doves made of fire; they explode outward and dive toward the grimspawns—hundreds of them piercing the rotting flesh of the terrible beings. They, too, burst into their own flames, emitting sounds of terror, smells of burning flesh, and tempered agony amongst the vampires floods me.

When time resumes and my feet find the ground again, I see one grimspawn remaining.

Why did he not burn?

He's standing by the fireplace, and as though he knows his death is subsequent, he runs up to Scarlet and tackles her to the ground; they both implode into a murder of crows made of smoke as they fly away.

"No!" screams Dom, who goes after them, vamp flashing out of the door in their wake.

Bash's eyes return to their standard, glorious blue, standing with his mouth agape at me as I stand over a pile of ash, nothing but black jewels twinkling from it.

Lights return to normal, the air in the mansion resumes its average temperatures, and I remain frozen, unable to fathom what the hell just occurred.

Allison's dead, her eyes unmoving and blank; the gaping hole in her neck is thrashed open, bits of flesh frayed where the creature had been eating her. Beneath her head, her brown hair is matted and thick with the pool of blood she lies in. Talora is still as well, paler than she had been before, her neck bent at an incongruous angle, her eyes utterly white as though she had tried to turn her vampire on while fighting for her life against the man she came here with.

Dom returns without Scarlet, his face contorted in rage and fear. "She's gone. They have her."

"Who has her?" Adaline asks, coming up to stand beside Everett, who has blood covering him from head to foot. "Sayah killed the warlock that spelled them."

"There has to be another one?" he asks ,or tells- I'm not sure.

"I need to sit down," I say, blustering, examining my hand. My skin is still lightly glimmering, but it's fading back to normal as I head over to the bar stools.

Dom is there beside me in an instant, hesitant to touch me.

"Does someone mind explaining what the hell just happened?" Jasantha says, eyeing all the bodies around.

"Ollie's dead," Bash murmurs, kneeling next to Ollie.

He's lifeless and still by the fireplace, a stake laced with silver driven through his heart. His eyes are wide open, blood seeping from all points of his face. The irises of his eyes are completely white, his skin mirroring that same hue.

Bash is crouched over Ollie, a tender vulnerability in his hardened jawline. He's touching the silver stake that's protruding from his heart, the thing that rendered him lifeless. Violently, Bash rips it out and tosses it aside, where it flings with a force a wooden stake shouldn't have and shatters into a million pieces on the wall.

Adaline flashes to Ollie's side and scoops him up, shattering her hardened demeanor. "No, not my Ollie."

I can't move, can't think. All that's in my mind is what just happened.

I'm the phoenix now, as I literally rose from the ashes.

And I have fangs?

What the hell is that about?

The psychic's words are suddenly in my mind again: *"One love will rise you from those ashes. And one will put you in them. Your heart will want the pain. The burn. The fire. That is the love that will consume you. The other is safe. It won't take you to the ends of the Earth, but it will protect you and keep you safe. When the time comes, you must choose which love you want. The love that ends you. Or the love that revives you."*

It had been Dom's blood that dropped onto my ashes and ignited the flame. So, Bash is the one who put me in the ashes, and Dom is the one who rose me from them.

Literal pain swells up in my mind when trying to figure out what this means.

What am I supposed to do now?

Am I the savior of the damned? Or the destroyer of them?

Tears again flow from my eyes.

"My mark is gone," Dom says and when I turn my head, I see him examining his arm. I move silently over to him.

"Is mine?" Bash asks, pulling down his collar.

No one speaks.

"What?" he asks, his black brows like checkmarks, "Is it bad?"

"It's darker," Dom reports.

"What does that even mean?" questions Bash incredulously.

"What does any of this mean?" Dom queries.

"There must be another warlock." That is Hattie.

"What do we do about Ollie?" Adaline laments, her voice cracking as tears threaten to fall from her eyes. Everett's rubbing her back.

As I crouch down to see the mark that's missing from Dom's arm, a tear falls from my eye that drops right onto the wound the stake had left behind in Ollie's chest.

The tear that fell creates a spark that lights the entire wound up, the charred and bloody flesh glowing red but then the light turns bright, bright white. The blazing light pools until it's blinding. The wound seals up, and his skin returns to the typical pale peach color, the blood staining his face and eyes fading. His eyes were that ghastly white suddenly turn to green and when he takes a deep breath in, a shock wave like thunder without sound emits from him and ripples out into the world, awakening something ancient that has been slumbering until now.

He begins to cough up blood.

"Ollie!" stammers Adaline, quizzically looking from him to me.

This is too much for me.

I run from them all, out of the back door and into the night. The psychic Quinlyn's voice reverberates in my mind, and I hear it as I run toward the water: *"Even though your choice will hurt you, you have something in you that will save a lot of people. Your pain will end other's suffering, and so this path that you're on is one that you're meant to be on. Others before you could not rise from the ashes as you have, and you will have to keep rising out of those ashes. For you are like a Phoenix. And your blood is powerful. There's a reason that you've been dealt the things you have. Your pain and suffering will not go unrepented. You have a magick within you that's unlike any other kind of magick the world has ever seen. Take caution when honing your power, but hone it all the same. Conquer it. And seek the advice of others who walk your path, for they will guide you to where you need to be."*

Reaching the water's edge, I fall to the sandy shore and scream.

"Who is it that walks my path that could possibly help me with what all this means?"

"It seems as though there's magick that you're playing with now that's stirring something ancient and powerful. Something is happening in your eyes that tells me you know exactly what I'm talking about. Just be careful with it. And that man you are seeing right now is part of that darkness that's seeping into your soul . . . I would leave him behind if I were you. Something in his energy is attaching to you and seeping into you. Careful if that's the darkness that will consume you..."

It's Dom who's at my side as I wallow in my sorrow and grief.

"Are you all right?" His concern is genuine for me. When I look at him, his green eyes are agonized, harboring a grief I know nothing about.

"Are you?" I ask, wiping my tears away.

"I don't know how to be," he says sadly.

"I hear that," I reply, my voice shaky and unreliable. "I don't know what the hell I am now."

"Well, I would say that you, clearly, are a phoenix."

"What the fuck does that mean?"

It's not anger I feel for him; it's anger at the situation that seethes through me. There's no one to tell me what I'm supposed to do now. I'd risen someone from the dead with my tears. I fucking glow! I have fangs. What the fuck am I? What does this mean? What am I supposed to do now? I am screaming inside.

"I don't know."

"I brought your brother back from the dead with a tear! What the hell is that?"

"It was mixed with a little of your blood. I don't know if that means anything at all. But it would appear—to me—you are magickal now. And your bite kills the warlocks that spell the grimspawns. Bash killed you—" His voice trails off with his eyes, somewhere to the depths of the lake before us. "Why did Bash kill you?"

"Why did your blood rise me?"

His eyes are back on mine. "What?"

"I rose up out of my body when I was burning. I watched the rest of that all go down. You ran over to the ashes of me; you were bleeding. The moment your blood dropped onto my ashes, the fire rose back up, and I was pulled back into them with my body."

Blinking wildly, he rubs his hands over his face, massaging his eyebrows, furrowing them, and then relaxing them again. "What?"

"Bash put me in the ashes, and you rose me out of them."

"I have no idea where to begin to figure out what that is."

"Do you think your mom would know?"

"I doubt it. But we can see." He hesitates, then his eyes lighten a bit. "What about your aunts?"

Thinking of Hilda, Maggie, and the grimoires they'd said they had at their house, that may be what we need to try to put all of this together.

"I can call them tomorrow. At least we can leave here now, knowing you're not marked anymore."

"But my brother is. We have to help him. And find my sister."

"How can we find Scarlet? And help your brother?"

"I don't know. But you are the key to breaking the curse. We have to help him."

It's a good thing Dom is showing emotions for his brother.

"Okay," I say tenderly.

Rising up from the ground, he offers me his hand. When I'm at eye level with him, he holds me still, and his eyes taper toward me.

"I wanted to tell you how sorry I am." As he says this, he moves my hair from my neck where Bash bit me and caresses where the two puncture holes should have been.

"Your bite," he says, and there's a questioning in his voice.

"What?"

"The marks, where there should be holes. They're gone."

I shake my head, unable to process any more of anything else. "Well, considering I just rose from ashes, it makes sense, in a weird 'you're a vampire' sort of way. Six months ago, and I wouldn't have believed any of this."

He kisses me like I'm as fragile as glass, and my heart swells. My feelings for him have not abated after all. These past few days, they've been hard to recognize with everything that has happened.

Pulling me by the hand, we walk back into the house.

Bash is pacing again in the kitchen, and the rest are in the living room around the couches.

As I approach, they all have coveted eyes for me now.

Ollie, who looks worse for wear but is up and sitting on the couch, rises and draws up to me.

"Thank you," he says sternly, his green eyes strong in their gaze on me. "For bringing me back to life. The place I went to was not somewhere I'd want to stay. Or to ever go back to."

I nod. "You're welcome, Ollie."

He hugs me, and it's a remarkably expressive hug.

None of them seem the hugging type.

"So what does this make you?" Jasantha says grimly, and her tone is imbued with a dislike for me.

"You'll have to excuse my sister," Bash retorts as he joins us in the living room. "She dislikes anyone that can out-power her."

Jasantha huffs and shoots him a disgruntled glare, her eyes flashing purple.

"Doesn't work on me, sister. I thought you knew that."

Her head cocks sideways as though this confuses her.

"I'm not sure," I say, ignoring their quarrel and sitting on one of the couches. "A phoenix, I believe, but I don't know what that means."

"Have you ever heard of anything like this, Mom?" Dom asks.

"No," Adaline says darkly. "I mean, I've heard of a phoenix before, but never what Sayah is here."

"Are you immortal now?" asks Everett, his gray eyes searching, his face and hair spattered with blood.

"I have no idea what I am," I answer honestly. "All I know is that Bash was marked to kill me. I burned. Dom's blood saved me. I rose. There was a power I felt within me; I knew I could overpower the warlock. I knew if I bit her, she'd burn. I could feel the fire in my bones. I feel it in them now. I did not know that my tears would rise Ollie. I don't know what I'm supposed to do now."

"You're our new secret weapon," says Bash. The sinister twinkle in his eyes rattle me. "You can get this, this thing off me now." He pulls at his collar in annoyance to show what he means.

We all knew what he meant.

"But," Dom says, "how are we going to get the other warlock here for Sayah to kill her and find out how to get Scarlet back before she does?"

"How did it come to be that the other warlock came here the last time?" Hattie asks, sitting next to Ollie and looking pensive.

"Bash and Dom were marked," I say, fidgeting with my fingernails, "they were fighting, and they were each ordered to kill me and Talora. My voice is what made him snap, what got Dom's mark to activate and want to kill me. I can only assume it has something to do with me."

"If we try to activate it now," Everett offers, cracking his knuckles, "by using Bash's mark, it may not work to summon the next warlock connected with it because it might call the grimspawns here. Since Dom was marked to kill Sayah, the phoenix, that may work. But Bash doesn't have any connections with Sayah."

Looking at Bash at that moment, the look in his eyes tells me now is not the time to bring up the dreams, even if it means linking us and maybe working to summon Bash's warlock.

"Well, I'll take his mark from him," Dom says, sitting on the arm of the chair.

"How will you do that, brother?" Bash asks disbelievingly, the tone somewhere between skepticism and curiosity. He sits down on the edge of the lazy boy.

"Kill you," he says with a smile and a wink at Bash. "Relax," he says to his mom, whose mouth has fallen open. "Sayah can bring him back. All we need to do is have me stake him with silver, take the mark, have Sayah bring him back, and then I'll be marked again."

"Dom—"

"It's to get her here so you can kill her."

"I can't let you do that," Bash counters, his mouth falling into a stern line.

"Why not? It's to get the warlock here for Sayah to kill her," Dom repeats.

"If it doesn't work, then I don't know what I'd do." The seriousness instilled inside of his voice leaves his throat and seems to level the rest of the vampires in confusion.

Collective looks from around the room give dubious glares to Dom, gaping between him and Bash. The two brothers that hate each other.

"Look, I'm the reason that you became a vampire to begin with. I condemned you to vampirism. It's my fault. And you taking this from me and taking a chance it doesn't work and condemning your soul again...I don't know if I can handle that."

The monster façade in Bash seems to fade. Sensing that his monster mask is crumbling, he fidgets with his fingernails.

"I didn't think you cared," Dom sneers.

"He didn't kill Sadie," I interject sharply. Bash shoots me a glare that could have ended me. Again. "What? They need to know."

"Need to know what?" Dom asks, anger raising his voice a few octaves.

"Tell them, Bash. They need to know," I say again. I know this is the right thing to do.

Keeping it a secret from Dom is wrong, anyway. There's no easy way to explain it, but they need to know Bash is not as much of a monster as he lets them believe.

He sighs and looks at Dom.

Retelling the tale he'd told me on the lake, I watch in rapt fascination as Dom's expressions rearrange from confusion to anger to sorrow and back to confusion again. All attention is on Bash as he weaves his tale of Sadie and her suicide and confesses to the dreams, to not killing Sadie, to not being susceptible to Jasantha's power—all of it.

"I let you all think I was a monster to keep my promise to Sadie," he concludes, pouring himself a rocks-glass of bourbon.

"And you two have been having these dreams of each other?" Dom asks me, his eyes pinched.

"Yes," I admit in a hushed voice. "I've been dreaming of him before I met you."

"And what happens in these dreams?" The way he looks at me tells me he's more concerned with the nature of the dreams rather than their message.

I look to Bash, who shrugs.

"He kisses me, okay? He kisses me, then he bites me. Then I burn."

"I knew you knew him when he walked in last night. He wasn't reading your mind when he called you by your nickname."

Dom is agitated. And it's pissing me off he's more concerned about this than of his brother baring his soul to him.

What the fuck is wrong with you! I want to spew.

"Dom," says Adaline, stealing my thoughts. "I think you're missing the point here."

Thank you, Mama Vampire.

"Right!" Hattie says. "I'm more interested in the fact that these phoenixes are being drawn to Bash and what that means."

"That," I say, "and Bash never killed Sadie. She killed herself. And she was being conditioned, but what does that mean? And am I Sadie reincarnated?"

"And that my blood arose you," Dom says, seemingly over the dreams, for now.

"Your what?" Adaline asks, her aquiline eyes beseeching.

"My blood. It dropped onto her ashes, which pulled her back."

"Well, that's curious," murmurs Adaline.

"Mean anything to you yet?"

She shakes her head. "Not that I am aware of, but once we get Bash's warlock killed, I can look into it."

"So, my siren song doesn't work on you?" Jasantha asks almost timidly, as though knowing there's someone her song doesn't work on grates on her.

"Nope," Bash chides, inhaling a sip of his bourbon. "But it has been super fun making you think it has all these years." He laughs, and her eyes turn purple.

"All right, I'm ready to kill you now," Dom says, rising from the couch. He walks over and retrieves a silver butter knife from the kitchen.

"Dom," I say, standing as well.

"You can bring him back, Sayah. And this will be fun. For me."

Bash shakes his head, and his dark eyes bore into Dom. He sets his glass down and walks over to the table. "All right. Just hoping this works, and she can kill this one too."

"Ready?" Dom says, holding the butter knife close to his heart.

"Wait!" Adaline says, stepping in between the two of them. "Because Bash dreams of Sayah, wouldn't that make him connected to her and able to bring the warlock here with that?"

"We can't trust that," Dom says. "It's safer this way; we know she'll come."

"Sayah, how exactly did you bring Ollie back?" She asks me.

"I didn't mean to. A tear fell into his chest wound."

"It was mixed with your blood," Dom reminds me.

"Then we need her to bleed a little bit, don't we," Jasantha says in a lofty voice she uses when wishing to wound, a devilish grin playing at the corners of her mouth. "I can make that happen." As she rises from the couch, her eyes turn purple, she holds out her hand and her fingernail grows, fangs protruding as she does. She hisses on her way up to me.

"J, stop," Everett commands.

The look on her face is that of disappointment. Her eyes return to green, and her fingernails and fangs return to their normal length.

An idea sparks in my mind, and I remember the way it had felt when my own new fangs protruded from my mouth. Wondering if I can simply wish them out or if there's some more profound force behind it, I say, "Let me try something."

Feeling a subtle tingle in my gums, the new power that lives in my bones is almost alive with buzzing, like I had swallowed a live wire that's now lodged in my veins. Beginning to pull at it, I focus on the fangs, squinting my eyes to force them to come to the surface. Feeling the razor-sharp pang of those sharp new teeth extracting from me somewhere, I open my mouth and gasp a little at the pain.

"I got this." I smile and bite my arm, feeling the terrible crunch. My skin tears open, and the taste of my blood spills into my mouth. "Ready?"

"That's hot," Bash says, and Dom is ready to kill him again.

Dom plunges the butter knife into Bash's heart, and Bash gasps with horror. Bash's dark crystal blue eyes go from light blue to white; his skin turns white and pale as a sheet, and blood pours from his eyes, his nose, and his mouth. It's horrific watching Bash die. A piece of me feels like it's dying with him. Falling to the ground, he writhes in pain for a second, and then he's still holding the knife that pierces his heart.

Dom extends his arm, anticipating the mark's appearance. However, the mark on Bash's neck remains, refusing to vanish. With each passing moment feeling like an eternity, Dom keeps a vigilant gaze on his forearm, hoping for the mark's manifestation, yet it stubbornly eludes him.

"It happened right away last time," he says with hesitation.

"Do you think it went somewhere else?" I ask, bleeding still, concerned about Bash and bringing him back.

"I don't feel it anywhere." He lifts his shirt, and there's no mark on his rippling stomach. Lifting his pant legs, there are no new marks, only tattoos.

"Dom?"

"I don't know. It's not showing up."

"We need to bring him back soon," Adaline pleads, her face panicked.

"Let him stay dead," Everett retorts, Adaline's gaze at him seething.

"Ollie was gone for a while before Sayah saved him," Hattie replies.

"Just do it, Sayah, save him," urges Adaline.

"Mom, the mark hasn't shown up yet."

"I don't care. I don't want to risk losing Bash!"

"There," Dom says, showing them his arm.

The faint crescent moon brand rises on his arm, faintly but enough to give me the green light.

Dom yanks the knife out, and I try to force myself to cry, but my eyes remain dry and unyielding of tears.

Dredging up events of the past few weeks to try and entice the tears as the family watches me, I feel more pressure to cry, and yet the tears will not come to me.

Do they have to be genuine and unbeckoned?

I think of my son, missing him and wanting to return to him.

Is it just the pressure of having to cry on cue?

I think of me having cancer and the baby I had to send back to the heavens to begin chemo.

Deep down, I know the thing that will bring my tears is the memory of my mom, and I don't want to reopen that raw wound, but the tears aren't coming on their own.

Closing my eyes, I remember everything about my mama, circulating through memories like a slideshow. Her laugh, the storms, unconditional love, the hard times, my cancer, her health scares, our bond. I think of all of it.

They come.

Tears pool in my eyes and down my face; I wipe the tears away and smudge them into the blood, smearing it over the gaping wound in his chest.

Again, the wound lights up and burns brightly within his skin, but this time, the incandescence scatters throughout his whole body, looking like fireflies that are alive and flittering beneath the surface of his skin. As they flit about, the awful white pallor of his flesh dissipates and returns to the color of apricots. The blood dries up from his nose, mouth, and eyes, and the wound in his chest diminishes and evaporates. Bash wretches forward, eyes alight with that glorious blue, and takes a long, deep, invigorating breath.

"Did it work?" he almost stammers, his voice sounding as though he'd been sucking on cotton.

"Yep," Dom answers, offering his hand and pulling him up.

40

DARKER SHADES OF DARK

SAYAH

"Once we get the artifact ready," Adaline says, "I think you two will have to fight again."

"No problem there," Bash retorts, brushing off his black jeans.

Dom's right eye squints in the projectile glare he whips at Bash.

"When will you two be okay with being brothers?" Hattie asks, the annoyance in her voice rising friction in the room.

"Never, apparently," Bash answers.

"All right," Adaline interjects, "let's get somewhere where we can be ready for the grimspawns bound to come along."

"I didn't think of that part," I say, remembering the dread when they entered the room.

"We'll be ready this time," Everett responds, arising from the couch.

"How will we be ready?" Dom asks, crossing his arms.

"Let's pick a room we control," Everett says, his wavy hair clumping in parts from the blood. "Have weapons ready. Attack on the offense."

"The spell room?" Jasantha asks, rising from the couch as well.

"I don't know," Adaline says, no doubt picturing all her jars and things breaking from the throes of war.

"The dungeon," Everett offers, his hard eyes growing like stone.

"There's a dungeon?" I ask, chills trickling down my spine, my ass puckering a smidge.

"Yes, well," Hattie answers, shooting me a devilish grin, "when you're a family of monsters, sometimes monsters come knocking at your door. When that happens, you need a place to put them."

I can only imagine what this dungeon looks like, complete with barred cages and torture devices and things of agony and pain.

A darker shade of dark.

"Well, let's get down there then," Bash replies, grabbing the bottle of bourbon. "Grab your witchy device and let the murder and mayhem commence."

"I need to grab the artifact," Adaline utters, "and some salt and candles."

We enter the spell room where Adaline gathers her things, and then we follow her to the far corner, where she quickly pushes aside her large bookcase and reveals a dark, damp-smelling staircase.

Descending, my mind is all but a wander, wondering what I will see in this dungeon.

Arriving at the landing, the stairway leads to a narrow hall crafted entirely of dark and weighty stone, reminiscent of a castle interior. The extensive hallway stretches across what appears to be the entire house, bars beholden to cells beyond them on either side. Walking the length of the corridor, I glance into each cell, seeing if there's anyone —or anything—inside. All cells are vacant, holding only lonely cots with metal toilets and no windows, mirrors, or furnishings of any sort. Reaching the end of the hallway, a spacious room opens up, maintaining the stone motif with a large fireplace featuring a black cauldron. The walls of this room are adorned with double and triple arrays of every conceivable type of weapon. Among them are modern weapons, such as guns of every kind, and then medieval weaponry—axes, scythes, maces, crossbows, swords, flails, halberds, spears, caltrops, and battle axes—all neatly arranged on the walls within their pegs.

On the wall with the cauldron are the weapons for the monsters.

Stakes of every size and wood laced with silver, crossbows and bows and arrows laden with silver heads, bronze and silver daggers, dried herbs which can only be Nightshade . . . this list goes on and on.

I find it odd that they have weapons that could kill their own kind within the walls of their house. But, when dealing with monsters, one could only be so prepared.

Adaline walks around the room with the salt and spreads a circle around the boundaries, laying the candles out. And with one swoosh of her hand, all the candles and the fire beneath the cauldron come alight.

"I love it when she does that," Bash says, picking out a few silver stakes from the wall. He tosses one to me. "Here, arm yourself. Just in case."

I hold the stake in my hand, and suddenly that nervous danger catches at me and makes me a little nervous. That fire in my blood tries to singe back the doubt.

But what if I can't kill this one?

Where's that power I'd felt the first time the white warlock came? I feel it buzzing, but how do I turn into that glowing, fire fissure being I was before? Will it just happen, or do I have to do it now?

Maybe the panic is suppressing the strenuous zap I felt ten minutes ago.

Holding the artifact in her hand, Adaline takes her place in the middle of the room. Hattie, with the vials of blood in hand, meets her there.

"Since we don't have Scarlet," Adaline says, "Sayah, we're gonna need you to chant with us. We must act like we're trying to break the curse."

I nod and meet them in the middle.

Everett pulls down a mace, handing Dom a silver stake, and Ollie takes up an axe.

They stand ready.

"All right. Make each other mad," spits Jasantha. An evil look twists within her eyes which flash purple.

"Maybe, don't use the weapons on each other, huh?" Adaline quips.

Dom stows his stake in the front of his pants, and Bash puts his in the back.

"Who's gonna provoke who?" Bash asks in contravention, squaring his shoulders.

"Doesn't take much for you to piss me off," Dom glowers, spreading out his stance.

"Awe, come on, brother, I think we've come a long way today." His voice is sharp with contempt.

"That does not make up for the last two-hundred years that you've been a complete dick. Why don't you have another dream about my girlfriend?"

"With pleasure," he answers with disdain, "as she will probably be dreaming of me, too!"

And this is enough to sear the anger in Dom to pounce on Bash. He flies up into the air and lands with a vicious blow to Bash's head. Bash falls back and cracks his head on the stone floor, blood spewing forth out of his wound.

Dom's eyes go white with the green rim, his teeth protract, and his skin turns pearly white.

Bash's eyes turn white with a dark blue rim around them, his teeth protruding from the gums, and he hisses ferally at Dom. He lurches up and runs at Dom with that speed, knocking him to one of the stone pillars. The whole house rumbles, causing loose stones to fall from the ceiling.

Adaline looks up worriedly. Everett sends her a quelling glance.

Dom rounds on Bash and pushes him to the ground with a thundering boom, savagely punching him in the face time after time, punch after punch.

Blood runs thick from Bash's nose and cut lip, he finally gets his teeth into Dom's arm, ripping a chunk of flesh from it and spitting it out to the side.

I feel lightheaded at the gore and try to look away, but I know it's essential to keep a steady eye on all that's happening.

The wound heals as fast as it came on and suddenly Dom's eyes go black, and he stops fighting Bash. His head goes still as though he's listening to something. His head turns toward me, and I feel that terror again that I'm about to die. He rises from straddling Bash and walks toward me, Bash getting up and holding him by the arms.

Adaline and Hattie pour the blood over the artifact, chanting magickal words, and I chant with them, the hieroglyphics taking on a somber glow.

Another shock wave emits out of the artifact, and right as that happens, a hissing sound engulfs us, and the candles flicker in the breeze it causes.

As the hooded figures find their way down to the dungeon, Everett and Ollie are ready with their weapons and flash after them. Everett ferociously swings his mace to one's head, making the most sickening crack as his skull caves in. Ollie takes his axe to another one, decapitating him with one swing.

The air changes again. The candles blow out, and a red glow secretes from the fireplace where this wraith of a warlock comes through, this time a man with diabolical red eyes.

His skin is as dark as the blackest night; his red and black dreadlocks hang around his fearsome and loathing face, framed by a dark goatee. He wears a black suit with red accents; the lapel and pocket square are that bright blood red. Atop his head is a black top hat rimmed with red, the skulls of small animals lining it, other bones in spikes reaching the top.

All along, we thought this warlock was a woman. But as it turns out, it is her male counterpart.

Adaline bends her gaze to me, and I summon my phoenix power. It becomes activated immediately when the warlock makes eye contact with me.

My skin cracks and fissures of gold emerge and glow. The fangs pierce through my gums, and the throbbing power within me propels me forward to the warlock.

Unable to tear my focus away from the man, the unequivocal fatality that rests within his aura staggers me.

Before I arrive at him to end him, his voice pours out of him, though his lips don't move.

"You!" he admonishes, his voice echoing with such asperity in the dungeon that it almost stings. "You are the one that killed my sister!"

"That's right," I announce vehemently in a warrior rogue, trying to hide the terror within me. "I did. And now I will kill you."

I make a move toward him. He holds up his hand; a long, spindly, dark, and terrifying hand.

"Before you kill me, Mederio, phoenix, know this," he hisses petulantly. "I have Scarlet, and you will never know where she is or how to get her back if you kill me right now. The only way that I will reveal Scarlet's location is if you give me the artifact."

Looking behind me for reassurance, everyone is unmoving. Ollie and Everett are covered in blood, the gristly head of the grimspawn still dangling from Ollie's hands. Bash is holding Dom back still, his eyes that black hue fixed on me. Adaline is poised with the artifact in hand, gazing from it to the warlock back to me.

"And if you think that by giving me the artifact and getting back Scarlet, you will be able to summon me again and kill me, it is there that you would be wrong as well. I have a hundred warlocks under the orders to mark your son should you be responsible for my demise."

Thinking of my child's sweet face wrapped up in this mess of a world I got myself into stills my heart and nearly drops me to my knees, feeling diminished. Nothing in the world can break me faster than threatening my son's life.

"On his twenty-first birthday," the warlock continues mutinously in his horrifyingly deadened voice, "should I reach my demise at your hands, he will succumb to his fate for a lifetime of darkness."

There's no way out of this. The warlock has won. There isn't a chance in hell I would give Gauge over to the darkness. My life's purpose is to ensure that he lives a long, happy life in the light.

"To safeguard that this continues past his twenty-first birthday, I will leave both brothers, Sebastian and Dominic, marked. One will remain inactivated to assure you kill no more warlocks. Should you choose to partake in any warlock killing, I will activate that mark and bring him over to the darkness, too. The other one will be activated, but he will not become a grimspawn. He will keep his mind for the most part and live his life, but he will belong to me, doing my bidding when and how I say. One mark is to ensure you do not kill more warlocks; the other is to have a marked immortal to do my bidding, killing when I say to kill, damning his soul with every murder. It is up to you to choose which brother gets which mark." The smile he gives me is pestiferous, his black teeth glistening in the candlelight. "I will give you twenty minutes to decide."

Panic sets my soul on fire.

What do I do?

There is not a single route around what he's asking for.

To get Scarlet back, I need to let him live. Handing over the artifact makes it impossible to break either mark on Dom, Bash, or anyone else with one. What's more, going beyond the artifact, this warlock secured his safety and a hundred others by threatening to mark my son on his twenty-first birthday. Even further, I now have to choose which brother gets which mark, saving one soul while condemning the other.

This is a fathomless choice with profound consequences beyond anything I've comprehended.

41

A FATHOMLESS CHOICE

SAYAH

Heavy is the unendurable assignment I have been tasked with to choose.

Turning to walk back to the fodder, approaching them is slow and rigorous, my choices heavily weighing me down.

Walking up to Adaline, there's a deep anguish in her eyes, but one that tells me that she understands what my choice must be to keep my child safe.

Dom's eyes have returned to normal, and he and Bash's face have stern looks, telling the tale that they'd heard the whole thing.

"What am I supposed to do?"

"You give him the artifact," Dom surmises, his posture rigid. "There's no other way to save Scarlet."

"And what of the marks?"

"I'll take the activated mark," Dom answers quickly.

"No," Bash interposes, his voice dredging smoothly through me. "Sayah, choose me. I already condemned my brother's soul once; I'll not do that again."

"What if I don't want to condemn yours?" Dom asks grudgingly, shoving him on the shoulder.

"You guys spent your lifetime hating each other, and now, when time is of the essence, you two can't decide which one of you wants to be condemned?" Everett asks harshly.

"Sayah, choose me, okay? Let me do this for my brother." Bash's eyes bore into mine, the supplication in them deciding me. "C'mon, I'm used to the dark. I'll run it. Choose me."

As Dom has said, Bash is always one befitting of the darkness. He thrives in it; it's becoming on him. Dom belongs to the light more than Bash does. He's the good one.

It makes sense to me.

And thus, the psychic's words never rang truer in my mind: *"When the time comes, you must choose which love you want. The love that ends you. Or the love that revives you."*

Although I didn't have any time with Bash besides my dreams and a few brief moments on the shore, I still have a love for him I don't quite understand yet.

Though it's nothing like the love I have for Dom.

He has made me feel safe and loved, and like I'm somebody when I'd been on the narrow edge of darkness after losing my parents.

I will choose Dom.

I nod.

"Sayah, no!" Dom says as Adaline presses the artifact into my hand. "Wait Sayah, don't . . ."

"J, do your thing," Everett says, and Jasantha's eyes turn purple.

"No, Jasantha, don't!" Dom begs.

Tears spill down my face as I walk back toward the warlock.

"Dominic, calm," comes Jasantha's capricious voice behind me, lulling Dom to let me do this.

As I walk by Bash, his lucent blue eyes tell me it's all right.

The warlock, his garish eyes aglow with red, awaits me patiently.

"Have you made your choice then, phoenix?"

I nod. "Where is Scarlet?"

"I will tell you the location," he begins.

"No. Bring her here now. I will not give you the artifact or make my choice until she is here."

"Very well," he intones, his aura smoking around him.

Tilting his head back, he spreads his arms and mumbles idioms that do not register in my vernacular. A few seconds later, dozens of wings flapping echo throughout the dark space. From the fireplace, smoke-like crows enter, swirling around the ground and rising upward like a dark inverted tornado. Slowly, Scarlet's body appears, from toe to hip to head.

The gaunt appearance of Scarlet is unnerving. She's bloody and beaten, chunks of flesh missing from her arms and legs that aren't healing. Her skin is almost gray.

Her appearance doesn't make sense for only being gone a few hours at most.

Adaline glances over her quickly, pulling up her chin to check her eyes, and nods at me to finish the deal.

The warlock holds his hand, and I place the artifact within it.

"And your choice?"

"Dom to have the inactivated mark. Bash to have the other."

"Your wish is my command." And the grin he gives me is so awful; his teeth are black save for one gold tooth, but the evil that emits from it freezes my blood.

Evaporating, pieces, and parts of him become those black smoke crows, each flying up and out of the fireplace until he is gone.

For a moment, I stand there, staring into the darkness, contemplating what I'd done. Although I know nothing of the phoenix blessing bestowed upon me, I'm sure that condemning one man's soul to darkness is not part of it.

The shaking in my arms and legs makes it impossible to stand. I'm so lost as to what I'm supposed to do now.

Dom is not marked—or it's inactivated—and that's the only good thing that's happened. But being the phoenix means I'm supposed to restore the balance, and I had thought that meant killing the warlocks who spell the grimspawns.

I can't turn to anyone and ask the mounting questions in my mind.

Except for my aunts.

Hilda and Maggie have to know something, or at least have a way to figure out what my purpose is with this whole new life.

When I turn back around, something's not right.

Scarlet's staring off into nothingness; Bash, Dom, and everyone else are around her.

"What is it? What's wrong?"

"It's not Scarlet," Dom answers solemnly.

"What do you mean? How do you know?"

"She's my twin. I can feel her soul is not in this body."

"So, the warlock tricked us?" I state the obvious.

"Yes," answers Adaline, her stoic face grave. "And now they have the artifact, and we don't have Scarlet."

"Then who is this? And where is she?" I query, sitting on one of the chairs.

"A grim," Dom says, leaning on the back of my chair. "Remember when I told you that they can take on whomever they—" His voice trails off.

"Whomever they eat enough of," I answer morbidly. "Does that mean she's dead?"

"Not necessarily," says Bash, walking to the table to get the bourbon. "They could have used dark magick and taken enough of her to not kill her but to become her."

"And how do we find out?" I ask, nervously worrying at a string in my jeans.

"I can do a locater spell," remarks Adaline, tugging the fake Scarlet's hands behind her back. "See if her soul is still on this plane."

"What do you need for that?" I ask as Dom rubs my shoulders.

"Dom's blood," Adaline answers, the fake Scarlet hissing at her.

"Have as much as you want. Let's go."

"But how are we going to get her back?" I query, utterly lost now.

"We'll find a way," Dom says.

"Did the marks appear?"

Dom rolls up his sleeve and shows me the faint crescent moon mark.

I look at Bash.

He pulls down his collar and shows me his.

His is entirely black.

"About that," Dom says, and before any of us can realize what he's doing, he jumps up, pulls out the stake from the front of his pants, and drives it into Bash's heart.

Bash falls back, the bottle of bourbon shattering on the cement floor, as he had done before. With sorrowful questioning in his eyes, they go from light blue to white, blood pouring out from them. His skin turns that awful white again, and his mouth falls open, agape with blood.

"Dom!" I scream, jumping up. "What are you doing?"

"I don't want to condemn his soul more than it already is, Sayah. Tonight is the first time I've heard my brother being human, talking about what he did for Sadie. This whole time, I thought he was a monster, and he let me believe that; he let all of us believe that.

"In time, you'll find a way to save us. I know you will. There has to be another artifact somewhere, and I know you won't rest knowing what that warlock said about your son. I know you enough to know that you'll find a way to kill him, to kill all the warlocks that threatened Gauge. But for now, until we can do that, save Bash and let me keep his mark, and he takes mine."

There's a pleading in his eyes that I've never seen before. I've known he's good all along, but never enough to take his brother's place in hell.

I'd seen nothing but anger and hate between them, and to see this love between brothers, enough for one to take a spot in hell for the other, or whatever hell means to them, is genuinely endearing and heroic. There's more light to these dark creatures than I could have imagined. My eyes well up with tears again for him, for his brother's dark soul, for all of them.

Nodding, I lift my arm. "Is his mark on you yet?"

Rolling up his sleeve, I watch for it to change.

Slowly, the embossed mark grows darker and darker, the mark on Bash's neck going faint.

Dom pulls the stake out and stows it again in the back of his pants.

I bite into my arm, shed the tears that had already welled up in my eyes, and let it fall into Bash's wound.

The same light swims up and down him before he wretches again. His eyes shoot open, the white darkens to blue, and he heaves a heavy air intake.

He sits straight up and grabs Dom by the collar of his shirt. "What the fuck were you thinking?"

"I'm saving your disgustingly dark soul," he shouts back and wrenches himself free of the grip. "Now get up. Let's go see if our sister is still alive."

"We need to put this one in a cell," adds Everett, grabbing the thrashing fake Scarlet from Adaline.

"On it," Ollie says, helping Everett maneuver the mindless grimspawn who wears Scarlet's face toward one of the cells.

A rushing sound fills my ears, and my vision turns bright white. I see my aunts in a dark room, lit only by candlelight. Maggie is leaning into the flame; it dances beneath her breath.

Sayah . . .

It's a gentle rush of a whisper that prickles and my hairs stand on end.

The aunts are summoning me.

This may be part of my new abilities.

"While you do that," I say as my vision returns to normal, "I need to make a phone call."

"Who are you going to call?" Dom asks, helping Bash up from the floor.

"I have to call my aunts. They are summoning me, and I feel that they know something."

"Summoning you?" His brows furrow in curiosity.

"Yes. I had a vision just now."

"Okay," he states simply, as though he already knew this is the new me, an all-knowing and vision-having phoenix.

Dom nods and comes to me, kissing me swiftly before heading back to the spell room.

Hearing him say that he's confident in me to find a way to break this curse, to save my son's soul in the interim, and to kill the warlocks makes me feel a little better, even though I'm still littered with that self-doubt I carried with me before my fire.

Now, though, a voice that's louder than my doubt is fighting against it, growing louder with every second.

Still, what if, when we locate Scarlet, we'll encounter more grims and warlocks to get me, and I'm unable to kill them, even though I'm the only thing I know of that can?

Sayah! The voice shouts at me now. *You are the phoenix! You are the most powerful being on Earth!*

It will still take a while to get used to this heavy new burden I carry.

Blindly, I walk through the dungeon by them all without saying a thing, eyeing the fake Scarlet in the cell Ollie and Everett had thrown her in, and float up the stairs, through the spell room, into the greenhouse, and out the door to the lake.

Pulling out my phone—which I'm surprised is not shattered or burned from all the shit I've been through—I sit on the bench down by the boat dock.

Finding my aunt's contact, I take a deep breath and hit call.

It rings three times.

"Sayah?" answers Hilda's voice.

"Hi, Aunt Hilda."

"Sayah, we were trying something out to summon you. Did you get our message?"

My aunts and their powers are still baffling to me. "I did. You have no idea what the hell happened. I don't know where to begin."

"If it's about the vampire you've been hanging out with, we already know."

My heart drops. "What? How?"

"You don't know many things about us, Sayah, including that we've known our fair share of vampires. Maggie was brokenhearted by one. But that's neither here nor there. Just know that we wear Lapis Lazuli dipped in Nightshade. It makes it impossible to be veil-weaved by vampires."

"So, you remember the whole thing with Dad and Dom?"

"We do."

"I'm sorry, I didn't—"

"Know how to tell us? We know. What I want to know is what has happened now?"

"I don't know where to start."

"Start at the beginning."

I spill the entire story to Hilda, leaving nothing out. Right up until the part that I'm at now.

"I don't know what the hell to do, Aunt Hilda," I sob, kicking a rock into the lake. "I am at a loss."

"Sayah, listen to me. I need you and Dom and Bash to get on a plane and arrive soon. There is something about the marks we need to figure out. It's best to have them both here if we can break it."

"Why? What do you know?"

"We'll go over it all when you get here. I also may know of a way to get someone else to help."

"Who?"

"Your mom."

My breath catches in my throat, and my blood drains from my limbs. "How?"

"Maggie and I have been dipping into our own magick since we came across your vampire. There are things in Grandma's grimoires, and we found a way to channel her. She has some things she needs to say to you, Sayah, and you have to come here for us to do it. We need the blood knot, which is a generational knot. We've gathered bits and pieces of what she's been trying to tell us, but we need you here to finish it."

"I'm coming as soon as I can."

"Let us know when you land. We'll come get you."

"Okay. Love you."

"I love you too, sweetie. Bye-bye."

"Bye." I hang up and about drop the phone.

My aunts found a way to channel my mom? And there are things Mama needs to tell me?

I'm both elated and saddened at the same time.

There have been so many times that I'd wanted my mother to come to me in a dream or as a ghost or something, anything, to give me advice or tell me what I should do or say, the list goes on and on.

Stowing my phone in my back pocket, I get up and run back into the greenhouse and into the spell room.

They're hovering over a table with a map on it, whispering words of magick to a drop of blood that has coagulated on top of it.

"Dom!" I call.

Seeing my face in utter shock and elation, he peels his eyes away from the map and looks up at me.

"Yeah? Is everything okay?"

"We have to go to Washington. Right now."

"Now? Why?"

"My aunts have been doing magick and were able to channel my mom. They said she has a message for me but they need me to complete the knot. They want you, me, and Bash on a plane right now."

"All right," Bash says calmly from the table he sits at. "Looks like we're going to Washington."

"Did you guys figure out if Scarlet is alive?" I ask, going over to look at the map.

"She is, but barely," Dom answers, pointing to where the blood traveled.

"Do you think your aunts will know how to save her?" Adaline asks, the desperate plea in her eyes softening her complex Viking-like features.

"I hope so," I say. "In the meantime, try to do the research and find another artifact. There has to be another one like it in the world. Hattie, can you do what you did to find the last one?"

Hattie nods, her face finally softer toward me—just a smidge. "I can try."

"All right, we need to go pack," Dom says, turning to leave.

"I'll grab my shit too," Bash says, standing. "It's with Talora's in..." He hesitates on the mention of her name.

She is dead.

And only a little has been said about it due to all the events of the past evening.

I can see now the grief creep into his handsome features; the sadness injures the hard lines of his face, and his blue eyes nearly shatter.

"We'll take care of it, son," Adaline speaks softly.

Bash nods and looks away, but not before I'd seen a glimmer of a tear resting in his eyes.

"Why do all three of you need to go?" Hattie asks flippantly, unmerited annoyance dripping in her tone.

"Because they were both marked," I say. "My aunts said there is something about the marks we need to figure out. It's best to have them both there if we can break it. But you two can continue to try as well. The more people we have working on it, the better the chances of bringing Scarlet home, saving Bash and Dom, and getting my son out of this story altogether."

"We will, Sayah," Adaline says, and for once, her eyes are lighter toward me, a genuine affinity for the witch who saved her sons.

Dom grabs my hand, tugs me away from the spell room, and holds it up the stairs.

As we're packing, his green eyes collide with mine a few times, and the anguish now harbored there has worsened, as bad as I've ever seen it.

At times, I'd seen the anguish and hopelessness linger about in his soul; the whole thought of being a vampire for him was something he hated. But now there's more to it than that. Now, there's the fact that his existence has brought me here to this precipice, and he blames himself for all the pain I'm in. The peace I'd brought him is now fragile.

I can sense it.

"I'm so sorry, Sayah," he says, and that anguish shatters his gaze.

Something twists inside me at the sight of him so sad. "Please don't apologize, Dom. There's no reason for you to be sorry."

I drop the clothes into the suitcase and walk over to him, sitting on the edge of the bed front of him.

His eyes are bleak and sightless. "It's my fault you're in this mess. And poor Gauge."

"I will dismantle the world before I let anything happen to him," I say savagely. "And it's not your fault I'm in this mess. This is, somehow or another, my destiny. You led me to it."

"That doesn't make me feel any better."

"I know. But despite all that is going wrong right now, I feel that everything will be okay."

"We have no idea how much time we have until my mark starts making me do things, Sayah. I'm afraid of what I might do to you."

"I'm not." I catch his eyes and hold them, trying to get him back from the ledge on which he walked out. "Dom, I'm not."

He nods, and I know he doesn't believe me. There's a darkness in him that lingers harder than before, and I will have to fight like hell to keep him from submerging himself within it.

I'll have to get Bash to help me with that, too.

"Dom, we're going to find a way to save you. *I'm* going to find a way to save you. To save you and Bash and my son, especially my son, and Scarlet. And I'll also find a way to kill those warlocks. Every. Single. One of them."

The fire in my bones stirs when I think, firstly, of Gauge and then of all the others, I'm going to save. The inferno that now lives in me that became alight when I became the phoenix has mixed with the storm that'd already made a home in me. The hurricane, mixed with a volcano, surges up and crashes into me and devours all the doubt that had seeped in when Mederio threatened my son. I'm going to save them all.

And be that savior of the damned.

"I believe you, Sayah," he whispers, putting his hands on either side of my face, caressing my cheek with his thumbs, "and I love you for it. But if there comes a time when I threaten you again, like I did earlier, I need you to kill me, okay?"

I'm not saying anything to this; I wonder if he's a threat to me now? I still have no idea what I am nor what would happen should any creature of the dark try and kill me.

"Sayah?" he asks, his eyes questioning where I'd gone.

"Yes, I will."

"I mean it. Earlier, when Mederio came to me in my head, told me his name and took over, I had no power over myself. He wanted you dead, and that is what I was veilweaved to do. From what he said earlier, I'll be myself but have to do his bidding; I imagine that's exactly what it'll be like. And I don't know who he's going to want dead and when. If we get to Washington and I threaten your aunts or anyone you love, take this." He pulls out the stake he had driven into Bash and puts it in my hands. "And drive it through my heart. I need you to promise me you will; I'll not be able to live with myself knowing I hurt you or anyone you love."

Reluctantly, I take the stake. "I will."

"Promise me?"

"I promise."

"Thank you."

"Now we have to figure out how you're gonna get that through airport security."

I laugh, and it feels good to have some light-hearted feelings bubbling up inside me in what seems like a long time. The dissolution of sadness abating even a fraction is calming.

"I'm sure they won't think anything of it if I put it in my suitcase. It's not metal. They'll think it's some sort of—"

"Some sort of what?" The devious smile he gives me tells me he knows exactly what I'm thinking.

"Sex object," I breathe, laughing at the way it feels to say it.

"Oh, if only we had time to explore that idea," he says, falling into me and kissing my neck, jawline, and lips.

Heat engulfs me and I kiss him back passionately, suddenly wondering if the throes of passion would be different now that I'm of the fire.

There's the sound of Bash clearing his throat at the door.

Dom slips off me sideways and eyes him.

"Yes?" he asks in a semi-mocked tone.

"I have a question for Sayah."

"Yes?" I ask more nicely.

"Ollie and I were thinking—wondering, really—if you could bring both of us back, wouldn't you be able to bring back Talora and Allison?"

I look to Dom questioningly. "I don't see why not?"

"They've been dead a lot longer than you two were," Dom offers, "but it's worth a try for them, I'm sure."

"We would be more than appreciative if you brought our girlfriends back from the dead," Bash sneers.

"Sure. I can try."

I rise from the bed and follow Bash back down the stairs to where Talora and Allison are.

The house is in complete disarray. Boughs are splintered, glass is shattered, and piles of ash where the grims burned lay savagely at our feet. Remnants of a battle.

Ollie's crouched over Allison, stroking her face, tears falling from his eyes. When he looks up at me approaching, there's a slight hope in his eyes, and I'm hoping too that I can revive their girls.

Arriving at Talora's lifeless body, her skin a pale white, I kneel down to her and look for her wounds. Realizing she had been drained of blood by two puncture wounds in her neck, I summon the tears again. Then, biting into my arm, which had healed from last time, I wipe the tear from my eye, drag it through the new blood on my arm, and smudge the two holes with the mixture.

Waiting for what seems like minutes, Bash has that hopeful look in his eye that his woman would wretch and come back to life as he had.

But nothing happens.

"Why isn't it working?" he asks desperately.

I shake my head. "I don't know. I did the same thing for the two of you."

"Maybe she's been gone too long," says Dom consolingly.

"But Ollie was gone for a while too, and she still got him to rise."

"I don't know, Bash. I'm sorry."

"Please try it on, Allison," Bash asks resignedly, so dejected my heart breaks for him.

Slowly walking over to Allison, I do the same thing.

Allison doesn't stir, either.

Why could I save two male Vampires and not two female ones? Does it have anything to do with gender or something more profound?

Feeling that these are questions that my aunts may know, I push them down within me, wishing we could teleport to Washington.

Does Vampire power work like that?

42

EQUAL PARTS DARKNESS AND LIGHT

SAYAH

The flight here was long and dreary between the two brothers, who hated each other but showed astounding and conciliatory love for one another in a few fateful seconds. They had been companionable while driving to the airport and finding last-minute tickets to Washington.

I slept as much as I could but would wake easily with turbulence.

I'm utterly exhausted, like I'm twisting up in a convalescence.

Arriving in Seattle around two in the afternoon, when my aunts see me and my two trailing companions, the look on their faces is a little bit of shock and whole lot of careful distance.

There's not much talk of anything important on the drive to their house in Anacortes.

The city of Anacortes is a beautiful, insular community in the upper northwest corner of Washington state.

The house they live in is an impressive five-story house located on the side of a mountain that overlooks the oil refinery. In the distance, majestic Mount Baker stands domineering and ominous, a volcano in slumber but threatening all the same.

They live here with my cousin Francine, her husband George, and their three children. Hilda and Maggie have their own apartment in the basement, separate from the big house.

My cousin's husband owns a local hotel, so luckily for us, the two of them are gone all day. I don't have enough energy to make small talk and feign niceties right now, so I'm thankful for the respite. My cousin and I have never been close. She's been a revolving door my entire life, tolerating me when I go out to visit and downright viscousness and hatred when I'm away. I was hopeful my mother's death would help close that door for me once and for all, but alas, here we are.

Upon arriving at their house, the aunts invite us all in—which is weird considering they're with us and they literally stopped at the front door and said 'Bash and Dom, won't you please come in—and then we head down to their apartment, where they pull us into a back room off the main floor, a room they use for storage.

Atop the cardboard boxes are the remnants of what I know to be a summoning spell, and my heart leaps at seeing my mother again, even if it is in the spiritual realm.

Black and white candles sit beside a mirror, salt, a picture of Mama and Janet, and sage. The room still smells of it.

Piles of what look like my grandmother's grimoires are lying haphazardly in one corner, and one is open on that same makeshift table.

The room is dark save for a small lamp in the corner covered with a red cloth, lending the space a formidable ambiance.

"So," Bash's cynical voice slices through the preamble, "what kind of witchy voodoo are we gonna do here?"

Hilda's gaze at him could have cut him. "We're doing a blood knot séance."

Even the words of it chill me.

"Oh," Bash adds, sauntering around the room, peeking in boxes.

Maggie slaps his hand away. "Sit," she commands him.

I know Bash won't hurt them, but still, to have a murderous vampire in such close quarters sits on the edge of me with unease.

Bash gets as close to her as he can, but Maggie's not swayed by his gaze. I wonder what the whole story is about Maggie's brush with a vampire and who that vampire was.

They're from around the same area, maybe it was one of the Sangravelli Vampires.

Entertaining the idea in my mind, Bash sits on one of the boxes in the corner.

Dom sits down beside me.

Hilda takes a knife and carves an intricate knot in her hand, wincing.

"Maggie," she beckons.

Maggie approaches her and takes the knife as Hilda lights the candles.

"Sayah," Maggie says when her knot is carved.

I hold out my hand and let Maggie carve the knot into it, watching as it fades as soon as she marks it.

"Well, isn't that interesting?" Maggie breathes.

"You're going to have to will it to stay open, Sayah. Long enough to make contact."

"What happens when it heals?" I ask.

"The contact with your mom will be lost."

Already, my heart breaks at the thought of losing my mom again. I take the knife and cut once more, willing it to stay open as long as possible.

With the knot formed, the three of us join hands in amalgamation.

Hilda starts scrying, chanting in a language I don't know. I close my eyes, picturing my mom.

Everything goes black, and the room disappears. I'm the only one there. Holding my hand before me, I'm glowing in the dark, shimmering gold. Blindly, I search through the darkness, hoping Mama will show herself at some point.

"Mom?" I call, my voice echoing, shattering the silence.

Two bright lights emerge from the darkness. One golden and one red. Amidst the swirling mist that seeps into the space I'm in, Mama stands before me on a plinth, an angel of bright white wings and a gown that's a pure sweep of elegant iridescent clouds. Her long blonde hair is wildly curly the way she always wore it, a diadem of pearls over her forehead, and her face is young again, her bright green eyes seeing me for the first time in what feels like ages.

The other one's red mist of wavy tendrils hangs loosely around her face, and wears crimson dress that's tight at the hip and gathered in folds beyond the waist. Her soft features are young again as well; my aunt Janet, her wavy red hair catching fiery blazes in whatever light source there is in this room. Her red wings rest gently on her back, and her soft blue eyes give peace and enduring love despite the fiery red colors.

"Mom? Aunt Janet?"

"Sayah," Mama speaks, her voice precisely how I remembered. "Oh, my sweet, sweet punkin pie. How I miss you so."

"Mommy," I say, knowing she's tangible and run up to her, collapsing in her arms.

Even the smell of her is as I remember. A mixture of summertime linen, rain, and wonderful earthy smells.

"I miss you so much," I sob, and the tears that fall from my eyes are heavy. I pull the tears away with my hand and see they're sinewy—thick, golden. "What's happening to me, Mama?"

"Shh, darling. Don't cry." Mama pulls my head up and holds my chin in her soft hands. "Everything is as it should be. You don't know that now, but you will." She looks at me levelly, the scintillating glimmer in her eyes surreal.

"Please tell me what all this means, Mama."

"Long ago, there began a time of darkness," my mother says, like the wind on a waterfall. "Where evil seeped into this world and made it into the hearts of men. They punished witches for being what they were, lovers of nature and all things pure. Because the witches were so good, the evil that came from heartless men killing them became the root of all evil.

"One of the greatest witches, Artemis, created a curse to undo that evil and created the first vampires to weed out the wicked. At first, it was as it should be, but then the lines blurred a bit, and demons got mixed up with the vampires.

"To restore the balance, the Witches of Artemis' coven made the different species, all put here to take out a portion of Earth's evil humans but also to be the other's undoing, to keep the balance. Vampires, sirens, witches, and formweavers. Vampires were meant to take out men and women with evil hearts, sirens were to lure crude sailors to their deaths, formweavers were to prey on vampires gone rogue, and witches protected them all. In turn, one was the undoing of the other to make sure they would not overrun the world, keeping the balance of good and evil. Formweavers are meant to undo vampires, vampires to undo witches, witches to undo sirens, and sirens the formweavers.

"The lines blurred further with having the crossbreeds of these beings, therefore taking away the ability to be the undoing of one, which was keeping the balance. Sort of like population control. Thus began the Gemini Covenant, the power of two beings, one being the darkness and one being the light, instead of one species being the downfall of the other—except the warlocks and the grimspawns.

"Artemis consulted an angel and a demon to create the incontrovertible Phoenix Blessing, setting forth the savior or the destruction of them all. A being that was equal parts good and evil to restore the balance, part angel and part demon.

"Our family line has been the line of the phoenixes, the bloodline of fire, for as long as time has been around. Yet, in the past four centuries, we've been thwarted and stopped from rising, so there is an influx of the grims. The warlocks have latched on to our familial line and stepped in to destroy the next phoenix in any way they can. That is why Janet, myself, and your grandma were killed. It's why Sadie was convinced she needed to be a vampire. A fae tricked her into thinking that so she would die before she could be turned."

"What do you mean you were killed? Who killed you?"

"Dominic," she says grimly, and my heart faints.

"What?" I breathe.

This can't be true.

"We are not mad at him. We forgive him. It put you on your path to rise from the ashes and become the first phoenix in four hundred years. But because of this, you must be extremely careful on your journey. There will be someone who wants you dead at every turn for what you stand for, what you are, and your power."

"I don't understand. If Dom was the reason you died, why was he the reason I rose?"

"He has pure blood, even through his darkness. Sebastian is evil; he has the blood of demons, but his blood is still mixed with that of the witch, so he is still allowed to live. Because he tried to bite you, his demon blood mixed with your fire, and that is why you burned. But Dominic's blood was the perfect elixir to bring your body and soul back from the dark and into the light again. You see, you needed them both to become what you are. You needed the dark as much as the light. That is why you are equal parts light and dark, phoenix."

"That makes no sense." My heart is bleeding; I feel it splintering, severing my thoughts and blood and bones.

Dominic killed my mama?

"It is all how it's supposed to be," Janet says. "We had to go before you to be your guide. You lived through all that was designed to kill you and came out stronger every time."

Still trying to wrap my mind around the fact that my boyfriend killed my mother, I say, "That still doesn't tell me what I'm supposed to do."

"The warlocks and the grimspawns," Mama continues, "aren't, nor have they ever been, meant to be a part of this world. Their magick is too dark; it is of hell and monsters, and that is who you need to kill. They will try to find ways to outsmart you at every turn. This will be a perilous path, Sayah. They will use the people you love to get you to bend to their will; but you, being of the dark and the light, will find ways to outsmart them every time. Warlocks can only be killed by the phoenix, which is your destiny. Kill the warlocks that spell the grimspawns, and they will fall with them. I know Mederio threatened to take Gauge's soul, but you will go to the ends of the Earth to save him, and you know that."

"And what should I do with the boys being marked?" Even though

I don't know if I want to help Dom now, I still don't need him going dark and murdering a bunch of people.

"Your light has already seeped into Bash when you saved him," says Janet, her voice like a fresh autumn wind blowing through crisp leaves. "That glowing light you saw when you revived him was your light swarming his dark, saving his soul a piece at a time. Until you get the warlock linked to them killed, you must save their soul by feeding them your light when it goes dark. Because they are spelled to darkness, you will never fully be able to bring them out of the dark. But so long as they don't stray on their own path and only kill the dark people of this world, your light in them will remain. Should they decide to stray, their darkness will consume them.

"Now that your blood has been awakened," Janet continues, "the shadows will worsen. When you arose and killed Matrasia, and with the shock wave you set forth to rise Ollie, awoke many more warlocks. The grimspawns and the warlocks throw the balance off completely and came to be because a warlock who wasn't immortal wanted the immortality of the vampires. To restore that balance, you need to rid the world of all the grimspawns."

"How do I save Gauge? And Scarlet?"

"Adaline's demon that she sought out to create Sebastian split into two and became Matrasia and Mederio," responds Mama, her eyes narrowing and her magic strong. "That's why he wanted one of them marked forever because that was what was promised to him when he gave her Sebastian. To restore the balance and save your son, you need to kill Mederio. But since Gauge's life hangs in the balance, that is where your light will come in.

"Since formweavers can become any predatory species, they can become what they need to get into the warlock's circles. The Gemini Covenant is the power of two; one being the undoing of the other but also being the strength, which brings light out of the darkness but can put out the light as well. Laureya and you have been at odds your entire life, and her path has awakened, too. She, too, has fallen into darkness, and although her path is different from yours, she rises from her own ash, too.

"Mederio said *you* couldn't kill any warlocks, but he did not say no one could. Laureya is your counterpart, the Bash to your Dom, the dark to your light. She has light within her, too; you have to help her find it. When you do, she will be what you need to help kill the warlocks. She is the other phoenix. Scarlet will be kept alive because she is immortal and a witch. Use your magick to find her and keep her alive, sending the grimspawn in her place—the one that's in the cell in the dungeon. Using Jasantha's siren power and some of your magick, you can devise a way to retrieve Scarlet and put the false Scarlet in her place."

"I have to talk to Laureya?"

"To restore the balance," Mama says, "you must find a way to forgive your sister and to save her soul."

"Am I immortal now?"

"You will exist for as long as you need to until all the warlocks and grimspawns are forgotten."

"And I'm part angel?"

"You are a tribrid now, too. You are part witch. Part angel. And part demon."

The words are opaque and foreign.

"I don't want to be part demon, Mom."

"Demons are not what story books have led us to believe they are. They are not of the devil, as the devil doesn't exist. They merely mean dark. The angel is the light. The demon is the dark. The witch in you is what holds them equally balanced."

There's a lot to process, but I feel the blood knot in my hand beginning to heal.

"I don't know if I can do all this, Mama," I say, choking back the tears threatening to engulf me.

"You can and you will, my darling," Mama says, and the light within them both begins to fade.

"Mama, no, wait! Don't leave me!"

"I will always be watching over you, my sweet girl. Always and forever."

I hold her hand as she fades and slips back into the darkness. "Mama, I love you!"

"I've loved you longer," she whispers, and then, in an evanescent whisper, she's gone.

Upon opening my eyes, I'm back in the dark room with my aunts and the Sangravelli brothers.

My face is soaked with tears as I pull my hand away, looking at my palm.

The blood knot has faded but will forever be indelible in my palm.

Maggie and Hilda exchange looks of gravity, not speaking with their voices, but their silence spills every word they think.

They had seen the whole thing.

"So," Dom asks, arising from his box, "what happened?"

"You killed my mom?"

43

BROKEN

SAYAH

"What?" Dom exclaims, every pane of his expression sharp and pinched, concentrating on the meaning of my words.

"My mom said that you killed her, my aunt, and my grandma."

"Woah woah, wait a minute," he says, rising from the box he was sitting on and stepping toward me. "What are you talking about?"

I'm still kneeling on the ground, the feelings of grief and sorrow violently mixing together with anger and rage. The undeniable facts are colliding so violently within me that I feel nauseous. "She said our familial line is of the fire to make the phoenixes, but there hasn't been one in over four hundred years because the warlocks have been stepping in and stopping them."

"Oh," Bash says, his eyes darting between us, "well, see then. It wasn't my brother."

"She said that Dom was the one who killed my aunt. My grandma. *My mom*." I'm seething. I can't see straight, and those sharp splinters of disgust and agony are gouging into me, making it hard to breathe down here.

As he glances back at his brother, Bash's eyebrows draw up to his hairline.

"Babe, wait," Dom utters, the concern in his forehead drawn so tight his face looks like it may crack, "that can't be true. How did your parents die?"

"Fire," I whisper to the candle in front of me. "They were killed in a house fire."

When my eyes track back to his, his expression rearranges from confusion to anguish. Something surfaces in his mind, for his eyes blow wide with sudden shock. "No. No, no, no, no, no," he stutters, yanking his phone from his pocket and turning so fast, throwing the door open, letting angry light in.

"Where the fuck are you going?" I yell as I rise in a breathless rush, ungracefully chasing after him.

His legs are moving so fast that I struggle to keep up. Bounding up the stairs in two steps, which takes me three or four, he's a blur of colors when I reach the first floor. Stumbling after him as he slams the sliding doors open, the sounds of his phone making a call echo through the house.

"Hello?" comes Adaline's voice as I finally reach him, catching my breath.

"Mom!" he nearly screams, his face flushed with fury, his eyes wild under folded eyebrows. "You remember a few months ago when you had me come to Colorado to set that house on fire you said was part of a grim infestation?"

"Yes," she says, her voice a collection of calm and curiosity, "what about it?"

"Did you know it was Sayah's mom and stepdad in that house?"

Silence unspools from the line, and his knuckles whiten as he grips the phone tighter.

"*Mom?*" he screams after a few more seconds of quiet. "*Did. You. Know?*"

"I didn't know it was her mom. No."

My chest compresses with a surge of emotions I can't decipher. Eerily similar to the grief I felt when I got that late-night phone call telling me my parents were dead. Along with that agony returning, as I look at Dom and he at me, something exists at this moment that feels too heavy for me to carry. The weight of this revelation is tangling together, morphing into a monstrosity I can't cage. I watch him in horror as he realizes that he is the reason I suffer. He is the reason for my rage. He is the reason my best friend was taken from me. He is the reason that my son lost his grandparents.

I knew something didn't sit right when I got that phone call.

"But you knew it wasn't a grim…?" his voice trails off, as if the words grow too complex or too big to fit into syllables.

A few seconds of stilted silence feels like an eternity.

"Fuck! Mom? What the fuck?"

"Dominic. Stop. I didn't know it was her mom."

"But you knew it was an innocent? You knew it was a witch?"

"Yes. I knew."

This time, Dom is silent before he takes the phone away from his ear and lets loose one of the most agonizing sounds I've ever heard. The keening sweeps into a scream and collides with fury, becoming a wail with such emotion that the grass lays down to weep at his feet. As his lament subsides, he leans on the balcony's banister and looks at his phone, his breath shuddering as he waits for Adaline to speak.

"We were told by a witch long ago to kill the witches of that bloodline to keep the balance. If I told you it was an innocent witch, you'd never do it. When you agreed to do it in the '70s to thwart the grims back then and again in the '90s, I didn't think to tell you anything different. We thought it was helping to stanch the swarm."

Tears fall from his eyes and splash onto his hands. "And when Ollie and I told you that Shayde and her energy spirit said to kill a witch in Colorado, you didn't think to bring it up?"

"I thought it was coincidental. I didn't ever think that the witches we burned in the past were her family."

"*Fuck*!" He says again and hangs up the phone.

He turns to face me, his eyes returning to mine.

The shift in his demeanor is immediate. His skin darkens, his eyes dilate, and tears have welled up and are falling down his cheeks. The brokenness set upon his bones is fracturing the features of his face, and while my heart shatters, the mutilated and reprehensible grief spills out in a deluge from both of us.

44

SHATTERED

DOM

"Sayah," I utter, though words are too weak a sentiment to explain to her how I feel. How sorry I am. They're lost in the hurricane of wretchedness and remorse. My stomach is tightening, a stitch in both sides almost has me keeling over, and I've forgotten how to breathe normally.

Sayah sets her jaw. "What did you mean when you said she had you *come* to Colorado?"

Fuck.

The stitches break and rip me apart. Physically, I have to grip my hand to my side to stop the ache, clutching the agony as it simmers to a boil.

I'm never coming back from this now.

"Sayah, wait, I can explain . . ." I step toward her, feeling her tear the truth from my throat.

"No!" she screams, her blue eyes are splintered with splotches of gray. The gray of them tells the story of her sadness, her anger at my betrayal. "What? Did you come out to Colorado to kill me, too? Is that why you were there?"

"No," I state, my voice languid, trying again to come toward her. She takes another step back. "I came to Colorado to save you."

"To save me? What were you saving me from, Dom?" Rage is coloring her face an angry red, and tears stream down her face. Bash and her aunts are standing in the background, staring at me. Judging me. They could be hewn from stone; there is no draw of breath, no reaction to my confession. They all just stand there and stare at me, watching me burn.

I feel my vision wavering, the threat of going dark getting more intense; like a sinister vessel on the horizon of my mind, looming large and wild and ready to attack. I swallow it back and try to remain calm, feeling myself spiraling faster than I can manage.

"Everyone wanted you dead," I respond softly as if whispering will keep the demon inside me quiet. "The warlocks, the witches, the vampires. My whole family. I talked them into letting me go out there to help you find your fire."

"And killing my parents was just another Tuesday?"

Her words sit in the air like smoke.

The memory of the fire is shattering my mind.

"I didn't know they were your parents," I almost whisper. I can't think. Every thought in my head is jumbled together, swirling and crumpling simultaneously. The demon is gnawing at me from within, mingling with the torture of feeling her slipping away. Losing her.

"I can't," she says, turning her back to me and walking away.

Is her blood bright red or that beautiful burgundy color? says a voice that is not mine.

"Sayah, wait," I plea, ignoring the voice and going after her.

The sound of Bash's boots thudding against the deck boards, blocking my way, enrages me further.

"Get. The. Fuck. Out. Of. My. Way."

If it drips in a spattering rush or is a slow, methodical ooze. Pinching the bridge of my nose, I clench my teeth to bite back that voice.

"Just leave her be," Bash says tersely, and the urge to punch him in his smug fucking face taunts the demon that teeters on the edge of my madness. "I think you've done enough damage."

"Fuck you."

"You're just mad that, for once, I'm not the monster. You are."

Turning his back to me, he flashes after Sayah, leaving nothing but blurred black lines and the smell of his cologne in his wake.

The only people left here now are me and her aunts. The aunts whose shrewd eyes are narrowing on me like they would like to see my head on a pike. The aunts who know now that I killed their mom. Their sisters. Their family.

Hilda hobbles up to the door, her wild white hair matching the madness in her eyes. "We rescind our invitation," she seethes and slams the sliding glass door so hard it should have shattered.

Fuck.

Rescinding their invitation means I'm no longer welcome on their property, which means I have to exit it immediately, or else I will burst into flames.

As much as I deserve that right now, I must stay alive a little longer to help Sayah finish her quest. To help save her son. To save humanity.

Maybe then my soul will be redeemed for the horror I've caused.

The calm wind rushes into my skin as I speed down their property's hill and continue going through her aunt's winding neighborhood. I don't care if anyone sees me; the feeling of the sky crushing me alive and the ground rising like quicksand, my life is hanging in the murky balance in between.

I didn't know that was her mom's house.

I didn't fucking know.

Tears stubbornly fall down my face, and I don't cry.

Sayah is my whole world, wrapped into a perfect package of kindness, grit, strength, and raw, unadulterated resolve. Nothing made sense, and my existence was one lonely line of one-night stands and hunger pains until she entered my life. The distress is beginning to devour my bones; I'm surprised my feet are still moving. I feel so heavy that my feet would melt if I stopped.

I should have been honest with her the moment I knew I was falling for her, and that is the one thing that will haunt me for the rest of my miserable days. I'm a planet that has spun loose from its orbit.

Nothing can break me faster than losing the love of my life. I have never felt more alive than when I am with her.

My one.

My end game.

Everything about her flickers through my mind as I lose myself along the spangled streets of Anacortes. The way her eyes light up when she talks about something she's passionate about or the way her cheeks flush when someone tells her she's beautiful. How her expressions rearrange with every emotion she feels and how she feels those emotions a hundred times stronger than most people. How her pain has sketched stars around her scars and how she wears those scars like battle paint. She has been strengthened by whatever she has gone through in her past. She is the parts of my story that I've underlined, the maps of realms I've memorized, the lyrics to songs that have embedded themselves within my soul. She is my absolute everything, and to be without her is like watching all the stars fall from the sky. Watching the moon go out, or the sun lay down with a sigh.

To know I'm the one who has caused her pain dismantles me. It breaks apart the atoms of my being and tosses them into a ravine so hallow and reverent, even the demons would lay down to die from the sorrow. Whatever is tethering me to sanity is fraying, eroding along with my resolve to keep going.

I've fucked things up beyond all recognition and have no idea what I'm going to do now.

I've lost.

I lost.

I've been running so long that the blue haunt of the mountains is looming before me, and trees surround me at every turn. Not knowing where the fuck I'm at, I stop and look back at the road I sped down. A blue Subaru slows down as they pass, and I see Bash and Sayah. Bash's glacial blue eyes collide with mine, but Sayah's remain fixed on the road.

I watch them as they pass me by.

Adding to my already twisted and mangled sense of reality is the fact that not only did I lose my girl, but my fucking brother is there to swoop in and pick up the pieces of her that I broke.

A BOND WITH THE BLOOD OF ANGELS

SAYAH

The water at the bottom of Deception Pass looks cold as it churns in the rocky depths of the cliff's ledge beneath us, representing the feelings that I have coagulating and warring within me.

Don't get me started about the fact that I'm sitting on a cliff named Deception Pass.

It only adds fuel to the raging fire within me.

My literal fire and the proverbial fire.

It's late spring now, and the trees bend together like cautious whispers, glowing green in the sunset's austere light. The wind's cold in Washington, causing me to shiver severely; my only means of cover is a light hoodie my aunt Hilda loaned me.

I sit on a rock at the top beside the bridge that goes over the two points, next to Sebastian, who is trying hard to say things that make me feel better, but they do not.

Everything was making sense to me, and I was starting to see the world before me in a crystal-clear clarity I hadn't had in all my life. All the suffering I'd experienced throughout my life has had a purpose, a more significant meaning.

I died.

The old me is gone.

In a tragic twist of fate, Dom is the reason that my parents are dead. That my grandma and aunt died. The whole reason why I met him was he had come to Colorado to hunt me.

I feel like I'm going to throw up.

"I know you're spiraling right now," Bash says softly. "But he didn't know it was your parents. My brother is a selfless martyr. He wouldn't have done it knowingly."

"He still lied about not living in Colorado and coming there to stop people from killing me. Things I should have been in the know about."

"Yeah," he says, picking at a rip in his black jeans. "That is true."

"I know you don't know me that well, but honesty is something that I *have* to have in any relationship. Once that trust is broken, it's never the same. Even if I learn to forgive him for what he did to my poor, sweet mom and stepdad"—I choke back the tears—"there will always be that fissure there. The foundation is cracked. It'll never be the same."

"Well, you'll have to figure out how to forgive him. We need him around to get that mark off him so he doesn't go dark and kill you and your son."

"I also have to find a way to get to Laureya and make amends with her so she will help me kill Mederio."

"Sayah," says Dom's voice from behind us.

"The fuck are you doing here?" I say, standing.

"Sayah. I know you hate me right now. Believe me. I hate me too." His voice is dejected, his eyes blown wide like dark saucers of midnight.

"What do you want me to say, Dom? Whether or not you meant to, you still killed my parents . . . my mama. I can't look at you right now."

"I know," he says, stepping closer to me. "Please, Sayah, listen to me . . ."

"You touch her, you die," Bash says, coming in between us, and I'm taken aback by his protectiveness of me suddenly.

"Really, Bash?" Dom says, squaring up to him.

Bash, in turn, puffs his chest out and steps into Dom's face.

For fuck's sake.

"Guys, not now," I say, separating them. "Please. I don't need either one of you going dark right now. That's the last thing that we need."

"We need to talk about everything your mom told you in that vision," Dom says, and it salts the wound now festering with anger.

"Really, Dom?" Bash snipes.

"Well, what the fuck else is there to do?" Dom yells. "I didn't fucking know it was her parents. The whole reason we are here and they died, and I'm in love, is because of us trying to get rid of the fucking grims! That is what we came here to do. If we don't do something about it, her parents dying and me lying and everything else will all have been in vain!"

"What do you suggest we do then?" Bash expands. "Sit down and have a pow-wow kumbaya and sing songs while holding hands?"

Dom's eyes go violently white and flicker to black.

"Stop," I say to Bash. "I have to keep you two from going dark."

"How are you going to do that?" Bash asks.

"By feeding you my blood."

Bash's eyes glitter and Dom's return to green. "That sounds nice," Bash says eagerly, and Dom looks over me and threatens him with a glaze so intense the Earth could've caught fire.

"You bite her, you die," Dom says now.

I know he's being protective, but part of me wonders if that's true now. First, he burned me; now, I could burn him.

"You're right," Bash concedes. "I don't want to find out. So, how will you get this blood into us then?"

"Vials, I'm thinking."

He sucks his teeth. "Vials of phoenix blood. Sounds tasty."

"In the meantime," Dom interjects Bash's silent reverie about my blood, "we need to return to New York. If Hattie finds another artifact, we may be able to break the curses anyway; then we won't need your blood."

"I will not be going anywhere near your family," I say, turning my back on both of them. I reach the cliff's edge and look at the churning and dark waters below. Shivering, I wish my power would come to light right now and those wings of fire would fly me far away from here and everyone.

"Sayah," Dom says from behind me. "You don't have to come back with us now. I know you need space and time to sort this all out. Take all the time that you need. But we do have to face this. Since you are the phoenix. We need you. Otherwise, the world will be overrun with those gods' awful things."

I turn to face him. "I know that, Dom. And I will help you guys. But . . ."

"But?"

"I don't know if I can be with you anymore, Dom. I know what you did was unintentional, and you didn't know it was my mo—" I choke up and the words come out all stuttered. "I know you didn't know. But you lied from the start. And I can't stay in a relationship like that. I can't. My last relationship was filled with lies, and I vowed to myself I would never do that again."

"Sayah," he says my name like it's his elixir, like he's dying of thirst, and my name is that last drop that his tongue missed. "Please . . . don't . . ."

He tries to grab my hand, his eyes red, rheumy, and shaded with tears. "No, Dom. I can't. Please. Let that be what it is right now. Let's get through this whole warlock shit and get my son safe and you two unmarked."

"And then?"

"I don't know, Dominic. Right now, nothing. Go our separate ways. Be done."

"Um, guys?" Bash says from behind us.

"What, Bash?" we both say.

When he doesn't say anything at all, I turn and see his face has gone pale. His gaze fractures at the sight of something over my shoulder. "Sayah, don't move."

"Why? What's wrong?" I ask, my heart dropping at the worry that paints his beautiful face.

"There's a wolf. Sitting. Up on the mountain, looking right at us."

Usually, this wouldn't frighten me as much, as we're in the mountains and can run to safety. But the look on Bash's face tells me it's not *that* kind of wolf.

Turning slowly and carefully, I see the wolf sitting on the mountaintop, looking right at me. A large, gray wolf with yellow eyes. I feel the wolf's waiting for something.

"We should go," I say, backing up toward the cliff's edge.

"Where can we go?" Bash asks, "The minute we head to the car, the wolf can pounce. Look," he says, pointing out how close the wolf is to the car.

"So where do we go, then?" I respond, my tone edged with fear.

"Down," Bash admonishes, pointing to the steep mountainside path. "Once we get far enough away, hopefully, the wolf will leave, then we can vamp flash back up."

"Okay," Dom says. "But we should go now because he's coming."

Without thinking twice about it, Dom absconds with me and moves me with him as fast as he can. I feel the world whip by me, the acceleration of his feet at his inhuman pace, the steep decline of the mountain making my stomach lurch upward as though I'm on a roller coaster. Visibility is non-existent while the evening mountain scenery flashes by me, and before I know it, we're at the bottom of the cliff we'd been on top of, a dark sandy beach in the shallows.

Bash arrives shortly after, looking around for the wolf.

"I think we're in the clear," he says breathlessly.

"Not so much," says a disembodied feral voice.

Turning around in shock, I see a woman, perfect shades of white ivory, in a red blouse, black jeans, red heels, and her fiery red hair ablaze with the sun setting behind her. Her green eyes are blazing into me, and I blink a few times to make sure I'm not hallucinating.

"Laureya?" I ask incredulously, blinking wildly to make sure.

"Miss me?" She gives me a dark and nefarious smile, the cloying scent of her insulting my senses.

Bash and Dom gape from me to Laureya, knowing as much as I do as to what the fuck is going on.

"How in the hell are you here right now?" I ask in consternation.

"Of course, you would know nothing that has happened to me," Laureya spits venomously, sauntering to me. There's something weirdly renewed about her. Not only does she look healthy and sober, but she also looks like she'd aged backward a decade. "When all your life shit happened, it happened to me too. Everything. And I know you've been running with vampires. I know because I am a formweaver."

The words pierce perfectly through me and shatter whatever calm and collective notions I'd been trying to gather. Gravity is pulling me into that depth again, and I need to regain my composure. I breathe deep, trying to cling to that calm with all of me. I am about to shatter.

"I'm sorry," Bash interjects and slides between me and Laureya, "I'm Sebastian. Laureya, is it?"

Her smile turns wistful. "Hello, Sebastian. Yes, I'm Laureya."

"Nice to meet you," Bash says, pulling her away from me and toward the water's edge. "Now, tell me again what you said to your sister over there. A formweaver?"

"Yes. And you are a vampire. Your brother, too."

"Yes, but LaLa, can I call you LaLa? Anyway, what's tripping me out about this is how you know all this and how you're here right now. I mean, I know you're part witch and all, but—"

"I'm not a witch," she answers.

I remain close to them to hear what she's saying.

I know that Bash is trying to keep me calm and Dom from going dark, which is why he pulled her away from us.

But I have to hear this.

Bash's brow furrows in confusion. "Come again?"

"Fran was not my real mom," she says, and like summer lightning, everything flashes in front of my eyes at Laureya's words.

"What?" I say, moving closer to her.

"You heard that right, sis; we're only half-sisters."

"Was it your mom who was the formweaver?" Bash asks. "Or your dad? Because you have to be born to or bitten by one to be one."

"I was born to one," Laureya says steadily, and my knees feel like jelly.

"And which one of your parents was the Werewolf?" Bash asks earnestly.

"We are not werewolves; we can weave into anything."

"Okay, sorry, which one was the formweaver?"

"My dad."

With everything that's happened in these few days, there isn't anything else that can shock me. I had died, for fuck's sake, and had risen from the ashes. But even then, the fact that my dad is a supernatural formweaver and I'd not known my entire life floors me. Gravity beckons my knees to hit the ground, and I fight that feeling, wondering idly what the hell else could possibly come up.

I try with all the power within me not to fall. "So what do you want? Why are you here?"

"Well, because your mom's mirror spelled you to me—I got everything that happened to you. All of it. So, you can see why I kept my distance and turned to drugs to get that shit out of my mind. I also did drugs to keep myself from formweaving. I began to turn into a wolf years ago, but it was so painful and excruciating. I found out that if I was completely out of my mind with drugs, I wouldn't have to formweave. Until Mark came around."

"Who's Mark?" Bash asks, a little sarcastic, but he's seemingly enthralled in her tale.

"Mark was a vampire."

"Was? Past tense?"

"I killed him. Unintentionally, I'll have you know. But because of his presence, my body couldn't resist the weave anymore on full moons anyway. I had to hunt the vampires. It was in my blood. Until I met a man who gave me hope and made it possible for me to fight the weave, to form into anything I wanted and whenever. When he was killed, my heart was torn. I went back to drugs, but then I met Ryan. He's the one who has my heart now."

"Excuse me, Snow White," Bash intercedes, "is there a point to this story of yours?"

The look Laureya gives him could have sliced him. "He's a vampire, but I can't be with him because the desire to formweave is getting more intense. Even stranger, a few months ago, I began to have visions of this one here." She points at me. "I saw the fire, I saw her meeting Dom, I saw you in her dreams, I snuck into the celebration of life for Fran and Dan to make sure it was true."

"I *did* see you," I state, astonished.

The realization wrings eye-rolls from Laureya as she continues unabashedly, "I saw bits and pieces of this last weekend, and I saw the artifact and the fact that it can break the lycanthrope's link to the moon. I saw this before but knew you would be here now to discuss what happened to her. So I came to confront you. I arrived here the other night, and I burst into flames when I was lying in bed. When I came to, I couldn't use my visions anymore. And now, it seems, I can set fire to people with my mind."

"Hmm. That's curious. So, *What* Do? You. Want?" Bash's tone is derisive now. He's done listening to her.

"I want that artifact. To get this curse off me, and I want to be a vampire. I can't be both a formweaver and a vampire."

"Why not?" Bash asks.

"Because my blood will kill anyone who bites me. I know. It's how Mark died."

"Well, too bad your visions are broken; otherwise, you'd know we don't have the artifact anymore."

"You don't have it?" Her gaze turns dark and worried.

"Yeah, that's what I said."

"Laureya," I cut in, realizing an opportunity here. "We're going to look for another one. But there are some things we need to take care of in the meantime. If you help us with that, we will help you get the curse off you and become a vampire."

Dom and Bash glare at me cautiously.

"What do you need my help with?" she asks hesitantly.

"Did you ever stop to wonder why you burst into flames last night?"

Laureya looks at me questioningly. "I figured it had something to do with the magick I'd been doing to prevent my formweaves."

"Well, it's not," Bash snides.

"You're a phoenix," I blurt, and everyone looks at me. "I'll explain later."

My head is spinning, and I need something cool to stop me from fainting, from spiraling into outer space and never coming back.

I walk away from the three people on the beach and go into the water to sting my toes enough to know that I'm still alive and this isn't a crazy dream.

I hear Dom clear his throat behind me.

"You okay?"

"I have no idea who either of my parents are, apparently. I mean, it makes sense that she's not my full sister, as she has hated me her entire life. But for my dad to be a formweaver? I've not had that feeling about him at all. I mean, not that I knew they existed a month ago, but still, there's been no signs of anything weird—" Feeling myself beginning to panic, Dom holds on to my shoulders, narrowing his eyes on me, and I know he's trying to calm me down with his power. But it isn't working.

Apparently, I can't be veilweaved by them anymore, either.

"What this means," he mumbles, "is that you are one too. And we need to figure out why you haven't known about it until now."

"Pretty sure all her other hero blood suppressed it," Bash contends, joining us by the water bank.

"How do you know that?" Dom asks.

"Just a guess. But I say we get back to crazy pants over there and try to convince her to help us. She's not boding so well waiting for you two to hash all this out."

I nod and move back over to Laureya.

"I would say I'm sorry for dumping that bombshell on you, but I'm not," Laureya says coldly, her eyes glowing with a wild smile.

"Either way, are you going to help us or not?"

"If I help you, will you help me undo this curse and turn me?"

"Yes," I reply.

"Okay. Now, what do I need to do for you?"

"Kill warlocks with your new-fangled power, using shifting to get into circles to track down the main one to undo our curse first," says

Bash casually. “Easy peasy. You said you can set people on fire with your mind, right?”

“Right,” she concurs.

“Perfect,” Bash replies, his eyes that desperately smoldering crystal blue.

“A Bond with the Blood of Angels. Just what we need.”

The End (ish)

ACKNOWLEDGMENTS

To Mama. Gosh. I miss you. I can't even explain, the word I feel for your absence is a word that doesn't exist in this reality. The depth of my sorrow for you is abounding, and although as time passes and I continue to move on with my life, there is a hole in the shape of you that will forever remain. I hope you like this story. It was inspired by you. I wrote it in the days after I lost you and kept writing to somehow try to process this huge, incomprehensible thing. Your death. In this story, you will forever live on. This story truly is for you, I hope it makes you proud. ILYFILYFALAILMMYB.

To my Dad and Lynda. I don't know what I would do without your unwavering support. Of every book I write, you two are always my hype team, my cheerleaders. You two are the voices in the dark that tell me I will one day see success as an author. Daddy—you've always been my rock, my hero, my main man. I adore you and just want to make you proud. I love you both to the moon and back.

To my son. You know you make me proud every day of your life. You are the most funny, handsome, smart, intelligent, wonderful person I have ever met and I am so honored you picked me to be your mama. Thank you for being my inspiration and listening to my stories first, before anyone else. Thank you for letting me put your story in this book. You are an inspiration and will be to many people. Your future is so bright! To the moon and back.

M. You know what you mean to me. I wouldn't be who I am without you. Whatever souls are made of, yours and mine are the same. You are my person. I can't thank you enough for your endless support, listening to me rambling about my book not having any clue wtf I'm talking about, but helping me with ideas anyway. Our 12 hour phone conversations are my life's blood. You are always in my ear, even when you're not. End game.

Amber Thoma. Girl. I couldn't have done half of the things I'm doing without your support. You are a bright shining light in the indie author community and I love you and your hustle so much. I aspire to be you. You, my friend, are going places and I'm here for it! Thank you for letting me put my poetry in Queen of Light and designing the bad ass covers for the ENTIRE series! I adore you!

Book Beasties, I love you and our chicken talks and your unwavering love and support. I am so glad we all joined that train together and have our chat that goes from zero to one hundred on any given moment.

To my booksta community, I have never felt as though I fit in—anywhere—until I found Bookstagram. I have found my tribe. I cannot tell you the amount of support and encouragement I found in this community, it has made me so incredibly happy. I love you all so much and I cannot thank you enough.

To the indie authors of the world. Everything I learned, I did so with you forging the path for me first. I want to give you all the thanks. Every bit of advice, every book put out there independently, every thing I have done has been because you all forged the path for me. Indie authors are tireless angels who only want to share their stories with the world. Support them always.

To my Alpha, Beta, and ARC readers and street team. Where do I begin? You all made ALL the difference in the world. I cannot express what your feedback and endless support means to me. You all helped make this book what it is today.

To my sensitivity reader, Holly. I adore you. You also a bright shining light in any community you enter. You are such a wonderful human and I am so happy I met you. Thank you for keeping me honest and sincere about a community I care so much about. I am just a visitor and ally in your community and I want to make sure I am authentic and respectful. Your insight has helped so much. #teamholly (iykyk)

Kendra. K-DUBS. Ma'am. You are amazing. Not only did you help me from the kindness of your soul, your reactions to this novel give me life. You are such a genuine soul and I'm so so happy I met you.

And lastly, to you, my lovely readers. Your love for reading new stories and getting lost in our tales is what pushes us authors to keep writing, to keep sharing, to keep doing what we love to do. Every author leaves pieces of themselves in their works and this one, by far, is the largest piece of my soul I've ever laid bare. I know that as readers, you find pieces of yourselves in stories that call to you and so I hope that this story left you feeling like you found a piece of yourself within my words. It will be my biggest honor to watch this story take flight and find homes on your shelves.

Yours always in magick and fire and thunder and storms,

Inara

xoxo

ABOUT THE AUTHOR

Inara Gage is an indie author based in Northern Colorado. She resides with her son Gauge, her mastador Khaleesi, kitty Nox, and bunny tWitch. After the first two failures of publishing her first book, A Witch's Aura, she went all the way through grad school to learn how to market herself in this crazy, incredibly hard, and immensely trying self publishing world. This is her third book baby and she learned so much from all the trials and tribulations with the first one, she has authored five more books since and hopes to continue putting stories out into the world that you all will love and enjoy.

SNEAK PEEK OF BOOK II

A BOND WITH THE BLOOD OF ANGELS

Chapter One: Love Triggers it

"So you can form into anything? Like air? Or a big cat, like a tiger?" Bash's childlike questions to Laureya ricochet off the rocks surrounding us, leading to the cliff's top, where we left the car.

"Anything, anything," Laureya answers methodically, her voice tinged with boredom by Bash's questions. "Watch," she says, and we turn our attention to her.

Standing before us, Laureya tilts her head back and closes her eyes, and her red lips mumble words I don't understand. Her skin and clothes tremble and shake, and her very appearance wavers a bit. The image of her folds in on itself and unfolds as a giant owl, flapping its beautiful wings before us.

"Now," Bash says, turning to Dom, "if she bites us as the owl, is it still lethal to us?"

Dom shrugs his shoulders. "Don't wanna find out."

Grasping onto my waist, that familiar shift of air and movement sweeps me up as we ascend the mountainside rapidly, the Earth, rock, and moss becoming a blur of colors as we jolt up the hill.

As the movement halts, we arrive at the mountaintop, Bash's blur of black arriving with the whooshing sound vampire movements make.

The owl lands on the hood of my aunt's car, the car they let us borrow to go for a drive hours ago to clear our heads.

"Laureya, don't, you'll scratch—""with the same unfolding of energy, she returns to her own body, sitting on the hood of the white Subaru— "the car," I finish as Laureya grins.

"Relax. It's fine."

"I don't care who you are; that shit's cool," Bash says, his heavy boots clunking on the pavement as he traipses over to the driver's side of the car.

Laureya flashes him a toothy smile, and I bite down on the vomit that comes crawling up my throat.

No matter that Laureya is going to help us with getting their marks off of them and killing the warlock that spelled them, I don't fucking like my sister, and I sure as hell don't trust her. Her flirting with Bash, even with just her eyes, makes me ill.

I don't exactly know why.

"So," I say, shifting my weight towards the car, Dom and I blocking Laureya a bit to avoid inviting her along, "you'll be at the hotel or?"

"You don't want me to come and see our aunts again?" Laureya asks, slipping off the car's hood, heels clicking as they hit the asphalt.

"You mean my aunts? My mom was not your mom, apparently."

"They don't know that," Laureya says, moving closer to me.

Dom, in turn, inches closer toward Laureya.

I smile at his 'touch her and die' attitude, even though I'm still furious with him, and also, we both know I can protect myself now.

"Still," I return, laying my hand on Dom's shoulder to tell him I'm okay. He moves to the left. "I don't think it's wise to come tonight. We've all had a really long weekend. Why don't you give me your number, stay at the hotel tonight, and we'll meet again tomorrow to review plans?"

"I don't know if you heard the bit about how I lit someone on fire with my mind," Laureya spits back at me, "but I can't go back to that hotel."

"So pick a different one," I say, squaring up to her. Dom moves in front of me again, and Bash advances to the front of the car to stand beside me.

Laureya lends them a devilish grin. "I'll just stay at the Lamplighter Inn. You know, the one our cousin owns."

Although I know Laureya's trying to grate on my feelings, possibly a ploy to get me to agree to her coming with us, there's no give a fuck left for my sister. I give no fucks if she goes to the motel.

My cousin Francine and I have never been friends.

But that's a story for another time.

"Go ahead, Laureya," I answer, turning on my heel to the car. "Text me. I know you know my number."

I clamber into the front seat and shut the door.

The silence of the car greets me softly. Trying to keep my mind from spiraling, I hug my legs to my chest and rest my chin on my knees. So many things have been added to my brain in the last few hours, it may explode.

The fact that my boyfriend killed my mom, that my dad is a supernatural formweaver, and I am the balance of light and dark, part angel, part demon, part witch, part shifter.

How had my dad kept that big secret from me all these years? How had I never known it, in turn, makes me part formweaver as well?

Watching out the windshield, I see Bash say something to Laureya that causes her to giggle. Of course, Bash would say something stupid and witty to her. In the short time I've known him, I know he's inclined to use his dark humor to lighten things.

Laureya looks both ways before she formweaves once more, this time to a raven, and flies away.

Bash enters the driver's seat, and Dom stands outside my window. He raps on the glass with his two knuckles, and I look over at Bash and nod, signaling that he should turn the car on so I can roll down the window.

"Is it alright if I come back with you?"

I hesitate.

I know there are things we have to discuss, and we need the aunts to answer some questions.

But I also know they want nothing to do with him right now.

"I have to go in first and make sure they're okay with it," I say softly.

Bash leans over me to see Dom better. "I'll vouch for you. See if I can smooth it over with ol Hildy and Maggie for you."

The annoyance that creases Dom's face is apparent in how the bridge of his nose crinkles. "Thanks," he says dryly.

He climbs in the back, and Bash puts the car in drive and takes off.

"Well, that was unexpected," Bash chides as the car sails back over the pass.

"Very," I second.

"It's been a very insightful weekend, to say the least."

"And it's Monday night even," I correct.

"Wow," Dom says from the back, "I didn't even realize it was Monday."

"I know. It's good that I took the week off this week for 'vacation.'" I make the air quotes with my hands.

"Gauge probably needs his mama something fierce," Dom says softly from the back.

"Yes," I answer, turning on my seat warmer. "First thing tomorrow, we should grab the first flight out of here. But for now, I have some questions I want to ask the aunts."

"What do you intend on asking the old Witches of Anacortes?" Bash asks, maneuvering the car around the twists and turns of Deception Pass.

"Oh, you know, about the fact that my sister is only my half-sister and that I am also part formweaver, you know, the small shit."

A small laugh escapes Bash's lips and catches my giggle in the same wind. Strangely, there's no returned laughter from the back seat, which makes me turn around to look.

As I rotate my neck, the light in the car shifts as though the sun went behind the clouds. The air grows dense and dark, and a chill ravages my skin when I see Dom.

His eyes have gone completely black.

"Dom!?" I gasp, blinking wildly as though trying to push the sight back to regular Dom.

Bash swiftly spins his head around, causing the car to swerve into oncoming traffic. The loud honk makes him right the car hastily, correcting the wheels into the right lane.

"Shit!" Bash exclaims, scanning the roadside for somewhere to pull over.

Dom is gazing out the window, nodding as though listening to something. The pounding in my chest takes me to another level, and I fight inwardly on what to do.

"Dom?" I ask timidly, cautious of what's about to happen.

Deliberately, he turns his head and looks at me. His eyes are a fathomless black, the pallor of his skin intensifies, blue veins are even more prominent in his face, and fangs protrude from his cuspids. The beating of my heart slams against my ribs.

Before I can even blink again, he bolts toward me and grabs my head, pulling it towards him as he bites down on my neck. Trying to break free of the hold, I feel my blood being siphoned out of me; he's too strong; there's nowhere to go.

The fire overcomes us quickly. It starts in my neck this time, burning Dom where he bites me. The red and orange tipped flames emit out of me with a fiery fierceness, causing his skin to melt immediately, the smell of charred hair and flesh and cloth tinging the aroma of the car. Although the flames come directly from me, they do not graze me an inch, merely floating around me. As they engulf him, his body flies to the back of the car with gut-wrenchingly agonized screams, flailing maddeningly and trying to pat himself out violently. Bash catches the same fire in a whoosh of flame that explodes outward, causing him to swerve the car into the rocky mountainside.

My eyes fly open, and I gasp.

The car's still moving, and we're passing through the small downtown area of Anacortes.

"Whoa," Bash says as I thrash around, swirling in the seat to ensure Dom is still Dom. "You okay?"

Dom's eyes are back to normal, his green eyes upon mine, questioning, though a bit of knowing at the same time.

His eyes tell me that he had seen the same fate.

"Dom?" I ask, still unsure if that was a vision or a dream.

"I saw," he answers, his voice brutal and indifferent.

"What the hell is going on?" Bash asks.

"We just had a vision," Dom answers quietly, as though he's still trying to comprehend it.

"What?" Bash looks to me, his face crinkled in confusion.

"He bit me. And he burned."

"As did you," Dom finishes cynically, regarding Bash with a tarnished glare.

"Well, what the hell does that mean?"

"I think," I say as I try to form my own thoughts into words, "that if he bites me, he will burn."

"And," Dom continues, "if I get the urge to bite her, I won't be able to control myself, and I'll die."

"Well, the warlock should know that, then, right?" Bash asks, alternating between looking at Dom in the rearview and at me. And not have her as your mark? I mean, the whole point of having a vampire as a grim is to be able to have you do his bidding forever. You can't do that if you're dead."

Bash's words make sense.

"But why would we both have the same vision if that was not the intention?" I ask.

"Maybe he wants her dead, and he was psychically trying something out," Dom offers.

"Well, it felt pretty real," I concede.

"Right. You weren't the one who was on fire. Well, you were, but you weren't burning."

"Do you think I need to give you blood when we get back to the house?" I ask.

"It may be a good idea," he says. "Just in case that was a sign of something to come soon."

"Yeah, I could use some, too, just in case." Bash's tone indicates that he's joking, but his face tells me he's serious.

"I'll give you some, too, just to make sure."

He grins and nods. "So, what will you say to dear auntie Hildie and Maggie?"

"I haven't really decided yet," I answer, turning back around. We're coming up in the aunts' neighborhood. "I think they should know about Laureya. I just don't know how they're gonna take it."

"Maybe they already know," Dom says.

"Very true. They seem to have a wealth of knowledge about things that I would never imagine they knew."

"Just feel it out," Bash says, "see how they take the Laureya thing first, then bring up that she's a formweaver."

"I gotta make sure that they don't kill that one first," I say, pointing to Dom with my thumb behind me.

"True dat," Bash says, and the heavy sigh from behind me lets me know that Dom is dreading this as much as I am.

Chapter Two: Corrosive Beauty

Bash pulls the Subaru into the driveway and kills the engine.

From where we sit, we can see the front door perfectly. The door cracks open a smidge, and Hilda's face appears for a second before closing again and reopening as she undoes the chain lock.

"Okay, you wait here," I say, turning my head to look at Dom.

He nods solemnly and looks out the window to the neighbor's hydrangeas.

Bash turns off the car, and we both exit the vehicle.

I approach the front door, and as Hilda opens the screen door for us, her eyes narrow to the car where Dom sits, still in the backseat of their car. "What's he doing with you?"

"Hilda," I say softly. "I know you're upset, as am I. But we still need to help him."

She is about to object when Bash takes her hand into his, and she stops.

"I know you're upset," he says gently and it sways me, seeing Bash being gentle. "You all are. And you have every right to be. But I know my brother. He would never intentionally hurt anyone, especially not someone like your sister. This was all my mother. And she was only doing it to protect our kind. But if you're going to hate anyone, hate her, not him. Believe me, no one will be harder on him than himself. That I can absolutely promise you."

My heart splinters a centimeter thinking of how Dom will punish himself, but then I think better of feeling sorry for him and remembering Mama, burning in the fire.

Shaking my head to relieve myself of the vision, I focus on my aunts.

Hilda's eyes pierce into Bash's, the objection sitting firmly on her tongue, when Maggie slides her arm through the crook of Hilda's. "Let's try to be objective. Bash is right. He will punish himself. Let's help them with what we can and get them on their way."

The silence wraps us all up in a sincere wind that is infused with an ancient pain, spiced with a sister's agony and a daughter's suffering and decanted with the anguish of a ten-year-old who lost his best friend.

Hilda nods and removes her hand from Bash's, retreating back inside.

I turn to catch eyes with Dom and nod.

As we all enter the quiet house, Bash's boots are the only loud clunk aside from the ticking from the grandfather clock in the entryway.

"Let's sit, shall we?" Bash says, barging between us and sitting at the table in the room full of windows.

Reluctantly, we follow Bash into the dining room and sit at the table.

"So?" Hilda asks, her eyes cautious on the vampires but curious on me.

"Laureya showed up," I blurt out.

"What?" the aunts ask in unison.

"Yes. We were sitting at the pass, talking, and she came."

"I don't understand," Hilda states, incredulous.

"She's a formweaver, aunties."

Hilda and Maggie exchange looks, and there's a knowing between them again. Something in their silence, an unspoken word, tells me they knew she was and had known all along.

I can't help the annoyance in my voice when I say, "You knew?"

Anger bites at me, and hard. Sometimes, I understand my aunts keeping things from me to keep me safe. And really, I just learned about all of these dark things recently. But still, once they had learned of me being the phoenix, they should have told me.

"Sayah," Hilda begins.

"No!" I stand, utterly trying to find the calm that keeps trying to relentlessly flee me. The sound of the chair scraping on tile assaults my ears, and I feel Dom's hand on my lower back, but I shake him off and walk toward the windows. Spinning around, I yell, "If you knew this, you should've told me the minute you knew I'd become the phoenix. That would've been the first thing to mention before letting me see my mom, so I could have asked her about it."

"That's why we didn't tell you," Hilda says, getting up from her chair and walking over to me slowly. "We didn't want you to waste your time with your mom asking her things that we could answer for you. We wanted that time you had with her to be everything you needed to hear, what we couldn't tell you."

"We were going to bring it up when you guys got back," Maggie offers, standing too, crowding me. "We wanted you to go get your air and think about everything, and then when you got back, we were going to tell you because you need a formweaver for your quest."

"Why didn't my mom tell me? Since she said I needed one, why didn't she tell me that Laureya was one?"

"I don't know the answer to that," Hilda says, taking my hand. "Maybe she needed you to figure that out alone too."

"Come," Maggie says, grabbing my other hand. "Sit and ask us all the questions you want."

I oblige them and sit down again as Maggie goes to the kitchen to retrieve the tea kettle, which begins to scream.

"So, tell me what you know. Everything."

"Your mom knew that your dad was a formweaver from the minute she met him," Hilda begins as Maggie comes in with five cups and sets them down in front of each of us. "He had been suppressing it for a long time but still had moments. Fran could tell things about people, regardless of whether they hid it. It was who she was. She confided in us that he was and had been using a talisman to keep the weave at bay. He used to formweave into things when he was a teen, getting into trouble because he learned to form into anything he wanted. Your dad's family is of the gene, but it is only triggered by something. Something that only your dad triggered."

"What did my dad trigger?" Thoughts are running rampant in my mind as I watch the steam from the kettle fill my delicate china tea cup as Maggie pours.

"Falling in love with a demon."

"But you said that he had been formweaving since he was a teen; if he didn't fall in love with a demon 'til he met Laureya's mom, that would've made him in his twenties."

"It wasn't Laureya's mom who triggered the gene," Maggie answers, filling her cup with the scalding water.

"Then who was it?" Bash asks, leaning on his fist, seemingly enthralled by the tale as the steam from his cup warps his beautiful features.

"A woman from his past," Hilda answers. "Not sure of her name. But when he fell in love with her, he began to formweave on the full moons. He hated it and brought it up with your grandma, who told him to suppress it. It was his father, not her, that gave him the gene. As you probably remember, your grandpa was a very hard and cold man. He used to beat your grandma; that's why they divorced. He couldn't turn to him because Larry would have never helped him with something like that. So, he sought out a preacher who gave him a crucifix spelled by a witch. Your dad didn't believe the witch part of it, or he didn't acknowledge it, but it helped him to suppress it. Sometimes the formweavers can get away with a lifetime of suppressing it if they don't encounter any vampires. Since formweavers were meant to undo the vampires, if there were none to undo, they wouldn't need to become the very thing that kills them."

"Then Laureya must have fallen for a demon?"

"She must have," Maggie says, sitting down again. "If she is formweaving now."

"Your dad met her mom, who was very much part demon. But she hid it with drugs. It wasn't just any drugs, either. It was Ether Dust."

"What the hell is Ether Dust?" Bash asks.

"A dust made from Feyfire crystals," Maggie states, continuing when we all look at her blankly. "Those are gems infused with the essence of the Luminara Court. To demons and fae, it's like heroin, or so I'm told." She awkwardly looks down and steeps her tea.

More questions mount as to how the flying fuck my aunts know all this shit. Just. Mind baffling. Who are these women? "And what does that have to do with Laureya?" I ask instead, so lost that it feels like my voice is coming out of the wall.

"She got pregnant with Laureya and refused to stop using it," Hilda says, spooning some sugar into her tea. "Your dad had no idea what it was doing to the baby and so told her he would take the child from her and raise it on his own when she had it. She also knew he was a formweaver and the baby would be too. Knowing that Laureya would be part demon and part formweaver, her mom didn't want anything to do with her. So when Laureya was born, your dad was on his own."

Hilda passes me the sugar, and I begin scooping in spoonfuls, catching glances of Dom, whose eyes search mine and then return to Hilda's.

"He was out buying diapers one night with the infant," she continues, cupping her hands around her tea cup. She was screaming, and he was lost when Fran found him. Her heart went out to him, and she helped him that night and many nights after. She fell in love with Laureya and him. She even helped him with his talisman and made him a stronger one so that he would not have to change. She tattooed it on him."

Hold up. "What!? My dad doesn't have any tattoos; he hates them!"

"His is invisible to the untrained eye," Maggie responds, watching as I slide the sugar bowl over to Dom. "Next time you see him, unglamor his left arm. It's there."

"So the tattoo on his arm makes it possible for him to fight the formweave?" I ask, observing Dom as his hands shake while he stirs in the sugar. "If that's all it takes, why can't we do that for Laureya?"

"'cause the aunts said the talismans only work if vampires aren't around," Bash adds, taking a drink of his tea and wincing. "Gah, this shit is gross."

"So why didn't he form when he was around Dom?" I ask, ignoring Bash's outburst about tea.

The memory of my dad's absolute uncomforted wince when Dom had shaken his hand at my mother's Celebration infiltrates my vision. I figured it was because he didn't like anyone I brought to him for a first meeting.

"It has to be constant for the talisman to ween down with a vampire presence," Maggie says, taking the sugar from Bash, who had passed on it.

"Why does Laureya not want to be a formweaver anymore?" Hilda queries.

"'cause she is in love with a vamp," Bash answers, sarcasm coated thick around his voice. He slams the tea back in two short gulps and shoves the cup away from him. "Neither here nor there. What about the part where Sayah is part formweaver?"

Hilda frowns slightly at Bash, then returns her gaze to me. "When Fran got pregnant with Sayah, she spelled her. She didn't know what kind of world Sayah would be brought into, and because she was a witch, she already knew that Sayah would have magick in her bones. So she put a spell on her that would protect her. But we don't know if it worked because—"" She trails off.

"Because I've never fallen in love with a demon?" I ask, rubbing my lips absentmindedly.

"Exactly," Hilda responds.

"Well, it's a good thing Domie here isn't part demon like yours truly," Bash chides and stands.

Dom throws a terrible look at him, and I wonder if the love I felt for Bash in my dreams is just that, something in my dreams.

"I wonder who it was that changed Laureya?" I mumble, more to myself than anyone.

"You said she's been mixed up in the meth world for a time," Dom responds, "maybe someone in that world was part demon."

"We're not hard to come by these days," Bash retorts, his voice dressed again in that cynical humor.

"Was it the fact that my mom was a witch and he was a formweaver that made them fall out of love with each other?"

"Maybe," Hilda answers. "There were a few times I spoke to Fran on the phone, and she was miserable. I think your dad inwardly hated that she was a witch, and a part of him disliked himself for being a supernatural formweaver. When they divorced, he delved deep into religion, as you have probably been chided for not believing in the same god as him, I am sure. He has been suppressing his formweaver side for so long; maybe there's a part of him that refuses to believe that side of him was ever real."

"And what of the fact that Dom fed him some blood when he had that episode?" I ask, my head swimming with questions. I take a sip of the tea and let it soothe me, the scalding hot liquid warming my throat and stomach.

"A vampire can feed a formweaver blood," Hilda answers; if the formweaver bites the vampire, it becomes fatal."

"But Laureya was bitten by a vampire, and he burned; what does that mean?"

"She's part phoenix," Bash answers, "hence why when I bit you, you burned."

"But the vampire burned, not her. I'm so confused."

"She's not the actual phoenix," Maggie clarifies, setting her tea down in its saucer. "She's protected by the blood because it's spelled to yours. You're the one who actually had to rise, and because you did, in turn, she mirrored what was happening to you."

"And what will happen if she becomes a vampire? I thought phoenix blood and vampire blood could not mix?"

"Guess we will see what happens when we go to make her a vampire." The look in Bash's eyes is something of a corrosive beauty, as though he enjoys the thought of someone dying.

"So, you two knew about the spell my mom put on Laureya to have her receive everything happening to me?"

"We did," Hilda answers softly, the steam from the tea fogging up her glasses. She takes them off and begins to clean them with her shirt. "From early on, Laureya showed her dark side. She was constantly mean to you and tried to light you on fire when you were a baby; she was only a year older. Fran still loved her, though, and didn't know what to do. She decided to put the mirror spell on her to see if it would stop Laureya from hurting you if she would learn her lesson and feel the pain she caused you."

"Well, it turned into everything. Laureya was able to feel every single thing that I went through, with cancer, almost losing Gauge and the loss of my mom. She said she felt it all."

"I don't think Fran meant for that to happen." Hilda's eyes flitter out the windows to Mount Baker's silhouette.

"She hates me, and now I understand why," I say quietly.

"At least you'll leave here the answers you were seeking," Dom says, trying to make it a little better.

"So, because Sayah is part formweaver now," Bash inquires, his crystal blue eyes shimmering, twisting his expression from one of confusion to curiosity. That would make her witch, demon, phoenix, formweaver? So she's all four?"

"She's all four," Hilda concurs.

"Wow," Bash breathes, his dreamy blue eyes zooming into mine, amazed at the power I never knew I had. "That would make you, like, the most powerful being on Earth then, wouldn't it?"

"She is," answers Maggie. "One of the most powerful beings on Earth."

"I wanna know how you two know so much about this stuff," Bash says, turning his attention to Maggie, his eyes still dazed and sparkly.

"Maggie studied about it in school,"" Hilda tries to begin.

"You already said she was broken-hearted by a vampire," I cut in, "start there. Spill that tea, Auntie." I grin at Maggie, who shifts uncomfortably in her seat.

"I was 19, he was an asshole, that's all there is to it," Maggie spits, annoyed.

"Mag," Hilda says soothingly, reaching out and stroking her sister's knobby hand, "you loved him dearly. It's okay to let that live."

Maggie's eyes drift off to another place, possibly while she recalls the face of her vampire love. "If I tell mine, you have to tell yours," she says authoritatively to Hilda.

"Agreed," Hilda says.

"I was in college," Maggie begins, toying with the little handle on her teacup, "I was working nights at the local pub in New Jersey. I was bartending one night and felt his presence before I knew he was there. There was something dark and sinister about him, yet his face was angelic; I immediately found myself drawn to him. He sat alone at the bar and looked like the world was ending. He was so sad. I talked to him and felt feelings for him instantly like I wanted to save him from whatever dark he lingered in. I talked to him and tried to find out why he looked so sad. There were a few things he offered, he had lost someone and all that. His eyes were dark brown, dangerous. I didn't see him for a few nights, and then he came in again, and he looked replenished; his eyes were green. There were a couple of strange attacks around town, people with weird bite marks on their necks and blaming it on kinky sex, but weird things, weird circumstances. This went on for weeks. I would see him, then I wouldn't, then when he returned, he'd be replenished, and more weird things were happening on campus. Finally, after a few months of this, I asked him things, and he divulged his secret to me. The way that his entire story poured out of him, it seemed as though he had been dying to tell someone, anyone, for a very long time. He thought he was veilweaveling me so I wouldn't remember what he said. Still, from my studies and stories from my mother's grimoires, I wore this always,""she pulls the chain up with the blue stone that I know is the Lapis Lazuli," "it's also coated with a pulverized Nightshade concoction so I could never be veil-weaveled. I didn't tell him this; I didn't want him to kill me for knowing his secret. It's dangerous to know a vampire's secret. But I couldn't help myself; I wanted to be in his world. One night, I decided to follow him, I don't know why. He never seemed interested in me more than a barkeep who listened to his tales. We were going down a dark alley; he was walking alone, his head hung and his hands in his pockets. The sound of my heart must have triggered him; he flashed up to me and pushed me against a wall, barring his fangs; his eyes had gone a white, cat-eye shape, rimmed by the green that his eyes used to be. I was terrified but not; I wanted him to bite me. He told me he could never love someone like me and that I didn't belong in his world. I told him that I knew his secret and didn't care, that I loved and cared for him beyond measure. He told me that it was his power; he drew people in and made them think about him so he could kill them. I urged him that it was more than that for me, that I truly cared and wanted to be in his world."

Maggie lapses into silence, her eyes glossy and scintillating as though remembering her greatest love story. Maggie has never married anyone, never had children, and, as far as I know, never had any boyfriends or love stories or anything of the sort. This tale is telling me something different. She loved that vampire and loved him with a force beyond anything she'd ever known.

"So what happened then?" Bash asks, slicing through her reverie and bringing her back from wherever her mind had taken her.

"He bit me. Drained my blood. Left me for dead. I never saw him again."

"Who found you? What happened?" Bash again.

"I did," Hilda answers, looking over to Maggie. "I knew that she had been mixing herself up with a vampire, she told me; we shared a dorm. I went to check on her, as I knew she was getting increasingly entranced by him. When I got to the bar, one of the waitresses said she had left twenty minutes before following the strange man she had been crushing on. I followed my instincts and found her lying in the alley, pretty much dead, barely clinging to life. I called for help, got her to a hospital, and could not explain to them what had happened, why she had two bites in her neck and needed a blood transfusion because she lost so much blood. I stayed with her that night as she went in and out of consciousness. I was half asleep, but I'm positive that same vampire came and fed her some of his blood, veilweaveling the rest of the hospital staff that was working on her that she had been attacked by a raccoon. When she finally came to, nobody said the real reason she'd been brought in."

"So, he saved me after he almost killed me," Maggie says solemnly. "I never forgot him."

"She was devastated by that for years and never really got over it. There were a few men in her life after that, but none she loved the way she loved him."

"And what's your story?" I ask Hilda, clasping my hands on the table before me.

"Mine was a sailor. I was actually in a relationship with him. Tim. He was the love of my life. The Navy took him away from me for months at a time, but every time that he returned, he would sweep me off my feet and promise me marriage and a life after the Navy. Well, one time, something strange happened to him during one of his deployments. When he returned, he was not himself; he was pale and strange and wouldn't get near me. He said many of his comrades had jumped ship to their deaths after hearing a strange song. He wasn't veilweaveled to jump in, but he said she came aboard and bit him and drained him nearly of all his blood, then fed him some of hers, snapped his neck, and left. When he came to, he was alone on the ship. He was transitioning into a vampire, but I couldn't understand it because he was bitten by a siren. The craving for blood was getting worse, and he knew that if he didn't feed, he would die. I offered my neck to him, and he bit me and drained my blood. I survived. But he said after that, being near me was too much for him; he always wanted more, to the point that he didn't know if he could ever stop, and he didn't want to kill me. So, he left me and broke my heart."

Bash and Dom share a look between them that signifies they, as well as I, know that Hilda's love had been turned by Jasantha.

"Wow, aunties, I am so sorry," I offer, staving off the urge to mention the siren. It's not pertinent and would make no difference now.

"Neither of us ever saw our vampires again," Hilda replies. "But that didn't mean that we ever forgot them."

The noise at the table lulls into silence as thoughts of past vampire loves capture the aunts, siren's dooming beloved sailors encapsulate the vampire's, and secrets dwelling within the minds of those aunts haunts me.

Chapter Three: The First Dark

"Well," Maggie says, batting a tear away and standing. "I'm going to go to bed. I trust you all won't be far behind?"

"Yes, I'm exhausted," I say, unable to hold back a yawn that escapes my mouth.

"I'll show you all to your room," Maggie says, "if you're ready to go now."

"I am," I say, arising from the table.

Bash's eyebrows furrow a bit. "Um, where are 'we' all going to be sleeping?"

"There's an extra bedroom downstairs, and the couch folds out to a bed in the living room. You can choose which amongst you."

"I can sleep on the couch up here," Dom answers, looking up at me like he's expecting me to say no.

"No, it's fine," I answer hesitantly. I honestly don't want him out of my sight. "You can sleep in there with me.

He nods slightly and gets to his feet, pushing in the chair softly. "Want me to help clean up?" he asks as Hilda collects the empty tea cups.

"No, I'm fine," she says coldly. "Thank you."

I go to her and hug her, squeezing her tight and kissing her cheek. "Goodnight, my sweet," she says, whispering into my ear, "Are you sure you're okay with him sleeping in there with you?"

"Yes. I don't trust him anywhere else," I say back, kissing her on the cheek.

She pulls away and glares into my soul, seemingly ensuring that I am confident that I know what I'm doing.

Nodding, I smile and nod again, letting her go.

Bash, Dom, and I silently follow Maggie down to the basement.

Maggie shows Bash to the couch that folds out in the small living room in their apartment, and Dom and I follow her to the little room on the other side of the storage room where we conducted our seance.

Maggie hugs me goodnight and leaves us in our plain room, which has a queen bed, a small nightstand, and an ancient TV.

Dom closes the door, then stands with his back against it, eyeing me beseechingly. "Sayah," he says, but I cut him off.

"No. Not tonight. Please," I say, slithering out of my hoodie and sitting on the bed to take off my shoes. "I have no more energy left to talk of anything more."

He nods and comes in, sitting down next to me. "Hattie texted me. She thinks she may have found another artifact in London. I think I'll fly to Denver with you and then catch a plane to New York from there."

I slip my socks off and stand to turn down the bed, "I'll have to get you a few vials of my blood to have on hand while you're there. And as soon as I can get out there, too, I will. I have to go back to work at some point."

"Are you sure you want to continue doing this?" he asks, going to the other side to help.

"I mean, I think I have to. We have to focus on getting Gauge safe, getting Laureya to help us, and getting those marks off of you. We can't part ways and forget we ever met."

The agony I feel in his stare stutters me. "I didn't mean to hurt you," he says, and I can feel him break.

I can't deal with this right now.

I may shatter.

"Dom,""

"Don't say anything," he says, grabbing my hand. "I was thinking, and you can tell me no if you want. . ." His eyes are severe and sturdy. "I can help with your mortgage and bills for a few months while you take a leave of absence. I think you'll need over a week to settle this."

"I don't know, Dom—" I don't like getting help from anyone. I've worked too hard and too long to accept charity.

And this better not be some ploy to get me to forgive him.

"Sayah, I know that you're independent and don't like asking for help," he says, and I'm not sure if he'd read my mind or if he knows me that well. "I'm saying that I have the means to help you, and I can. I'll pay your mortgage for a year and whatever bills you need, and—"

"I accept," I blurt out. There's no mistake that I do need help; I don't want to lose my job, but I need the time off to get this whole mess sorted out. "I have some insurance money coming soon, so I'll be able to pay you back."

"You don't have to pay me back," he says, stroking my hand with his thumb. "It's my pleasure."

"Well, thank you." I let go of his hand and get into bed. "But I will pay you back."

He nods silently, turns off the light, and gets into bed without saying another word.

The air stirring in a whooshing rush around my face relieves me from the deepest sleep. I open an eye and see a black silhouette of someone kneeling right by my face.

Rising with a scathing bolt of energy and backing up to the headboard, I gasp as both eyes open and adjust to the dark, kicking out to the mass next to my bed.

"Ow!" Bash yells as he comes into focus.

"Bash! What the fuck are you doing?"

He's rubbing his forehead where I kicked him. "Did you not notice that your prince charming has gone for a late-night sleepy walk?"

I turn and see that the spot next to me is empty. The sheets are ruffled and pulled down to the foot of the bed.

"Shit!" I exclaim, throwing the covers off me and swinging my legs to the side.

"Whoa!" Bash exclaims, still rubbing the spot where my foot met his face. "You might wanna put on some clothes!"

I'm only dressed in a tank top and some tight-fitting shorts. "Oh, stop," I say unashamedly. Did you see where he went?"

"No, I heard a noise and figured it was one of you getting up to get some water."

A scream spears through the silent house that sounds like Francine's.

My heart drops, Bash's eyes glaze, and suddenly, he's moving at his speed up the flight of stairs toward the screams.

I struggle to keep up with him and curse vampire speed again as I take the stairs two by two all the way to the top and then again to the next staircase that leads to the bedrooms upstairs.

Bash has burst into the master bedroom, and as soon as I enter, Dom hovers over George, blood covering him, the sheets, and the walls. Dom's eyes are black. Francine's screaming and blindly looking for her phone. Bash is already starting to veilweave Francine, getting her to calm down before he flashes to Dom and pulls him off George.

"Sayah! Phoenix blood stat!"

Dom is thrashing around, trying to get back to George as I focus on the fangs that now live beneath the surface of my gums. I close my eyes and force them to come out and feel the still unfamiliar sting as they elongate and puncture through the tender skin.

Biting into my own arm, the crunch of my skin rattles my stomach, but I push back nausea and run up to Dom, shoving my dripping, bleeding arm into his mouth. The blood smears across his face as he tries to shake me away, but one sniff of my delicious angel blood and he's hooked. Bash holds him still as he wraps his hands around my arm and drinks, the black of his eyes fading back into green.

As Dom calms down and continues to noisily slurp from me, Bash bites into his own arm and kneels down to George, feeding him his blood. The bite in his neck is profound, not just two holes, but as though Dom had ripped an entire chunk of skin and consumed it.

I have to pull my arm away from Dom before he bleeds me dry.

Blood is covering his entire chin, dribbling down his shirt, all over his arms and hands.

"I went dark, then?" he states, his eyes holding the guilt he feels when he does something that he hates about himself.

"You did," I say.

"Well," Bash's voice cuts in, "the good news is that A. Georgie here is going to make a full recovery, and B. either the aunts didn't hear, or they want to stay out of it."

"What are we going to do about all this blood?" I ask, glancing around the room. "The wound in his neck?"

"The neck wound will heal quickly with the blood he drank," Bash states, his white muscle shirt darkened with crimson. "The whole ass murder scene in here?" he strains his neck, looking up to the blood on the ceiling, "That I'm not sure of. . . unless you have a vanishing spell in your Witchy repertoire."

Nothing comes to mind, but something has to be done.

We can't leave it like this.

Francine is sitting on the bed, blankly looking at the floor, and George is about to be veilweaved by Bash. His neck wound is healing before my very eyes. Dom is brooding by the corner, looking at his hands and the scene before him.

I remember the spell I'd done with water when I was learning how to weave the elements together. In that spell, I had gathered water out of the cloth in droplets hovering before me into a ball before guiding it to a glass of water. This could work the same with this blood.

Closing my eyes, I call to all the power I hold in me now, bending my head back and imagining all the droplets of blood arising from the bed, the sheets, George, Dom, and the walls, coagulating together in the middle of the room and hovering there.

When I open my eyes, the room shudders, the walls shake, and the lamp on the bedside table flickers. The drops of blood slowly rise up, out of the sheets, off the wall, slithering off of Dom's mouth and hands. They arrive together, floating in a ball in the middle of the room.

Bash's watching me, awestruck, and Dom seems to have a slight glimmer in his eye for me, but he's too upset with himself for hurting my cousin's husband.

"Bash?" I ask. "Dinner?"

"Absolutely," he affirms, walking up to the blood ball hovering in the air and slurping it down like an astronaut would slurp hovering water in space.

"Well," Dom says, getting ready to leave the room, "I believe I need to shower."

Bash and I follow him out the door and down the stairs.

When we arrive back in the bedroom, Bash comes in with us.

"So," he says nonchalantly, "I think you're going to start giving him blood every, like, 8 hours or so, I would say. Don't want something like that to happen again."

I nod in agreement.

"I'm so sorry, Sayah," Dom says, sitting on the bed.

"I know you didn't mean to," I answer, trying to keep all the hurt I feel out of my voice. "It was that wretched mark."

"Speaking of," Bash says, "Hattie got any news on that?"

"Yes, she thinks she found one in London. I was going to head straight there from Denver."

"You think it's wise to leave her that far away?" Bash asks, leaning against the doorjamb.

"I'm gonna give you guys some vials to take. And then I'll be there after the weekend. I need to see my son and spend some time with him. You guys should be okay with that, right?"

"Should be." Bash eyes Dom dubiously. "You good brother?"

"Yeah," Dom says quietly, picking out some clothes from the suitcase the aunts had brought down. "I am going to take a shower."

He moves to leave the room, and Bash slides out of his way. He comes in and sits down on the hope chest at the foot of the bed.

"Will the vials be enough?" I ask quietly, sitting next to him.

"I hope so," he says softly. "If we hadn't gotten there when we did, he would have killed that man. And when he kills someone, he can't handle the high it gives him. He goes off the deep end. It would not have been good."

I don't want that to happen.

For either of them.

My gums tingle as the fangs emerge again and bite into it, offering my blood to Bash.

He looks at me curiously. His beautiful features fold in on me in questioning, maybe questioning himself as to whether he wants to do this or maybe questioning me as to whether I was sure I did.

"Take it," I say, urging my arm closer to him. "I don't want to risk you going dark too."

Angels only know what will happen should Bash go back to the darkness.

Eyeing the blood on my arm, his eyes turn white, fold into the vertical slits, and the fangs come out, but he does not bite me.

It's part of the blood, I'm sure. It makes the fangs come out.

He puts his lips to my arm and opens his mouth over the wound. I feel him sucking my blood, it leaving my body and entering into him. There's something almost erotic about it; I feel hot and tingly in places that I shouldn't be for my boyfriend's—or ex's??—" brother. Maybe it's letting someone drink my blood; it's a very intimate thing.

Blood sharing.

He continues to suckle my arm until I start to feel faint, then I pull away.

Reluctant at first, he lifts his mouth from my arm and looks at me, wiping away the excess blood that dribbles down his face.

The blue of his eyes returns, and he sits there, inches from me, not saying anything at all, but something in those eyes spills mountains to me. The beating of my heart becomes very erratic, and I feel faint again, probably from the loss of blood, but neither of us moves, and I remember the way I felt for him in my dreams.

Those feelings come flooding back with him so near me, and all I want to do again is run to the ends of the Earth for him, to feel that fire and burn with him, to find that darkness and dwell in it with him.

When he doesn't speak either, I swear he's going to kiss me, and I back away a bit, not wanting to give in to that temptation that I feel too.

"Your blood," he says finally.

"My blood what?"

"Is the most delicious blood I've ever had."

"Thank you?" I say as a question.

"No, I mean it. There's something about it that tastes unlike any blood I have ever had. There's a fine sweetness to it, almost like honeysuckle. But it also gives me weird feelings in my head, like I drank eight bottles of bourbon."

"Well," I respond, arising from the hope chest. "Don't get too used to it. You need to share the vials I will give you with Dom, and once we get this mark off you, you won't need it anymore."

But there's something in his eyes that tells me there's more to his mere observance of what he's saying. It's like watching someone try a drug for the first time. There's an air about him now that tells me he's high off of my blood.

And he likes it.

www.ingramcontent.com/pod-product-compliance
Lightning Source LLC
Chambersburg PA
CBHW020451310726
48979CB00016B/2608/J
* 9 7 9 8 9 9 0 6 9 9 7 1 7 *